RUBBERMAN'S CITIZENS

1st Edition

Joseph Picard

This page has been intentionally made a liar, as it was going to tell you it was intentionally left blank. The page has been reprimanded, and feels bad for its behaviour. But it brings to mind Schrodinger's Cat. It is simultaneously blank, and marked.

But now it has been observed. It was both blank and marked until you looked at it. It is now obviously marked. Don't check on the cat, there's still hope; that smell could be anything. Technically, all the pages you haven't seen yet are, at this moment, both blank and marked. You might have a couple of hundred pages of blank in your hand.

Better quickly flip through the pages to make sure I haven't ripped you off, and in the act of observing each page, decide on a quantum perspective that they are marked. (Probably.)

Come to think of it, some pages *are* intentionally blank, so that the chapters all start aesthetically on the right side. Except page numbering. Let's blame that on string theory. It'll take the blame, it's cool like that.

–Unless you're reading the e-book version. *You* people can't appreciate the science of this situation as much. The people with the paper versions have bigger, prettier covers, too. – I pity you.

Referencing that cat officially makes this a science-fiction book. Maybe this page is more like light, both a particle and a wave.

More science. That's a bonus for you.
Free science lessons.

You're welcome.

Disclaimer: The rest of the book is 96% more serious than this page.

......89%.

© 2017 by Joseph Picard.
1st Edition

ISBN-13: 978-0-9813960-4-0
ISBN-10: 0-9813960-4-6

Wad of legal crap: (You knew it was coming)

With the exception of quotes used in reviews, this book may not be reproduced or used in whole or in part by any means existing without written permission from author. Warning: The unauthorized reproduction or distribution of this copyrighted work is illegal. No part of this book may be scanned, uploaded or distributed via the Internet or any other means, electronic or print, without the publisher's permission. Criminal copyright infringement, including infringement without monetary gain, is punishable by up to 5 years in prison and fines of up to $250,000. Please purchase only authorized electronic or print editions and do not participate in or encourage the electronic piracy of copyrighted material. Your support of the author's rights is appreciated. This book is a work of fiction and any resemblance to persons, living or dead, or places, events or locales is purely coincidental. The characters are productions of the author's imagination and used fictitiously.

Thank you for respecting the hard work of authors.

For information, feedback or other questions, contact the author.

Joseph Picard joe@ozero.ca

Cover art by Joseph Picard
Other books by Joseph can be found at www.ozero.ca

/// WARNING! \\\

This book is written using 'u' in an honorable manner. I have in the past claimed to write in a 'U.K.' manner, but as I don't call an *'elevator'* a *'lift'*, nor a *'flashlight'* a *'torch'*, I am forced to concede that I write in Canadian.

It should all still be *more or less* Queen-approved.

Also, pregnant ladies in the U.S.? A *'sontimeter'* is a metric thing, you're just mispronouncing *'centimetre'*. You're using the metric system. I hope I didn't just trigger early laboUr with that mind-blowing fact.

My apologies.

And of course *'Z'* is still *"zed"*.

Heartfelt thanks to:

Gilles and Dolores Picard, Meggin Dueckman, and Adam Zilliax for their feedback and keen eyes, as ever.

Michelle Patricia Browne, whose expertise and kindred spirit has been a steadfast aid throughout the Rubberman series.

Alan Seeger
Supporter and proponent of independent writing, music lover, humble student and wizened teacher of life. The core of Five59 publishing, giving new and seasoned writers a chance to be heard, and a positive force in the many, many things he touched. His passing will be keenly felt.

Rest proud, Alan. You enriched us all.

Contents

Foreword...7

One: The Actual and his Messenger.....................9

Two: Gathering...11

Three: Being Real..27

Four: New Friends, New Hobbies......................39

Five: Disastertunity...53

Six: The Usual Way After All...............................63

Seven: Reparations...75

Eight: The Sweep...91

Nine: Peace..101

Ten: Two Lofus...107

Eleven: Stand...135

Twelve: Farewell..149

Thirteen: Empty Hand..159

Fourteen: Full Hand...171

Fifteen: Run..179

Sixteen: Some Truths...189

Seventeen: The Big Truth...................................199

Eighteen: The Big Lie...203

Nineteen: The Awakening...................................207

Twenty: Purpose...209

Foreword

Welcome to the second tale of the Rubberman series. Don't worry if you haven't read *Rubberman's Cage,* you won't get lost here. Through the story in *Rubberman's Cage*, readers were given a tour across most of the many areas in the world of this series.

One such area was the Citizenry. During the visit there, we heard of the area's troubled history, and we left it facing its hopeful, yet uncertain future. *Rubberman's Cage* then continued on with its own central focus, independent of the Citizenry.

Rubberman's Citizens takes a bit of a step back into that cruel history, and fights through it (then briefly through the events that were covered in Rubberman's Cage), then moves forward into Citizenry's own destiny.

Those who have read *Rubberman's Cage* might feel a bit of déjà vu half way through *Rubberman's Citizens* in the chapter *"Two Lofus"*. Indeed, it mainly covers the same events, although from a different point of view, and carrying the disposition of a Citizen, (Leena) – not a *visitor* to Citizenry. After that chapter, *Rubberman's Citizens* continues on, independent of *Rubberman's Cage* once again.

Rubberman's Citizens moves the world forward as this story comes to conclusion, but when things here are done, other areas have yet to tell their tale...

Chapter One

The Actual and his Messenger

The Grand Elevator shaft reached through the very centre of Citizenry. From the distant domed ceiling eight storeys up, it pierced through to the loading bay building, and down further to where the Lessers dwelt.

The concrete dome housed the largest part of the Citizenry, called the Commons. Most Citizens lived in this vast space, in scattered shacks made from metal scrap that had been around and re-used longer than anyone living remembered.

It is believed quite firmly that at some unknown distance above the Commons, resided the *Actual*. The source of all things. Food, light, water, clothing, everything.

From time to time, Actual's servant, *Messenger,* would come down in the Grand Elevator. He would bring gifts that Actual deemed necessary. He would take the dead up to be with Actual and live again with him.

Most often, however, Messenger would bring food from Actual. Enough for all.

The Grand Elevator would shake the loading bay, and the Citizens knew to back out, and lock the bay shut. Messenger would not open the Grand Elevator's door and emerge if anyone were in the bay. To *see* Messenger was rare, although over the years, some had gotten small glances through the little slot that he occasionally peeked through into the loading bay...

Through the locked door outside the loading bay, the Citizens must wait patiently, and could sometimes hear Messenger delivering boxes of food. At last, the door would unlock by Messenger's will, and as the Citizens drag the bay door open, the Grand Elevator would be rumbling away.

Then it was for the Citizens who were considered leaders to hand out the food, and the Citizens who called themselves leaders were cruel indeed.

Chapter Two

Gathering

Sledge, his function served, staggered back from the ravaged, battered woman that was tied by her wrists to the pole. He called out what most of the audience had already figured out.

"She's dead." The brute's voice carried more irritation and disappointment than anything else.

The hundreds of members of the audience, most here unwillingly under the threat of starvation, had mixed reactions. Some jeered at the deceased 'guest of honour', or consoled Sledge, her rapist. "Don't sweat it," "Did *that* one right!" or "She must have been a weak one!"

Most of the onlookers were silent. Some fought tears.

The great and all-important Warren stepped down from his raised platform. The people parted before him with fear, backing away, shoving a little to give Warren a path to Sledge and the deceased. Hands at his hips, Warren wore a smile of resignation, and shook his head.

"Sledge, I told you this was why I don't like you performing at the Gatherings! You get too excited, and people get hurt!"

In the Citizenry, people were not some infinite resource. You could beat them or abuse them, but doing *permanent* physical harm was not looked upon kindly by Warren. New people to replace the dead– be they new arrivals or infants– were rare, and it was not in Warren's interests to shrink the population.

Controlling them *was* his interest. 'Gatherings' were his favourite way to assert that he could do nearly anything to them. His most loyal of followers could do what –and who– they pleased in general. The Gatherings were a chance to be seen doing someone, an unwilling someone, in front of a crowd.

The type who enjoy that are not kind. They are feared. And they thank Warren for their freedoms over others, such as the freedom to carry a blade.

"Well, that didn't go as planned," Warren called to everyone, "but it went all right, I guess, and she was just a lofu. Who here had fun?"

A muted cheer surged from the crowd.

Warren was not satisfied. He grabbed the arm of a nearby woman. "*Was it not enough? Was this Gathering too short?*" He yanked at the woman's neckline, but the zipper of her standard blue bodysuit held for the moment. He shoved her in front of himself, with her facing out to the people. His hands grabbed her front strategically as she squirmed and whimpered. Fighting back too vigorously against Warren generally backfired.

"*Didn't we have fun today?*" he screamed at the people. They cheered again, this time with more force. He sneered at them, and whispered in the woman's ear, "Maybe next time. Don't worry, Sledge won't be doing it. Probably." He shoved her away, and she scrambled into the crowd to go find escape.

"Very well, Citizens! I release the food shipment!"

The crowd left the circle of the Gathering. Some ran, some slogged along slowly. There really was no difference. If Warren's men were letting people through, early or late, everyone got their share.

It was controlled.

This was control.

This was normal.

"Untie your dead girl," Warren said to Sledge. The cloth used to tie her up was a commodity as well, and cutting it would be a waste. "Your punishment is to take care of it. Drag her to the Grand Elevator. I'll call Messenger later. She'll be with Actual soon enough."

Sledge picked up his nearby sledge hammer. With his free hand, he took the body by the wrist, to drag her to the Grand Elevator.

With the gathering over, the days resumed.

Most of the Citizens lived in the Commons. Scant shelters had been built from any available scrap. The shacks were only for privacy. No roofs were needed. Nothing fell from above, and they would just block the light of the Commons. Insulation was not needed, as the Citizenry was always warm enough. Some shelters were much bigger than average, built against the edges of the Commons. When they were big enough, people affectionately referred to them as a 'stack'. A respectable-sized stack could contain many shacks within its walls.

Warren's stack was the largest, and many of the men loyal to him lived in it –as well as whatever women could be convinced, through threats, or promises of dizzy water and sniffing jars.

Far from any stack, one of the humblest shacks was the one built by Leena and Mike. Leena had other men than Mike from time to time, and he likewise had other women, but they were each others' favourites by far.

"Behold, my lovely! I have found... a thing!" Mike came home from a walk, swinging a bulky, padded brown satchel by its long strap.

"Wow, Mike," Leena said, sitting up from her scrap-cloth pile of bedding, "Generally, the only thing you care about finding is in your pants! I give up. What's this?"

Mike tumbled down, rolling with the large package. As he came to a floundering stop, the thing rested in Leena's lap. His body coiled around behind Leena, poised to grope, should the whim strike them.

"I dunno. It's full of little things, though. Meds, I think." Mike purred, now far more interested in Leena's curves than anything.

"Where'd you find it?"

Mike shrugged. "You know that little dark crack on the edge of Commons over past the Grand Elevator, with all the little tunnels and stuff, where lots of sniffers hang out?"

"Ugh! Were you sniffing crap jars?" Like almost everyone, Leena had tried the high of smelling the carefully fermented fumes produced by contained excrement, but her disgust was stronger than any pleasure the experience awarded. *Sniffers*, people addicted to sniffing jars, were looked down upon in general.

Mike shook his hands in denial. "No, no. A sniffer came out asking for help. I figured he was hallucinating or something, but he seemed harmless. I followed him in, and his buddy was pinned under some scrap that had collapsed from the wall. When we... well, mostly me, got him out, I saw the bag under some of the debris. That place is a wreck."

Leena huffed. "Perfect place to get wrecked, then." She looked at the big white symbol on the bag, and the words below. Like most Citizens, Leena was mostly illiterate. She opened the buttons which held it shut.

Inside was an array of little flat paper packages, in various sizes and shapes, and a multitude of small bottles, neatly stored lengths of off-white cloth, a packet of fuzzy, fluffy white things. Half of the things had an insufferable amount of words on them. "Oh, and look, it has a booklet. Dandy," she said as she flipped through it.

"Hey Mike, this one's got a lot of pictures." It showed people using strips of the cloth to wrap around arms, legs, on heads, and so forth.

"Strange." Mike grabbed one of the cloth strips out of the bag and tried to imitate one of the illustrations, but he wrapped it around his head too loosely. It dropped around his head, resting around his neck. He got up on his knees and spread his arms out. A long end tumbled down his chest. "What do you think?"

Leena ran her finger across the tops of the dozens of little bottles. "I think Warren will want to see these meds before you go playing with them."

Mike slumped, and sighed. "Warren. Why can't I just play with this stuff without Warren getting involved?"

Leena gently pulled the cloth strip from Mike's head with a soothing smile, and started rolling it up neatly, to place back in the box. "Because this thing is unique, and these meds might be special fun, and –"

"And if we mess up Warren's special fun, Warren's special friends will do special things to us," Mike said grimly. Warren's special friends helped keep order. Warren's order. Warren's friends also did other things.

"Take this thing to him, and get it over with. I'm not going anywhere near that place," Leena murmured.

"Oh, come on, you'll be safe with me. Besides, did you hear them a while ago? They had to be sniffing or on dizzy water. Half of them are going to be passed out, and the other half will be in no mood to be rowdy."

Leena huffed, and shook her head. "Sniffers. Who got the bright idea that storing crap in a jar for a long time would get you a stench that could give you terrifying fun?" Similarly, someone had discovered that leaving a food disc rotting with a bit of water could get you dizzy water which could get you pretty silly. It stank too, but not nearly as bad as the crap-sniffing jars.

Mike shrugged. "I don't know, but yeah, I know they can be dangerous if they start seeing things, but they're all quiet over there now. They had their fun for a while. Come on."

Leena shook her head slowly, and pushed herself to rise. She zipped up the front of her jumpsuit to avoid any unwanted ogling when they went to Warren's area, then tied up the cloth strap she used to keep her dark, scraggly hair out of her face. The strap, and her bedding were both made of old clothing.

Messenger provided clothing in different sizes, but all were the same blue body suit: legs that went most of the way down the calf, and short sleeves, every one of them blue.

Some were modified for fashion, to make blue hairbands, blue scarves, blue robes. Only a few cloth items were known to exist that were not blue, and they were treasured.

Leena stepped out of her shack. Although she could see the ceiling of the Citizenry before, being clear of her shack's walls gave her a better view of Citizenry's width and breadth. To run from one side to the other would take several rest breaks, assuming you could find a path clear of scrap and shacks.

The vast, off-white dome that encompassed the Commons was separated into eight sections, the dark seams between them running from the ground, all the way to where the Grand Elevator shaft pierced the top. About half-way from top to bottom, four balconies mounted on the dome's walls could theoretically be accessed by long ramps. Two ramps were in terrible disrepair, and not considered safe. The other two were destroyed entirely. This left the balconies – and the rooms that many of the balconies led to – neglected.

Leena grumbled. "I wish I could bring a knife," she said. Not that she had a knife. Mike only smirked. They both knew that having a knife was forbidden for all but Warren's most loyal people. To do things like cut hair, they had to make due with any sharp edge that Warren's men didn't see as a weapon, such as large, cumbersome hunks of sheet metal.

Warren's stack loomed in the centre of Citizenry's Commons – almost the centre. The true centre was the building housing the loading bay for the Grand Elevator. The Grand Elevator's shaft reached up out of that building to the apex of the Commons. And near that building, the notorious Gatherings happened whenever food came.

Leena, and a great many of the Citizens dreaded the gatherings. At best, it was a speech reminding everyone to thank Actual, Messenger... and Warren... for the necessities of life.

At worst... well... this last one, the guest of honour died. But the public abuse, and often sexual assault before the food was released was effectively mandatory for people to watch. If attendance was not as high as Warren wanted, he'd been known to wait for more people, or order second or repeated 'events'.

He wanted the people to see. It crushed the spirits of the masses, and fueled the zeal of the loyal. After a Gathering, Warren's men might have little gatherings of their own, grabbing an available victim as desired. Such things were not ordered, but Warren was quite fine with his men doing as they pleased – as long as they didn't cause lasting physical harm.

Leena glanced up to the top of the shaft, and gave a small thought to the unseeable Actual. No thought was needed for where the Grand Elevator went below Citizenry; those were places belonging to the lofus, and the lofus were not important. That was why they were called lofus. *Lesser ones from under.* No, the true importance of the Grand Elevator was that it also went up.

Up, up, up, all the way to the centre of the Commons and beyond. Out of the Citizenry. Above, where the Actual lived. And to the Actual, all is owed. Did Actual see? Did he know how things happened here? Or would he care? This was all... *normal.*

Leena inhaled sharply to gather her courage as they got closer to Warren's stack. Like most stacks and smaller 'shelters', Warren's stack was open to the light of the Citizenry, but the walls were sturdier, made of more, better scrap.

At the front opening stood two guards. They carried spears that were slightly taller than themselves: long chunks of metal, one solid piece, with the top thirty centimetres bashed into a blade. Their guards' clothing was augmented with additional padding, making their shins, forearms, and shoulders look all the bigger. They wore black headbands – once blue, then stained with blood and let to sit until they faded to black, and the stink was gone.

They said nothing to Leena and Mike, but stared at them –and the bag – expectantly.

Mike lifted the bag up to his chest, and smiled. "I found something Warren might like! Let me in."

"Leave it here, we'll see that he gets it."

"Oh, I'd like to talk to him personally, Warren knows me." Leaving it in the care of the guards seemed like a risk.

One of the guards shrugged. "Big deal. Warren knows everybody."

"Well, Warren knows a lot of people, and he's probably *seen* them all, but I think that —"

"He's sleeping."

"Well, I'll just bring this thing back later."

A weary voice came from one of the shacks inside the stack. "Hold on, hold on." Along staggered Warren. Bleary-eyed, sluggish, but awake. "I'm right here. Mack, right?"

"Mike."

"Right, right. And this little curve is, of course..." Warren pointed at Leena, waiting for her to say her name, but her distaste for him supplied only an awkward silence.

Before awkwardness became fuel for Warren to slide into a bad mood, Mike spoke up. "Leena. She's my favourite." Being someone's favourite didn't mean they couldn't favour other people as well, but it was a polite way to say *keep your mitts off. Imposing on my favourite is imposing on me.*

It didn't mean much to Warren, in general, but it was something. Hopefully it didn't simply mark Leena as a prize.

Her breathing became a little faster. *Why did she come here?*

"What are you doing so close to the front of your stack, Warren?" Mike asked with a smirk.

Warren smirked back. "Oh... yeah. I started out in my usual den, but a girl I was getting cozy with left, and I chased her to her shack," he gestured to a shack just inside, "and when I was done, well, you know how it is." He raised an eyebrow towards Leena.

"Dizzy water?" Mike asked.

"Ha, yeah, there might have been some. Anyway, what ya got there, Ma... er, Mike?"

"Big bag with, among other things, mysterious meds! I thought you might want first crack at it." Mike held it up for inspection. He knew he would be lucky to walk out with any meds at all, but implying he wanted to leave with the bag and *most* of the contents was a good place to start. Better than keeping it secret, only to risk having it found out later. A person could get hurt that way.

Warren nodded sagely, opening the bag to give it a cursory look. "Come back to my den. We can pick it apart, maybe do some sampling."

"Sounds... sounds like fun!" Mike patronized with skill.

"Ooh, not too much fun," Warren said with a wince, "I'm still a little dented from dizzy water." They headed deeper into the stack.

Leena was not invited, nor rejected, but she followed along a few paces behind.

She slowed at the opening to the shack where Warren had come out of. Inside was a heap of bedding in the corner (made from re-purposed clothing, of course,) with a foot sticking out one side. Leena looked to the guards, and to Mike and Warren, still walking away. No one was watching her, nor seemed to care.

Leena went into the shack and put a hand on the pile of blankets. "Hey, are you all right in there?" she asked softly.

The reply came back even softer. "Yeah. Yeah, everything's fine. I'm okay."

"Marissa?" Leena asked, "Rissa, is that you in there?"

A chestnut-maned head popped out of the blankets on the opposite end from the foot. "Leena? What are you doing here?"

"What am *I* doing here? Rissa, what the fuck are *you* doing here?"

Rissa curled up into a seated ball, and Leena put an arm around her. Rissa swallowed hard and took a trembling breath. "I was going to go see if anyone wanted to play box-throw, when a couple of guards ... invited me to Warren's stack."

"What... did they hurt you?"

"No, no, I obeyed, I'm not an idiot. But I lost my nerve and ran as things at his den got more rowdy. I thought a whole bunch of them were going to..."

"But Warren caught you."

"Leena, I let him. When I saw it was only him chasing me, I let him get me. He was so drunk, I could have gotten away, maybe, but his men were out there roaming around, and... but ... at least now I'm not a *new* thing to him anymore. Maybe if I'm not new, he won't pick me to be a guest at a gathering. I... I did it on my own terms."

Leena squeezed Rissa as she started to cry. "Okay, Rissa. It's okay. You were smart."

"I didn't know what to..."

"No, honestly, Rissa. I don't know what else you could have done. You got out of a bad group situation, and that's a victory. You were smart."

"Walk home with me?" Marissa asked meekly.

"Of course. Let's go back to my shack and eat a bit. You did well, you were smart."

Holding Marissa's hand tightly, the two headed towards the exit of the stack.

"Leena!" came Warren's voice. Damn. He remembered her name. It would have been better to be forgotten. "Leena, I thought you were coming along! And I guess Rrr...she can come along too!" Mike was behind Warren, looking apologetic.

Rissa grabbed Leena's hand, painfully tighter. "Oh, Warren," Leena called back, "my friend is feeling sick, I wanted to take her home."

"Oh," Warren said, deflated a little, "well, she can go. If she throws up, better to do it farther from the stack, okay?"

Leena began to turn with Rissa, but Warren spoke up again. "Leena, she's perfectly capable of throwing up on her own. You should come to the den."

"But I —"

"I insist," Warren said. Mike was suddenly wide-eyed, his attention darting between Warren and Leena.

Leena turned to Rissa, hand on her shoulder.

"Rissa, I think I have to go," Leena said in hushed tones.

"Don't. You'll get—"

"I'll get chased if I leave. Mike's with me, I'll be okay." Leena looked over to Mike for a moment. He was looking particularly useless, standing there all droopy and stunned. She'd told him she didn't want to come. Idiot. She turned back to Rissa. "Are you good to get home?"

Rissa pulled Leena close and squeezed her for a moment. "I'm okay. Just make sure *you're* okay."

Leena offered a muted smile, and an extra little squeeze before parting. "Go now."

When Leena walked up to Warren and Mike, Warren was still watching Rissa go. "Leena, are you and she... friendly?"

"Not like you're thinking, Warren."

"Pity," Warren said.

"Well, Rissa knows I don't share my favourite," Mike said, putting an arm around Leena's waist. A lie, but in present company, Leena welcomed such precautionary lies.

Warren shrugged. "Well then, let us go to the den, and start sampling that fancy bag you brought."

The three of them headed deeper into Warren's great stack, passing progressively bigger, and better made shacks. As they passed one, a young blonde woman barely dressed in scraps shuffled out.

"Hey, Waaaaaarren. Is it tomorrow yet?"

Warren stopped, and looked around. "Darling! Tomorrow? Now? Right now? No, this is not tomorrow. Maybe it will be tomorrow – tomorrow."

"Lookin' forward to it, Warren. What's going to happen tomorrow?"

"It will be today."

"Again?"

"Always now is today, Darling."

Leena leaned over to Mike and whispered, "I'm not sure if she's in on the joke, or just..."

Mike only shrugged, but smirked about it. No big deal; this was a common enough type of denizen in Warren's stack.

"Who are your friends, Warren?" the woman asked.

"This is Mike and Leena," Warren said, gesturing towards them, "and this girl is..."

"Darling." the woman said.

"Your name isn't actually Darling..." Leena said.

"Eh... why not?" 'Darling' slurred with a sheepish grin.

"Darling it is!" Warren declared, taking her by the hand. "Darling, we're headed to my den to sample some of this-and-that, which Mike found in an odd, old bag. Would you care to come along?"

"We can wait until you're dressed," Leena said, hoping that Darling would choose to cover a little bit more of herself.

"Nah! This is good."

The trio, now a quartet, continued on the journey for only a little while before Darling hollered at a couple in another nook of the stack.

"Jen! Dan! You're awake! Come on! We're going to try something at Warren's!"

'Jen' and 'Dan' looked at each other, and it was hard to tell which of them was pressuring the other, but they came along. Maybe it was the implied authority of Warren's presence that made them comply.

Leena didn't know Jen, Dan, or this Darling girl. The Citizenry wasn't all that huge, and '*everyone knew everyone*'. Except that they didn't. Most people, especially women, avoided and often hide from any of the boys lurking out from Warren's stack. The women who lived here had their own reasons, but Leena felt that few were here out of the purest free will.

All of this did not lend itself well to casual social behaviour. And yet here Leena was, dragged in by Mike, on her way to sample mysterious poisons.

"Well, you have enough people," Leena began to say while moving slightly away, but Warren jumped in with a dangerous smile, and a tone that rode a manic edge of friendly anger.

"Yes. Yes, we do. Now let us proceed." He turned his back, and walked onward in a more decisive stride.

Mike grabbed Leena's arm, and tugged to get her moving. "Super," Mike whispered to her, "you made him all... 'grr'."

Darling either didn't notice the change in Warren's demeanor, or was simply brave. She flounced to his side. "Warren, Warren, do tell; what yummies are in your den?"

"Eager," Warren commented, "have you been sniffing?"

"Not in a while - why?"

"Nothing. I just want you to be able to tell if one of these 'yummies' are doing anything, and it's not just the effects of a sniffing jar. Any dizzy water?"

Darling hopped a few steps ahead of the procession, then turned around, stopping suddenly, and staring intently into nowhere. "Not dizzy! No headache! I'm healthy, and rrready!"

"You sure are," Dan said, leering at Darling's bouncing.

Leena looked to Jen for a reaction Dan's flirting, but Jen was stoic. Jen seemed determined not to look at anyone.

The group continued on in haphazard formation. The most stoic member was Jen, doing her best to be unnoticed, and the most chaotic member was Darling, flouncing about, giggling, and prattling on about nothing in particular.

"Does she ever shut up?" Mike murmured to Leena.

"Don't pretend you don't like the bounce, Mike."

Mike smirked, and tilted his head, taking a moment to focus on Darling's buoyant endowments. "Breathtaking," Mike said.

"Uh huh." Leena felt a mix of wanting to slap Mike for being a lech, wanting to slap Darling for being an airhead, wanting to have a *feel* of Darling for novelty's sake, and wanting to have a chest like Darling's. All of these blended and faded into a backdrop of apathy for Darling in general.

Getting through this little social gathering without attracting undue attention from Warren or one of his goons was a much more pressing matter. In that regard, Darling might be a good person to have around– as distraction. Darling was bound to get a lot of attention if she kept behaving this way.

But that could mean a very bad time for Darling– if Darling cared. Either way, Leena felt a bit guilty. It wasn't worth thinking about; she couldn't affect it. She could scarcely affect her own situation. *Focus, simplify, get through this, and go home.*

Warren's den was a fairly large room. Around the outside edges, a long, continuous bench built into the wall surrounded everyone, covered with padded cloth. Blue, of course; re-purposed clothing. The floor was upholstered in a similar way. Just walking on it, Leena could tell it would be more comfortable to lie on than her own usual bedding heap. Knowing Warren and his reputation, the room was doubtlessly used for a lot more than sleep. The entire room had a notable odor of dried dizzy water.

The bench was nearly a metre high, and when Dan and Jen hopped up onto a section, their feet dangled off the floor.

"People," Warren said in his most congenial tone. Leena found his voice to be unsettling with any disposition. It was peaceful, but not entirely friendly. Not entirely. "People, come down off the edge. Sit closer to the middle. It will make it easier for all to partake!" He gently tossed the medical bag into the middle of the room. The glass containers inside made muted clinking sounds.

Darling laughed, and danced around it, and gave it the odd tiny kick just to hear the glass containers jingle a bit. Everyone else formed a loose circle around it, except Warren, who knelt in front of it.

Jen had found herself closer to Leena. Jen and Leena exchanged a glance, confirming that they both understood the situation. Thankfully there weren't a lot of random men in attendance, but it would only take a holler from Warren to change that in an instant. That was half the threat of Warren. Not Warren himself, but the number of loyal men he could call at almost any time.

"Do you live in Warren's stack?" Leena asked Jen quietly. Before Jen had a chance to reply, Warren spoke to everyone.

"What we have *here*," he said as he opened the medial bag up, "is a little treasure found by Mike here. It was where, exactly, Mike?"

"I was helping some sniffers in one of the cracks, and found it in some scrap. The wall was falling apart." Mike said.

Warren perked up starkly. "A wall opening? You discovered a new room? A new hallway, maybe?"

"No, no, nothing that grand," Mike said, "I was hoping it was something like that, but nope."

"Ah. Well, no matter. We have this interesting bag to explore, and I guess we should be thankful for that. Did you try anything in it before you brought it to me?"

"No."

Warren eyed Mike carefully for a moment, then turned his attention back to the bag."Then let's see..." Warren pulled out the different objects. Some things that couldn't be eaten, like the strips of cloth, were put to the side.

A bottle, roughly a litre in size, earned an interested hum. Five little tubes with sharp ends were laid out. A thin little cardboard box rattled when shaken. Two different glass jars, roughly a quarter the size of the first bottle, with at least a hundred little tablets each. Another shorter, wider one with white powder inside. A few tiny glass bottles with a metal cap. Those metal caps had a soft spot in the middle of them.

"Gifts forgotten by Actual?" Warren posited as he spread his arms. "Sit, sit. What looks interesting to each of you?"

"If Actual stuck this stuff behind a wall," Dan said, "maybe we're not supposed to have them."

"Nonsense!" Darling collapsed her body around the first bottle, and stuffed it between her cleavage. "Actual's. Own. Dizzy water. Mmm hmm. Mine!" She rolled away from the other items, bottle held tightly.

"We are *trying* them," Warren reminded her. "Until I say otherwise, these are no one's but *mine*. Is that understood?"

"Yes Warren," Darling cooed, eyelashes fluttering at full power. A disgraced sigh came from Jen.

Dan reached for one of the jars of tablets, Jen got the little box before Leena could stake claim, Mike took up one of the tubes with the sharp end, Warren took the jar with the white powder, and Leena ended up taking one of the little bottles with the metal tops.

Darling had the top off of her bottle, and was quickly chugging down the contents... before the taste registered in her brain. "This tastes... I mean... not *horrible*, but *not* dizzy water." She put the lid back on.

"Thank you, Darling," Warren said, "Let me know if you feel anything."

Jen opened up her box, took one of the tablets out, and swallowed it. "All right. Now I guess I wait."

"That looked a lot like mine," Dan said, getting a tablet out of his jar. He downed it, and shrugged contentedly.

Leena looked to her own jar. She tried to flip the lid off, she tried to unscrew it. Nope, nope. "Okay, here's my report. This one's cute. And doesn't open."

Mike took it from her. "Wow, it's not just tight- I think she's right. It won't open."

"Here," Warren said, holding out his hand. Mike passed it over, and Warren poked a finger at the top. "I think it opens from this soft spot." Warren picked at it with his fingernail, and grumbled when it wouldn't obey. He pulled out a knife and stabbed it. After a little work, he'd carved out the soft spot, leaving it open. "Good enough."

Leena gave a minimal grimace of a smile when she got it back, then took a sip. "It just tastes... I don't know. Stale."

"A little sip like that won't do much, probably," Warren said. "Drink the whole thing. We have a few of them."

Leena looked down at the little jar. "If it's this size, it's probably pretty strong. And with a difficult lid like that, I don't–"

"Drink it," Warren said brusquely, with a smile that didn't reach his eyes.

Leena sighed, and raised the jar, letting the bulk of the clear liquid dribble into her mouth. It tasted more nothing-ish than nothing. Hopefully it wouldn't knock her out, but if it did, at least she'd sleep through anything too horrible that could happen. It was small comfort.

Warren nodded, and looked to Mike. Mike held up his tube. "Huh. This thing has some kind of liquid in it. Looks like the un-sharp end might open." Mike fiddled, and a tiny dribble of clear liquid oozed out a previously unseen hole on the sharp end. "Oh. That's odd." He leaned back and held it over his open mouth. He pressed the dull end, and the sharp end squirted out the liquid. Most of it got in his mouth, but some sprayed as far as his shoulder. Mike giggled. "What a dumb thing to drink from. That sharp bit could poke a person."

"How does it taste?" Warren asked.

"It tastes like I fell asleep on my mouth." Mike giggled again.

Warren smiled. "And it makes you feel happy?"

Mike's eyes widened. "I... yes? I don't know. I feel. Huh. Hehehe."

Warren put the other tubes with sharp ends back into the bag. "I'll have to give one a try later. Let me know if the feeling changes." He opened up his own jar with the white powder. He took a pinch, and put it in his mouth.

"Oh. Ah. Hm. Ah hah. Yes. Yes? Oh yes! Oh this is good." He put the jar down without putting the lid back on. "So so so so far, two things have had an effect. Two things. Not bad. I think not bad - has anyone else felt anything? Does any one else want to feel anything or be felt? Hee, hee, ha. I have things I want to feel. Darling? Darling? Come here so I can feel you. What are you doing?"

Generally unnoticed, Darling had fallen rather unusually quiet in the time since she drank from her bottle. She had moved towards the benches, away from the group, and was curled up. Her eyes looked afraid. Unsure.

"Darling," Warren called out fervently. "I want to do hard fun things to you! I need it now- I thought you would be happy to!" He was far more enthusiastic than he generally was. Smiling, with wide, insane eyes. His movements were quick, almost non-stop, but most served no purpose.

Darling leaned forward, and opened her mouth to reply, but instead of words, a violent spray of vomit shot out. The others backed away instantly in shock and disgust.

"Woah!"

"Never seen it like *that* before!"

"*That's* gonna stain."

Indeed, roughly half a metre's area in front of Darling was covered, and doubtlessly already soaking into the floor's upholstery.

Warren approached with huge exaggerated steps, as if stepping over unseen obstacles on the way. He stopped, inches from the vomit pool. He jittered and fidgeted, and pointed at Darling, looking around at everyone.

"I'm not doing her now! Not now, no, no, maybe in a week or something, not now, no, no, no, yuck. Darling, that's horrid. Was it that drink that-"

Almost unaware of anyone's presence, Darling's body convulsed again, louder. Leena had heard quieter births. Another spray of vomit burst out of Darling, but her mouth wasn't wide open this time, resulting in a bit more of a spray. Again, her body heaved, and some more vomit short forth. The sound of her heaving shattered into sobbing, as she rocked forward and back, arms wrapped around her middle.

"*Bitch got some on me!*" Warren screamed, marching backwards a couple of steps. "Not touching that! No! But I need what I need!" He frantically scanned the room for other female volunteers. Neither Jen nor Leena were stepping up to the call for sex, so Warren lunged at Jen, who was slightly closer. He grabbed her by the top of her clothing, and yanked her over.

"*Gathering!*" Warren wailed, "*gathering time!*"

Jen's eyes widened in terror. "B-but gatherings are for when the food comes! And—"

"I! Said! I! Still! Need what I need!" With every syllable, Warren jerked Jen around, her feet coming off the floor a couple of times.

"Dan!" Leena turned the man that Leena had figured was romantically connected to Jen. "Dan, aren't you —"

"Meh." Dan shrugged. "It's Warren. So I guess I'm okay with it."

By now, Warren was yanking and dragging Jen out of the room, into a more open area of the stack.

"Mike, stay with Darling," Leena said, "I'm going to follow Jen."

"You can't help her! The crowds will be coming!" Mike said. "You stay with Darling, I'll follow Jen."

"Nope." Leena gently shoved Mike in the direction of Darling, and jogged after Jen, Warren, and Dan.

Leena made it to the clearing just in time to see Warren strike Jen, knocking her down. Sledge was already there with his trusty hammer, and people, mostly men, were coming steadily. Easily ten already.

Warren looked to Sledge, and pointed at Jen. Sledge obeyed, stood his hammer nearby on its head, and knelt by Jen's head. With a little struggle, Sledge had both of Jen's wrists held above her head.

Warren cackled with the influence of the white powder. "Usually this is done out in the Commons, and you're right, usually on food days! But today is special! I feel..." Warren grabbed her clothing, and ripped it apart, tearing the seam along the zipper, and exposing her.

Her kicks proved fruitless, and the one she did land on Warren didn't seem to bother him at all. Warren yanked her clothing off the rest of the way, laughing at her flailing legs.

They had what Warren likely wanted — a large audience. Twenty now? Leena wanted to jump in, and stop this, but history had proven that women who took such heroics usually met with the same fate from spectators.

Jen looked to her, tears streaming, and all Leena could do was return a look of sympathy, and wish her strength.

What was about to happen wasn't that uncommon. In some ways, Jen had already resigned herself to it. Everyone in Citizenry knew there was always a chance. A big chance that it would happen to them. Some, many times over in a lifetime. This was worse than what she'd imagined. The enthusiasm and fury coursing through Warren was a new, dangerous variable.

Leena backed away from the crowd, trembling. She was about to run; she could feel the cowardice building in her. She could rationalize it easily, but it felt like cowardice when she ran.

When a cheer erupted behind her, she screamed. When she got back to Mike and Darling, Darling was still heaving painful-sounding convulsions, but her stomach had nothing else to give. The pool of vomit in front of her now sported brilliant green patches, and the whole room stunk of it.

Mike held an arm around Darling's back, giving what comfort he could. "Leena," he said quietly, "are you..."

"Take the white powder," Leena said grimly, "it only makes him worse. We'll get it, and Darling out of here, and I'll come back for Jen when it's..."

Darling heaved again, almost falling forward into her own mess.

"I don't think she's ready to run yet," Mike said. "And what do you think will happen when Warren comes back and finds his powder gone?"

The lid to the powder's container was still off. Leena growled at it. "It's a shame that he accidentally kicked it over when he ran at Jen." Leena kicked the jar, spilling the powder out so that most of it landed in vomit. There was still a notable amount safe inside, much more than Warren had taken, but any further action would be far too suspicious.

Outside, another cheer erupted from Warren's show.

Mike looked to Leena. "So. Does one of us stay here to make sure Warren takes the blame for the spill, or do we just focus on getting out?"

"Someone should be here. You, I guess. I want to be there for Jen when it's over."

"So then, I guess we stay."

"You saw how he was, though," Leena said. "He might hurt Jen more than the usual treatment." Warren didn't have *respect* for people's lives, but he understood that the Citizenry had a limited population. Besides, from his perspective, a woman you could use once, could be used again later– if alive.

"We can try to show some effort, to save the powder." Mike picked up the jar, and scooped in whatever dry powder he could. "There. We can say *'gee, Warren, we tried to save your stuff, but you kicked it pretty good.'* That... might be the best we can do."

"I think I'm do– HUAGHhhh!" Darling was getting better. Slowly.

"Leena, you didn't feel anything from yours?" Mike asked.

"Nope. You?"

"Nope."

"Yaaaaay!" Darling weakly chirped.

"Darling, do you live in Warren's stack? I mean, do you have anywhere else to go?"

"Why? Warren has stuff. Always best stuff," she whimpered.

"Darling, do you sniff the sniffing jars a lot?"

"Used to. Kinda stopped working, didn't need it anymore, kept working. Kinda."

Leena and Mike gave each other knowing glances. This wasn't unheard of. Darling's mind was a permanent mess. At some point, Darling's "dumb girl" behaviour was probably an act. A tactic to keep the ruffians happy, and less violent. Over time though – and enough getting high on jars – who knows how much was still an act – and how much was now simply burnt into her?

"Darling, when Mike and I get out of here, do you want to come along?"

Darling chuckled. "No, I think I have a chance with Warren! You know, minus the throw-up thing."

Mike pointed forcefully out of the room. "*That Warren out there?*"

No one had really noticed that the ruckus outside had calmed down a bit. It was around then that Warren and Sledge, with hammer in tow, walked in.

"You'll love this stuff, Sledge! I ate like a pinch of it, mind you, a big pinch, and–" Warren stopped walking forward, but his compulsive jitters kept him in motion. He pointed at the significantly depleted jar. "*What? What happened?*"

Leena spoke with the most honest-sounding voice she could muster. "On your way to grab Jen, you kicked the jar over. Most of it landed in vomit, but I saved what I could."

Warren grabbed Leena roughly by the shoulders. "You. You are one of the good ones. There's only so many, you know. Good ones. I'll keep an eye on you. Thank you."

"Ah- you're welcome?"

Warren turned to Sledge, clicked his tongue, and pointed at Darling. In an instant, Sledge levied his hammer and brought it down on Darling's head. She went down bleeding, but whether she was conscious or not didn't matter. The second strike came quick, and buried the hammer's head deep in Darling's.

"*Stop!*" Leena screeched.

"Already done, Leena. Don't worry. She wasn't one of the good ones. In fact, I have doubts if she was real. I mean real, real."

"That looks pretty real to me!" Mike said, staring at the bloody mess spreading across the vomit.

"It's been a while since the room was re-upholstered," Warren said, "this is a fine reason to get it done."

"We... we're going to go." Leena murmured.

Warren was ignoring Leena and Mike entirely. He knelt beside Darling's body, and groped her most pronounced curves, which were decorated with her warm blood. "Kind of a waste. She cleaned up nice."

Leena and Mike headed out. She wanted to just run, but feared that it might attract attention. When they came to the clearing, there were still some spectators. Dan was on top of Jen, and Jen looked about willing to die.

"Dan, right?" Mike asked.

Dan stopped, and looked up. "Wh,,, what? Warren was done."

"I was under the impression you cared about Jen," Leena said, almost in a growl.

Dan backed off sheepishly, kneeling between Jen's knees. "I do, sure. I just... well, seemed like a good time as–"

"Just stop," Mike said. Leena knelt beside Jen and took her arm, helping her to her feet. The audience grumbled in disapproval. Some shouted complaints, but none seemed motivated enough to do anything about it.

Leena gathered the wreck of Jen's clothing, and helped her get it back on as well as could be managed at the moment. "Come on, Jen," Leena said quietly, "we're leaving Warren's stack. Sound good?"

Jen just nodded in agreement, and they started walking with Mike as a rearguard. Dan just sat there wordlessly, watching them go.

Chapter Three

Being Real

"Where's Rissa live?" Leena asked, remembering Marissa's departure from Warren's stack shortly after they had arrived.

Mike looked back and forth across the Commons, as if a flag would pop up conveniently. "I don't know. I wouldn't worry about her though. She seemed mostly okay."

"I don't want to go home," Jen peeped quietly.

Mike and Leena glanced at each other, and Leena spoke up. "I thought you lived in Warren's stack. I'd totally under–"

Jen shook her head. "I live with Dan, in a Commons shack. He just likes to go to the stack sometimes."

"And you don't want to see Dan, huh?" Mike said, nodding sagely. "I get that."

Leena rolled her eyes. *Yeah, no kidding, genius.* "Jen, if you want, you can stay with Mike and me, at least for a while," Leena said.

"Really?" Jen said, looking down, barely audible.

"Yeah." Leena put an arm around Jen's shoulder, and was surprised when Jen grabbed her close, and started crying into Leena's shoulder.

"Whoa, woah, it's okay, Jen. It's okay. You're safe."

"And I'm nice, too," Mike stated.

Fearing he was looking to get in on some group-hug action, Leena shot him a little scowl. Mike staggered back. "I mean, I'm nice. I'm not like the kind of guy that works with Warren. I won't do anything to you. I'm nice."

Jen looked up at Leena, and Leena nodded. "He's got a big mouth, he's an idiot, but he's nice. That's why I put up with him."

"And I'm good at scaring off and/or rescuing crap-sniffers!" Mike proudly proclaimed.

When the trio got back to Leena and Mike's shack, Mike hopped in first with a little bit of heroic flair. "Nobody here that we didn't want. Nothing looks messed up."

Leena led Jen in, and looked at the recycled-clothing bedding.

"Bedding's going to have to be spread a little thinner for the three of us," Leena said. "I'm not sure where to get any more right now. Gonna make for a bit of a hard floor."

"I... I don't mind sleeping closer, if it helps." Jen said.

"Might help. Me in the middle, so you don't have to risk waking up cozy with Mike." Leena assumed that Jen wouldn't be too quick to get overly snug with any men after the events of the day.

"Thank you." Jen squeezed at Leena's arm, and started softly crying again. "Thank you, thank you so much. Oh, both of you, really."

"Actually," Mike mumbled, "if you want, I could just find a totally different place to sleep. If you want, Jen."

Jen thought about it for a bit. "If... if you're nice, it's safer with three people than two. And you can..."

"Protect you ladies heroically?" Mike said with a smile.

"More like stick your head up if trouble comes around so you can scare them off with your face," Leena said. A joke, but in all seriousness, seeing a man first could discourage roaming troublemakers. Could.

"Have a seat, Jen. Relax a bit, okay? Mike, our food supply's okay for three people right now, yeah?"

Jen let out a tiny gasp, realizing that her share of the Citizenry food was back at Dan's.

"Yeah, we're fine," Mike said. "Maybe it's not a horrible idea if I take a stroll to see what I can find. Cloth, food, whatever. Not *too* far."

With a meek smile and nod shared between Leena and Mike, he set off into the Commons. Leena sat down on the bedding near Jen, and sighed. "Want something to drink? Water. We don't have any rust flakes for water right now, but we have some dizzy water around here somewhere. Nice stuff. Could ya use a swig?"

Jen sniffled. "Might be an okay idea."

"Good," Leena said, "I'd feel like a scumbag drinking on my own!" She reached for a jar with murky liquid in it. The pieces of food discs that started the fermentation had been picked out well, and lifting off the lid released a pungent invitation, qualifying it as 'nice stuff'. Leena took a swig, and passed the jar as she let it burn in her mouth.

Jen looked down into it. "Wow, it's almost pretty."

Leena swallowed, and gasped. "Yeah, Mike makes it a hobby. His stuff's always well done."

"It's a lot better than the stuff they choke down at..." Jen grimaced, shook her head, and took a gulp – a big one, straight down the hatch.

"Heh. Easy there, Mike doesn't make it weak."

Jen nodded, eyes wide, coping with what she'd just swallowed. "Yup, I mean nope. Wow."

Leena quietly took back the jar, and considered sipping a little more to catch up with Jen. Instead, she resealed it and put it back in its nook. She looked over at Jen, who was staring into the floor.

"So, Jen, what do you want to do?"

Jen glanced at Leena only momentarily before refocusing on the floor. She put her arms around herself and shrugged. "I don't know. I don't want to do much. I want to wait for the dizzy water to get to my head. Sleep. I don't know."

Leena nodded with a soft smile. Soon enough, Jen had curled up and was taking a nap, maybe with light alcohol poisoning, as Mike did *not* make weak stuff.

After a while, Leena got bored of waiting, and wanted to go find Mike. She couldn't leave Jen, however, so she settled on standing outside and surveying the Commons.

People passed by here and there. In the distance, a young girl was helping her mother scrape rust from a scrap of metal, probably to be added to water for taste. Mundane activities.

It turned into a typical span of time in the Citizenry. She considered where she might go some time and attempt to paint something on a wall. Besides finding an ideal spot that hadn't been painted already, it took blood for painting, and it wasn't as if she could easily summon some blood at will.

Then, she saw a group of men, maybe half a dozen. They were still far off, making their way around some shacks. They were walking with purpose, not just idling about. She couldn't make out who they were yet, but Leena got the feeling they were headed for their shack. She got the feeling they were Warren's men.

She rushed to Jen's side and shook her. "Wake up. I think we should clear out of here."

Jen moved and gave a moan, but didn't seem interested in what Leena was saying.

"Look at me!" Leena held Jen's face, and gave it a little shake to encourage Jen to open her eyes.

Reluctantly, she did.

"World's kinda spinny right now," Jen mumbled.

"Well, that's going to make it hard to run. Get up! Shake it off!" Leena dashed back to the doorway to peek at the group of men. She could now see that leading them were Mike and Warren. "Sack of stupid!" she hissed. Mike waved like an idiot, and Warren was carrying something.

Warren turned back to his four escorts, and presumably said something. They backed away, letting Warren and Mike get a bit of distance ahead. Leena watched the four men carefully, expecting them to split up and surround her shack, but no. They just maintained a distance several metres behind Warren and Mike.

As they got closer, Leena could see that Mike was wearing his "sorry" face. When they were a few metres in front of Leena, she looked back and forth at them both, suspiciously.

"Warren, if you're here for Jen, don't. Just don't. She's resting."

Warren smirked. "You could have told me she wasn't here. You could have played *dumb!*"

"Yes, I could have, and then what? My shack gets searched, you find her, and then it's beatings for everyone."

Warren smiled wide, and leaped up a little, stamping on the floor and pointing sharply at Leena. "Yes! You don't *play* dumb, do you? You play *smart!* It fits, it fits!"

"What fits?"

Warren tossed the bag he'd been carrying at Mike. "Here, food and things for your new little friend. Go inside and play with her. Leena and I have to talk."

"What?" Mike blurted, fumbling with the bag, "I'm staying by Leena, and–"

"*Ah! Ah!* I forget, she's your favourite. And well she *should* be!" Warren's disposition was a little like after he ate some of that white powder. Not as intense, but similar. "Fine, Mark, I mean Mike. Stand there and keep an eye on us. We'll go for a walk, and talk. Just over there. Nowhere near my men; just out of earshot of everyone."

Mike shifted his weight awkwardly, glancing at Leena, Warren, and the four goons.

"No, no, it's good, it's good," Warren said, "peace is good. It's that, or I have the boys beat you while Leena and I have a private chat. Frankly, a nearby beating is just not a good mood setter!"

Leena huffed, and patted Mike's arm. "It's okay. Do as he says, don't be stupid, and be good. Count what's in the bag here if you're bored."

Mike nodded grimly, and watched as Leena and Warren walked away. Warren had noticeably more spring in his step.

"Where'd you find Mike?" Leena asked.

Warren waved his hand dismissively. "Oh, he was rummaging Jen and Don's place."

"Dan," Leena corrected.

"Whatever. I asked Dan where I could find Jen, so–"

"So you could put her through another quick gathering?" Leena tried not to throw too much anger behind her voice, but it was terribly difficult.

Warren seemed to be in too good of a mood to take offence either way. "No, Leena, I wanted her to lead me to *you.*"

Leena came to an immediate halt. Warren turned to face her, and clued in. "Oh, no no, Leena, I'm not considering you as special guest at a gathering or anything. That's *absurd!*"

Leena was silent, but resumed walking along.

Warren slowly turned on his heel, and held an open hand towards the apex of the common's dome. "You know who lives up there, yes?"

"You mean the Actual?"

"Yesss." Warren maintained his gaze upwards, but clasped his hands in front of his chest. "We know of the lesser ones from below, and obviously, Actual is better than the average Citizen, right?"

"Yeah, okay..."

Warren's stare snapped back down to look into Leena's eyes. "But haven't you noticed that some Citizens are just better than others?"

Leena held her tongue, and let Warren continue.

"Even ignoring the over-sniffers who do nothing, there's a lot of useless people here. I don't think they're real."

"Not... real? Hallucinations?"

"No, I mean they're real, they exist, but they're not as real as others, Leena. Not like us!"

Leena cocked back her head and raised an eyebrow. "Like us?"

"Leena, I had a feeling when I first saw you. When you saved most of my new powder jar, I *knew*, and the way you didn't lie about where Jen was to me. So smart, I *knew*, it was *confirmed!* You're like me! We're real, we're Actuals!"

It was insane ramblings, but Leena had little choice but to play along. She gestured to the rest of the Commons. "Everyone else is fake?"

Warren's face turned serious, and he gave tiny, sharp nods. "Probably not all of them. There could be some Actuals I haven't met yet, or noticed. But most of them? Yeah, no better than lofus. Want to know my theory?"

Leena sighed."Sure."

"Citizenry. Is where Actuals come from. We were all born from who? Other Citizens? But we know that now and then, a lofu comes to live here. What if we are all children of children of children of lofus?! And from us, sometimes one of us becomes an Actual. That's what Citizenry is! From up there," Warren pointed to the top of the Grand Elevator shaft, "Actual can see us! Judge us! See who has become like him!"

"Fine, fine, and then what?"

Warren became sombre once again. He held his jittery hands close to his chest, He faced the Grand Elevator's loading centre. His voice became as soft as a parent wishing a drowsy child a good sleep.

"And then, those of us worthy need to wait, I suppose. Wait for our deaths in the Citizenry, so we can be taken by the Messenger to go *up*."

Leena gave Warren a moment, in case more insanity was about to dribble out, but he seemed to be waiting for a reaction. "So, Warren, do you think maybe the Actual up there now- may have been a Citizen at some time in the past?"

Warren bounced away backwards, and outstretched his arms. "Who's to say? Maybe our Actual has been eternal, and new Actuals are sent off to other places to do Actual things. Maybe they all become new parts of Actual's being, like all in one and stuff. Maybe they sit around getting wasted on some *unimaginable* dizzy water and screw all day! I don't know!"

Leena didn't ever think Warren could be this entertaining. And friendly. Maybe the key to making a friendlier, safer Citizenry was keeping Warren on just the right amount of the white powder. Enough to make him happy- not so much as to make him a manic, spontaneous rapist and murderer. As stupid and overly optimistic the idea was, it was worth exploring.

"Warren, you're on that white powder right now, aren't you?"

His expression changed again, chin high, eyes wide. "See! Oh, you're clever. You're an Actual for sure!"

"That wasn't too hard to guess. You're not as crazy as last time."

"Yes, yes, that turned unpleasant when it wore off. I've taken to smaller doses."

Unpleasant when it *wore off*? For him, maybe, but Jen and Darling seemed to dislike it a *lot* when it was at its peak. Leena's sense of pity for the women that Warren had abused and even killed over the years bubbled into a quiet anger, reminding her that the jovial fool in front of her was the same man who made abuse part of his regular activities.

"If you're so eager to go be an Actual with Actual," Leena said, "why not just kill yourself now? We all get sent up!"

Warren nodded and paced. "Yes, yes, I've considered this, but it sounds unpleasant. I've given this thought. But just so you know, I've been thinking about this whole thing for a long time, long before the white powder. It might be giving me clarity... and more *motivation*, however."

"Motivation to kill yourself? If it's a problem, Sledge could help, I'm sure."

"And then I'm dead, and I go up, and it's all good for me, but the Citizens learn nothing of the truth of it all! At least not with proof."

"I didn't think you cared so much about the education of the masses, Warren. So how will you teach us all?"

He held out his arms as if ready to embrace the entire Commons, or at least the ceiling of it. "I will not wait to die to go. I will go up without death because I am an Actual, and the Citizens will know. I'll be a legend!"

Leena suppressed a snort. "So if I'm an Actual too, am I invited?"

Warren raised an eyebrow, but his expression didn't say much. "Oh, oh, for now, go back to your man Mark over–"

"Mike."

"Whatever. Go home. I might be in touch."

As Leena walked back to her shack, and Mike, she passed Warren's four subordinates, who were heading to meet up with Warren. Everyone was eyeing everyone else with caution.

Except Warren, who waited for his underlings; merrily, lazily pacing in sloppy circles.

When she got close enough to Mike that he could he heard by her, and not the goon pack, Mike spoke up. "Leena... what was that all about?"

Leena smirked and shook her head. "I'm having trouble digesting it myself. Our great and fearsome leader is going crazy. Did you know that you don't exist?"

"I what?"

"Oh, how did he put it... you're... not real."

"I'm not?" Mike felt his chest, then spread his arms and turned, trying to look at his back. "Looks as real as ever."

Leena giggled. "Oh, don't take it personally. This is apparently a condition shared right across most of Citizenry. *He is* real, though."

Mike raised his eyebrows. "Of... course!" he said in a near-monotone voice, "Which entitles him to treat us all like piss. Oh thank goodness, now it all makes sense!"

"Well, not me, maybe."

"Not you what?"

Leena smirked. "It seems that he has determined that *I'm* real too! Oh wait; even better, he and I are *Actual*."

"As in..." Mike pointed up.

With her best snob-face, Leena waved dismissively at Mike. "Yes, yes, cut from the same cloth. Myself and the Actual, giver of all things. We are... practically family, I suppose!"

"And Warren, too?"

That deflated Leena's act. "Well, crap. He's not really family. We found him in a crap-sniffer's den, and took the poor lad in."

"And raised him to be the Warren we all know and loathe?"

Leena turned to the ceiling, and reached out to the peak of the Grand Elevator's shaft. "*O, Actual! Where did we go wrong as parents?* I blame you, always so distant! When's the last time you took Warren to go play box-throw?"

Leena's rant was cut short as she noticed Jen sitting up, looking not-so-worse for wear from her little dizzy-water overdose. "Oh, hi guys. Mike, you're back. How did it go?"

Mike nudged the bag from her previous residence with his foot. "I got everything we need. And you'll ever guess who helped me carry it home."

Jen's lip turned up in a bit of a sneer. "Dan?"

"Warren."

"*He was here?*"

After explaining to Jen what she'd missed while she was out cold, including the fact that she wasn't real, she was a little less amused by the whole thing than Leena had been. "He's lost every bit of his mind now, then, hasn't he? What makes you so 'Actual', Leena?"

"Not sure," Leena said with arms flopping out with an exaggerated shrug, "He mentioned some stupid little things I did that he thought were unusually clever, but I think his stupid white powder could have something to do with it. Yeah, he's pretty bonkers right now."

Jen pulled her knees up and rested her forearms and chin on them. "I... I noticed."

"Yes... well... it goes further than what he did to you. That was just slightly different than the kinds of things he and his men do all the time anyway. But you should have seen him when I was talking to him. He was... happy and basically *friendly*."

"Well, he'd be friendly to another Actual like you, wouldn't he?" Mike said.

The three of them sat silent for a bit. Pondering. Decompressing.

Mike jerked up to perfect posture. "Well! I've had a busy day, Leena, you woke up late, and Jen just had a nap. I'm going to catch up." He grabbed a swig of the dizzy water, and flopped onto the bedding. The violent, insane people had gone away for now, without incident. It was a god day.

Days went by quietly. Jen just sort of stayed around, and without a word about it, she became a third occupant. Dan was nowhere to be seen, but they hadn't gone looking for him, either. He was likely living between where Jen used to live, and Warren's stack.

Without any meaningful form of calendar, the Citizens watched the days dwindle away by the count of their own food supply. As the standard little food discs grew less and less, the Citizens had faith that the great Actual would soon send another shipment down with Messenger.

It also filled most Citizens with a quiet and familiar dread, for it meant that Warren would call another Gathering when it arrived. It likely meant that one way or another, a 'guest of honour' would suffer in front of a crowd.

Leena looked into the pouch holding her own supply. There were a few days worth of discs left. "Jen, Gathering is soon. You can skip it and just stay here, okay? I'll pick up your share when Messenger comes."

Jen smiled softly, and shrugged. "I'm not weak. You know it gets worse if there isn't enough of a crowd."

"Forget it. It's not that long since your... encounter with Warren. You don't need to watch that crap, or worse, get selected. You might be a popular option if he sees you there."

"Me, a target? Leena, with him thinking of you as an 'Actual', you might be a desired victim. Who knows how much of that white powder he's been having, or where his brain's gone to?"

Leena lowered her head in thought. "I have a theory," she said, looking up to the peak of the Commons dome, and then back to Jen, "I might be immune, as an 'Actual'. Maybe he feels he can abuse most people because he doesn't think they're real. If I'm real, maybe it wins me enough respect to get odd things, like rights."

Jen grimaced, and shook her head slowly. "That's a lot of assumptions, there."

"Yeah," Leena said, returning the same expression, "maybe it's all chance, but you know what? Do me a favour. I'd feel better if you sat this one out. Can you?"

"I didn't actually need a ton of convincing." Jen moved over to Leena, and gave her a long squeeze. "Thank you. You've helped me so much since we met."

Leena giggled, and backed away. "Not that much, really." It nagged at Leena that she was of no help at all to Jen when Warren had dragged her away.

Jen put on a mildly stern face, and sat back down on the bedding. "Oh shut it. You've done a ton, and you know it, so don't deny it."

It was another day before hints of the inevitable Gathering met their ears. A typical little group of Warren's men walked slowly along, striking their spears against anything that would make noise, quite often the side of someone's shack. A few of these groups wandered separately around the Commons, to spread the word quicker.

Today, however, the four-person group that approached Leena's shack was led by Warren, who stepped in a cheerful, nearly sprightly manner. Sledge was also in the group, toting his pet hammer as usual. Two other goons followed behind.

"That creep's coming," Mike said, leaning out the entrance of the shack to see. "Looks like he's on his happy-powder."

Still a few dozen metres away, he could be heard exclaiming in a sing-song way, "*Gathering, Gathering, a very special Gathering! Everyone come to the Gathering!*"

Leena peeked out groggily. "I can't believe his goons are still putting up with that."

"Why wouldn't they?" came Jen's voice, lightly laced with spite, "they're all hoping to be picked to 'enjoy' the guest of honour."

Unsurprisingly, Warren ended up at Leena's shack, and Mike was standing in place to greet him. "We're coming, okay? Relax."

Warren seemed to look right through him. "Oh, Mark, thank you, but frankly, I don't care where you are. I'm more concerned with your master, Leena."

Leena sputtered a laugh, stepping up to Mike's side, "Fetch me my dizzy water, will you, boy? Mark, right? Was that your name? I heard someone say it was Mark."

"So," Warren said in awe, despite Mike's lack of motion, "you *do* command him! As I command my men. This must be linked to us being Actuals! Oh, Leena, you must come to this Gathering! It's as important to you as it is to me!"

"As Mike said, we're coming."

This was creepy. Warren, commander of Citizenry, and the rape-happy army, was a step away from saying 'please'. Leena and Mike got moving, apparently going alongside Warren, when he spoke up.

"Oh, and your little friend, isn't she coming?"

"Jen?" Leena could nearly feel Jen cringe behind her. "Jen isn't feeling well. I told her she could stay here."

"I see, I see," Warren said with a thoughtful nod, "I'll trust you to know what's best for your underlings, but she'll be missing out!"

"She'll just have to cope with only getting told about it later."

The group headed towards the Elevator loading bay building. Warren still jittered about, in a way that betrayed his use of the white powder.

"So, Warren, how much of that powder stuff have you been eating? Are you running low yet?"

"No, no. It's a concern though, it seems unlikely I'll come across any more. I've been rationing it. I think I've found the amount that doesn't get things all crazy, but still gives me *pep!* Gets me *motivated!*"

"Motivated for what? Gatherings?" Leena asked.

"*This* Gathering?" Warren glanced up to the Grand Elevator. "This Gathering, oh yes."

When they arrived, the crowd had already begun to form, and guards were posted to prevent access to the loading bay. By this time, he *usually* had Sledge and a guard or two taking point, and he himself briskly walked along with a menacing smirk. Sledge moved forward to take his usual position, but Warren waved him back. "Not this time!"

As Warren approached the edge of the spectators, they parted, giving a wide berth. Warren sprung forward into the provided path, arms outstretched, smiling gleefully.

"*Citizens! Are you hungry?*" Warren asked as he spun to get a look at everyone. A confused murmur came from the people. No one was out of food quite yet.

"I *know* you're all hungry!" Warren spoke as jovially as anyone had ever heard, prancing towards the pole where guests of honour were often strung up. "You're all hungry for the *truth*! Truth you don't even know you were hungry for, because you're all ignorant, meaningless, *nothings!*" He laughed in a way that could make a person think he was joking– yet everyone, especially Leena, knew that's how he really felt about them.

He leaned up against the pole, and the Citizens got even quieter. He looked up at the pole, and tapped it affectionately. He gazed up at it with a nostalgic smile. "Nah. Nah! I'm too excited for the main event, and Messenger will be here soon. How about we skip the girly-fun time?"

The Citizens sighed with a mix of relief- and mistrust.

With unwavering glee, he put his hands on his hips, and declared, "Yeah, you all *know* I could have any one of you ravaged raw at any moment, and for now, that's enough! Let's move on to the loading bay! Leena, it might be best if you stayed close. Bring Mark if you want, but guards? Guards, keep the masses a couple of metres back from me while we go in, okay? Okay! Let's go!"

Leena felt the confused stare of every other Citizen there. She just hoped that none of them thought that *she* was complicit to Warren or this strangeness. She looked back with an expression and a little head shake that hopefully told people that she was almost as confused as they were.

Leena, Mike, and Warren walked through the few short halls into the building before coming to the outer loading bay door. Warren yanked on it, and it slid slowly out of the way. "Ah, excellent. We're not too late."

The inner door that joined with the Grand Elevator was locked; no one felt the need to test the fact. Warren stopped square in front of the door, a couple of metres back. Leena and Mike stood nearby, then a line of guards, then a lot of curious Citizens.

"Messenger?" Warren called out, "Are you there? Are you here yet?" He leaned forward without actually going any closer to the door, and listened. He turned to everyone else. "He's not there yet, we have to wait a bit."

Leena went to the side, and leaned on the wall. "So, what are you going to talk to him about?"

Warren giggled a hissy giggle. "It's a surprise!"

Murmurs and timid (ignored) questions came from the Citizens for a while. Then they were silenced, when Warren shot a hand out towards them to signal "stop". His gaze was locked to the top edge of the door, and he bounced a little.

"I hear him!" he whispered. "Listen!"

Sure enough, the hum and vibrations grew louder and stronger until it was plain that the Grand Elevator was right there on the other side of the door. As it stopped, the Elevator shook the bay with a decided, low impact of metal.

Warren sighed deeply, which was interrupted by the voice of Messenger. "All Citizens clear the loading bay."

Warren grinned, and hopped a little. "Mm! No! I mean, I have great news! I am an Actual!"

A new wave of murmurs came from the Citizens. Messenger was silent.

"Messenger, I figured it out!" Warren excitedly pleaded, "I figured it all out! When I die, and you take me up, I won't just be *among* Actual, I'm one of his kind! We are *above* the idiotic masses!" He flung his hand behind him at everyone. "Take me up, take me home- before my death, so they can all understand!"

Messenger could be heard to sigh before repeating, "All Citizens clear the loading bay."

Leaning over and bouncing as if he had to go pee, Warren begged in a whine, "But they have to witness me rise above! I promised them truth! Oh! And this woman over here, she's an Actual too. You can take us both up at the same time! Spare her the need of dying a stupid Citizen-death before going up!"

"Oh, how kind!" Leena said sweetly while Mike snickered.

"For the final time," Messenger's voice came again, "All Citizens clear the loading bay."

A lot of the Citizens were making their way out. Many already had. Warren might be boss, but Messenger was Messenger, sent by the great Actual.

"No! You fools!" Warren shrieked, "You'll miss when Messenger lets me onto the Grand Elevator!"

And then there was a smell. A quiet hiss and a smell. It wasn't a strong smell- not offensive at least.

"Oh... how are people feeling?" Leena asked, feeling the need to sit down. Mike seemed tired as well, and steadied himself against the wall.

"I'm! Fine!" Warren yelped, staggering. "I'm! Fine! And! Ready! To! Meet!...."

And the world went dark.

Chapter Four

New Friends, New Hobbies

Leena opened her eyes to see Mike, and several other Citizens waking up. Also present were a multitude of boxes; the usual amount for one of Messenger's food deliveries. They were not as neatly stacked and arranged as usual, seemingly due to the Citizens in the way, passed out all over the floor.

Many of the boxes were stacked haphazardly, and the most chaotic pile was right where Warren had been standing. Leena realized she didn't see Warren anywhere.

For a split second, she thought that Messenger had taken him away. The foolish thought was gone as quickly as it came.

A moan came from that most chaotic heap. "Where am I?" Warren groaned groggily.

"Still with us nothings, in Citizenry," Mike replied. "My sincerest ... condolences." He turned to Leena, "*Condolences?* Am I using that word right?" Leena only replied with a non-committal shrug-and-nod combo.

Warren freed himself from his burdens, and stood. "*Why? Why? Can't he see what I am? Do I have to wait until I die in this...*" He looked around at the other Citizens sourly, his eyebrows, mouth and nose scrunched up as if his features were racing to the spot between his eyes.

"I need to think clearer, I need some of my white powder." Digging through a pocket, he pulled out a crude little 'sealed' packet that looked like it was made of cardboard, and held shut by a thin strip of cloth. He opened it up carefully, so as to not spill, then dumped the contents into his mouth. Then he licked the cardboard patch clean.

"Better?" Leena asked, trying to control her sarcasm.

"Better." Warren sighed deeply. "But now I have to understand why he didn't take me." He staggered towards the back door, where Citizens in the loading bay had just unlocked it. On the other side, other Citizens shambled in for the food delivery.

"How did this get locked?" Warren asked one.

"Messenger told us to close this door, leave everyone who was sleeping where they were." Obeying Messenger was a very good excuse. Food was at stake, after all. "As soon as we had it closed, we heard it lock. Then I guess he started unloading the food."

Warren grumbled, and trudged his way along, with Citizens jumping out of the way when they saw who was coming through.

Leena watched him disappear into the masses, then turned to join Mike in getting their share of food.

Then, joyful yelling could be heard from outside. "*Of course! It was so obvious all along! I...*"

"Was that Warren?" Mike asked.

"I guess the white powder's doing its thing," Leena replied as she stepped away from the food box she was loading up from. Taking a fair share was based on the *'honour-or-you'll-end-up-beaten'* system. It worked pretty well.

The guards usually served another purpose on Gathering days. They regulated the flow of Citizens coming and going to pick up food, but today, things were screwed, so now there was an unorganized mob in the way. A generally peaceful mob, but a mob none the less.

"Come on." Mike led, being taller, and more suited to cutting a path through the slow-moving horde of food-seekers. Leena clutched her bag of food discs, and followed closely.

Not closely enough, it seemed. Someone bumped into her hard enough to stagger her to the side, and the glacial flow of Citizens didn't seem interested in letting her catch up to Mike.

Mike looked back in concern, but after some fruitless effort, and losing sight of him for a moment, Leena called forward, "*Screw this, get home- I'll see you there.*"

With a worried look, followed by a grimace, Mike nodded, and continued on, disappearing into the flow.

It wasn't as if Leena was at risk of getting trampled or anything- she was just stuck in traffic. The trick was getting into a faster bit of the flow than the rest. And in the right direction. That helps too.

Shortly after she cleared the building, a man approached Leena. He was older, but not yet old. The beginnings of grey peeked from his hair. He spoke quietly while discretely looking about.

"So. You're Warren's favourite? You're Leena?"

Leena looked him up and down. "No to the favourite, yes to the Leena."

The man put an arm around Leena's shoulders, and tried to guide her away, in the direction opposite of Warren's stack. Leena spun free, and took a combative stance. "Woah, buddy, where do you think you're taking me? For that matter, who are you?"

"I'm sorry," he said, "my name is Edgar. You can relax. If I wanted to do anything bad to you, I could have brought one or two of my cohorts to assist."

Leena walked beside him out of arm's reach. So far they weren't going towards any place he could yank her into, but she kept her guard up. "Cohorts? What's that? Like followers?"

Edgar made a non-committal tilt of his head. "How could I have followers- when Warren is the leader to all? For that matter, you have your follower. I know of one or two. But I suppose you're allowed, being an Actual."

Leena stopped, arms hung loose, and sighed. "Okay. First of all, I don't have followers, I have shack-mates. Mike is my favourite, *certainly* not Warren, and only *he* thinks I'm an Actual, whatever that's actually supposed to mean."

"What exactly is your relationship with Warren?"

"Oh. I don't know. He's just some rapey nut who dragged me into a little 'tasting party' of newly-found meds, and after he went crazy on his selection, he dragged Jen... " Leena stepped back, hand on forehead, and sighed. "Look, I'll summarize. He's just plain dangerous, and seems to think I'm special for a list of dumb little reasons."

"You sound like you don't *like* him," Edgar said.

Leena only replied with wide eyes, and hands out to her sides. "Duh."

"And yet, he trusts you. Because he thinks you're an Actual?"

"Yeah, looks like. If everyone else in Citizenry isn't 'real' in his eyes, I guess I'm special. Whoopee. I humour him, cuz... well, if he gets upset, bad stuff happens, right? Gotta be careful."

"Leena, what would you do with a knife?" Edgar asked, looking intensely across the Commons.

"Excuse me?"

"Oh, hypothetically. If, imagine you had a knife, maybe even a good one, what would you do with it?"

Leena snickered. "Nothing that would get me killed by a pack of goons right after, thank you very much. Keep fantasizing, or go kill him yourself."

Edgar looked up as if he were discussing something light and mundane, like techniques for making dizzy water, "Ah! Well, who can see the future, yes?"

Leena turned serious as Edgar got light. "Are you planning something?" she asked quickly in a low tone.

"Oh, I'm planning many things. I plan to clean out my other clothing tonight, eat, have a little read, and go to bed!"

"Don't be coy!" Leena said. "Wait a minute. Read? You have stuff to read?"

Edgar smiled. "Between you and me, of course." Warren's greed might demand that such things be his, for no reason other than their rarity.

"No one needs to know. I understand." She nodded.

"True. And 'no one' needs to know about any idle chat about a knife, do they?"

"Knife?" Leena smiled. "Why, you know only Warren's men are allowed those. We had a discussion about it? I don't remember."

Edgar sighed with a smile, and stroked the stubble on his chin. "So, your followers. Could they be trusted with those ideas that we didn't discuss?"

"Shack-mates. Mike's loyal to me as a favourite. Jen... she's probably pretty darn loyal, too. And she has extra cause to..."

"Of course." Doubtless, the word of Jen's encounter with Warren had gotten around.

"*Hey!*" not far off, Mike was running towards them. "Leena, are you okay?"

As Mike closed the gap, Leena gestured a downward pat a few times. When Mike arrived, he looked Edgar up and down. "Who's this? Is he causing problems? I got worried when you weren't showing up home."

Seeming to approve, Edgar looked to Mike, and then Leena. "I think I should go. I'll let you fill him in a bit. I'll be around." And with that, he turned and began walking off.

Mike staggered a bit, looking back and forth at Edgar and Leena. "Fill me in? You're all right though, yes? You're all right?"

"Let's head back to our shack."

When they arrived home, Jen was just finished sorting her share of food, which Mike had delivered just a bit ago. Leena told her and Mike about the chat with Edgar.

"Do you think he's really planning something?" Jen asked. "It would be suicide!"

"I don't know," Leena said as she sat down on the bedding and grabbed the dizzy water. "He sounds kind of careful about it all. Oh, and of course you can't tell anyone about him or his plan, right? I can only tell you guys, because as an Actual, you're my followers."

"*What?*" Mike hollered. "Don't tell me he's into Warren's theory."

"No, no. I'm kidding. But he seems to think you're both trustworthy due to your... well, closeness to me. Also, I think he feels he's safe because he can just deny everything. You know, should I decide to tell Warren."

Mike scoffed. "And Warren would believe him over you, an Actual?"

"Yeah. Either Edgar didn't think that through, or he just decided to trust me."

"You could just be worth the risk," Jen said. "Someone who can get close to Warren, and wouldn't mind him dead? You're a real prize, you are."

"Goodie."

A couple of days later, Leena heard some yelling, not far away. She peeked her head out of the shack.

"Be glad we're giving you this *cardboard!*" a guard yelled at a Citizen at a shack about a dozen metres away. Another of the four guards had a sheet of metal, which he threw onto a rough sled carrying various metal pieces.

"Cardboard isn't as good as my metal!" the brave Citizen complained.

"Sure it is!" the guard said cheerfully, "It's better, actually! Sound doesn't get as loud through it, and if you wanted, you could rip it into whatever shape. Oh, and– " The guard punched the Citizen as hard as he could in the face, sending him flat on his back before scrambling back from the guard.

"– And Warren says that's the way it is! If it were up to me, I wouldn't be handing out cardboard. You can all live in the crap-sniffer dens, for all I care."

"Might be safer," Mike said quietly to Leena.

The group of guards continued to the next shack. It was made of cloth, mostly, and deemed unworthy. The shack after that was made of only metal siding walls, and was soon replaced by an all-cardboard affair, much smaller than its predecessor.

Then it was Leena's turn. As the guards and their sled drew closer, Leena asked. "So. What's Warren want all this metal for?"

"Construction." The guard that answered earned a small slap on the arm from another.

"Shut it."

"Oh yeah?" Leena asked, "Is he improving his stack? Adding rooms?"

Leena's question was ignored, and the guards looked at the outside of Leena's shack. "Your shack has some nice-looking metal chunks on it. Hey, I think you're the one we're supposed to skip. Are you the one we're supposed to skip?"

Leena looked towards her freshly-ransacked neighbours. "No, I haven't heard about this." She held her hand out behind her to stop Mike. It seemed pretty obvious that Warren would have picked her to be exempt from these cardboard renovations. Living alongside the newly-raided neighbours could prove to be awkward if she was spared.

A couple of guards helped themselves to chunks of her wall, and another handed her flattened-out boxes from the food shipments.

"Don't you think this leans a bit towards stupid?" Mike asked, directing the question at the guards and Leena. Jen held her tongue.

Leena stared at the collection of metal on the sled and quietly replied, "Very stupid." Stupid but interesting. But it wasn't like the thin metal walls were so great, barely able to make something stable enough for leaning on. If they could make cardboard walls stand about the same height, in about the same places, it would be about as good.

"What's going on with Warren? Is he still on his white powder?" Mike asked the guards bluntly.

One of the guards huffed, and lowered his head. Another one answered. "What Warren's doing isn't any of your business. Shut up, and go rebuild your shack before I shut you up and toss you in a box."

"Cardboard! Wave of the future!" Leena sarcastically cheered as she picked up the first flattened box, thinking about how to put it together with the others.

"That's the spirit, tight-top! I'll have to remember you're the co-operative type." The guard smiled greasily, and winked.

"Just go," Mike said. He traded nasty glances with the guards, who trudged off with the sled.

"Lotta boxes they're handing out," Jen said, trying to help in the reconstruction, "If they gave us this many, how many boxes is it going to take to 'compensate' everyone they take metal from? More than a single food shipment's worth. Someone was hoarding them or something. Hey, with such a light wall in front, we can just use it like a door."

"Yeah," Leena said in a tired voice. She put little rips in the edge of some cardboard to make it interlock with another section. "We can make this work. Crap-face Warren."

"Why'd you let them take the metal, Leena?" Jen asked.

Mike jumped in before Leena could answer. "Because if Edgar is wondering if Leena's in league with Warren... there's bound to be others with that same notion. By denying a perk that Warren granted,"

"It makes me look like less of a bitch to my neighbours." Leena said.

"True," Mike said, tilting his head. "I was going to say it sends a message to everyone that you're not one of Warren's faithful."

"Ooh, Mister Strategy, here," Leena commented. He was right, though.

"Wow. How's Warren going to feel about that?" Jen asked.

"Before or after he has someone beaten for not sparing us from the metal scavenging?" Mike joked– sort of joked.

"Oh, I'm an Actual, remember? If Warren gets cranky about it, I'll talk my way out of it." Leena said, putting on an aloof tone.

"Don't push that too much," Jen said. "How long do you think he'll be so friendly with you?"

Leena turned up her nose with an evil glance, and rubbed her hands. "For the rest... of his short... life."

Mike snorted. "Ooh, Miss Strategy, here."

The new cardboard shack was soon up, more or less, and could indeed serve its purpose. In the process, they had shared little tricks with the closest neighbor for making it all work

Baseless theories about what Warren was going to do with the metal flew back and forth- from improving the Gathering area, to making a huge metal statue of himself. No one knew, and given Warren's recent change with the white powder, even the stupidest theory was plausible.

The sound of metal woke Leena the next morning. Distant, a clang, a bang, and general racket rang out across Citizenry.

Mike was already up, standing casually in the doorway. (If the doorway were still made of metal, he might have leaned on it.)

"Mike," Leena mewled, still groggy. "wuh shgoin' on out there?"

"I think I know where our metal is!" Mike chirped. "And everyone else's, I guess."

Leena pushed herself up, grabbing a couple of food discs for breakfast, and joined Mike outside of the shack. Jen was already there. The occasional distant metallic sound continued.

"Is it coming from Warren's stack?" Leena asked.

"Close," Jen said. "I just got back from a little stroll. It's coming from the Grand Elevator building.

"*What?* He's going to break something, and we'll all suffer for it!" Leena broke into a brisk walk in the direction of the Grand Elevator. Mike and Jen kept pace.

"What's your plan?" Mike asked. "Going to send him to his room? Take away his white powder? Tell him you're very disappointed in him?"

Leena just huffed, and threw up her arms. When they got to the loading bay building, they saw about a dozen of Warren's men fussing about, taking metal pieces up a crude ramp, onto the roof. Giving orders, Warren's voice came from up on the roof somewhere.

"*Warren!*" Leena called out, "*What's all this?*"

Warren walked to the edge of the roof, with his white-powder-fueled shakes, and smiled widely. "Ah! Don't worry, it will take a while. It's not like I was going to exclude you!" He walked away, disappearing past the edge.

"*Warren!*" she yelled up to him.

"I think he has a crush on you..." Mike quietly teased in a sing-song way.

"Ew."

"Hope he doesn't," Jen said.

Far from the edge now, Warren yelled back down to Leena. "*Leena! Come on up!*"

Leena just sighed.

"Maybe we can get some real answers from him," Jen said.

"Yes," Mike added, "because now he's in his special thinking-place, building his special thinking-fort!"

The trio begrudgingly went around to go up the ramp, mindful to stay out of the way of men carrying up metal pieces. Once up top, a little more of the operation was visible.

A scaffolding of metal chunks tied together with thick black wire sat at the base of the Grand Elevator's shaft.

Near the other end of the roof, Sledge was using his pet hammer and a spike to punch holes in metal– holes to allow the wire to be tied more securely.

"Hey, no *nothings*!" Warren said to them as they came towards him. "As an Actual, you have every right to be up here, Leena, but your subordinates need to go away."

Leena looked up the Grand Elevator's shaft. Wayyy up. "Warren, you're not..."

Warren ignored Leena, and elaborated on his point. "Mark! And what's-your-face girl, get off. You're not Actual people!"

Mike tried to keep a straight face, and Jen simply failed to find it funny. "What about Sledge!" Mike said, "and the guys bringing stuff up, and stuff? Are they Actuals?"

Warren scooched over to Mike, but kept facing Sledge. Warren turned his head to speak softly to Mike. "No, he's not any more real than you, Mark, but I don't want to bring it up around him- I'll hurt his feelings."

"Don't my feelings count?" Mike laughed.

"Nope!" Warren twirled away, then pointed at Mike and Jen. "But if you can haul metal up here, and work, I'll make a temporary exception! So... work, or piss off!" Warren spoke with such congenial glee, it was hard to tell if he knew he was being rude.

"Let's just go," Jen said.

Immediately, Warren twirled to Jen's side, and grabbed her upper arm. "Ohh, if you didn't belong to Leena, I could really do with a hard-"

Leena gently took Warren's hand off of Jen, and took Jen's hand. She locked eyes with Warren, and could feel Jen's hand tremble. "Warren, I think you might have had a little too much of your powder. Or not enough."

Warren backed away, soft as a cloud, and smiled darkly at Leena. "Oh, you might have a point. Why sully myself with someone who's not real, anyway?"

Mike stepped close to Leena and Jen. "So, we were talking about leaving?" he said quietly.

"Oh! You're going?" Warren said, seeing the trio head for the ramp.

"Yeah, probably for the best right now," Leena said.

"Yes, go for now," Warren hummed, "this is... going to take a while. It's a long way up, and I've never built something like this before, so, you know... learning and such."

Leena got half way down the ramp before turning towards Warren. "Just so we're totally clear, you're trying to build that thing up to the top of the shaft, to go see Actual?"

Warren hopped once. "*Actually*, yes!"

The trio headed back to their glamorous cardboard abode, and settled in. "Jen, you okay?" Leena asked.

"Yeah, why?" Jen's voice was casual enough, but her distant eyes didn't match. She saw that Leena was still looking at her, and finally confessed. "Fine, yes, I'm still rattled by that little moment with Warren. I'm sorry, you had to-"

"No. No sorry," Leena said. "Be as freaked out by that creep as you want to be." Leena supplied a hug.

"Does your favourite get a hug, too?" Mike asked afterward.

"I suppose," Leena said with a bit of a purr. She went to Mike, and lazily wrapped her arms around his waist. "Are you suffering from a 'hug' shortage?"

"Oh, you know me, I'm always up for a good 'hug'." Mike replied with a rather personal little squeeze.

"See?" Jen said, breaking the mood, "This is what I, well, everybody needs to see more of. A nice, healthy relationship. Consensual and everything."

Mike raised an eyebrow. "Exactly how much were you hoping to see?"

"Perv," Leena chuckled, backing away and giving his chest a playful slap. "Hey Jen, would you be okay if I went for a stroll and left you with big, bad Mike?"

Jen was mid-shrug before Mike spoke up. "Stroll? To where?"

Leena scratched her cheek, and looked to the doorway. "Well, given Warren's new hobby, I just kind of wonder if Edgar feels like a talk."

"What? How would you find him? And are you sure you want to go alone?"

Leena gave a hopeful-looking grimace. "I was just going to go in the direction he and I were walking before you showed up. Maybe ask around. I don't know."

"Fine, but I'm coming." Mike glanced to Jen. "We all are, I guess."

"Nah. I think he'll be more open with me if I'm alone." Leena said.

Mike scoffed. "What if he wants you to be more 'open' with *him?*"

Leena shook her head. "If he was going to try something, he could have done it before. We were alone for a while, and-"

"You weren't that alone, Leena. You guys were walking to *somewhere*. He might have been waiting to get you there, and then jump you."

"Whatever. I just don't get that vibe from him, okay? Stay here. I, the great Actual Leena say so."

"That Actual thing is fake, remember," Jen said as she sat down on the bedding. "It's not like it makes you stronger or something."

"Yeah, well, I wouldn't mind having a knife, but here we are. Seriously, it'll be okay. I'll see you all in a bit." She went over to Mike, and gave him a soft, slow little kiss. "Stay, okay?"

Mike frowned a little, and crossed his arms. "Fine. But I won't stay forever. If I get overly worried, I'm coming to find you."

Leena smirked, and nodded. "Fine, deal." She waved to Jen, and headed out.

She walked to where she'd last seen Edgar, then kept going. She spotted a man looking at her, but he quickly looked away, and went about his business.

She wandered about, stopping to ask a woman if she knew Edgar and were he might be, but she was of no help. A boy she came across also didn't know. She was starting to feel silly about it all, and turned to head home, when Edgar stepped out from behind a shack.

"Follow." he said, turning around, and disappearing around the corner of the shack.

"Hey..." Leena didn't have time to question it, or think too much. She followed. The other side of the shack had an opening, with another woman and Edgar inside. The woman looked a little like Leena. Similar hair, similar build, but up close, she looked quite different.

Edgar pointed in a somewhat right-side direction from where Leena had been walking originally. "Leena, that way on the edge of the Commons is a passage. After I leave with your decoy, count to two hundred, and then go there. A man will be there. Tell him the dizzy water is sour. I'll catch up."

"What?" But it was too late. Edgar and Leena's stand-in walked out of the shack, and were gone. Leena tried to remember all Edgar had said. *Count to a hundred? Two hundred.* As she silently counted at a moderate pace, she visualized which way he'd pointed. Remembering the sour dizzy-water was easy enough.

Passing thirty or so, her thoughts went to Mike. Maybe Edgar would send her 'double' back home to explain, so Mike wouldn't feel the need to run around and look for her.

That could be hilarious, but eventually she wondered... if Edgar was going to kidnap her, would a messenger calming down Mike just buy Edgar time? Would Mike believe any of it, or rush out right away?

Frig, what number was she on now? Let's call it fifty.

Deciding that her little theories were pointless without further clues, she decided to follow Edgar's plan, and focus in the counting. Impatient, her silent counting became gradually faster.

"-*Eighty-eight*," she continued in her head, "*eighty-nine, eighty- Edgar's lucky I know how to count this high.*" Many Citizens could not. "*-Wait... eighty... ninety, ninety-one, why don't I just stop now? Like nine more counts will make a difference. Aw crap, I'm supposed to be going to two hundred. One hundred and one...*"

Leena went on, trying to not let distracting thoughts derail her count, and failing regularly.

But given that Edward didn't specify how fast to count... *Whatever, close enough. Screw it.*

Leena peeked outside. No one was particularly looking her way, so she headed in the direction Edgar had indicated, passing by the scrap and occasional common shack.

It wasn't long before she found the edge. Facing a plain wall (which hadn't been painted on much... maybe a place to paint something some time.) she looked to the left and right. To the right, there was a doorway and some guy standing by it.

She headed over, and said... *oh, what was it again...?* "The dizzy water is spoiled. No, wait. Rotten? S... something with an S.. it's not 'spilled', uh..."

The man smirked. "Sour. You don't need the passwords, Leena. Everyone knows who you are."

"Oh. That's kind of creepy, y'know? Anyway, now what? My shack-mates are gonna get concerned."

"Head back in there for a dozen metres or so. There's a room to the left, Edgar will find you there."

"Uh huh. Hey how many of you are-"

"Go, go. Get out of sight of the Commons." The man spoke with an urgent tone, but his body language only showed boredom.

"Okay, okay." Leena headed down the hallway, which had a similar ex-white tone as the loading bay. It was a fairly narrow hallway, mind you, and if she didn't know better, she'd swear she was in a crap-sniffer's den.

One of the light fixtures built into the ceiling was broken, making the passage just a little bit dimmer than a Citizen was used to. Broken lights like this were usually reported to Warren, who apparently told Messenger somehow. A replacement part would eventually come, but only if all the broken parts were provided back to Messenger.

Some saw this as unfortunate, since the long light-stick thing inside was made of glass, that was sharp when broken apart. Citizens had considered using it for other purposes, but when even a shard was kept from Messenger, he wouldn't provide a replacement. Only the tiniest, most useless bits had ever been salvaged.

And yet, here sat a dead light, up in its beveled fixture, neglected. Unreported. Warren didn't come here, apparently. And no one who frequented here felt like bringing it to Warren's attention.

The doorway to the left opened up into a room about ten metres wide, and nearly twice as long. Here and there were piles of bedding. The one at the far end was a lot bigger. Some of them were lumpy enough to have a person under them.

"Anybody home? Wakey wakey!" Leena hollered. No reply. She walked over to the biggest one, and gave it a polite little kick.

Clank.

Clank? Leena nudged it around a bit more, and more metal-on-metal sounds resulted. She bent down to lift the edge of the bedding, and saw narrow pieces of metal, almost as long as a person was high. They were fitted with cloth grips, none quite the same, because the materials used were not uniform. They used what they could get. The ends were all sharpened in one way or another. One was a pipe, the end mashed flat, one was a moderately thick rod with the end cut off at an angle, and so on. All together, there were easily over a dozen spears.

"Now you know we're serious," came Edgar's voice from the doorway.

Leena spun to face him, surprised. "Heh. Yeah, and I know why you were so careful getting me here."

Edgar nodded. "I can't be sure if any of Warren's men have been in the area, but hopefully if there were, they followed me and the decoy around to nowhere. So, '*can I trust you*' is the question."

Leena leaned towards the spears, and rolled her eyes. "Well, you must, if you went to the hassle of getting me here."

"I still have the option of killing you here."

"Yeah, true. I'm closer to all the spears, though-" Leena said.

Edgar pulled a very nice-looking knife out of a secret pocket hidden under the empty food pouch attached to his waist. "And how fast are you?"

Leena shrugged, and tossed up her hands. "Bah! I must be super, super amazing fast. Don't you remember? I'm an Actual! Heck, even if you managed to stab me, your knife would probably shatter, or melt, or bend around and poke you, due to my awesome power! Cut the crap- I'm here, we'd both rather see Warren dead. What's the plan?"

With a chortle, Edgar put his knife away. "Well, I have about as many people willing to fight as I have spears. Especially after Warren's little metal-harvest, I fear there won't be many more spears to come. I know most people would support us, but getting people to join is risky. The more people with questionable levels of loyalty know, the more likely that Warren will find out and squish us. Right now, he still has a lot more people ready to fight than we do."

"Which is when I sweep in with my Actual powers, and... wait... Warren's pretty well out in the open right now. Why not attack now?"

"Most of his men are busy helping him built that stupidity," Edgar said. "There would be a lot of deaths on both sides, and no guarantee of victory."

"So... Actual powers?" Leena offered.

"Sort of. Would you say he trusts you?"

Leena shrugged. "Well, more than you *not-real* people, probably. I mean, he talks to me like... like I'm his buddy. As long as he has his powder, and eats the right amount."

"White powder?"

Leena had to tell the story of the med-tasting party, how his first try of the white powder made him more violent, but less made him merely jittery and a bit too happy.

Edgar seemed to know parts of the tale, but not by any means all of it.

"And where does he keep it now?" Edgar asked.

"I've seen him carrying a little bit in a package, but the jar? No idea. Somewhere in Warren's stack, I guess. Frankly, the rate he's using it right now is probably the best for us."

"You're probably right," Edgar said. "As insane as he is at this stage, if he's as pliable as you make him sound, it could work to our advantage. And we don't need him going on a rampage. Not that we could *change* the amount he uses, short of finding the jar and getting rid of it."

Leena looked to the doorway. "Hmm... I wonder what that would do. Would it give us the same old cranky, mean Warren?"

"Good point," Edgar said. "Maybe he wouldn't be the same. Have you ever seen someone who's done a lot of sniffing, or drinks too much dizzy-water, suddenly stop?"

"It can get pretty rough for them." A hint of sorrow crossed Leena's face. "For all we know, cutting him off could end up being our worst option, even if I *could* get in there and find it."

Edgar waved his hand in front of himself dismissively. "So, we keep him as we know him now. No need to drive ourselves crazy for a result we can't predict. If he's committed to his new project on the elevator shaft, that will make him all the more predictable."

"You know what it is, right?" Leena said, giving a glance upwards.

"He wants to get at Actual. Insanity. If he gets to the top of the Grand Elevator's shaft, then what? It's not all that easy to see, but it doesn't exactly look like there's a door up there."

Leena shrugged. "He might get up there, find it was pointless -"

"And we'll see how he deals with that," Edgar said. "There has been word that a few of his men are becoming disillusioned with him."

Leena huffed with a smirk. "Yeah, go figure. So what, we sit and wait to see if him failing ends up making a good time to attack?"

"Depending on what happens, it may require us to think quickly. If we're very lucky, he'll simply *off* himself. To react in a timely manner can be difficult with our fighters scattered around the Citizenry." Edgar paced idly, then pointed at Leena. "And you. He thinks you're an Actual as well. What if he finds a door up there, and opens a way to *the* Actual. What would you do?"

Leena reeled back a bit. "You don't believe his ideas about him and I being Actuals and whatever, do you?"

Edgar huffed, and straightened his posture. "Of course not! It's pure blasphemy! There is but *one* Actual, and he is infinitely above and separated from us. The notion that he's a person resembling us is laughable, or it *would* be, if it were not insulting." Edgar let his indignant pose relax again. "But the question stands... if Warren opens a door... what do you do?"

Leena had to think about that. "Well... I'm not so keen to wander into some unknown little corner of things with Warren. I'd be curious, though. Maybe bring Mike, and go exploring with him. I mean, he found that interesting-but-awful bag of meds. Who knows what else could be out there?"

"And if you anger Actual? Or Messenger?" Edgar paused, and stared into Leena's eyes. "I can't pretend to know of their will, but I'd be very careful treading in places we weren't meant to go."

When Leena left Edgar's little hideaway, she was instructed to take a wandering path, and not to walk too quickly, nor too slow, to hide the importance of the doorway she came from. She was a little surprised that the decoy wasn't used again. Edgar never gave her any instructions on what she should do to aid the anti-Warren cause. The whole thing seemed to be aimed at finding out her intentions. Whose side she was on.

From somewhere across the Commons, a scream called out. Some women didn't bother to scream for help. Everyone knew what was going on. Some of Warren's men were having a bit of fun, and no one dared a rescue.

Leena didn't dare either. They would have knives or spears, where she had none. She almost asked Edgar if she could have one of the spears, but being seen with a weapon would earn a beating or worse.

Whose side was she on? Not Warren's, but she felt guilty as the distant screams quieted.

She could do more.

Everyone could do more.

Warren's men were outnumbered by everyone else. But who wanted to be first to get skewered by a spear over it? Maybe Edgar. So they'd wait for Warren to build his own failure, and see what happens.

When Leena got home, Jen was there, but not Mike.

"He went out looking for me, didn't he?"

"Yup," Jen replied. "Are you okay? Where were you?"

"I found Edgar, eventually." Leena leaned back to peer out the doorway for spies, as if there couldn't be one listening through the back wall, being cardboard and all. "It sounds like he had a group getting ready to fight Warren and his guys. Edgar wants to wait until Warren gets to the top of the elevator shaft, and see what happens."

Jen leaned over, and spoke in urgent whispers. "Seriously? You..." Jen sat properly and smiled. "Leena, you're silly. Really. What were you off doing?"

"He's got a pile of spears, and I met a couple of his followers. There's at least a dozen of them," Leena said.

"You're being serious!" Jen exclaimed.

"I should have asked him for a knife. He had a knife that he hid pretty well in his clothes."

"*He had a knife?*"

"Oh yeah, and did I tell you about the spears? He's got a bunch."

"If Edgar's so well-armed, why not just attack now?"

Leena shrugged. "Mostly to wait for a chance that won't involve a lot of Warren's men, and everyone getting gutted. And if you ask me, I think Edgar's a little curious about what Warren might find at the top."

"*Leena!*" Mike came in, eyes wide. "Where have you been?"

"I thought I told you to stay home. *Bad*, Mike, bad! And now I have to tell the tale all over again."

Chapter Five

Disastertunity

Days went by, as Warren and his men fumbled around to build a climbable structure against the Grand Elevator shaft.

"It looks like …. like a toddler designed it." Warren said, looking at the work so far.

Sledge looked at their scaffolding structure. Men brought more pieces, and did their best to climb efficiently while carrying bulky chunks of metal.

"Who *did* design it?" Sledge asked. Indeed, with a dose of the white powder in Warren, his organizational skills were less than exacting.

"Oh, shut up."

Many pieces had the same colour, or size, or other attributes, but they weren't arranged all that attractively. Many pieces had been bent or dented by the Citizens to adapt pieces to their shacks. Various sizes of metal sheets and various sizes of piping constituted the bulk of the materials.

"This piece won't stay on this other piece!" called one of the men from above.

"Why not?" Warren snapped. "Doesn't it have good holes? Did you bring up a chunk of that cabling?" As he spoke, he made fidgety jerky hand motions, poking the air in front of him for the holes, smoothing out an imaginary cable and dangling it.

"That's all fine, but this piece is too heavy for the piece below it," the worker said. "I think this piece should go near the bottom!"

Warren looked at the offending piece, then looked at the base of the scaffold. "You're just lazy! You want it down here so you don't have to carry it up there!"

"But I've *already* carried it up here."

"Well then, you'll have no problems carrying it back down!"

Many a piece had to be taken off to be used lower down. Then another, and another. Nearly everything had to be taken apart, so that they could put the big heavy things that should go on the bottom, and lighter stuff on top.

Warren was pleased. Fidgeting, and smiling widely, he talked to himself or anyone who might happen to hear. "See? This is a test! No one has done this before, because no one's been a motivated Actual to make it happen! He'll be so proud of me. I hope he doesn't think less of Leena because *she* didn't think of this. No, an Actual is an Actual, and deserves to ascend!"

Construction went on, some days better than others. Leena didn't want to stroll over casually to Edgar's hidey-hole, since apparently that would be a risk. Edgar didn't feel the need to contact *her* either.

One day she *was* approached by Marissa, who Leena had last run into before the tasting party at Warren's.

"Leena? It's you, right?" Marissa was a few years Leena's junior, and this time seemed downright enthusiastic. It beat the state she'd been in before.

"Yeah. Hi Rissa."

"Leena, is it true that you're an Actual?"

"Well, Warren says so, anyway, whatever that's worth."

Marissa bounced a couple of times, grinning. "I think you should be the next actual Actual. Warren is... you know... Warren."

"What? Last I heard, Warren just wanted to go live with the Actual above, not replace him."

This made the Marissa even more excited. "Then the way is clear for *you* to be *the* the Actual!"

Leena smirked and shook her head. "I don't know where you get your information, but we don't even know if the Actual is anything like us! And who suggested he's willing to give up being the Actual, anyway?"

Marissa deflated a little, but bounced back. "Oh! If you go there, and Actual offers, will you do it?"

"Ugh, as if I want the job. Rissa, right now, I don't even know if there will be a way up. Let's all take this one step at a time, okay?"

"You're gonna be the Aaaactual," Marissa sang quietly.

"No, no, no. Stop saying things like that. Imagine if that idea got back to Warren."

"Oh, right... right, I see... maybe he's your competition... dangerous. I'll keep this news to myself." Marissa said.

"*There's no news to be had here!*"

"Got it. Got ya, loud and clear. No news at all."

"Rissa! There isn't!"

"Uh huh..."

Then, the sound of scraping, then the sight of Sledge appeared a few dozen metres away. In one hand, he carried his pet hammer, and the other hand grasped the wrists of a dead woman.

There was a portion of cloth over her face, but her blonde, blood-matted hair stuck out around her shoulders. From this distance, Leena and Marissa couldn't make out much else.

Sledge was dragging her in the direction of the elevator loading bay, to be taken by Messenger. Sledge hadn't come from the direction of Warren's stack, but that fact that Sledge was taking her away narrowed down the list of who killed the woman. Sledge would likely only do this for himself or Warren.

Leena and Marissa watched silently for a bit. Leena tried to think of who it could be under the covering. She was glad to be able to rule out Jen, and obviously Marissa. Was she the source of the screams she had heard the other day? No, the direction and timing would be all wrong. Just another victim.

Marissa was still staring blankly towards the distant body and Sledge. Her jaw was trembling, tears welling up. "That could have easily been me," Marissa said. "For all I know, it still could be, any day at all."

"Riss..."

"Leena, I don't know what might change if Warren becomes the one Actual, but I get the feeling it wouldn't be good. So don't let him, okay?"

"It's going to be soon." Edgar said. He'd found a way to 'randomly' run into Leena during a run for some water one day.

"What? Your attack?" Leena blurted.

"Hush, keep your voice low. Bad enough we're seen together."

"Why," Leena said as quietly as was reasonable. "As far as anyone knows, you're just some guy, right?"

Edgar wavered his head back and forth a little. "Warren and I have had words a few times. I am not considered a friend."

"What? And you're still alive?"

"My words were clear, but not harsh. I was a fool to attempt reason. I had my beating, and was sent on my way. I was lucky, but I wouldn't put any faith in the notion that he's forgotten me."

The inevitable day arrived, and Warren stopped by Leena's shack with a compliment of four guards. "Coming to watch us break through?" he said with giddy glee, cruising on his white powder.

"Oh, you actually reached the top?" Leena had seen the progress, like everyone else, including Edgar.

"Actually made it to the actual top to go see Actual? Actually, almost. But within minutes! Leena, you're so funny!"

"Yes, I'm Actually pretty witty," Leena said dryly. Warren erupted into laughter, while Leena, Mike, and Jen traded little glances of bewilderment.

"Of course you are, you're an Actual! Let's go!" Warren bounced on the spot in excitement.

"Hey Warren," Mike said, "are you on a bit more of the white powder than usual?"

"Uh huh! I don't need to conserve it like I have been. I'll soon be with Actual, and I won't need it! He probably has a ton of it!"

"Did you have a bigger amount the other day?" Leena asked, thinking of the dead woman she'd seen being dragged toward the elevator.

Warren's eyes went from mildly frantic to inwardly intense. His smile barely faltered, though. "Now and then... I don't know. I forget I took it already, or the white powder in me makes me want more. I don't know. Things happen, everything's fine. *Fine!* Even better, because today is the *day!*"

As they were departing, Leena looked towards Jen, who was still seated on the bedding. Leena didn't want to speak, and risk drawing Warren's attention towards Jen, so instead, she used a head bob in the direction of the Grand Elevator, with a sympathetic smile. She wasn't surprised when Jen meekly shook her head 'no'.

From seeing a white-powder-filled Warren so close by, Jen's eyes were a little distant- but she managed a timid smile for Leena, and waved her off.

When they got to the roof of the elevator's building, and stood below the tower of scrap, men were having arm wrestling matches below. Lacking any table, the competitors were just lying on the flat roof, facing each other. Sledge was winning handsomely.

"What's this?" Leena asked.

"Oh, at the top is no clear door," Warren said, "but the sections of the Commons dome has those large 'seams' that all meet at the top. Sledge is giving people a chance to prove they're stronger than him, for the right to take his hammer up, and try to smash through between the edges, to go up."

"Wow, I didn't think Sledge would part with his hammer," Mike said.

"My idea," Sledge hollered over as he planted the current challenger's hand down flat. "If someone can better do the job, I can lend out the hammer. As long as I can keep an eye on it. Ready for the next one!"

Warren's brow crunched inwards in seriousness, and he grimaced, making sharp little nods. "Good man," he said quietly to Mike, "He's got his priorities right, above his affection for his hammer." Warren looked Mike up and down, as if suddenly realizing that he was speaking congenially to 'one of the not-real' people – And totally missing that he'd called another not-real person, Sledge, a good man. Perhaps he was simply a good 'not-real' in Warren's eyes.

A new challenger got down to face Sledge. This one was actually of comparable size, unlike some of those previously defeated

"Greg! About time!" Sledge grinned as he put his arm in position.

'Greg' put his arm into position as well, and smirked. "Sorry, I would have been here sooner, but I was ... busy." He smirked again.

"Oh yes? On who?" Sledge asked.

"Never asked for a name."

"Fair enough. Okay, *go.*"

Banter was abandoned as both men struggled against each other. There was no slow buildup. Both were putting everything into the match from the first moment. Their faces turned red quickly. Veins were seen in necks and foreheads. It was all ridiculously manly.

"I could take 'em both," Mike whispered to Leena, "at the same time. As soon as they go to sleep, drunk, and I have a good knife."

Leena raised an eyebrow at his failed joke.

The match between Sledge and Greg went on longer than was terribly interesting. Neither of them had given more than a centimetre, and no signs that either was weakening more than the other.

Finally, suddenly, Sledge gave up with a groan, rolling onto his back, stretching out his arm.

"Okay, Greg," Sledge gasped, "you can gloat, but keep in mind how many matches I was tiring out my arm with before you even got here."

Greg sat up, and stretched his arm out in a similar way. "Fine. Fine, a rematch another day. But if your arm's so tired, it's not ready to go smashing through the top of the world anyway."

Sledge flopped his arms to the side in defeat. "Buuuaaaaahhhhhhh. Take good care of it, Greg!"

Warren handed Greg the sledgehammer, and Greg held it upright with both hands, against his chest. "Sledge, when your hammer returns, it will tell you all about the glory!"

"I can see up there from here, you know."

"Here," Greg said, "hang onto my knife for me." He took a very shiny knife out of a sling built into his clothing, and tossed it on the floor, so it would slide over to Sledge. The handle was a very perfectly shaped piece of black.... something, and the blade was about fifteen centimetres long, slim and gleaming. It was not made by Citizens. It was assumed to be a gift from Actual, like the hammer. Such treasures were Warren's to award to his best men.

Sledge shrugged, storing the knife on a loop on his waistline, and Greg started climbing. Warren was beside himself, bouncing and shaking.

"I figured *you'd* want to have the honours, Warren," Mike said.

Without slowing his little fidgets, Warren mumbled under his breath, "An Actual knows how to delegate. Delegate means–"

"I know what it means."

"Of course you do, don't you? Leena must teach you well! Or you're lying. Whateverrrrr..."

Mike grimaced, and shook his head slowly. "Oh, I'll miss you if you leave us to go up."

"Ha, of course!" White powder apparently blocked the sense of sarcasm– at least when operating alongside a sufficient ego.

Mike went over to Leena, and held her hand, giving it a squeeze. Leena squeezed back, and looked to Mike. "Hey, favourite boy, what's up?" she asked quietly.

"Just had a stupid thought," Mike responded just as quietly, "and I felt like holding your hand."

She frowned slightly, and looked into his eyes, even if his stare was on the ascending Greg, coping with the hammer as he went. "What kinda stupid thought?"

"Would you go?" Mike asked, "If a way opened up, and you had the chance?"

"Oh, Mikey," she said, moving a little closer to put an arm around him. "I'm not about to run off without you. And if it happens I do, I'll be back quick."

Mike looked less than at ease about that. "So, you assume that if you run off to the Actual place, that you'll be safe and *able* to come back?"

"You're right. I should bring a stick. A big one."

Mike smirked. "Now you're making fun of me."

"Yeah, pretty much. But you're my favourite, and I take *that* pretty darn seriously."

Mike held her a little closer, and put a slow little kiss on her forehead.

"Behave, love," she said with a soft smile.

They both turned their attention to everyone else. Warren didn't seem to notice the intimate moment, or if he had, he found it irrelevant.

Greg was nearly to the top, and it was hard to make out every detail. Finally at the peak and in hammer-swinging distance of the ceiling, he yelled down, "*Here we go!*"

The hammer was seen to swing down, pause, then swing hard upwards. The impact of the hammer made less noise than the scaffolding tower's groans.

"How safe is that, Warren?" Leena asked as a second swing produced the same result.

"Yes, yes, it's fine, fine," Warren said, waving his hands at Leena dismissively while still staring up at Greg. "It was made by my finest men."

"Uh huh..."

Another swing, more groans from the tower. Another, and another.

"Look, look, it's working," cheered Warren. "that black long bit between the panels came loose a little!"

Indeed, the next few swings, even though not aimed at the black bit, shook it loose. The top end of the thin black part now dangled down. Then it fell loose further, and about six metres of it dangled from underside of the dome.

"*Hit a different one!*" Warren yelled up. "*If another comes loose, maybe the panel between them will be weak enough to break, or pry open!*"

Greg heard, and adjusted his stance before striking another spot by the elevator shaft. Something about Greg's new stance made the tower groan *and* rattle in a different way.

"By your best men, huh?" Leena murmured, "all of them with years of experience using junk to build towers to Actual, right?"

Then, a snapping sound rang out. A few metres below Greg, a long chunk of scrap toppled outward, and began falling. Greg yelped, and dropped the hammer to free both hands, and hung on. The section he'd been standing on was now too steeply slanted. His feet balanced on the edge of it.

The hammer fell onto something about eight metres down. That section of the tower began to sag. The sudden jolt caused the piece Greg was standing on to collapse, leaving him dangling from the piece he had snatched onto. It was not strong enough.

While the Hammer continued its own noisy, destructive descent, Greg became a much heavier projectile, coming straight down, breaking apart pieces, many of them falling outward from the elevator shaft.

By now, people below were panicked, most unsure of which way to run. It looked to be coming down everywhere.

Leena fell as structure chunks surrounded her, and many others. Thankfully a vary large part of the tower that had fallen near her was acting as a meagre shelter to keep out other things. Mostly. She could still hear a few things falling. People yelling. Mike was still nearby, but also very nearby stood Sledge, crouching down with his hands on his head.

Facing away from her.

A bent bit of broken metal bar sat nearby. This was an amazing opportunity, and she could blame the tower's collapse. She'd had to defend herself in the past, but this was going to be a bit more extreme.

She held her breath, and lunged at Sledge, jabbing the jagged end into the side of his neck. As Leena hopped back, he tried to swat at her, but all he managed was to make his wound worse. To compound this, with a raspy yell, he yanked the metal bar out of his neck, and fell to his knees.

"Sorry. Warren's next," she whispered. She kicked his head, knocking him over onto his side, wound down.

"Leena...?" Mike gasped quietly.

"Heh... didn't even get blood on me, I ... wait... what's going on outside the wreck of this tower crap?"

The wreck obscured their sight and confounded passage around it- but the sounds of fighting came through loud and clear.

"Edgar's people are here. Where do you think Warren is?" Leena asked.

"Not here. But I also wonder where that Greg is." Mike went over to Sledge's body, and liberated Greg's knife. "I want to go out and help Edgar, but I want to track down Greg first."

"Do you think he survived the fall?" Leena asked.

"Doubt it," Mike said. "If he did, I'll bet he wishes he hadn't. If he's all wrecked and in agony, I'll finish him."

"How kind," Leena said.

"I'm just a big softie, you know that. Come on."

Leena looked toward the noise outside. "Eh, you go ahead. It's quieting down a bit out there, I want to get a peek, maybe make contact with Edgar."

"Oh, for crying out loud. I'll worry the whole time. Just –"

"I'm not an idiot, Mike. I know how to keep my head down."

Mike grabbed Leena, and hugged her tight. "You'll drive me mad yet." He handed her Greg's knife. "You might have more need of this than me."

"What if you find Greg, he's okay, and in a fighting mood?"

"I'll have to be resourceful," Mike said with a smirk. "Besides, I'm not an idiot- I know how to keep my head down too." He headed into more wreckage, moving chunks and climbing around things as he went.

"Be safe, moron."

"Love you too, idiot!"

Leena found she had a similar plight ahead of her, navigating the wreck. In five minutes, she hadn't gotten far, but she found one of Warren's men- half crushed by one of the heavier pieces. It looked like he'd died instantly.

This much death was not how Citizenry usually worked. Under Warren's rule, death was supposedly a last resort, because he might be able to use you later. She didn't expect it to take as long as it did to escape the wreck, and things had gotten quieter. No one was fighting nearby, but people were talking.

"I can't believe it," a voice was heard to say. "Barry's dead. So's Lyle. Others are just missing, and where the hell did Warren end up after all this?"

Leena didn't know those names. The person speaking could be on Edgar *or* Warren's side.

"We should remove ourselves from this place." That was definitely Edgar.

"Edgar!" Leena called out.

"What? Who's in there? Leena, you're alive?"

"Yeah, yeah, I'm coming out... uh... as soon as I wrangle over this chunk of... *well damn*, I think this used to be *my* shack's wall! Eh, I'm coming, I'm fine, hang on."

Edgar and his subordinate helped clear that path a bit, quickening Leena's egress from the wreck.

"Leena, oh, I'm so sorry, is Mike-"

"Mike's fine. He's still crawling in there, looking for Greg. Oh, by the way, Sledge is dead."

"You found him in the wreckage, hm?" Edgar guessed.

"If Warren or his people ask, yeah. But nah, he was fine, with Mike and me, and I just... took some initiative."

"*You* did?"

Leena shrugged. "Amazing Actual-powers, remember? Or not-so-amazing sharp metal pipe chunk... powers. You don't know where Warren is, I hear?"

"Ah... no. Today will change things. If Warren's alive, he knows we're against him. We've both taken losses, but Sledge will be a loss I think he would feel deeply. For better or worse."

"Yeah. Well, we'll see what happens." Leena backed towards the wreck. "I'm likely still seen as an ally, or at least a non-enemy by Warren's people. I'm going back in the wreck, to meet up with Mike, and ... go home, I guess."

"Yes," Edgar said, "I should go before the wrong people see us talking."

"Stay safe, Edgar. I might have an idea, so in the meantime, don't take any risks."

Leena headed back into the wreck. She thought of trying to take a path that might go more directly to Mike, but that would be a guess at best. Besides, the path she had come out was already mostly cleared.

She'd forgotten that it meant going by the half-crushed corpse, and eventually to Sledge's body. A pang of guilt tried to sneak up on her, but then she remembered some of the things he'd done. The memory of seeing him kill Darling brutally rushed back to her. Yeah, that alone scrubbed her guilt away too well.

Focus. She looked to the direction Mike had gone, and started to follow. She called out to him. There wasn't much fear of attracting some hostile individual. Her biggest risk right now was running into a goon that was content to ignore Warren's wishes while he wasn't around.

A metal clamour sounded before Mike answered. "Leena! I'm coming to you. Come to me!"

"Yeah, yeah. Find anyone in here?" she said as she followed the voice, worming her way around chunks of debris. Squeeze under this, crawl over that, bit by bit.

"Yeah," Mike called back- now closer, and a little quieter. "Greg. He was... wow *so* killed in the fall. No one else though. I mean, could be others in this mess somewhere. What did you find?"

"Edgar," Leena said, now face-to-face with Mike. "He had one of his guys with him, too. They're getting out of here now. Both sides lost people, and no one seems to know where W.... Mike, is that...?"

Now close enough to see it well, Mike held up the other thing he found. "Behold!" Mike cheered, "I have the *treasure!* The hammer of Sledge! I must now change my name to Sledge, because I have a sledgehammer that I'll become way too attached to, and am too dumb to remember the name of the hammer, *and* my own original name!"

Leena suppressed a smile. "Oh, be nice to the dead."

"If he was nice when he was alive, I might be."

"Fair enough. Let's go look for another 'nice' friend. I have a bit of a plan."

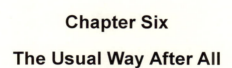

Chapter Six

The Usual Way After All

"*Just get out,*" Warren yelled at his guards, and the woman they were offering him. "I need to be alone right now! Make yourselves useful and find Sledge!"

Once alone, Warren threw himself into his misery and screamed with rage and sorrow. One concerned guard poked his head back in, only to get yelled at again.

"*I said go!*"

Where was that blasted jar now? He could still feel the white powder strongly, but *more* white powder would make him feel better, or at least different. If it was indeed from the Actual, maybe enough of it would give him the clarity of thought to finally find a way up.

Where, where? He tossed around the many layers of his bedding, finding a few empty cups, a sealed crap-sniffer jar, a book of nonsense that didn't even have any bloody pictures in it, useless piece of crap.

"*Where the fuck is it?*" Readying his knife, he stormed out into a larger area of the stack, looking to interrogate someone- anyone, about the location of the white powder.

One guard was brave enough to venture forward a little. "Everyone thought you'd be gone by now, so maybe someone thought they could take it, and..."

"And what?" Warren growled as he stalked towards the guard, knife at the ready.

"*Warren!*" Leena entered, with Mike beside her.

"*Leena!*" Warren lost all interest in the guard, who now retreated discretely. "Leena, you're all right! Bah." Warren hit his head with his free hand. "Of course you're all right, you're an Actual. You saved your servant Mark here, I suppose, and- wait, what does he have?"

Leena held out her hand for Mike to hand her the sledgehammer. She held it solemnly, lowering her head.

"No, no..." Warren whimpered.

"I'm sorry. He wasn't close enough to save." She pulled out Greg's knife. "This one also, of course, from so high up..."

Warren shuffled close, and leaned over so his face was right next to the head of the hammer. "Sledge, Sledge," he lamented, "you dumb non-real thing, you should have run as soon as it started collapsing, like I did."

"Warren, did you even see the fight that started?" Mike asked.

"What?"

"After the collapse," Leena chose not to mention Edgar or any organized group, "quite a few Citizens attacked the guards who weren't caught in the wreck. You lost a few, and some other Citizens died as well."

Warren nodded, with a furrowed brow. "Yes. Yes, I understand. The Citizens blame my men for making such a terrible tower. I understand. Next time there's a Gathering, I'll ask the Citizens to forgive my men for failing me."

"That sounds wise," Mike said, trying hard to keep a straight face.

"Warren," Leena said calmly, "may I give the hammer to Mike? He's like my 'Sledge'."

Warren looked Mike up and down. "It is right, it is good. But can your skinny little man wield it?"

Mike took the hammer from Leena, and swung it a couple of times. "It's a slow-moving thing, but I'll get better at it."

Warren stood upright, and spread out his arms. "The hammer will teach you, Mark!" He cackled a bit, jittering, "You will become stronger, and mighty! Worthy of being any Actual's man!"

"Ah... huh. Thank you?" Mike said.

"Warren, I have more important things to discuss," Leena said, "I have a plan to get you up, but we need to do it now."

Warren's expression snapped from a white-powder-fueled version of near-regency, to a white-powder-fueled version of ultimate hope, eyes welling up almost instantly.

"Leena! Leena, Leena, do not tease me! Tell me you aren't joking!"

"I'm not," Leena said. "We have a fair handful of dead now, right?"

The light began to flicker in Warren's head. "And where do they go... indeed. But how does that help me?"

"Simple. You play dead, and go with them. Messenger might not check everyone to make sure they're dead. If you're in the middle of half a dozen dead people, he might just bring you all into the Grand Elevator."

Warren lowered his head in thought, eyes darting back and forth. "And... and to look dead, I could take some blood from one of the bodies, and smear it on myself. But can Messenger even be fooled?"

"It's your only chance now, short of actually dying," Mike said. "We'll cover your face with some cloth too, like we often do with bodies. Then you don't have to be so careful not to move your eyes and such. Be careful not to blow the cloth off with your breath, though."

"Maybe we can skip the blood smearing though," Leena said, "that's taking it a bit far."

"No, no," Warren said intensely, "the greatest effort must be made. Will you be coming with me, Leena?"

Leena sighed. "Might be extra risky, trying to slip two people through."

Warren nodded again, and took Leena's hand. "Oh, oh Leena, you make such a sacrifice for me. But if getting me through works, you can try next time. We have a lot of dead bodies!"

Leena reclaimed her hand, and nodded politely. "I wouldn't be able to take my favourite with me, anyway. I think I'll stay in Citizenry for some time. Shall we?"

The trio headed out, with a customary quartet of guards... who kept a little more distance from Warren than usual. At Warren's instruction, Mike carried a strange box with knobs and other strange bits. While he was unloading cargo, he brought out his personal knife.

It was another of the treasured items, not made by Citizen hands. While Greg's knife was pretty enough, Warren's was compact. A blade that *looked* a little short, only because of its thickness. It had a little rectangular hole near the tip, a bit of a smooth valley running down most of the blade, and jagged bits on the non-cutting edge of it. The handle was thicker, and filled a clenching hand well. The end of the handle had a little hole for... hanging it on a wall? Overall, it had been designed with a purpose.

"Leena, I want you to have my best knife. From me to you, as Actuals."

"Well...! Uh, thank you, Warren, it's very impressive!" Leena's first thought was to gut him with it on the spot, but her original plan was still better.

It wasn't far from Warren's Stack to the Grand Elevator loading bay, but all the way, he announced things like, "Citizens! All Citizens! Come see my ascent to the Actual, and know I became among him!" leaping and flouncing madly with joy all the while.

While it was not said that attendance was mandatory to get food, a mix of curiosity and plain habit to obey-or-else, brought out a great deal of the Citizens in earshot.

The dead had preceded them. When they arrived at the Grand Elevator's door, a few guards were there, having recently laid out a row of the dead- both Warren's and Edgar's people. The row took up most of the width of the bay, with bodies snugly against each other, feet towards the elevator, faces covered with scraps of cloth.

"Oh, these lucky few," Warren said in awe, "When the Actual brings them to their new life, they will be among the first to see that I stand beside the Actual. This first to know what I truly am!"

"Oh, lucky Jen," Mike said quietly to Leena, "to have had the sense to have stayed home. This is all... I don't have the words."

Leena had seen dead bodies before, in the past and very recently, but seeing so many lined up in a matter-of-fact manner made it seem all the more... impersonal. Dehumanizing.

The Citizens and guards who were in audience were near silent. Despite the cruelty sanctioned by Warren over the years, killing was never an intended result. Inspiring suicide was another matter, but this row of brutally killed people was a sight that staggered and daunted almost everyone.

That didn't stop Warren from doing a tiny bit of re-arranging so that he could happily squeeze in a place to lie down around the middle of the row, which happened to be next to Sledge's body.

He reached over to Sledge's neck wound with a gentle smile, and pressed his fingers beside it, to cause more blood to ooze out onto his fingers. He brought it to his own forehead, and smeared it across. Then some on his cheek.

"Warren..." Mike said as he rested the hammer near the side wall, "we're going to be covering your face anyway, remember? That's... that's not necessary." He looked to the Citizens, who couldn't entirely hide their revulsion. One turned away and pushed through the crowd to leave. Another unconsciously shook her head slowly.

Leena chose to face away from Warren, so he could not see the rage building within her. She only shared looks with the Citizens, feeling a common empathy for each other, at the memories of all Warren's gatherings.

She could read their faces. How could anyone see them as not-real?

She walked closer to the crowd, stopping by a woman who looked particularly distressed, tears quietly running down her face. Leena took her hands, and said softly, "He's leaving us today. Sledge is dead, Warren is leaving. Things are bound to get better."

The woman sniffled and nodded.

Meanwhile, Warren had gotten more blood from Sledge to smear on his own clothes and forearm. "Mark, that box I had you bring? Time to use that to call Messenger. You should do it, because I'm supposed to be dead."

Mike drew the box closer. "And I wouldn't want to get blood on it," Mike quietly said. "I've never seen this getting used."

"It's easy. First, that little tab on the side? Flip that up. Don't ever touch any of the other things on the front of the box. It's set perfectly right now."

Mike followed the directions, and a little green light lit up.

"Good, good. By the way, if it didn't light up, or ever doesn't light up, there's a couple round pieces you need to take out of a little door on the back, and leave for Messenger. He'd take them away, and later bring them back. When you put them back in, the box will work again.

"Now, that chunk hanging on the side, attached with the funny string thing? Pick that up. There's a button on the side that you have to *hold down* while talking into the side with the little slots. Your words will find Messenger. Now- tell him that there are dead to take away. Repeat it a few times, and don't talk too fast. That's the way I was taught to do it."

Mike looked at the piece in his hand, looked to Warren, then to Leena and the Citizens. He held the button down.

"Hello. Hello, Messenger. I am Mike," he began slowly. Not slowly because he was instructed to, but because the weight of it dragged at his words. "There was a fight. There was a fight, and many died. Our leader, Warren, is among the dead." Mike stood with the box, and faced the Citizens. "Since Warren is dead, we will need a new leader."

He walked over to the hammer, which stood nearby. "I repeat, Messenger, we have many dead for you to take. It will be difficult for us to adjust to life without them. Please come, and take our dead. Thank you, Messenger." Mike released the button, and sighed.

Mike looked towards Warren.

"That should do it!" Warren chirped.

Taking a cloth from one of the guards, Mike draped it over Warren's face. Warren was smiling madly the whole time. "And ta-da! I'm dead." Warren joked, "I tried asking Messenger nicely to go up, I tried building my way up, and now I outsmart Messenger as my final test! Watch and marvel, my Citizens, as I go to join the Actual – as another Actual!"

Mike turned off the box, and put it down beside the hammer. He picked up the hammer, and looked to Leena. Leena gave a small, troubled smile, and nodded.

Carrying the hammer in both hands, Mike walked to the middle of the row of dead, near Warren, and faced the Citizens. "People. Soon, we'll have to leave here, and Messenger will take them all away... including Warren. He will be gone from us." Mike lowered his head a bit, and frowned a little. "Citizens..." Mike raised the hammer over his head with one hand and tilted his head. "What do you say we give Warren a proper send-off?"

The Citizens were silent for a moment. Mike stood motionless with the hammer held high.

"Yes." came a voice from somewhere in the crowd, very quietly. Murmurs of approval followed. "Sounds right," came another voice, louder. So far, none of the handful of guards nearby had said anything, but Mike spotted some nodding among them. Warren's new white-powder self had perhaps cost him some loyalty.

"Show him our appreciation!" yelled a voice. Cheers and more yelling erupted– indistinct, but all in agreement. A smile cracked on the face of one of the guards. Another joined in the cheering.

"I'm so moved, even if they don't exist!" came Warren's voice from under the cloth.

Mike turned to face Warren, and grabbed the hammer with both hands, steadying his aim. The cheering surged, and the hammer came down with all the force Mike could muster.

The head of the hammer crashed into Warren's head, pushing the cloth in about ten centimetres. The entire room seemed to shake with a thunderous sound. Thanks to the cloth, the unavoidable mess was minimized.

Mike stared at the hammer's head, driven deep. The impact seemed to echo, and quiver through the whole loading bay.

He barely heard the crowd erupt. Only when he felt Leena's hand on his shoulder, did he move again, pulling the hammer out. Despite the cloth, the hammer's head was bloodied.

He rested the head of the hammer on the floor, and perched the handle up. He expected to see the cheering. He didn't expect to see so many tears of joy. As he slowly walked away from the dead, some people came to him, throwing their arms around him, and more followed. He reached to Leena to keep her close as the crowd surrounded them. They shared a kiss, and the cheers grew.

As the overall clamour began to fade, Mike raised his hand.

"*I have some good news, and some bad news, depending on who you are, and how you see things,*" he hollered. The people grew notably quieter to be able to hear Mike better.

"*Rapes? Rapes are over.*" A cautiously optimistic up-swell ensued from people. "*If you're a person who might be a target for a rape, I think that's probably good news.*"

Mike paused to quickly make eye-contact with a few of Warren's nearby guards.

"*If you're a person who likes rapes, there's going to have to be some changes in your behaviour.*" Mike tapped the head of the hammer on the floor a couple of times— not seen by many, but heard by all.

"I don't have time to go hunting down everyone who's done awful things before today. They might deserve it, but it's not practical, I'm sorry. But from today on?"

Mike looked around with a smug grin. "From today on, that kind of thing will. Be. Dealt with."

The crowd remained fairly quiet, but most smiling, some also crying. Leena leaned over and whispered something in Mike's ear.

"Yes... that's exactly what I was thinking." He raised his voice again to address everyone. "You're all thinking, 'how is this one man going to stop all the cruelty alone? Simple, I'll have help!

"Firstly, I know there is a group that has opposed Warren and his way for some time. They were they ones who attacked his men when that tower thing fell. I know giving them any official responsibility might make some of Warren's ex-guards uncomfortable. Tough."

Mike changed his expression from smug, to compassionate, and made eye contact with as many people as he could. He spoke quieter, and the previously quiet crowd was now absolutely silent.

"Second is all of *you*. We've all heard attacks in progress, and done nothing for fear of arriving, and being beaten or stabbed, accomplishing nothing of any benefit." Taking a stiffer stance, he raised his voice again. "*That ends today! From now on, if you hear someone in trouble, run to it! Everyone who hears it, run to it. You'll be many. You'll be unstoppable.*"

Leena chirped up, "And let's ditch that knife-law, too. Twenty or more knife-wielding Citizens should make any rapist think twice!"

The crowd erupted in cheers.

Yes, they had just enabled mob-justice... but it was a lot more justice than they'd had before. Feeling that the important things had been covered, Mike gave the crowd his best smile. "Tell everyone, everything that happened here."

Cheering, tears and hugs were moving through the crowd, as if the feelings were entities with their own will. The crowd slowly began to disperse.

A few people went to go say some final goodbyes to a few of the bodies; a few stragglers came to thank Mike.

"So, he wasn't an Actual?" one younger man asked.

"If he was an Actual, then I'm a jar of sniffing-crap." Mike said.

Leena spoke up. "Yeah, I'm not into being a jar of crap, but I'm also not an Actual. As far as I care, Warren can go rot with the lofus, but I guess the real Actual will judge him."

The handful of people who heard that seemed pleased with the answer.

The room shook a little, and Mike clued in that the echo of the hammer hitting Warren was not his doing; Messenger had already arrived.

"Oh... hi." Mike said.

"If you are done, all living Citizens please leave the loading bay." came Messenger's voice.

"Did... did *you* hear everything that just happened here?" Leena asked quietly.

"Yes. I waited to let you all sort it out. Actual will approve," Messenger said.

"Actual..." Leena said softly. "He really knows what happens here? And he cares?"

Maybe, just maybe, there was a breathy trace of a laugh in Messenger's voice. "Many, who are not here, who are not Citizens, take interest in what happens here. It is displeasing when you hurt each other."

"Yes, Messenger." A familiar voice surprised Leena and Mike from behind. Among other Citizens who hadn't left yet, they turned to see Edgar, down on one knee, head low. Had he been in the crowd, or had he just recently come in? He and four of his people were in the loading bay now.

"Edgar!" Leena said, "were you here to hear everything?"

"I heard enough. Messenger, if I may have a moment still to visit with my fallen?"

"Very well."

Recognizing which were his friends by their clothing, he lifted the cloth from their faces. Then he kissed his index and middle finger, and solemnly touched the foreheads of each one of his friends. He put the cloth back over their faces, and stood back. "Thank you, Messenger. May your travels be safe, and may Actual smile upon you."

When they exited the building, one of Warren's ex-guards stepped up to Mike. "So. Are you intending to move into the stack? I don't really want to leave it. Lotta guys probably feel the same way."

Mike looked towards the stack, and scrunched his lips. "A bit too much bad history in there for me. Stay there. Or strip it down so you can all go have separate shacks from the materials. I don't much care."

"Lotta guys gonna hold a grudge anyway," the ex-guard said.

Leena looked in the direction of their own shack, which was still far off. A steady stream of Citizens carrying metal from the tower wreck could be seen. A disproportionate number of them were headed in the general direction of Leena and Mike's shack.

"Your 'lotta guys' are outnumbered, I think," Leena said. "Right now my boy Mikey is pretty damned popular. If he gets hurt, I think they'll be a lot of hurt back."

"Look, look," Mike said, "I think I've been really reasonable with Warren's men today. If 'a lotta guys' seem itchy to make an issue of it all, remind them that Warren was leaving them anyway. Remind them how messed up he'd become with that stupid white powder. We're all better off."

The ex-guard looked towards the loading bay building. "Maybe. Maybe some guys aren't so smart. Will miss the Gatherings and stuff." It was difficult to tell if he was including himself in that category.

"Well, if some guys become too much of a problem, they're going to be up against me, and a whole bunch of Citizens." Mike walked on by him, and Leena kept up. When the ex-guard was out of earshot, Leena quietly said to Mike, "You're putting an awful lot of faith in the Citizens to stand up to stuff."

"Yes. It might be wishful thinking right now," Mike said. "They're used to being scared. But, if I insist that they're braver than that, tell them I trust they can do the right thing, they might start believing it too. And then it simply becomes true."

"Optimistic! Hey, you've put a lot of thought into this, haven't you? Your little speech back there was pretty impressive. I wouldn't expect you had it in you! Or that you wanted to be any kind of leader, for that matter."

"Me as leader?" Mike laughed. "I hadn't given that a lot of thought, but I thought about the Citizens a lot. We always outnumbered Warren's goons. It just took some important deaths to give them a chance to see some hope. And I can thank you for Sledge, and your plan for Warren. You should be leader, my love!"

"No, no no no," Leena said, "I don't think there's much chance of a lot of these guys ... Warren's people especially, to want a woman leader. Instead, I'll just tell you what to do, and control you for my own *evil* purposes!"

"I can live with that."

At their shack, a minor commotion was underway. Citizens had brought a generous share of metal from the wreck already, and a couple of more Citizens were coming with premium pieces.

Jen stood outside. On spotting them, she ran over, took a moment to decide who to hug, then just yanked both Leena and Mike together, to hug them both. "I heard! Is it true?"

"What, is it true that people didn't waste any time to salvage the tower? Because– woah," Leena answered.

"No! I mean about Warren!" Jen insisted.

Mike swung the hammer up, so his grip was near the head of it, then held it out to Jen. It was still a bit of a mess from Warren's blood. "I don't know, does this smell like him?"

"Ahhh! Gross! And... yay! And get that away from me!"

"Classy, Mike," Leena said.

"Yeah, Jen, it's true. Assuming they memorised everything I said, and told it all to you."

"I.... I only heard about you killing Warren," Jen said, "sorry. What'd I miss?"

"Much!" Edgar had caught up with them. "You missed him assuming leadership of the Citizenry, and volunteering me and my people to be his underlings."

"Ahh..." Mike blushed, and smiled meekly. "I wouldn't put it that way, I didn't call you my underling. You weren't there to ask, and I figured, you're anti-Warren, we're on the same side of things, and..."

"And you assumed you would be the best leader," Edgar interrupted.

"Ehh, it was the moment, you know?" Mike held up the hammer again as part evidence, and part explanation. "Emotions were high, things were going so fast..."

"Quite."

"It's not like I planned it. I was just going to kill him, and things just... one thing led to another..."

"And now Citizens are offering you far more metal than you need," Edgar observed, as a couple of more pieces were delivered.

"Yeah," Mike turned to look at the growling pile, and the most recent delivery man. "Guys, tell 'em that's more than enough, and thanks." Mike turned to the little pile again, and mumbled. "Yeah, what am I going to do with this all?"

"All because it was your hand that killed him," Edgar said. "Not because you've been carefully planning, and organizing people. Not because you led a large attack on Warren that cost good people their lives, but because you were in the right place, and the right time, with a big hammer."

"Huh. Yeah, funny, that."

"Hilarious," Edgar said dryly.

"No, no, don't take it the wrong way, I'm sure your attack was uh... super important in giving Leena the chance to kill Sledge, and... yeah!"

Edgar snapped his direction to Leena, and looked her up and down. "Oh yes, that... *you* did actually kill Sledge?"

"Yeah," Leena said bashfully. "I told you at the wreck. He was looking the other way, I had a sharp thing..."

"Lovely," Edgar said. "So you sneaked up on him. And Mike killed Warren while he was playing dead. Such honour."

"Hey, hey now," Mike spoke up, "I don't know about honour, but what's more important? How it gets done, or *why* we do it? *What* we try to get done? And the plan that finally got Warren was all Leena's quick thinking."

"And the people were saved by lucky sneak assassins." Edgar said to no one in particular. "And where do you go from here, Mike?"

Mike looked at Jen, and back at Edgar. "Well, Jen didn't hear my whole talk. Most people didn't hear my whole talk. I think I need to tell everyone."

Hammer in tow, Mike headed back to the loading bay building. Beside him walked Jen and Leena, examining her two new knives, (Greg's and Warren's.) A few Citizens followed along. Edgar wasn't too far off, following, but not quite directly 'with' them. Edgar had a couple of his *own* people with him to chat with.

By the time Mike and his entourage were climbing the ramp to get atop the building, he'd attracted quite a bit of attention.

"People? People?" Mike called out from about half way up the ramp. "I can see more people coming this way. Maybe I'll wait to say my thing until they're arrived."

The growing crowd had some impatient members. *"Is it true you killed Warren?"*

Mike held up the hammer as he and Leena finished climbing the ramp. "Yeah, yeah. I still see some of the poor bastard's blood on Sledge's hammer. At least he gets to be with his buddy Sledge as Messenger takes him away!"

"Is he going to be our Actual now?" someone hollered.

With a laugh, Mike started briskly pacing atop the building, looking out over the crowd. (And Edgar, who stood stoically on the sidelines.)

"Do any of you think he was special, other than his brutality? Many of you have met him, and know he was not right in the head, especially lately. He thought he was so special, an Actual! Do you know why?"

Mike held his hand out to the people for an answer to "Why?"

Answers spoken, but not yelled, came back. Answers about him having his stack, about him having followers, things of that nature.

"No! No, no." Mike waved away their suggestions like a stench in the air. "No. He thought he was special, because he though *you* were nothing." Mike pointed at a random Citizen. "Thought *you* were nothing. Thought *I* was nothing." He pointed to someone in another direction. "That you weren't real, not in the same way *he* was real." Mike waved his pointing finger across everyone. "No one's life mattered, no one's feelings, no one's safety. I have news for you all. You exist! You're real! You know your fellow Citizens are real! They all feel in similar ways as you!"

"What about her?" someone asked, pointing at Leena.

"Uh, yeah," Leena said, "I'm real too. And not any Actual. He thought I was one because he thought I was clever. He... he was crazy."

Laughter bubled from the crowd.

"For the record," Mike said, "Leena *is* quite clever. And I think she's special. She's my favourite. But all of you are special. I apologize however, that I won't be getting around to sleeping with all of you."

Another volley of laughs came forth, a little braver than the last one.

Mike smiled at them all, reveling in the kind of merriment he'd never seen before. "Damn, I think I love you people," he said, not trying to be heard. Only those closest to the building could have heard it. He stood with better posture, and wore a serious but gentle expression, just the softest bit of a smile, eyes shining.

"Let me tell you my plan. The plan I told the people in the loading bay right after Warren died."

He then outlined his innovative "no rapes" policy, and how Citizens no longer had to be afraid to help each other. Strength in numbers, and an end to the knife ban. He was careful not to volunteer Edgar or his people, as Edgar was watching with an impossible-to-read face.

Cheers were cheered when cheering was expected. A few more tears of joy trickled down.

"So go home, get any metal you think is yours. And also look in the pile kindly taken to my shack. I can't imagine needing that much. The cardboard is actually working out pretty w–"

Leena slapped Mike's arm.

"Ow, okay," Mike said. "Maybe I need *some* metal."

A few laughs came forth.

"You're not still going to live in your old shack, are you?" a Citizen asked.

"Well... well yeah," Mike said, "I'm sure not going to be moving into Warren's stack. Where am I *supposed* to live?"

"Build your own stack! Get your guards to do it!" someone else called out. Another Citizen was pointing to some windows on the top end of one of the long, dilapidated ramps that led half-way up the side walls of the Citizenry dome.

"No, no", Mike waved the idea away with his hand. "And I don't have guards! I have all of you! Lots of people wanted to kill Warren; *he* needed guards! I hope that if any of you have a problem with me, you come talk to me. I promise I won't have my non-existent guards drag you into the farthest room in my non-existent stack, and beat you senseless. That's what we just won against. We. All of us. *We* won! Guard each other! We are *all* now guards of *everyone!*"

Mike and Leena descended the ramp and walked among a cheerful crowd. They had more hope than anyone could remember seeing in a long, long time.

Some older woman Mike didn't know grabbed onto him from the side, and squeezed, teetering back and forth a little. "Good boy here," she said to Leena, "you found a good boy!"

They exchanged smiles and small laughs as another stranger patted Mike on the back. Even small children that might not understand the whole situation could feel the general good mood, and were cheerful for it.

"Gonna need a bigger shack if all these people are coming," Leena discreetly joked to Mike.

And that's when Edgar found them. "Well!" he said, loudly enough to make it clear that he'd be happy if everyone heard him, "they seem quite enamoured with you."

"Well, that sounds overly personal of them!" Mike said, not having heard the word 'enamoured' before. A typical Citizens' vocabulary was often lacking.

Edgar lazily glared at Mike. "It means,"

"I get it, I get it," Mike interrupted. "I kind of 'enamour' them too!" He looked around the people surrounding him.

A swell of positive responses came from them. "Yeah!" "Me too!" "Enamble!"

"Yes!" Edgar declared, "they like you! I'm not questioning that! It's all well and good, but can you *lead?*"

"Can I?" Mike said, slightly quieter. Nearby Citizens strained to hear. "I didn't plan on it, but so far, things seem to be going okay."

"*Heroic bravado and popular proclamations!*" Edgar said, flustered. "It takes more than that! I've spent years studying the writings! I understand the difficulties!"

A Citizen who had been in the loading bay when Warren was killed spoke up, "Messenger said it was good!"

Mike nodded a few times, and looked back to Edgar.

Edgar was unimpressed. "I heard what you refer to. What exactly did he say that Actual would approve of? I didn't hear him endorsing any new *leaders*. It seems more likely that Messenger was simply referring to the death of the old one. I have a plan for the future, and you do not, beyond *'be excellent to each other'*."

"I like it," Mike half-mumbled, nodding to other people, some of whom nodded back in the same way. "sounds like a good plan that should last a good while. Seems like a plan that doesn't need changing."

"Child," Edgar said, nearly spitting, "do what you want. I will proceed with my plan. I will build a stack for me and my people. Others are welcome, but in my stack, my refuge, *I will be leader*." He stood defiantly before Mike, physically bracing for rebuttal, bearded chin held forward, hands on hips.

"Huh." Mike said. "You gonna be killing people in there?"

"What? No!" Edgar looked a tiny bit insulted.

"Aaaaand you gonna be raping people in there?"

"By Actual, no!" Now Edgar was notably more insulted.

"I didn't think so! Then have fun! Can't wait to see it!" Mike patted him on the shoulder, and continued his way among the surrounding Citizens, with Leena by his side.

After getting a little distance from Edgar, Leena pulled Mike closer, and with a sly smirk, she said, "Cold, man." She followed it up with a peck to the cheek.

"Cold?" Mike said. "Cold? No! Warm! Have I ever been anything but entirely friendly to that guy?"

"He might see it as smug and sarcastic."

"Bah. If he wants to see my being 'friendly' like that, I can't help it. I'll go help for a while on his stack or something when he gets it going."

"No you won't." Leena said.

Yeah, I probably won't. Sounds like effort."

74

Chapter Seven

Reparations

When they got home, the pile of metal was different. While some people had taken both his suggestion, and what they needed, others added to the pile. "We should just declare this place a metal supply pile or something, and move somewhere else," Leena said.

Jen stepped out of the shack to meet them, and another young lady followed her. "Hi, guys."

"Hello Jen," Leena said, "Who's your friend?"

The new one was similar in many ways to Jen- her build, hair length, and friendly but meek expression. Where Jen was blonde, the new one had very black hair. Where Jen was pale, the new one's skin was decidedly darker.

"This is Tara," Jen said affectionately, "she..." Jen blushed, and smiled, lowering her head.

"Oh, my, Leena, could it be?" Mike said in his smoothest voice, "Has our little Jen brought home her new favourite?"

Tara, now embarrassed as well, hid her face in Jen's hair, while grabbing Jen's hand.

"Mike, don't embarrass them... *too* much." Leena said.

"And where did you two meet? How long has this been going on?" Mike asked with a smile.

"Warren's stack, actually," Jen said, "kinda a long time ago, and we kinda couldn't. You know?"

"Uh, not really." Leena said.

"I had this man," Tara started to explain.

"You mean *he* had *you,*" Jen abruptly interrupted.

"Ehhh, yeah," Tara agreed. "He didn't like me being with anyone else. He was... strict about it."

"You lived with him in Warren's stack?" Mike guessed.

"Yeah. And now he's dead. Thank you so much, Mike." Tara moved in, and gave Mike a huge hug.

Mike raised an eyebrow, and looked to Leena, who shrugged.

"What... was it Warren?" Mike asked.

"Hm? No, no, we just lived there."

"But I only really recall killing Warren, so..."

"He died when that tower collapsed," Tara said. "And that wouldn't have happened without you."

"Totally *would* have," Leena said in a blasé tone.

"She's pretty much right," Mike said. "If he died in the actual collapse, you can thank Warren's men's sloppy construction. I didn't affect that. And if he died in the fight around it, you can thank Edgar, or one of *his* guys."

"In the collapse," Tara said, "but thank you anyway. I don't think there's going to be another like him now, and that's because of you."

"It wasn't Sledge, was it?" Leena asked. "Cuz I would totally take thanks from you if it was Sledge."

"Are you flirting?" Mike said, amused.

"What?" Leena scoffed with a laugh. "You're my favourite, but I can still play with others!"

"I'm going to be selfish here, guys," Jen said, gently pulling Tara away from Mike and Leena.

"Fair enough!" Leena said, chuckling.

"Do *I* get any sort of say?" Tara yelped.

Jen stood there, slowly leaning back and forth. She finally said, "Well... I mean... I'm not going to say you *can't* or anything-"

"I choose selfish, too!" Tara grabbed Jen close, and gave her a kiss lasting a handful of seconds.

"Awwww..." Mike said. "So, what now, is Tara moving in, or what's going on here?"

"Kinda... the opposite," Jen said. "Tara and I are going to move out."

"Oh." Mike said, looking dejected.

"Oh, well, I'm happy for you guys!" Leena said. "Just the two of you?"

"Uh huh!" Tara said.

Mike took a heroic stance, and stared off to nowhere. "But do you have some strong, burly man to protect you?"

Jen rolled her eyes. "Tara found us a spot with lots of good neighbours."

Mike leaned over to Leena, with a finger raised. "See?" he said softly, but with exaggerated intensity. "Citizens looking out for Citizens. Already! And Edgar says I can't lead."

"Before we head out. though, we're going to help you rebuild your shack," Jen said, "Especially since you have this handy pile of metal to pick from."

"Well! Thanks guys!" Leena said.

Reconstruction was a small task for a modest shack, but the quartet had fun picking and choosing metal sheets, rating them on size, rigidity, stability, cleanliness, beauty, sense of humour, conversation skills, and several other attributes that no hunk of metal is expected to have.

All the pieces scored quite poorly in several of the categories, except one piece of sheet metal whose rust stain looked vaguely like an interesting piece of male anatomy. Mike gave that one credit for 'manliness', and the ladies attributed it to 'humour' and 'pity'.

When they were half-done the actual 'reconstruction' part of the reconstruction, a young, darkly-blonde-haired man came up to Mike. "Mike? Hi? My name is Cody. Uh, can I ask a favour?"

"Huh? Ask away!"

"I had an idea... to make something."

"Something?" Mike asked. "Something bad, or something good?"

"Something good! You'll like it, I hope! I want it to be a surprise, uh... for you."

"Uh, thanks, maybe. Telling me that you're going to make it makes it less of a surprise, though." Mike said.

"Yeah..." Cody said, "but I kinda need some metal from that pile."

"Of course! I've already said that people can take what they need for their shacks."

"I think I'll need a *lot*." said Cody quietly, with a forced, nervous grin.

"How much is a lot? Other people might still need some from here."

Cody took a deep breath. "Well, I won't be taking it all at once, ha ha, I'm not that strong, so people will have lots of chances before I'm done, and if anyone needs some after the pile is gone, they can ask me for some back, but maybe when they know what I'm building, they might think that *my* thing to do with is more important than the thing *they* want to do with it. They might even give me some more, I don't now yet, I haven't even started yet, but I think people will really–"

Mike grabbed Cody's shoulders. "Stop. Take a breath already!" Cody did, and found that he'd talked himself right out of breath.

"Sounds … tiring." Mike said with a smirk.

"You can trust him," Tara said. "I've known Cody forever. He's nice."

"I only just met *you,* Tara," Mike said, "but you *seem* nice, and *Jen* likes you. And *Jen* is nice. And if *Jen* thinks *you're* nice, and you think *he's* nice..." Mike turned to Jen, and pointed at her nose. "If this guy destroys everything and kills everyone with whatever he's doing, it's all...your...fault."

Jen stared back at Mike, and gave a moment's thought. "If we're all dead, how are you going to blame me?"

Mike pointed up. "When we all get up there! All of us, every Citizen newly dead, and brought to Actual, and I'll tell him that it's your fault that your friend's friend killed everyone."

Cody was having problems keeping a straight face. "I'll tell him it wasn't on purpose!"

Mike sighed dramatically. "All right, take metal to make your whatever-it-is. *And don't kill us all!*"

The next morning, sounds of metal could be heard in the distance. Not seeing anything immediately when she stuck her head outside, Leena pulled Mike to his groggy feet, stuffed a food disc in his mouth, and led the way.

A few chunks of metal were gone from their pile, which was to be expected. They're heard some being taken now and then, and never saw fit to bother seeing who it was. Cody, or other shack-keepers, it didn't matter.

They followed the sounds until they found the site of it all. Several Citizens were moving around chunks of metal, quite a few of them, around a large area against the edge of the Commons.

"Huh. Cody was busy," Mike joked. This endeavor had much more metal than was missing from their own pile.

"Look again," Leena said. She nudged Mike, and he followed her gaze towards Edgar. When not hauling metal himself, Edgar was directing his people.

"He hauls that scrap pretty well for his age," Mike said.

"Oh, he's not *that* old, Leena said, "Let's go make nice."

"Sounds fun. Let's hope he feels nicer today."

They went over to Edgar, who noticed them as the approached, but continued talking with his worker about the best uses for a particular big hunk of piping. Once that was decided, he to Mike and Leena, who'd been waiting patiently.

"And yes, hello," Edgar said in a polite but brusque tone. "How may I help you?"

"Help?" Mike asked, confused, looking to Leena. "Did we ask for help?"

"Mike, you mentioned something before about helping a little bit with Edgar building his stack?" Leena reminded him.

"I did?"

"He did?" Edgar echoed.

"Yes, he did," Leena said, "and I think it's a wonderful idea. If nothing else, it would show the Citizens that there's no resentment between you two after yesterday's little chat."

"Oh, they know," Mike said cheerfully, brushing away the notion.

"Yes," Edgar said, making firm eye contact with Leena. "Mike and I, yes. Resentment, a little bit."

"What?" Mike exclaimed.

Edgar held up his hand, with thumb and finger separated a bit, and silently mouthed, "little bit."

"Oh, play nice," Leena said. "Put my boy to work, Edgar, it'll do him good."

"What about you?" Mike asked Leena.

"Your idea involved *you* working, not *us*, I thought I'd go check on Jen and... Tara was it? If I can find them."

"Without me?" Mike made an exaggeratedly pathetic face.

"Sweetie, you're my favourite, not my third arm. You'll survive."

Leena walked through the Citizenry and felt safer than ever before. Maybe it was just Mike's optimistic view, or maybe it had actually infected most Citizens, becoming real. She had to remember to ground herself.

The new freedom wasn't devoid of danger, she knew that. Warren's men hadn't all disappeared the moment he died. They were out there, and habits can be hard to break, even knowing that the good people around them were doubtlessly finding or crafting their own knives.

She carried the knife that Warren had given her in a sheath made of cloth. She planned to later add a cardboard lining, so the knife was better housed. But she was carrying a knife, and it gave her a notable boost of confidence.

She looked towards an unexpected noise whenever she heard one, she still tried to choose smarter paths. But now she found herself also keeping a keener eye out for strangers- be they potentially a threat, or someone who might need help.

Here and there, she asked if anyone knew where Jen and Tara were. Just looking for a newly-created shack wasn't helpful; almost every shack had been, or was in the middle of reconstruction.

After having drifted a fair distance from Edgar's stack-in-progress, she heard another project on the go. A shack doesn't typically take *too* much bashing, or yelling, but she could hear both. Not as much as with Edgar's stack, but similar... she followed the sound, and before she arrived, she could see that people were working on one of the heavily damaged ramps that led around the Commons outer wall, up to one of the neglected balconies.

The three workers were on a section roughly thirty metres along the ramp. This only got them a few metres up from the floor below, but it implied that they had repaired things to that point.

She jogged the rest of the way, and was not surprised to see that it was Cody leading the little workforce.

"Cody! Is this your surprise?" Leena called out.

Cody turned abruptly to face her. "Ah! Aw, you've seen what I'm doing now! Don't tell Mike, okay?"

"He's going to figure it out soon enough," she said, "it's not like you're quiet, and sooner or later you're going to be visible from anywhere in Citizenry!"

Cody shrugged in concession. "Yeah, but I wanted to make sure I was able to repair this reliably, like, past the old big supports attached to the walls ... test a few things before I get anyone's hopes up."

"Wow. I'm guessing you weren't one of the people building Warren's tower. It's as if you're being *careful*, and want to *prevent* it from collapsing and killing people!"

Cody chuckled. "That's the idea. This one's for Mike. As far as I can tell, it leads to the biggest space at its top. Hard to tell from below." He wiped his brow with a rag, and pointed at the three other broken ramps around the sides of the dome. "When I'm done here, I'll probably get working on the other ramps. Like... we have these spaces waiting for us up there, so..."

"So why hasn't it been done before?" Leena asked.

Cody shrugged. "I dunno... There's a lot of scrap running around right now, for one thing. Almost everyone's stopped taking scrap from the fallen tower thing already, and have been carving up Warren's stack. Besides, I never got the impression that Warren would have much use for the ramps being fixed. His guys might have taken to beating me up over it."

"Wait a second," Leena said. "People are taking Warren's stack apart? What about the people who still live there?"

"Not many do. Between women who had felt trapped there, and men who think it's dangerous now to be associated with anything 'Warren', a lot of it's empty. Some are setting up their own shacks, some are talking about joining Edgar, some are just staying where they are. Eh... it's still early to see where everyone's going to land."

Leena snorted. "Imagine one of Warren's goons asking Edgar to let them move in... there's a conversation I'd like to hear. Hey, Cody, has anyone found a brown bag full of weird meds, or a jar with some white powder in it?"

"Not that I've heard of, why?"

"Well, the jar came from the bag. The white powder messes with your brain. Warren was using it, and is why his behaviour … changed."

"Huh," Cody said as he pulled a piece of scrap into place. "Seemed like he was a lot friendlier lately."

"Sometimes, yeah." Leena scrunched her mouth, and looked in the direction of Warren's stack. "Other times... well, you'd have to have been around him up close to see the mess he was even when he was friendly. That white powder, whatever's left, should probably be sent away with Messenger or something. The bag, too. It had a lot of stuff in it, and we didn't even try it all. Who knows what the other stuff in there might do to a person? The puke-drink was bad enough."

This led to a handful of questions from Cody about the 'tasting party', some of the things in the bag, and how the party all went bad by the end. Leena made a mental note that some time, maybe at a Gathering, she could tell the tale to everyone at once, and not have to bother telling it again.

Three other Citizens carrying or dragging metal showed up.

"Hi guys!" Cody greeted them. "Who's the new guy?"

"Just joined up!" one of the Citizens said. "Thought it sounded fun. I'm in."

"Cody..." Leena asked cautiously, "how many people do you have on this whole thing?"

Cody looked around, pointing to each person as he counted them up silently. "This is everybody, so looks like five, plus me."

One of the workers on the ramp called out, "and my favourite, who's joining up once he's done with our shack!"

"How about you?" Cody asked Leena.

"Me? Yeah, sure, but I want to go check on a couple of friends first. That's who I was looking for when I heard your noise."

"Who ya lookin' for?"

"Jen and Tara."

"Over that way," the other worker on the ramp pointed across the Commons. "I can see it from here, barely. If you head that way, look for a shack with a dark green wall facing you."

Leena trotted up the ramp to get a better look. It shook in unsettling ways.

"Careful!" Cody yelped. "Some pieces aren't tied in so tight yet!"

Leena froze, and looked around her. It wouldn't have been much of a fall if it collapsed from under her, but she imagined falling from the *top* of the ramp. "Sorry! Careful, careful. Careful stepping!" She looked out and spotted the shack with the dark green wall. "Got it. Thanks guys. I'll be back in a bit."

With soft steps on the way down, she then broke into a jog again towards Jen and Tara's.

On arrival, Leena found the two passed out, curled around each other.
"Awwwwww," Leena said, loud enough that it might wake them.
Sure enough, Tara opened one sleepy eye. "Whu?"
"Just checkin' on you ladies. Things seem good."
Now Jen was awake, and frowned at her own morning breath. "Heyyy Leena. How's it goin'?"
"The Commons is under *con-struc-tion*! Mike is playing nice with Edgar, helping on Edgar's new stack, and your buddy Cody is 'secretly' repairing one of the big ramps as a surprise for Mike! Don't tell Mike, and we'll see how long it takes him to notice, I guess."
"Muhhh?" Tara responded.
"Yeahhh," Leena said. "I was thinking of asking you guys if you wanted to join either construction site, but...go back to sleep, and keep being repulsively cute together! Bye...!"
Leena almost started heading towards Edgar's stack to go see Mike, but remembered she'd said she'd go help Cody's project. And given that some of them could see her from where they were, it would be bad form to wander off.

Soon enough, Leena was holding a chunk of metal in place, while Cody secured it, bending a bit to grab on here, running a cable through a hole to tie it down there, and so on; chunk after chunk. They were still in the lowest sections of the ramp, but they were slowly creeping up.
"This is actually going faster than I thought it would!" Leena said.
"Yeah, this section looks good, but now, we test. Back up." Cody started with little hops that didn't quite get him off the surface of the ramp. Then slightly bigger hops. A corner of one section made a scraping noise. "Right there. Weak. I have to secure it."
"Gee, actually making sure it won't fall down again? Slows things down...!" Leena joked, handing him a blunt piece of metal that he'd been using as a hammer.
"Yeah? Wait until I repair my own ramp! I'll probably take even longer, and do a better job, because I did my learning here," Cody said.
"Ah, you're evil after all!"
"Haha, sure, I guess so. But don't worry. Before I'm done this one, I want it to be strong enough that a bunch of people could be running on it at the same time."
Leena grabbed his head roughly, and kissed the side of it. "Oh, you're a good boy, huh?"
"Not evil?" he chuckled.
Leena shrugged, leaning her head to the side. "Could be both. That usually works pretty well." While she held the piece in place firmly, Cody got to work fixing it, and hammering bits in.
He was cute. A bit younger than Leena generally aimed at... but cute. Seemed like a solid type of person. "*Oh Mike would laugh at me,*" Leena thought.

Eventually, Jen and Tara showed up. Each was soon paired with an experienced member of the crew, and apparently Leena qualified well enough... with *some* supervision.

Soon Jen was holding pieces still for Cody, while Tara was holding things still for Leena to attach by whatever means the pieces seemed to suit.

Leena looked at how far they'd come, and how far was left. "This is going to take *forever!*"

"Oh, I don't know," Cody said, "this is less than a day's work so far, and it's doing well. If it's done right, it'll *last* forever. A week or two is no big deal compared to the benefit."

"*A week or two?*" Leena blurted out.

"A week or two for what?" Mike was approaching, with a few people tagging along. "A week or two before you remember you left me with Edgar, and... what's going on here?"

"Aw, crud," Cody mumbled. "Surprise."

Mike pointed at the ramp, then up to the balcony that the broken original ended up at. "Neat! What's your plan for up there?"

Cody sighed, and broke into a smile. "Well, I was hoping to keep it secret from you until the ramp was passable and safe, but when we can get up there, we'll see what's there. See how there's doors on the balcony going into the wall? Eh, it's easiest to see from the middle of Commons, but I'm *hoping* inside is a space large enough to be used as a 'stack'. But who knows? It could lead into a whole new area as big as the Commons."

"Or, it could be barely big enough for a crap-sniffer's den," Leena said.

Mike's awe faded to a troubled stare as another thought came to him. "It could have *dangerous* stuff. Like that bag of meds– or worse. Could be 'treasures' of Actual sitting in there. When we get up there, we have to be careful."

Soon, they all resumed work on the ramp, including two of the Citizens who'd followed Mike here, but it was tiring. Mike had done a lot at Edgar's stack, and the ramp crew had been working most of the day. Cody's enthusiasm only carried the crew so far before the consensus was that the time for rest had come.

Most of the crew, including Cody, Jen and Tara, ended up at Leena and Mike's shack. Many made stops at their own shacks to bring out their own dizzy-water.

To the surprise of no one, Jen and Tara found a corner in the shack to curl up together. Everyone settled in for an evening of talk, and getting plastered.

By now, friends of friends had joined in, and their numbers were great enough that the shack could no longer house them all. With a minor recharge thanks to the general merriment, a few people decided to give the shack a minor expansion with the dwindling pile of metal pieces nearby. Others were happy to supervise.

"Edgar's building a fancy stack, and we're slapping together a super-shack while drunk." Cody was amused, but continued fine-tuning things well after everyone else had decided it was good enough.

That's when Edgar showed up. "So, this is why you didn't come back to the stack," he said in a somewhat judgmental tone.

Mike gracefully extended his arm and pointed at Edgar. "Ah! I'm sorry about that, but I'll have you know," he said, pausing for a small wave of dizziness to pass, "I'll have you know I ended up at another construction... thing. I'll come back to the stack tomorrow," he said, trying his best to maintain a serious tone, even if he found it amusing to be speaking in such a serious tone.

He pointed toward Cody. "And later in the day, I'll go back to help Leena and her newest boytoy to work on the ramp!"

Cody was stunned to be called Leena's boytoy, and Leena burst out laughing– laughing even harder when she saw the look on Cody's face.

"But tonight!" Mike hollered, standing tall, jar of dizzy-water held high, "tonight, we celebrate! We celebrate the end of Warren!... and his ways." The party-goers cheered, and cheers were heard from people farther off, who were not (yet) part of the party.

"We celebrate the beginning of new construction!" Mike declared, putting an arm around Edgar and reaching out for Cody to join them. Cody was too embarrassed to stand and join them, but he offered up a hand for Mike to hold. Leena rose to give Mike a hug, and Edgar deftly evaded being caught up in it.

"I think I'll leave you to the celebration, then," Edgar said, clearly unmoved.

"What?" Mike said. "If you must, but first have a swig of *my* dizzy-water, I make fine stuff!"

"He does!" Leena confirmed.

"Hey," Mike said. "Did you know Edgar's getting most of his metal from Warren's stack? He could have moved right into it, if it wasn't... Warren's stack, but no, that would be creepy, so he's moving all the metal he needs to his new stack."

"I've been thinking about that," Edgar said, glad that the notion of trying the dizzy-water was lost on the flow of conversation. "As much as I didn't want to move into Warren's stack, I might want to move away from calling my own a 'stack'. It carries too much association with Warren's stack."

"Oh yeah? Whatcha gonna call it?" Leena asked, still clinging onto Mike.

"A pile?" Mike suggested.

"A heap!" Jen offered.

A friend of Cody's from the crew spoke up. "A thing that's big and made of the metal, and is big, so big, and you hope the metal doesn't fall in on you, because it's so big, and *no one* needs a repeat of Warren's tower thing, because *wow*, that was just a mess, and it was big and made of metal, and you'd need to take *refuge,* away from all the metal, and curl up in some bedding, because bedding is way more comfortable than metal, and everyone knows that, so it's no surprise at all, of course somewhere in between is cardboard, but given the choice, I'd rather sleep on bedding than cardboard of course, you can't curl up in cardboard, at least not easily, and it's not as warm, of course, curling up with a person helps a lot, but that leads to other complications, but oh, sometimes so nice, you know what I mean, I haven't had a complication like *that* in a while."

A moment of silence followed, excluding the extended party that had formed around the shack as people joined. Everyone in earshot of the drunken spiel waited for some other wisdoms and amusement. The silence broke as Mike erupted into giggles, allowing Edgar to make a discreet escape.

Leena growled, and dragged Mike to the floor, next to Cody so that she could sit comfortably, and put an arm around each of them. Cody looked embarrassed, but not inclined to move away at all.

Mike nuzzled up to Leena, and planted a kiss behind her ear. He leaned forward to see Cody.

"I think my favourite's taken a liking to you," Mike said to Cody. He'd used the word 'favourite' deliberately, to make the relationship between he and Leena clear. "But you seem okay, you know? If you hung around her and whatnot... I'm not saying she's interested in *whatnot*, I wouldn't speak for her, but you seem okay."

Leena lowered her hold on both of them to be more snug around the waist, giving them both a squeeze. "Yeah," Leena said with a smooth smile, "you seem okay."

Giggling came from Tara's direction, and bemused glances were shared between her, Leena, and Jen.

Cody swallowed hard. "You... you seem pretty okay, too."

Morning came, and so did headaches. Leena felt this wasn't such a bad one. Lots of people had passed out in and around their shack.

She walked over to the Jen and Tara pile, and nudged Jen with her foot. "Hey, you," Leena said quietly. "I thought you moved out. Now there's pretty girlies littered everywhere."

"Shap," Jen mumbled with her eyes still closed, waving her hand at Leena lazily. "Comfy. Go 'way."

Leena tousled Jen's hair a bit, got swatted at, and went outside.

A bit of noise could be heard in the direction of Edgar's stack. No hangovers there. She wandered over, and saw two Citizens putting pieces on an outer wall. Edgar had outlined a significant amount of space that his stack would take up, so even with all of yesterday's work, there was a lot of wall left to be made.

Edgar stood in the stack's open space. Nearby, a woman with dark blonde hair knelt over some strange bedding heap. Or maybe it was just a heap of cloth strips.

"Whatcha got here, Ed?" Leena asked.

Edgar turned to face Leena, with a look of disdain which softened when he saw that Mike wasn't with her. He turned to the bedding and the woman tending them. "Tapestries," Edgar said, almost with a smile.

"There's a lot of kinks and wrinkles in them, but I can flatten them out," the woman said. She was a beautiful one... Leena looked between her, the bedding, and Edgar.

"So, this thing is for doing the thing with her?" Leena asked.

Edgar rolled his eyes a little with a huff. "Clara, spread it out, so we can see."

Clara obeyed, dragging the corners out until it was a long rectangle- with slices in it. Through these slices were strips of cloth about three centimetres wide. They were coloured different shades of the omnipresent blue of clothing.

Once Clara straightened it out, the strips made a crude image of a man's body. "I've got one for a woman, and ones of faces for a man and woman, and my attempt at showing the Citizenry, with the Grand Elevator shaft."

"Wow. So do you sleep on them, or...?"

"No," Edgar said, "they are tapestries. They hang up so people can see them."

"I actually made them for Warren," Clara said. "Well... I made them just because, but if I *didn't* offer them to Warren, and I put them up where everyone could see them, he might have..."

"Been upset. Got it," Leena said. If a person made or found anything of note, it had always been good for one's health to offer it to Warren first. "So where did he hang them?"

"Nowhere," Clara said grimly through a forced little smile. "They ended up forgotten in a pile somewhere in his stack. I made the mistake of asking about them, and... well, used your imagination." Clara made the smallest unconscious glance towards where the Gatherings used to take place.

Leena sighed, then knelt in front of the 'tapestry'. She put her hand on it and looked to Clara, who was making busy work for herself, flattening out the cloth with her hands. "I'll make them better again," Clara said quietly. "I might use water on them to soften them up. Then it might flatten sooner."

"Where will they go now?" Leena asked.

"Somewhere in Edgar's refuge, I guess," Clara said.

Edgar spoke up. "Yes. I picked a name for here, by the way. Edgar's Refuge. So people can come here and feel safe."

Leena pointed her thumb back to the rest of the Citizenry. "Not a whole lot of danger out there right now."

"Give it time," Edgar said gruffly. "When trouble happens, as it eventually is bound to, I want good people to know they are safe here. The gates will be guarded by men with spears, and other men will be available to help keep the refuge safe."

"Guards..." Leena said slowly. "And inside, can anyone carry a knife, or spear?"

"Yes. But people waving them around will be watched."

That didn't sit well with Leena, but it sounded somewhat on the reasonable side. She still preferred the *'everyone looking out for everyone'* plan.

She turned her attention back to Clara. "Would you like some help with that? If you have five of them, you know. It'd be a nice change from hauling metal, and still helping."

Clara stopped working, and looked at Leena with somewhat wary eyes. "Why do you want to help Edgar so much? I thought you were close with Mike."

Leena tilted her head. "Yeah, I am. But I can help Edgar also. His 'refuge' idea sounds okay."

"Meanwhile, Mike and his men drink dizzy-water, and make fools of themselves," Clara said, working harder now to flatten the fabric. "Like Warren's men always did."

"What?" Leena sat up straight. "It's not like last night was one of Warren's style of thing. It wasn't just men. There were as many women, and they were even there by choice. And everyone gets a little stupid on dizzy-water now and then."

"Clara does not," Edgar said in a low, serious tone. "And that will be a rule in my refuge. No dizzy-water, no sniffing jars, and no coming in if you're drunk or high."

Leena stood. "Huh. Well, I'm behind you on the jars, but so strict with the dizzy-water? I know it's not good to overdo it a lot, but. Well, whatever. Your spot, go for it. It's not like those rules will do any harm, I guess. So... where should I help? If Clara doesn't want my help, I can get back to metal stuff, and–"

"It might be best if you go," Edgar said, stone-faced.

Leena looked at him, trying to fathom the attitude. She said nothing, he said nothing.

"Well. Huh. Okay then. See you around... I guess."

In coming days, construction continued for 'Edgar's refuge' and Cody's ramp. Edgar had managed to rally a good handful of solid workers, while Cody needed to turn away volunteers, just because there wasn't room for them all.

This allowed Cody to pick the ones that looked strongest, and seemed most competent. Citizens that supported Mike who were not picked to work often just loitered around the repair site. A few moved their shacks nearby.

Repairs were going very well– much faster than Cody had initially hoped, thanks to the enthusiastic Mike-supporters.

During this time, Cody's salvagers found the medic bag that Warren's white powder had come from, but the white-powder jar was still missing.

One day, both Edgar and Cody hit a milestone.

Edgar erected the front gate to his refuge, (despite the main wall being far from complete,) and the final, most critical chunk of the ramp was laid into place.

Leena wondered if Edgar's premature gate erection was timed to take some of the glory away from the ramp being usable.

The Edgar site cheered. The Mike site thundered.

"Would you like to do the honours?" Cody asked Mike from the top of the ramp. He leaned his head towards the five doors, which were metal frames around the edges, and glass in their middles. The glass panes were all broken to various degrees, from 'badly cracked' to 'one big dangling shard left'. Broken glass littered the floor, and a couple of the metal frames had some rust forming on the bottom edge.

Leena peeked in through the glass. "A sink! Cool, that's handy. And some big … heap of cloth?"

Mike knocked down the lone big shard from the most-empty door frame. A quick little jab sent it to the floor. Carefully, he crossed into the room. There was a passage to the left that looked like it headed to another room. He kicked the strangely organized pile of cloth.

"Ow! It's hard!" he reached down to feel it. "Soft on the outside, and hard on the inside. Hey, this cloth is attached to it! And really well."

Leena stepped into the space, with Cody behind her. She tested the sink. After spending some time noisily coughing up air, it worked and everything. She grabbed one of the nearby cups, and inspected it. It seemed fine, other than being dusty.

Cody ventured to the cloth pile, stared at it, and carefully sat on it. One wide part in the middle was low, and soft to sit on. Behind was a taller piece to lean back on, which he did, and a similar part to his side to rest his arm on. The other side piece was too far away to reach.

"I think this is for a few people to sit on. It's not even, though."

"Not even what?" Leena said, flopping herself down to sit on it.

"Get off, get off," Cody said as he himself scampered away and got down to face the bottom section. "Yeah, look. This side has a couple of hard brown chunks of something that... well, it reminds me of cardboard more than anything, but way harder. The other side has them too, but they're crushed sideways. Ooh, metal pieces in the other things, and more of that weird material... I think all the hard parts in this thing are made of that material! Hold up the end, I'll try to fix it."

Mike lifted the one end with both hands and a bit of effort, and Cody got tinkering. "Ooh, look. On the other side, they're in tight, but on this side the metal pieces in the brown pieces have ripped apart the st-"

"Cody," Mike said, "enough exploring under the thing I'm trying to not drop on your head. Finish up and get out from under there."

Cody pushed the two pieces back into place, trying to wiggle them in securely. "I don't know how well that's going to work. They might just come loose right away when any weight is-"

"Okay! Get clear already!" Mike snapped.

Cody recoiled from the sitting-thing. "Okay, gently..."

Mike didn't exactly drop it, but it was rough enough that the two freshly repaired pieces collapsed instantly.

"Hey!" Cody protested before considering. "Well... people will be sitting on it rough enough anyway. I'll have to figure a way to stick those in there better."

"Or we could just put a thick hunk of metal under it."

By now, several other of the crew had come in, and were checking things out. Trying the sink, poking this and that. One was knocking out more broken glass bits from the door frames into a folded piece of cardboard, to carry them away.

"Hey guys," Leena called from the next room. "Are you coming, or what?"

Mike and Cody filed into the next room. It was about the size of the last one; six or seven metres wide one way, a bit less the other way.

"What's that?" Mike said, pointing at a wider, flatter cloth-ish looking thing on the floor.

"What's that?" Cody said, pointing at a tall piece of furniture against the back wall, made of the same light brown material discovered minutes ago. Beside it stood a table made of thin bits of metal, with the new material for its top.

"Well, I think I figured this one out already." Leena jumped backwards onto the twenty centimetre thick cloth-ish thing. She landed on her back, and bounced a little when she hit, perfectly comfortable in it, and able to spread her arms out almost wide enough to touch both sides at once. "For sleeping on! Or other activities that involve lying down!"

Mike went to her, putting one knee on the object, and took Leena's hand with a hint of a mischievous smile.

Cody decided to mind his own business, and go look at the tall thing made of... whatever it was.

"Looks like it's meant to just hold stuff," he said, feeling the texture of it. He used his thumbnail to dig at the material's fibrous surface. "As hard as it is, the surface is kind of... oh! I just chipped off a bit!"

"Well, don't wreck it," Leena said.

"You were saying about bad news?" Mike said as he sat straddled over Leena. Leena reached back over her head, and pointed at the next doorway. Cody carefully walked over to it as Mike got up to join him.

"Oh." Cody said.

"That's it, huh?" Mike wandered into the small room, with no other doors out the other side. "Two and a half rooms isn't quite stack-like in scale, even if there's interesting stuff here. Sorry, Cody, the great discovery is a little smaller than you were hoping."

Cody smirked a bit, and shrugged. "I knew this was a possibility. Still glad I did it. So. Are you two going to move in? I mean, it's got a working sink, a neat thing to sit on which needs a thing to balance it out, this sleeping thing, this.. other thing... and did you get a look at the view?"

Mike blinked. "So- you're just giving it to us?"

"Yeah, of course," Cody said. "I didn't mention that was one my hopes for this project? That's why we had too many volunteers. They were doing it for you! And curiosity, I'm sure. I'm going to work on another ramp next, and see what *it* has. We'll see how many volunteers follow me to the next ramp..."

A meandering Citizen spoke up, "I'm in!"

"Me too," said another. Most of the crew had made it inside to explore, and a dozen people started to make things a bit crowded.

Leena was still alone on the rectangular bedding thing, sitting up. She called out for everyone to hear, "*Who thinks Cody deserves a reward for starting this project?* Not to mention being so kind as to give it away..." She stared into Cody's eyes from a couple of metres away.

Controlled cheers and positive responses came from all rooms.

"Okay then, kind Citizens! Go away, so I can reward him!" Leena reclined back onto the bedding, holding herself up by her elbows. She squirmed a little, still staring at Cody with a coy smile.

Laughs and a few excited sounds of titillation came from people.

Among those who gave a laugh was Mike. "Leena, I think you've been thinking of 'rewarding' him for a while now!" He gently ushered people out, and as a group, they kept going, heading down the ramp.

Leena arched back to tease her cleavage a bit as she slid her outfit's zipper down. "Maybe. Hey Mike, did you want to stick around? Cody?"

Cody was still a little stunned, staring at Leena's tiny bit of newly exposed skin down her middle. "Uh- yeah?"

Leena settled back, and grasped the opened edges of her zipper tightly, closing her eyes. "I thought I'd ask Mike if he wanted to join in- what do you think?"

Mike laughed again. "Dear, you know I'm not the first in line to play with guys. And it's *his* reward, not yours."

Cody was hard to read, trying to be polite, but Leena figured Mike was right. "Okay, Mike. Go amuse the crew or something." She arched hard as she yanked the top of her outfit wide open, and pushed her cleavage up. "I'll catch up with you later."

"Love, you put thoughts in my head," Mike said, admiring the body of his favourite. "I might end up in the arms of another lady shortly, to vent some energy!"

"Have fun, love," Leena said to Mike before kissing the air in his direction. Mike left with a smile, and Leena turned her attention to Cody.

Chapter Eight

The Sweep

Mike went down to talk and hang out with the crew.

"Guys, I really need to thank you all, too. Cody was nice to give the space to Leena and me, but *all* of Cody's guys worked like crazy on it, too. As far as I'm concerned, come by any time, y'know?"

"Damn Mike, I'm not one of *Cody's* people, I did it for *you*." said Natalie, a woman with long auburn hair.

"Me?"

A few others nodded. Another said, "Me too."

Mike was dazed, so Natalie elaborated in a more sombre tone. "Do you know what he did to me? What his men did to me?"

It took a moment for Mike to realize that she wasn't talking about Cody. "I was the guest at a Gathering, you know." Natalie looked to all the other women of the crew. One of them tapped her collarbone, and silently mouthed *'me too'*.

"I'm... I'm so sorry," Mike said.

Natalie held out her hand to silence Mike, but kept her face down. "I don't know if you were there. You probably were. Most people were. But wanna know where else I was?"

Mike was silent, so she went on. "I was with you in the elevator loading bay. When you raised that hammer... I swear I could feel the handle in my own hand." She swallowed audibly, and sighed. "All my hate, all my revenge was in your arm. Mine and a lot of people's. I mean, I was glad he was leaving, one way or another, but people expected his men to just keep doing the usual."

She looked up and grabbed Mike by the forearms. "But when that hammer came down..." she squeezed his arms tight, "and then you told us it was over..."

Natalie seemed to have a lot more to say, but words were failing her. Mike got his forearms loose from her grip, and pulled her in for an embrace. She gripped back harder. One of the crew joined in the hug, then another. One man laughed at himself as he did so, tears on his face. "I'm not crying, you are!"

"Shut up," came a laughing reply.

"Leena thinks I came out here to find someone to have sex with," Mike laughed, "but dammit if hugs aren't better now and then."

Group composure slowly coming back together, the group hug began to dissolve, leaving Natalie holding Mike just a bit longer than needed. As she withdrew, she whispered by his ear, "I can hug- and that other thing." She held eye contact with Mike, and smiled softly.

Mike raised an eyebrow, then frowned. "Would you be okay with that? I mean..."

Natalie smiled. "My Gathering was a long time ago, I've... I've moved on. And maybe your hammer helped, huh?" By this time, only half of the crew were snoopily listening in.

Mike looked around. "I'm glad everyone's so happy with how things worked out, yeah? That's great, it's amazing... but I don't want to take advantage, right? I don't want to end up like Warren."

"I told you," Natalie said, "I'm all right. My choice. Your shack or mine?"

Mike's hand was just getting comfortable on Natalie's hip, when a scream came from the distance.

"Later! Totally!" Mike started running, and most of the crew were following. As the group hunted the source of the scream - now another- Citizens would see them running towards it, and many joined.

Then the screams changed to yells.

By the time Mike got to the destination, the entrance to a sniffer's den, a woman was sitting nearby with someone at her side. Her attacker was getting beaten by five Citizens as many others watched.

The attacker was on the ground, trying to defend himself. The avenging group had one metal club among them, and the one who wielded it stood back, and watched the others. "Is... is that enough?" he called to them. They kept beating him, and his yells were deteriorating into helpless sobs and apologies.

"Okay, okay!" Mike called. The group slowed, and left the attacker to cringe on the floor. "I don't think we need to kill him, do we?"

The question wasn't simply rhetorical. Did they need to kill him?

"James was one of Warren's men," said one of the men who was beating him. "it looks like he couldn't break that habit."

Mike turned to the victim of the initial assault. "Are you okay?"

"Yes. I... I just want to go home."

"What do you think we should do with him?" Mike asked her.

She shook her head. "I just want to go home." She stood, and her friend put an arm around her.

The attacker, James, was still on the ground, squirming in pain. "My arm!" Every time he tried to move his arm, he yelled as if he were being hit.

Leena and Cody showed up, having started out behind Mike and his group, and probably having to put clothes on.

"Wow. People really took your suggestion," Leena said, looking around at the mob that came to assist. "Yeah... good job, people! But now I need to figure out what to do with him."

"Messenger? It's me, Mike," he said into the communication device, "I hope you can hear me. I hope you can help. For the first time since Warren's death, someone has attacked a woman. The Citizens came together and helped her, stopped it before it got...worse... but now I have a problem."

Mike shifted his weight, and looked around his shack at his friends. He then held the button on the communication machine again. "The guy who attacked her... we didn't kill him. His arm is hurt. I don't know if he should be killed, to keep the Citizens safe, or if we give him another chance.

"I'm going to take him to the Grand Elevator very soon for you to take away. If you get Actual to heal him... and bring him back, like has happened with hurt people in the past, I'll take it as a sign to give him another chance. If he just never comes back... well, it will tell me what I should do in the future if something like this happens again."

"Tell him about the bag," Leena whispered.

"Oh yeah. We found a bag of strange meds. The things inside caused some trouble, and we don't know what to do with it. It might be best if you took it away. Oh, and I haven't seen any of the normal meds in... a long time. I'm wondering if Warren never asked. I guess that's not important. Not compared to the attacker,"

"You're rambling..." Jen said.

"Right." Mike said, speaking into the communication machine once more. "So... We'll trust in your wisdom and Actual's wisdom about the man. Okay. We're heading to the Grand Elevator right now."

"Why don't you just ask Actual over for some dizzy-water some time, Mister-Chatty!" Leena said.

"Yes, yes," Mike said, collecting himself. "Let's get going."

The prisoner, James, was brought before the Grand Elevator, and they waited in silence as James wincing in pain. It did not take long before the Elevator could be heard, humming and scraping closer until the clatter and boom of it stopping.

"All Citizens other than the injured, leave the loading bay," came the authoritative voice of the Messenger.

Mike nodded. "You heard me? About what he did? And the bag? Bag's right here..."

"Yes." was the reply, followed by silence.

Mike moved away from the Elevator, and followed the others who had escorted James here.

"You don't seem afraid at all," Mike said to James.

"I'll see Actual. Warren is there. I'll be *just* fine. You'll see."

The next day found Leena and Mike settling in to the new home atop the ramp. The smallest room was a little bit useless. A person could sleep in there, but the middle room with the big mat of bedding was much better. Leena had dragged the bedding cloth from the old shack, and tried to spread it out neatly on the mat.

Mike had brought the little table from the mat-room into the little room, and put the communication machine on it. "Okay! Communication room!"

Leena made herself comfortable on the mat, and called to Mike. "So... what do we call *this* room?" Mike peeked out of the newly dubbed communication room, and saw Leena posing seductively for him, and not in any subtle manner.

"Oof, Leena, your playtime with Cody put you in that kind of mood, huh?"

Leena rolled her eyes. "He's a sweetie, but we never really got anywhere before the attack drama. If I chase him down again, I'll have to teach him a little, maybe."

Mike knelt down on the edge of the mat, and rested a hand on one of Leena's raised knees. "Hm. Can *I* have a lesson?"

Grabbing Mike's wrist, and pulling him down on top of her, she growled. "Dear, you don't need lessons."

"Then maybe I should just get to work..."

"Mike?" came Jen's voice. She was walking in from the balcony.

"Aw man, really?" Mike whined. "Last night I was headed for some fun with Natalie, and now this?"

"Jen, what's up?" Leena said, patting her poor, neglected favourite on the cheek. "You sound a little stressed."

"Messenger's back," Jen said.

"Already?"

"He wants to talk to you, Mike," Jen said.

"Me?"

Leena got up, dumping Mike on his side in the process. "Well, you're the one that's been talking to him. I think you told him your name. I guess it's official in the eyes of the Messenger. You're the leader of Citizenry."

The outer door of the loading bay was unlocked, and Messenger was back in the Grand Elevator.

James lay still, a new bag sitting nearby. Mike went over to James, intending to find out if he was alive. Before he could reach out, Messenger's voice stopped him.

"Let him sleep. He'll be fine."

"He's alive then?" Mike asked, "well of course. If he was dead, you'd have taken him anyway, so... now what?"

A bit of silence passed before Messenger answered, "He is of your people. He is for your people to judge."

Mike released a heavy sigh, and nodded. "I guess I'll call a Gathering and ask them. It's... fair, I guess." He picked up the new bag. Where the old one was brown and lumpy, this one was bright yellow, and firm- almost like a box.

"Is this a replacement for the other bag?" Mike asked, opening it up by a zipper.

"Yes," Messenger said. "There are no medications in it besides a light pain-killer. Primarily bandages and the like. There are also instructions on their proper use."

Mike pulled out the little book, and flipped through the pages. "Lots of pictures. That's good- I'm not great with the paper words. Thank you, Messenger."

"Farewell, Citizen."

The Grand Elevator groaned to life, and soon faded into the distance.

Mike slung the bag over his shoulder, and looked to the sleeping James again. He looked to the Citizens who'd occupied the other end of the loading bay, including Leena.

"So, what do we do with him?" Leena asked. James began to stir...

James stood, wrists tied behind his back to the pole that many a woman were tied to for Warren's gatherings.

"No, no, no," Mike said to the crowd that had gathered, "We're not here to make a show of killing him. But he might die."

The crowd murmured. Indistinct things were said in Mike's general direction. Mike spread his arms, and tried to hush them.

"I sent him to Messenger, hoping that Messenger would decide if he lives or dies," Mike said, only to be interrupted.

"He's been with Messenger?" a man called out.

"Yes, and he came back with his arm all better," Mike answered.

Questions from the crowd bombarded James immediately

"Where did you go?"

"What was he like?"

"Did you *see* Actual?"

The questions overlapped, and James decided to answer as well as he could, and shut the crowd up by telling the story.

"Okay, so I was in the loading bay, with my arm hurting like crazy. Messenger told every else to go away, and the door closed behind me. I was alone, locked in the loading bay, and I started smelling something funny. I started getting sleepy. When I woke up, my arm was better, and I was in the loading bay. Wherever I went, whatever happened, I slept right through it."

The crowd grumbled in a mix of dissatisfaction and disappointment. A question rose above the murmur. "So, Messenger didn't kill him, if he..."

"Ah, see that's tricky," Mike said. "Messenger basically said it was up to us. A second chance, kill him, throw him in a box for a month. I don't know, but it's –"

From the crowd, Natalie dashed forward, knife bound for James's gut. As she rammed the blade in, Jamie buckled forward as far as his restraints would allow. She pulled the knife out and took a jab at his throat, spilling more blood before Mike could pull her away.

As James slumped dying, Natalie dropped her knife, not resisting Mike's hold on her. She spoke to Mike, but yelled, so everyone could hear. "*You wanted to forget the things Warren's men did? As if they'd just behave?*"

"Natalie..."

"They're not even Iofus!" Natalie hollered. "I say we find every one of Warren's men, and kill them before they harm anyone else!"

The crowd was quickly becoming a mob. Agreement came from both men and women, but it was a woman who first took her own knife to a nearby man she knew to be one of Warren's men.

Guilty men could soon be spotted trying to get free of the group, to flee, but most were caught. Even those who were caught by someone meaning only to detain them, found themselves vulnerable to the blade of someone more wrathful.

By now, Natalie had gotten free, and picked up her knife again. "Sorry, but this needed to happen. It's for the best. You said that Messenger said it was up to us."

Mike staggered back, in awe of the anger 'his people' still had for Warren's people. Stunned, he did little as the crowd including Natalie, dispersed to chase those who had escaped.

"What do we do?" Leena asked Mike.

"I don't know- this was... unexpected. They're arguably justified."

As if out of nowhere, Edgar made himself known. "And what of the innocent who are bound to be harmed in all of this?"

"What? They're chasing down men who are far from innocent, but..."

"And if someone takes this confusion to kill someone they simply don't like?" Edgar asked.

"Fine!" Leena exploded. "How would *you* be handing this?"

"It's too late," Edgar said, "They should have all been judged as soon as Warren was dead."

"And what, killed one by one in an organized manner?" Mike growled.

"I... maybe not, but –"

"You're right," Leena said. "You should have brought up that kind of idea long ago! We could have discussed it!"

"Would you have listened to me?" Edgar smugly said.

"You think maybe I was helping out at your stack... Refuge, whatever, because I liked moving metal? I was trying to work *with* you!"

"Well," Edgar said, surveying the now-distant ring of chaos around them, "you needn't put yourself out to help in the future. The Refuge will do just fine." And with that, he turned and left.

Leena and Mike made their way home to the new den atop the ramp, finding a handful of people there, including Cody.

"What's going on?" Leena asked of them.

"So much rage," Cody said. "It's justified rage, I know, but I can't... I can't keep up with it. I just wanted to so somewhere quiet. Maybe I don't feel like killing anyone because I've never been on the receiving end of the *worst* of Warren's men, but..."

"I have," Leena said meekly, "but I'm not out there killing right now. I..."

"You had your moment of rage against Sledge," Mike said, "just before I had mine against Warren. What do you mean, though, that you've gotten the worst of Warren's men? You were never featured in one of his Gatherings."

"A Gathering no, but –" Leena shied away, backing against a wall to sit down.

"But what? What... what happened? When? ... Who?" Mike, Cody, and a couple of others stared at Leena with sympathetic faces.

She stared back at them, knowing they where quietly guessing the crimes that had been committed against her.

"Talk to me..." Mike pleaded.

"No. Not now." Leena got to her feet, and unsheathed Warren's blade. "I'm going back out."

Mike nodded, and checked his own knife.

"You don't have to come," Leena said.

"If there was a time when you needed me, and I wasn't by your side, I'm sorry, Leena. But I'm not going to sit here and do nothing while you do what you need to."

"You didn't even know me then, so don't go feeling guilty."

"Don't care, I know you now. So lead on."

Running to join the nearest hunting group, Leena, Mike, Cody, and one of his friends were in time only to help corner one of Warren's men, and witness his death. Leena cheered, despite fighting tears. Having missed some of the hunt, the numbers of Warren's men were shrinking. The group Leena and her friends had joined migrated to join another group, to corner another of Warren's men, arriving too late to be of help. Groups merged over and over as prey became less and less.

It soon seemed obvious that barring any terrific hiding spots that had gone unnoticed, the deed was done.

Mike's presence was noticed by many, and many were lingering around him, waiting for him to say something.

Natalie found him before he thought of something to say, and looked at him expectantly.

"Maybe this had to happen," Mike said, glancing over at Leena.

"So... are you going to blame me?" Natalie asked.

Mike looked around the crowd. There were some new killers today. Ones fueled by revenge and rage for Warren's days. "No. I mean... you got things rolling, but I'm just... I feel disappointed."

"*Disappointed that I didn't want to spare –* "

"No, no," Mike interrupted, making sure that others could hear, "disappointed that my... optimistic idea that everything could be just fine after Warren died... didn't work out. It wasn't going to happen. A lot of the men who died today might never have ever done anything wrong again, but it doesn't erase what they did before."

"Assuming everyone who died was guilty," Leena quietly admitted, "or not mistaken for someone else."

Mike nodded, and Natalie couldn't find a rebuttal.

"*What happened today... might have been necessary,*" Mike hollered to everyone, "*but it was dangerous! Now that as far as we can tell, all of Warren's men are gone, we won't need this kind of chaos again. If someone needs punishment...*" Mike shook his lowered head slowly for a moment. "Bring them to me."

Edgar stepped forth. Whether he'd recently arrived, or was part of the hunt could not be known. "What then, Mike? You kill them yourself?"

"No... *we* decide what happens. I'll... call a meeting, and everyone can help decide. I don't know exactly how it will happen, but giant, angry groups can't be the answer, and neither can one person. We need to find a way in between. Though hopefully, we won't have to any time soon."

"That easy, hm?" Edgar mulled with a sarcastic tone.

"No. That hard," Leena said. "It should never be easy to decide if someone dies."

Mike put an arm around Leena, and waited for anyone to say anything else. None came. "Look, people, if anyone has a better idea- today, tomorrow, whenever. Let me know. We work together!"

Positive mumbling came from the crowd.

Natalie, perhaps feeling lucky to have dodged repercussions, raised her knife high and yelled, "*We work together!*"

Leena followed suit, raising her own knife. "*We work together!*"

A few in the crowed now copied the gesture, knives and larger blades held high. "*We work together!*" quickly became a joined cheer, repeated by almost everyone.

The most notable exception was Edgar, who just rolled his eyes, and left.

Roused by the community's support, Mike's love for them swelled, and with Leena already on his arm, he turned to her for a deep, dramatic kiss. Those who could see it, broke the chant into a general cheer, and the chant of the group fell apart from there.

"Oh!" Leena said, "the bodies!"

"Ah!" Mike raised his voice to everyone again. "*We can't leave their bodies laying around. If you know where one is, help get it to the Grand Elevator. I guess I have a talk to Messenger...*"

98

"Messenger? Are you there? It's me, Mike. We have more dead. Quite a few. Men who'd done terrible things under Warren's lead. I... I didn't call for their deaths, but the people... they kind of spontaneously decided that James had to die, and things just kept going from there. It was out of control for a while."

Mike sighed. "I can't say I approve of what happened, but I can't say I entirely disapprove, either. Maybe it needed to happen. I guess. I don't know." He tapped the communication device idly a few times, hoping he was being heard. "Either way, I think this is pretty much all of Warren's men. Every one the people could find. I told them that we couldn't behave like that any more. They seem to understand. We're working on a way to deal with future problems in a... a more organized way, I guess. Okay. That's it. I'm heading over to the Grand Elevator now, and if you have anything to say to me, well, I'll be there."

The walk to the elevator was quiet. Most of the Citizens he spotted made little or no fuss as he passed by. One or two looked away as if in shame. Especially when they saw those who had just carried a body to the elevator.

When Mike got to the loading bay, the dead were lined up and waiting, just as they had been they day Warren had met his end. Today, there were even more bodies.

Leena stood grimly at the doorway, offering Mike a hand as he approached. "Hey."

"Hey, you." Mike brought her closer into an embrace, looking over her shoulder at the bodies. "Why are you hanging out here?"

"Just in case Messenger showed up before you did."

"Hard to hate them while they're dead," Mike said. "Most of them look kind of peaceful now."

"Forgiving them?"

"I'd rather just forget them."

Leena only responded with a sigh.

Moments later, Edgar entered the loading bay, wearing some sort or robe made from the usual re-purposed clothing. He gave Mike and Leena only the slightest glace before walking between the rows of bodies, taking time to look at each one until he stopped at one.

He bent over, kissed his own fingers, then touched the body's forehead. He then placed some trinket in the body's hand, and held the hand silently for a few moments. He placed the hand on the deceased's chest, and stood to leave.

Leena turned to face him as he passed. "Edgar–"

"Will you be celebrating drunkenly tonight, as you did after Warren, and many of my people died?" Edgar ruefully mumbled.

"I don't think anyone's in the mood for that."

"Indeed," Edgar mumbled as he left.

When his footsteps grew silent with distance, Leena ventured over to the body Edgar had stopped at, and looked at his face. "Mike. Do you think this looks like him?"

Mike looked down at the young man. "I ... maybe. Other than new arrivals from the lofus, everyone's somebody's baby."

Leena looked across all of the dead bodies. "All used to be babies. That's... *and look at the bastards they turned into.*"

"I guess it's *not* so hard to hate them when they're dead and peaceful." Mike said.

Leena kicked the body nearest to her in the head. "Not in the slightest."

"I think Dan's laying over there if you want to kick someone you know."

Sniffing sharply, Leena corrected her posture. "I think I'm done, thank you." Her eyes still darted about, looking for faces she knew to hate more than others. "Besides... I think I hear Messenger."

Mike strained to hear, and yes, the elevator was near. The sound grew closer, and ended with the noise and rattle as usual.

"Hi, Messenger," Leena called out.

Mike raised an eyebrow. "Really? '*Hi Messenger?*'" he murmured to her. Leena just shrugged back.

"Citizens," came Messenger's voice, "is there something you need to tell me beyond what was communicated?"

"...Not really," Mike said. "I just wanted to be here in case you wanted to say something about this... about all these bodies."

Silence, for a while. Leena shifted her weight, glancing around the dead, lingering her eyes a bit by the one that was likely Edgar's son. Mike folded his hands in front of himself, and looked down, awaiting whatever reprimand Messenger might see fit to give.

Messenger finally said, "No. I think you made the situation clear over the communication. Leave the loading bay."

"Messenger, it's a lot of bodies to move," Leena said quietly. "Would you want some help with —"

"No," Messenger interrupted, "please. Just go."

Leena and Mike turned to leave, but Mike paused. "I think it will be a long time before we need you for any dead again."

"Good," was the only reply.

When the bay door closed behind them, Leena couldn't help but imagine Messenger in there, dragging body after body onto the Grand Elevator all alone.

"I feel bad for him," Leena said.

Mike looked back at the door. "Yeah. I hope he understands why it happened."

"Let's go do something productive, Mike."

"Like what?"

"Like maybe Cody is building something. Working on his new ramp repair or something. I want to go check on Jen and Tara first. Wanna meet at Cody's ramp in a bit? I just need to go somewhere else."

Chapter Nine

Peace

"Hello?" Leena called as she breached Jen and Tara's doorway.

"Oh, hey, Leena," Jen answered. She was seated and busy adjusting a set of standard clothing.

"Where's Tara?"

"She went out to get some rust flakes. I find 'em disgusting, but she grinds some into her water regularly."

"Eh, I do that sometimes," Leena said.

"Ew. And then they're like... in your body. Can't be good for you."

"As if dizzy water is."

Jen shrugged sheepishly. "Yeah. But it's not rotten little chunks of metal."

Leena took a moment to gauge Jen's overall mood, until Jen looked at her funny. "Yes?"

"Oh, nothing," Leena said, sitting down. "I mostly came by to see how you two were doing after the big... uh... Warren-man-hunt."

Jen chuckled softly. "So you came to check on your pets, huh?"

"I have never petted you!" Leena countered.

Jen rolled her eyes with a smile that began to fade steadily. "So... Dan's dead."

Leena sighed. "I was going to ask. In a subtle kind of way. Did you..."

Jen shook her head, holding her hand out. "No, I didn't kill him. Someone told me that a mob had gotten him. Technically, I don't think he was one of Warren's men."

"Everyone knew what kind of man he was."

"Well, no," Jen mumbled, "he wasn't just about the bad things he did. He had some good qualities, and..."

"Would you rather he be alive?"

"He *meant* something to me," Jen said. "I didn't want to see him ever again, but he meant something good for me for a long while."

"Don't make excuses for a rapist."

"I *know*. I know. But death? I don't know. He wasn't as bad as Warren's main group. I just don't want to see him so... easily lumped in with them. I don't know. It's complicated. I'm glad he's not here, but I can't be glad he was killed. He meant something to me."

"So, he's better than Warren's men because he raped you exclusively, and not any woman he came across, and merely watched when Warren had you, and didn't help Warren out directly."

"I feel like I'm feeling the incorrect feelings or something," Jen said weakly.

Leena took Jen's hand, and gave it a squeeze. "Well, he's now officially and completely part of the past. You have something so much better now. Even if she drinks rust now and then."

Jen moved to give Leena a hug, but tossed her aside when she saw Tara approaching. Jen dashed over to Tara and wrapped herself around her. "Tara! You're great, did you know that?"

Leena stood up after being unceremoniously discarded, and smiled at the couple. "Tsk, tsk... I was just about to get some hug action, when you show up and ruin my evil plan!"

"Yes?" Tara eyed Jen with mock suspicion. "What have you two been up to?"

"Leena just came to remind me how awesome you are," Jen said.

"Well, I was just checking on you both," Leena explained, "but one thing led to another, and before you know it, I'm assuming the hug position like some kind of hug-tramp. You know how it is."

"It's been pretty chaotic lately," Tara said. She smiled sadly and looked over Jen's shoulder at the open Citizenry. "Do you think it's all over? Warren and his guys are gone. Things could stay safe for a while, if I had my way."

"With any luck."

***

Indeed, in the coming months, Warren's name was spoken less and less. Violence was not outright gone; personal conflicts sometimes came to blows or worse, but nothing that resulted in having to send a body away. Nothing that couldn't heal- other than grudges, perhaps.

Around the same time that Cody completed his own ramp-top den (which turned out to be three times larger inside than the one he'd made for Mike,) Edgar's Refuge reached completion at last; a section of the Citizenry separated by a wall which was up to five metres tall in some spots.

A gate opened on one end, guarded by two of Edgar's loyal people, holding spears. Inside lived Citizens who felt more or less as Edgar did about Mike. Not hating Mike, but not entirely trusting him, for whatever various reasons.

Mike and Leena were welcome to visit there. Welcome, but not wanted. Tolerated.

"This is a place where people can feel assured that they aren't under the omniscient gaze of the great and mighty Mike," Edgar had been heard to say more than once. Because to some people, being under Edgar's gaze was better, apparently.

One day, five of Edgar's more fanatical followers went to Mike's ramp to shout at him. Calling him the new great dictator who was unfairly imposing his will, and so on. One was armed with a sword-like weapon.

Mike stormed past them, walking off across Citizenry.

"Where are *you* going?" one of the mini-mob members demanded. They followed him, and many random Citizens followed the commotion. Any who stood against the noisy crew to defend Mike were waved away by Mike. "Don't cause anything," Mike would say.

Soon, Mike had led the noisy little mob to Edgar's Refuge. He addressed a guard, and pointed at the five angry Citizens. "Are these ones yours?"

"Ah, I know a couple of them, but..."

"So you didn't send them to come yelling angry crap to wake me up? Did Edgar send them?"

"I don't know if–"

"Go ask him. I'll wait."

"I can't leave my post."

"Fine." Mike walked through the gate, with his five angry irritants behind him.

"You can't enter the Refuge without authorization!" one hollered, despite the guards not caring much.

"Fine, fine. I'm not bringing my army," Mike said. He turned to the random scattering of Citizens who'd followed along. "Anyone who doesn't live in here, wait outside, or go home, or whatever, okay? No mass invasions into the Refuge. It's a refuge. Okay? Are we okay? I'm going to see Edgar, and ask him about you goons."

Mike noticed that one of said goons had excused himself, having lost interest or nerve. Going further in towards where Mike knew Edgar had made his nest, he saw several of the Refuge Citizens. They had normal shacks within the Refuge.

They were like any other Citizens... except what...? They saw Mike as a potential threat? Or maybe they were more comforted by Edgar's age and experience. And armed guards.

103

One Citizen looked obsessively concerned with a couple of thin, colourful books, and mumbled to herself about the pictures therein, holding them up in front of herself. Another Citizen prepared a bottle for dizzy water. (Wasn't that against one of Edgar's rules?) Two others were wrapped about each other in the doorway to a shack.

These were normal Citizens. Citizens who felt better being inside the wall than outside of it, whatever that meant.

Before Mike got much further, Edgar approached to meet him. Edgar walked with a new spear, one adorned with cloth decoration where the shaft met the spear's head.

"Edgar!" one of the five– make that four– rabble-rousers chirped up. "We're keeping an eye on Mike. He came marching right here to cause trouble!"

"What kind of trouble?" Edgar asked, eyes on Mike.

"I don't know, he–"

The Citizen was silenced by Edgar's raised hand. "I was asking Mike."

"Are these guys yours?" Mike asked, pointing a thumb over his shoulder at them.

Edgar looked them over, to make sure. "Yes, I believe they live in the Refuge."

"Then why did they feel the need to come up my ramp, yelling all kinds of crap about me? Sounded like the kind of crap I'd expect to hear from you, but only if you were really drunk. Did you send them?" Mike asked.

The leader of the little group spoke up, "We wanted to let Mike know that he wasn't the boss of everyone, that we have the right to–"

"The right to make fools of yourselves, and start a riot?" Edgar asked.

"We–"

"Hush," Edgar said with a stomp of the end of his spear on the floor. "So the four of you–"

"Five, they lost one somewhere when we arrived at the Refuge," Mike corrected.

"Five of you decided to cause a disturbance at the home of someone you figured was your enemy, surrounded by masses of people fiercely loyal to him? Oh, you're lucky to be alive. Do tell, how did you survive hundreds of Mike-loyal Citizens attacking you?"

"They didn't attack," the leader of the mini-mob answered.

"Ah. There were what, a dozen of them? A hundred?" Edgar guessed," all scared away by one of you having a blade? How brave of you- how cowardly of *them*."

In an awkward silence that Edgar and Mike were both enjoying for essentially the same reasons, Mike finally offered, "A few Citizens felt the need to shout back at them, but I told them to back off."

"Surely, Mike, you sent your hundreds of followers away, as you were concerned that your giant group would all be slain by these five brave heroes."

"Surely."

A smile tried to break Edgar's stern expression, but was quickly brought under control. He went over to the Citizen with the sword. "Give it to me."

The Citizen obeyed.

Edgar looked at the sword. It was nothing too fancy. Some tool's long handle, hammed down along most of its length and tip to make a blade. He turned, and held it out to Mike with both hands.

"Please accept this as apology for the disturbance."

"All right." Mike said. He held it up. It was really unimpressive to him, but he was willing to play along.

"And you four..." Edgar said, turning to the delinquents, "—and pass it on to the fifth. You're all banned from weapons for ten days. If I, or a guard sees you with a weapon, it will be taken away, and given to Mike or one of his people."

"Oooh, nice," Mike said quietly. "Nice fair little punishment, I'll have to remember that one, I might have use for it some time or the other."

Edgar looked to the four. "All of you, go to your shacks."

"Thanks." Mike said, improvising a little salute with the hilt of his new sword."

"Thank you for not killing those fools," Edgar said.

"They were behaving like little brats, so I dragged them home."

Mike headed back out of the refuge to discover Leena at the head of twenty or so Citizens. She had modified her outfit, the legs ripped short to show more skin. This was the kind of thing one would simply not do when Warren's men were about.

"Hey," Leena said. "These guys wanted to rush in and save you." Leena rolled her eyes discreetly.

"And if I'd needed help?" Mike said, walking up to Leena and putting an arm around her waist.

"I'd have dragged you home, listened to your story, then maybe beat the crap out of you for your stupidity," Leena said with a squeeze.

"Oh my. Well, I'm glad it didn't come to that!" Mike said.

"Don't relax yet, pal. I still haven't heard the full story."

By now, groups of Citizens loyal to Mike were staring at a group loyal to Edgar, who'd clustered around the entrance to the refuge.

"Okay, enough sour faces, everyone. Let's go home."

And this was peace. Imperfect peace, but peace none the less. In effect, but not design, if someone disliked Mike or Edgar, (but not so much as to inspire violence,) they could go align with the other. It would lead a Citizen to essentially the same life, but secure in the idea that they were with people who had similarly ill-defined ideals as they themselves did.

Edgar didn't ban dizzy water within the Refuge after all, although he made his disapproval of it known. He *did* ban sniffing jars.

Mike had no problem with dizzy water as long as your behaviour didn't hurt others. He didn't outright ban sniffing, but no one really publicly approved of it anyway.

Being outside of the Refuge made access to water a bit easier. In or out of the Refuge, life was different only in the smallest degrees, but small degrees felt a bit bigger when the old, greater threats – like Warren's ways – became more and more a distant memory.

105

Chapter Ten

Two Lofus

"I'm going over to the Refuge to swap books," Leena said, flipping the pages of the most recently borrowed one. Even before Warren had been in power, Edgar had been hoarding books. Now that Edgar felt a little safer, the books weren't a *secret*, but they weren't just tossed out to the masses, either.

"Oh! I wasn't done with that book!" Mike sarcastically said, lazing upon their sleeping pile. "What is it again? Lee-Enful Riffly five muk I?" Mike sucked the last bit of dizzy water out of a jar. It had been half full not long ago, and the silliness was starting to set in.

Eventually, over the course of uncounted weeks and months, Leena, Mike, and a handful of others could claim to be able to read, even if only barely. It would sometimes become a game to go through a book and pick apart a word here or there, usually with little or no context, occasionally even getting the meaning and pronunciation right. Occasionally.

"Lee-Enfield Rifle No.5 Mk I," Leena corrected, waving the small but thick tan tome around. "Yeah, it was boring. At least it had a lot of pictures. Boring pictures, though."

The book could tell a person (especially a person who was notably more literate) how to take a *Lee-Enfield Rifle No.5 Mk I* apart, but never actually mentioned what the thing did. Mike had some sort of theory that it could be used to attack a person with little bits of metal. Lame. What a lot of hassle to throw little bits of metal, when a good knife threw quite nicely. It had to have some other purpose. It was a moot point, though, since they only had the manual, not the *Lee-Enfield Rifle No.5 Mk I* itself.

"Tell you what, Mike, I'll see if I can get another of the colourful ones."

"Ooh!"

Mike liked the colourful flimsy ones, even if a lot of pages were damaged- or missing entirely. They had a lot of pictures to help tell the story, and they were some crazy stories, from what anyone could understand. A lot of them had very interesting clothes. Colourful, and often skimpy. Colour options were limited in the Citizenry, but Leena had been inspired by one or two of them to modify her clothes to show more skin.

Leena ripped off the legs of one of her outfits very high to expose a lot of thigh, and around home, she became prone to walking around with the top part zipped down very low.

Her exposed thighs turned more than a few heads, though. In the time of Warren and his type, it would be considered dangerous. Now? Not everyone saw it as prudent, but Leena and more than a few women had become more confident- in both dress, and attitude. Not that Leena had a long way to go with her disposition. She was strong, and everyone knew it.

Some women followed her lead, daring to be more suggestive in their dress. Some chose to keep the usual outfit configuration. Now and then, you'd hear a comment disparaging the new ways, or the old. Too brash, too shy, too suggestive, too repressed. It generally came to no ill will, generally, but little grudges would stick here and there.

She looked at the manual and considered Mike's request. "I kind of wanted one of the ones with more words, but since this one was kind of a flop, sure, I'll get a colourful picture one."

"Thank you," Mike said, getting up to embrace Leena gently. "They still have lots of words to play with, and they don't make any more or less sense than the ones that are all wordy."

Most books made little or no sense, even if you *could* manage to decode the words. Many had pictures of things that simply didn't exist. One common fantasy was a huge room, bigger than Commons, with a blue ceiling.

"Oh, you've heard Edgar. They're all from Actual, and of course have more meaning than we lesser Citizens could ever understand!"

Mike ran his hand up into the unzipped upper half of Leena's outfit, and caressed one of his favourite curves. "I understand some of those colourful pictures," he whispered in her ear, with a hint of a dizzy-water-fueled chuckle.

"You tend to do a lot more than those pictures," Leena purred.

Mike growled back playfully, only to nearly get his wrist caught in the zipper as Leena closed her top back up most of the way. She honestly didn't care a lot if someone other than Mike got a bit of an eyeful these days, but she found it sometimes made conversation awkward, and sent mixed messages.

"Later, big boy," she consoled. "I want to pop in on Jen and Tara before I swap the book, and when I get back, I might be convinced."

"Tease," he said, finding consolation in a fresh jar of dizzy-water.

"At every opportunity!"

Leena's visit to Jen and Tara was a little on the short side. Some women in the Citizenry would regularly bleed from a very private place now and then. It hurt them inside, kind of, but never did any permanent harm. It was inconvenient as heck, and a bit messy for days at a time. Tara and Jen had been bleeding on more or less the same days as each other for a long time now, and they were less in the mood for company than usual. Especially Tara.

"Aw, don't be so chipper, Miss *I-never-have-to-put-up-with-that,*" Tara snapped, half-joking. Leena resisted teasing them by accusing them of too much crap-sniffing as teenagers. That was a popular rumour about why some women started bleeding, but honestly, no one knew.

Some said it started after too much sex, not enough, or whatever. And for that matter, men never seemed to have that.

This led to women who bled, occasionally teasing women who didn't bleed, noting that non-bleeders almost never bore children. Such teasing was generally done with great care.

Leena was nearly to Edgar's Refuge when she realised that she'd left the book at Jen and Tara's. As she was cursing her stupidity for departing for Edgar's without the very purpose of her visit in-hand, she heard a shout.

"The Grand Elevator's here!"

Well, it was about time for a food delivery from Actual. Leena was heading back to Jen and Tara's when she spotted Mike heading for the elevator with a growing following.

Oh, why not go to the Elevator, too? Leena finally decided.

When Leena arrived at the loading bay a minute or so after Mike and his group, about two dozen Citizens were clustered together in the way. Messenger had already left, leaving behind the usual boxes of food discs, and something else that had the Citizens excited.

She heard Mike's voice on the opposite side of the group. "Oh my, young man, you certainly have come up in the way of things. Welcome to the top!"

It sounded like Mike was making friends with a lofu. Messenger had brought lofus before, and it never ended well. But that was under Warren's rule. This might turn out different.

"Oh yes, oh yes," Mike continued, "but of course, you know there is a fee to enter, correct?"

"A fee?" came the voice of the lofu. He sounded nervous.

Mike chuckled. "Oh, no, we wouldn't expect you to have any material possession worth trading, but entertainment, on the other hand, would do nicely."

Oh crap, Leena thought. *What kind of crap is Mike up to now?*

The lofu didn't say anything, so Mike continued, "Well, my boy, there's two interesting things you can do, and we can provide a partner for either," Mike said, then turning to the others. "What do you think? Will we make the baby 'Provider' fight, or ffffffornicate?"

That dizzy water was putting words in Mike's mouth. Fornicate? *Fight?* Where had that come from? A lofu might be lesser, but it didn't call for violence– much less encouraging it from Citizens. If Mike were sober, he'd be thinking more than this. How much dizzy-water did he *have* earlier?

A lot of the Citizens began chanting, "Fight, fight, fight." This was bad. Leena resolved to chew Mike out later, and keep the dizzy-water away from him for a while.

The lofu backed away from Mike, nervously looking around at everyone and taking a defencive stance. This was getting bad, and Leena needed to stop it. Well, Mike had given her the seed of a distraction- for the lofu, and everyone.

She took a deep breath, and rallied her nerve. Zipper down half way, she pushed through the other Citizens towards the lofu.

"Yer not gonna let anyone bloody up this pretty, pretty boy, Mike. It's not like shiny lofus pop up every day! I want a turn with him!"

The Citizens by the door cheered and goaded her on. Okay, play it up. Confidence, sass, pour it on. She did a little bit of a dance as she closed in on the lofu, and pressed herself up against him.

He backed away, but she kept close, stopping him by putting her arm around his waist. "Afraid of a little slippery fun, 'Provider'?"

Was that his name? Mike had called him that. Lofus are weird. She growled softly. Okay, maybe she was having a little fun. The lofu seemed fairly harmless, and not ugly, so the act was easy enough.

Actually, he looked scared. Leena looked back at the Citizens, then again to the lofu. She leaned closer and whispered in his ear. "Don't worry about them. You don't even have to take your clothes off. Just get on with it, yeah? And our audience isn't into softie-style, so feel free to rush and get it over with."

She could tell he wouldn't, but found herself suddenly terrified that her bluff would backfire. *Ugh... follow through,* she thought. A fight would be worse than having to play up comedy if she were forced to physically reject this lofu. And surely Mike wasn't so drunk as to let anything happen if she showed distress. Right?

She leaned back far, a thigh coming around the lofu now, her head almost upside down, her cleavage threatening to escape the unzipped top. Eek. The 'audience' reacted to her showmanship with a wave of lewd cheers.

Coming back up, she found his other ear to whisper into. "I'm making myself the show here, kid. Don't stress it. We all earn our place in our own way. Just enjoy it, you'll be fine." As they came face to face again, her glossed-over demeanour cracked a little. She dropped her smile briefly and shrugged just enough that the lofu would notice.

She started to feel bad for him. He backed away, holding her back with a soft push to her shoulder. They locked eyes. Where did it go from here? The Citizens needed to go home and forget all of this.

Cries of protest rang out from the Citizens. "Come on!" "Make her scream for it!" "Maybe he's into guys." "Whip it out!"

Crap. This was a mistake. A dozen much more logical ways to diffuse this situation came to mind, and all of them needed to be started the moment she entered the loading bay. She'd done this to try to stop violence, but she'd just painted herself as some sex object.

"Maybe you were more interested in the fighting option?" Mike said in an accommodating tone. Definitely still drunk. He was in *so* much trouble.

The lofu shrunk away from everyone slowly, taking timid little steps backwards towards the elevator. "Maybe I should just wait for Messenger to come back," he mumbled. Moans and boos from the Citizens only pushed him back towards the elevator further.

One of the food boxes began to move. Grunts came from inside as it wiggled around a little. The top finally burst open. A fist holding a knife shot up as smashed food discs spilled in every direction.

Up rose another lofu, with an unsavoury look in his eyes, and a knife in each hand. "Lenth!" he called to the first lofu. "I thought these *'Citizens'* were supposed to be the best of us! They just seem like a different kind of awful than the Providers!"

The knife-wielding lofu spotted Leena, and quickly dashed behind her with an arm around her throat, knife by her face. "Well! I've heard enough to know that *you* obviously work for your keep! Maybe you're the exception!" He pointed the other knife at Mike and the other Citizens. "Anyone want the soft one dead?"

Leena sneered at herself for letting her guard down. She wasn't expecting some lowly lofu to make a lunge like that.

"Six! Don't make this worse than it already is!" the first lofu, apparently named Lenth, pleaded.

"Friend," Mike said, "you're clearly out of your depth here. I don't think you under—"

The lofu 'Six' wrenched his arm against the Leena to enforce his leverage. She struggled, but the lofu Six was really strong.

"Out of my way! I'm leaving," Six said to the Citizens clogging up the hallway. He walked towards the Citizens with his free knife waving at them. Between a lack of organization and room to move, the group wasn't moving nearly as fast as Six was hoping for. "This is garbage," he seethed at them.

Six threw Leena at Mike as forcefully as he could to slow them both down. Before she even landed on Mike, Six had turned again. With two free arms and knives to wield, he charged at the Citizens, screaming.

The first lofu, Lenth looked at Leena and Mike, then moved closer to the other one, Six. Lenth seemed as stunned as everyone else, and his body language seemed like he wanted to stop Six. Too late, really, Six was already slashing wildly. His third rabid slash into the crowd of Citizens at the doorway sent an arc of red across the wall, as did the fifth.

Three Citizens were on the floor already. One scampered away backwards from the commotion as he held his bleeding upper arm. One Citizen was kneeling, guarding a third who lay motionless in a growing pool of blood.

"Six! What are you doing? Stop!" Lenth's cries went ignored, if Six heard them at all over the swarm of chaos he had created – and was still cutting his way through.

Lenth tried to get closer to Six, but more wounded and panicked people made it impossible. "Stop it, Six! You don't have to do this! They haven't done anything to you!" Lenth disappeared through the Citizens, giving chase as well as he could.

In a relatively calm moment, Leena zipped back up, and turned to the nearest injured Citizen on the floor. His arm was cut and bleeding, and it seemed like an injury she could do something about.

She pulled off her headband, and used it as a bandage to tie around his arm.

The lofu Lenth wandered back in, looking stunned. He knelt down by Leena and asked her, "Are you all right?"

Without taking her eyes away from her bandaging job, she drew breath to answer, but was cut off.

"I'm fine, thank you," Mike said, strolling leisurely towards them. "Oh, you meant Leena." He smirked smugly at his own joke. He was still far too stupid with dizzy-water. Lovely.

"I'm fine," Leena said quietly. "I've been through worse." She lifted her chin towards the two dead men visible from where they were, and a half dozen other Citizens tending to each others' wounds. "I guess I was lucky."

Lenth looked at the fallen Citizens, then back to Leena, then to the doorway. "I can't believe he...I knew he'd killed, but this..." Lenth looked Leena up and down. "Maybe Six didn't want to hurt a pretty woman. If he's like me, he didn't grow up around any."

"You know that energetic young knife enthusiast?" Mike said, gazing down the hall. A few unhurt Citizens had begun getting into the food crates...carefully.

Lenth stood, fists forming as he looked at the casualties. "We've...run into each other a few times. Before this, he's killed seven? I lost track. A Rubberman and a bunch of Providers. I kind of understood his reasons for that, but Citizens? He's crazy. We have to stop him."

Mike shrugged. "Go ahead. As far as I'm concerned, that fellow's little show was more than enough entertainment for the day. Consider your entry...granted."

"Entertainment?" Lenth looked at Mike with a wrinkled brow.

Leena's patient was bandaged as well as she could manage, and as he stood, so did Leena. She put her hand on Lenth's shoulder and said in a tired tone, "Welcome to the Citizenry."

"Who's the leader around here?" Lenth asked.

Mike reached out with a theatrical shrug. "Leader? A lot of people do what I say, so maybe I am!"

Lenth still looked a bit confused. "So, how long have you been kinda-leader?"

Mike counted on his fingers. "Hmm, a hundred... -hundred and fifty days or so? More? The guy who figured himself to be leader before was a real prick. I caved his head in, people cheered. It was a big thing."

"He did a lot of things, that guy before," Leena said with a distant gaze. "His buddies, too. They..." She smiled, and pinched Lenth's cheek. "You're a damned virgin, aren't you? I shouldn't go trying to confuse a kid like you." She pulled out her food bag, and wandered over to the crates to fill it up, then secured it to her hip through a couple of small holes in her suit. By now, the

112

flow of Citizens coming and going to secure their own stash had steadied, still slowed by the injured and the residual chaos.

"He made a lot of use of spaces above the ceiling," Lenth said. "The ceiling here was solid with no special 'above', and offered no hiding places. "Where could he go to hide, and maybe move around? You know, where he might not be seen."

Leena snickered a little. "So you want to go crawl into wherever that guy and his two knives went?"

"I can't believe how relaxed you all are!" Lenth said. "Look at how many people Six hurt and killed!"

"Someone will kill him," Leena said quietly, "or he'll end up being the leader or something." She paused to make eye contact with Lenth. "—And for the record, I highly doubt that will happen."

She shouldn't joke with the lofu. He seemed to have no clue. But as much as violence had been curbed in the Citizenry since Warren's men were hunted down, the remaining Citizens wouldn't tolerate some madman for long. With a little luck, some kind of group would form and surround this 'Six'. Someone would take him down eventually. Hopefully 'Six' wouldn't do much damage before it happened.

"This...this is normal?" Lenth asked.

Leena shrugged. "It's not everyday or anything, and the fact that it's a lofu causing trouble is unique, but this kind of thing happens."

"Not where I come from," Lenth said. "Nothing like this at all! I didn't even know what death was most of my life, let alone this! Hey, where's Mike gotten off to?"

"He's probably gone to get his medical stuff. He keeps a bunch of it, and looks like a big hero when he comes along with a bandage and pain pills."

"But not heroic enough to go after Six, huh?" Lenth asked.

Leena shrugged. "He might. Mike's never been much of a brawler."

"But he caved in the head of the old leader? What, was he asleep?"

"You're pretty close to the truth," Leena said. "Someone needed to do it."

Leena began to wander down the hall, and Lenth followed. "Oh, Leena, Six isn't a Provider, by the way. He came from a couple of floors below that. Unit Subject. Like I was, but in a different Unit. I guess I'm a Provider now."

"I have no idea what you're talking about," Leena said.

"Units. I lived below the Providers and Rubbermen. Among other things, the Units grow food. Well, the food that the food is made out of."

"Grow food?" Leena chuckled. "What are you talking about? Food doesn't grow, dummy."

"It does! I didn't know either. My Unit doesn't grow anything, but I've seen the 'trees' that they get the papayas from, and the papayas go into the food. And don't even ask what they feed the trees– not if you want to sleep tonight!"

Well, that sealed it. Lofus were crazy.

"So, Provider guy..." It clicked in Leena's head from Mike calling him Provider as she had entered the loading bay, and Lenth's own rambling, that this might be a word lofus used instead of 'lofu'. Or something. "Are you following me for a reason? Showtime is over. Are you thinking of some nekkid grunty fun? Because to be totally honest, I'm not in the mood after your buddy did his stabby thing."

"I...wasn't really thinking about that. I just...the only two people I know around here are you and Mike, and between the two choices..."

Leena scoffed in amusement. '*Drunk-Mike*' hadn't made a great impression, and '*distraction-Leena*' maybe made *too* good of a first impression. "Gotcha."

"And I'm not quite really a Provider, I think. My name is Lenth."

"All right, *not-quite-a-Provider-I-think-Lenth*, what's your grand plan?"

The surrounding Citizens, some dealing with Six's attack, and some heading in for a resupply of food, were thinning out a bit. Leena and Lenth were almost out of the Grand Elevator building, toward open Citizenry.

"My plan?" Lenth said. "I was looking for answers about my Brother's death. Found 'em, too. But I guess while I was looking, I started finding things. Things I didn't know were out there." He chuckled and looked Leena up and down. "Like women! I never knew!"

"What? I was right? You've never..."

"Nope. I learned about it recently, though," Lenth said.

Leena couldn't help but laugh. "What, you learned about it? How, from a magazine?"

"What's a magazine?" Lenth said. "I learned it from a video."

Leena laughed at the strange fellow. Lofus were nuts, but at least this one seemed harmless.

"How is that funny?" Lenth asked. "How is a person supposed to learn it?"

Leena forced her laughter down to a dark, rolling giggle. She pressed Lenth against the wall, unzipping her top a bit again. "Have a peek," she said darkly. "Are you telling me you need instructions to get ideas?"

Lenth looked, but quickly looked away, blushing.

"See, you get it," Leena said, zipping up and continuing down the hall. "It all figures itself out."

Lenth composed himself as well as he could and trailed along behind her. "I don't understand how you...and I guess I mean all Citizens I've met so far, can be so casual about sex and death. I mean, what Six did was horrible! I'm still expecting him to jump out and attack again! He could be anywhere! And you're teasing me and showing—"

They came out into the open Citizenry. Lenth slowed down to stare about, and up around Citizenry's dome, gradually coming to a stop.

"Lenth. Wake up," Leena said.

Lenth snapped out of his gawking. "Oh? Oh! What's going on?"

"Mike's feeling important and doing his thing."

Ahead was a crowd of about fifty Citizens around a big chunk of random scrap that made a sufficient platform for Mike to talk to everyone.

"Attention, people," Mike called out. He seemed less dizzy now. Hopefully he wouldn't say anything too stupid. "Many of you know what's happened, and some of you know bits and pieces. I was there, I saw it all, and I want to make sure truths are known before rumours get confused and muddied, as rumours tend to do.

"First, the good news. Yes, food has arrived as expected. I see many of you have already gotten yours. I don't have to remind anyone what happens if people get unreasonably greedy, so good is good." His tone then grew a good deal more serious.

"Second, I see some of you are bleeding. You've met one of our newest inhabitants, an angry fellow who likes knives. He's from really deep down, a bottom-rung lofu, so we can't expect much in civility. I saw four dead people on my way out, and a lot more hurt. I've sent runners to go fetch some medical necessities, and we'll get right on treating the injured as best we can.

"Thirdly, good news on that front. We also have another new inhabitant, at least for a while: a Provider!" Evidently Mike had decided to use that word to be polite for Lenth. Still a lofu, but maybe a slightly better type.

Mike held his hand out to point towards Lenth. The crowd turned to look at Lenth. All Lenth could do was shift uncomfortably. Mike quickly took the attention back.

"Our new friend Lenth here will take care of our little stabby-man problem, after which," and Mike paused for emphasis, "after which, I'll summon Messenger with the communication box, if Lenth wishes. Then he can go about whatever other adventures await such a hero! Ah, I see my runner coming back with medical supplies, so I'll just get to business. Oh, if you see that stabby lofu, do tell Lenth here."

The gathering slowly started to dissipate as Mike stepped off the platform, stopping to talk to various people.

"Leena," Lenth asked quietly, "what's a lofu?"

Leena rolled her eyes with a smirk. "Lesser Outsider From Under."

"Lesser outsider?" Lenth asked. "Are there better outsiders?"

"You're a riot," Leena said mirthlessly. "Outside of the Citizenry. Lesser as in not as good as us."

"Ah." Lenth stuck out his chin and nodded slowly. "So I guess that counts for me, too."

"He didn't call you that," Leena said. "Maybe he counts you as a Citizen now. Or maybe you're just useful."

"Useful but lesser?" Lenth asked.

Leena smirked. "That attitude, minus the sarcasm, will get you far with Mike." Actually, Mike loved sarcasm, so maybe Lenth would do as well to pour it on.

"And the people that make your food? Are they lesser, too?" Lenth wondered aloud.

"I guess!" Leena paused for a moment, only giving it real thought for a split second before her Citizenship reasserted itself. "They're not as lesser than other lessers, I guess." This fellow was confusing. Food came from Actual, not lofus, but what use would it be to explain everything to a lofu?

Lenth pressed the issue. "And Messenger? And Actual? Are they outsiders, or lesser?"

"You have odd thoughts, Lenth." Leena looked back at the elevator shaft that reached up to the lofty ceiling. "They're...outsiders for sure. But they're not like us. They're..." she stared at the ceiling, looking for the right words.

"Better outsiders?" Lenth offered.

Leena looked at him in all seriousness, and studied his face for a moment. "Yeah. Yeah, maybe that's a good way of putting it. We're..."

"Do you think they call you Citizens 'lofu'?"

"Stop thinking so much, Lenth."

The group was nearly dissipated, and Mike wandered towards the two of them.

"Well, that went well!" Mike said, grinning. He accepted a large medical bag from his runner and slung it over his shoulder.

"Subtle, Mike," Leena said, "how you spelled out that Lenth can't go until he's gotten rid of the other guy."

"Liked that, did ya?" Mike chuckled as he did a quick little inspection of his bag's contents. "I thought it sounded right leaderly of me!" That dizzy water couldn't wear off fast enough.

"His name is Six," added Lenth quietly.

"Who?" Mike closed his bag, apparently satisfied. "Oh, oh, Mister Stabby. Right. Six, whatever. Hey, do you have a knife, Lenth? I hope you have a knife. It might help."

Lenth shook his head.

"Ah. Pity. Leena, can you take our brave boy here up to our den and let him pick something out from the pokey-rack? Not my best ones, of course, but the rack should have *something* that suits him."

"Sure," Leena said.

"You're a doctor, Mike?" Lenth asked.

Mike had pieced together what a doctor was, mainly from the manual for the medical bag. He patted the bag. "Nope. No one here is, but I've figured out enough. I've read a couple of manuals. Lot of pictures."

"You can read!" Lenth said, partly as a question, eyebrows high.

"Yes," Mike said with a fairly smug look. "I've been able to read for a long time! I've mastered it! Well. Mostly."

"Don't tease the lofu, Mike," Leena said. "Mike reads well enough to get by. As well as anyone."

"I bet 'anyone' is better than me at it," Lenth said. "I'm pretty new at it. The Providers, though, they all seem great at it. Probably better than any of us."

Mike coughed. "I highly doubt any 'Provider' is better at anything than a Citizen is."

"Come on," Leena nudged Lenth. "Let's go get your pokey-poke."

Leena led Lenth towards home. They crossed paths with a few Citizens.

"Leena, food's here?" one of them asked.

"Yeah," Leena said. "Hey, you guys haven't seen a stranger in the last little while? Besides this guy here. Probably has bloody hands and stuff? Did a lot of damage, some dead people."

The trio looked surprised and didn't have any useful information. Leena gave them a brief warning before she and Lenth continued on their way.

"Who were those people?" Lenth asked.

"I don't know. I mean, I've seen them around, but I don't know their names."

Lenth looked back at them as he walked, then back at Leena. "They knew you."

"Yeah, most people know me. I'm with Mike and stuff, and, well..."

Lenth looked around, still seeming a bit in awe of the Citizenry. "I only knew about four people all my life, and I know them all. Not knowing people that you live around..." Lenth glanced around, spotting others in the distance. "It's just really weird for me. I guess I'm weird to you and the other Citizens."

Leena shrugged. "Hadn't thought about it much. Four people all your life, huh? Does that have something to do with why you couldn't get a girl?"

"Pretty much. There were no girls." Lenth chuckled nervously.

Leena whistled a long, low note. "Boy. That sucks. Wait. Am I the first girl you've ever seen?"

"No, no, I met some Provider women. You're nothing like them, though."

"What, they got no...?" She swayed back and forth and ran her hands down along her body in an exaggerated way.

Lenth stared at her, shaking his head. "I'm not even sure what that was."

"Oh, you poor boy, you," she said sullenly. "Gonna have to get you an education."

They passed a few more Citizens as they approached the ramp, and asked them if they'd seen a stranger with bloody hands. No luck.

Lenth looked back across the huge Commons. "Six was good at hiding in tight little spaces. I was hoping he wouldn't be as good in a *wide open* place."

If Lenth's stare across the Commons was one of awe, Leena's was one of quiet disdain. "I think I know enough hiding places to get us a good start."

Leena turned her head from time to time, looking around the ramp and down in the Commons. A lingering habit from when Warren's men roamed about.

"I should keep a better eye out for Six, too," Lenth said.

Leena looked surprised for a moment. "Huh? Oh. Yeah, Six. Him too."

"Him too?" Lenth asked. "Who else are you looking for?"

She shrugged. "No one special. Just habit. No one messes with me since Mike became such a big deal, but then again, it might make me a target for anyone mad at Mike for whatever. But most people are pretty okay with him. Oh, look out; there's a loose chunk right here." She tapped her foot on a piece of the ramp as she kept walking.

Lenth took care to not step on the hazard, but his stride slowed. Then stopped. "Is that how it works up here? Really? People just...kill? What Six did doesn't seem to even have anyone that upset!"

Leena turned halfway around and looked at Lenth with a sad smile. "You're cute, kid. People mind if they get killed, but it's not like it's unheard of. Your buddy, though, he's made an impression, I'm sure. So much violence, and no real purpose? Yeah, that's going to unsettle folks." Even in Warren's day, a stab-fest like Six had done would have been rare. Not unheard of, but rare.

"I don't get it," Lenth said, resuming the climb.

Leena shrugged. "Most people who get killed—they had it coming. Or at least there was a reason of some kind. People feel safer if they keep their heads down and don't piss others off. But some jerk like Six starts causing problems with no reason?"

"Do you mean...you're always in danger of getting attacked? Everyone is? By anyone?"

"Ha. No one lives forever," Leena said, continuing on.

"Yeah," Lenth said quietly as he followed, "and then they become plant food."

Leena stopped. "What food? Citizens don't eat dead people. We eat the food that Messenger brings."

Lenth shook his head. "So, Leena, what do you do with people when they die?"

Leena continued up. "We send them off with Messenger. He brings them to be with Actual."

"To be with?" Lenth asked.

Leena recited the common notion, despite her common doubts: "To live again- with Actual. Actual is not like us."

"He is separated from us," Lenth said, "as separated and above Messenger, as Messenger is from us."

Leena smiled. "You know all about it, then."

Lenth looked troubled, and gave a glance to the centre of the Commons, where the Grand Elevator's shaft reached the ceiling. Maybe he was on some kind of dumb quest to reach Actual, like Warren had been.

"Welcome to my place!" Leena said when they got home. "Well, Mike's place. Whatever." It had been given to Mike, though Leena's half claim was assumed by all.

She got some water from the sink, and scraped a bit of rust into it from the door frame for flavour.

"There's other cups over there if you want." She said as she retrieved a new headband from under the sofa to replace the one that she'd used to bandage someone earlier.

"You drink rust?" Lenth asked.

Leena shrugged. "Didn't feel like water, didn't think the dizzy stuff was a good idea right now either." She was still a bit irritated that Mike was drunk when things got crazy, but it wasn't his fault that something unexpected happened. She'd still give him a hard time later. Hopefully he hadn't done anything too stupid while she wasn't keeping track of him.

Lenth poured himself half a cup of water and downed it.

"Ah, we came here for the hurty kind of pokey, didn't we?" Leena waved Lenth to follow her as she put down her cup. Lenth did the same.

The sleeping room had that chunk of tall furniture that Mike had designated the weapon rack... it had collected a good handful weapons. Some was stuff Mike and Leena had used, or carried for protection. Many were gifts from Citizens, many of those made or modified by Cody. Warren's knife was here, as well as the sword Edgar had given Mike.

Lenth went to Sledge's hammer, standing on its head, handle sticking up. He knelt next to it and felt along the handle, picking it up with a bit of a grunt. He looked at Leena, who was looking at him with a raised eyebrow.

Leena ignored the memories behind the hammer, and tried another tease. "Like it *nice and big*?"

Lenth heaved it up with both hands. "People fight with these? Seems kind of stupid. By the time you get it swinging, the person you're trying to hit would like...not be in that spot anymore."

"That was supposed to get a reaction out of you," Leena said.

"Huh? I answered."

A little puzzled, Leena sighed, unzipped her top past the navel, and arched back to nudge out a bit of cleavage. No seductive smoothness. Just quick, blunt, and almost clinical. "Okay, a girl unzips in front of you, alone in a room with bedding. What does that make you think?"

"Oh. Oh! I'm sorry, I'll pick a better weapon and leave so you can get changed or whatever. Gabe taught me about privacy," Lenth said apologetically, turning back to the weapon display.

Leena shrugged. She mumbled. "It's no fun telling you I'm not interested in actually fucking you when you don't even take the bait."

Lenth dropped the sledge-hammer where he'd gotten it from and turned back to Leena. "I'm confused."

Leena shook her head. "Yeah. Yeah, don't worry about it, I'm just wasting your time anyway." She flicked her hands dismissively at the weapons. "Go ahead, pick what you want. Don't rush on my account."

"Well, hold on. What's 'fucking', and why would I do it to you?" Lenth asked.

Covering her mouth and reaching out with her other hand to some imaginary audience, Leena turned about the room until she faced Lenth once again. "Sex!" she yelled. "Fucking means sex! Have you heard of sex?"

Lenth nodded and pointed at Leena. "Yes! I have. I leaned all about it, but I don't think creating children right now would help. Having more people helping me find Six would be good, but I also learned that children take a long time to grow inside—"

Leena screamed in exasperation, shutting up the idiotic lofu.

After a moment, Lenth rallied his courage to speak again. "I'm pretty sure I remember being a child, and it was a long time to—"

"Hush," Leena said flatly, shaking her head.

"And I've seen some children recently in the Provi—"

"Just. Just stop now, Lenth."

"Leena. Have you done a sex?"

She put her hand on her forehead and nodded, biting her lip. "Yeah. Yeah, Lenth, I seem to remember doing a sex a couple of times."

"Oh! So where are your children now?"

Leena squinted at Lenth. "When I first met you, I said I needed to educate you. I had no idea how bad it was. Just pick a weapon already." After a bit more urging, and listening to him debate about the benefits and drawbacks of everything he touched, he finally settled on a pair of gloves with spiky wire wrapped around them, a sword, *and* a knife, which he found he could carry in the arm-guard section of the gloves.

Leena smiled quietly and took in the sight. "Hmm, lofu, that's not a bad look on you," she said. Despite his dawdling about, when he was finished, he looked about ready for anything. Assuming he had any talent in using any of the gear.

Leena equipped herself a bit lighter from a box holding her current favourite load-out; a belt which carried a slender machete and a flask. "Let's go."

They went looking for the dreaded 'Six', asking Citizens they came across, with not a lot of success. One was a tired old crap-sniffer hanging out in a dark crawlspace that had been found adjacent to the ramp. Lenth seemed especially disgusted by it, and felt the need to get talkative again.

"You get everything from the Providers and Units," he said, "fresh air, clean water, food ... I guess if you don't have to work for it, you have to fill the time somehow."

Leena had resigned herself to Lenth going off on nonsensical bouts now and then. He was just a lofu, after all. "Sniffing, art, games, fucking, dizzy water. Yeah, it's pretty good overall," Leena said. "Aside from violence, rapes, that kind of thing, being a Citizen is great!" Her mock-enthusiasm surprised even herself.

Lenth staggered and stopped. "Violence and what?"

Leena stopped, and still facing away from Lenth, lowered her head. She scoffed lightly. "I guess you wouldn't know," she said softly, "given your...lack of experience."

"But what is it?" Lenth asked cautiously.

"It's bad." She turned her head towards the middle of the Commons. "It doesn't happen nearly as much as before Mike took over, though. No public exhibitions of it either. So that's...that's good."

Still not informed on what 'rape' was, Lenth asked again. "What is it?"

Leena turned to face Lenth with a sad smile on her face. She gently pinched his nose. "You're cute, lofu. I'll explain it, but not now, okay?" Leena turned away and continued on. Lenth took the hint, and didn't press the question.

They continued the search, stopping to ask some people playing, or just watching a game played with a ball made of tightly wound clothing and a raised box. Leena was loath to go into the box-made enclosure that it was played in. It reminded her too much of places where Warren-approved, semi-private 'parties' used to take place. Lenth's ignorance of such things just brought the memories up all the stronger.

She made the lofu pull his weight a bit, and sent Lenth to go in and ask. She could listen into the conversation, which proved how socially-awkward and clueless Lenth was. One of the players said he saw a couple of people that had blood on them heading towards Edgar's Refuge. Lovely.

When Lenth came out, ready to go, he asked, "So... who's Edgar?"

As they approached Edgar's Refuge, Leena noticed Lenth squinting at the sign above the entrance – attempting to read it, probably. She rolled her eyes, and huffed. "Edgar's Refuge," she told him.

At the gate, still several metres away, stood two guards, one on each side. The guard outfits had been improved recently- extra padding around the shins and stiff armour plates strapped to their shoulders and forearms. And of course, they both held a spear.

Leena nudged Lenth. "Just try not to cause problems, Lenth."

"Me?"

"Yeah. Let me do most of the talking, yeah?"

"I guess, Leena. Sure. So what's the deal with this Edgar guy?"

"A lot of people respect him, treat him like a leader. A lot of people think that Mike's a jerk, which, face it, he can be," she said, specifically thinking of his inebriation today, "and that the only reason more people like Mike is that he mashed up the last leader, who was...a lot more than a jerk. All the worst rape-happy people disappeared or were killed after that."

"Again, what's rape?" Lenth asked.

Leena sighed forcefully, and stared at a spot on the floor. She didn't feel like explaining this, but he seemed likely to keep asking. "It's sex, all right? It's forced sex. At its best, it's terrible. It stays with you." Her voice became slowly weaker as she spoke. "It's humiliating; it's a wound in the brain. At its worst, it's...worse. And the old leader and his people did that a lot. Bunches all at once. Holding down—often out where everyone could watch. Some girls didn't live."

Leena hoped that would shut Lenth up. He looked kind of shocked... but his silence was short-lived. "Leena. I...met a woman, a Provider, who had visited the Citizenry before. Her name's Diane. She had a really bad time. I think she was here when the old leader was still alive. Have you heard of her?"

Leena shook her head. "No. No, I can't say I have. But back then, I was a bit more into keeping myself out of the way, and less about meeting new people, you know?"

Lenth nodded. He might get it after all. "Right." he said

"Right. So, anyway," Leena sighed again, recovering much of her confidence and poise, "Edgar was more or less on Mike's side and all, but now he's just...the second most popular leader."

"And that makes things hard?"

"It makes things uncomfortable at times. The Refuge people will be all right with us, but they're not all going to be our best buddies."

The guards at the Refuge gate held their spears in a very official fashion as Leena and Lenth approached. They reminded Leena a bit too much of Warren's guards. They were a little bit of a hassle, and it seemed they were somehow given the impression that Mike had started attacking Six before Six got violent.

Lenth and Leena tried to correct them, but they were at best skeptical even after Leena explained what they'd witnessed, and that Six had a history of violence down with the lofus. They were convinced enough to let Leena and Lenth head in to find Edgar.

Walking through the interior of the Refuge these days wasn't all that different than the rest of the Citizenry, except a tiny bit more densely populated. The walls were built where they'd originally been laid out, and the people who chose to live in the refuge just had to be a bit more cozy. It wasn't anywhere as crowded and cluttered as Warren's old stack, though.

They encountered the known lunatic Patricia, who rambled on about whatever crap she'd seen in whatever picture book she'd most recently convinced herself was real. Patricia wasn't a crap-sniffer, and she wasn't stupid on dizzy water- it was just the way she was. Not to rule out her past. For all Leena knew, she'd grown up in a sniffing jar or something.

Before they shook her, Patricia mentioned Actual as part of her mumblings, and how Actual would save them from the things she saw in a book.

Lenth followed along behind Leena listlessly, giving a glance back towards where Patricia had been. "My friend Gabe...he said that some people think that above Actual is a place where a war happened, and lots of people used something to kill each other." Lenth glanced up at the top of the elevator. "I don't know if he believed it, but he seemed...bugged by the idea a lot." He then mentioned something about Patricia's nonsense. "Yeah, it's all silly," Lenth said. "The only things that are *alive* are people and the six kinds of plants that make the food."

"You say the stupidest things sometimes," Leena said. "What the heck is a plant?"

"I saw some that are way taller than a person, and have big huge green hair. It doesn't have any arms and legs, though, and never move. I heard that others are small and flimsy, and also green, and they—"

"Stop sniffing, Lenth."

"I wasn't sniffing! I'd never even heard of sniffing before I met you."

"Ugh, whatever lofus get stupid on."

"It's real. Food is made of plant chunks!"

"Whatever, Lenth."

They arrived at the huge doorway in the Refuge at the edge of the Commons, a bit smaller than the doorway to the Grand Elevator. One could see holes and grooves in the floor and ceiling where doors had once stood. Hanging there now was a wide curtain made from clothing shreds, a closed flap in the middle.

Leena pulled the curtain aside for Lenth to enter. A pair of guards stood quietly inside, watching but not interfering.

On the far wall, twenty metres or so away, the 'tapestries' Leena had seen being prepared during construction of the Refuge now hung from the ceiling. She'd seen the one on the far right, depicting the full body of a man, on that day. On the far left was a woman. Next to those were heads, not detailed enough to look like any specific person. The ones farthest towards the middle depicted the Elevator shaft and the top of the Commons.

In the middle of all those sat a throne of large, tightly-bound bundles of cloth, upon which sat Edgar. Nearby on either side lay a naked woman, both of whom casually covered themselves when they realized they had company.

One of the women was Natalie, the girl who'd arguably triggered the big hunt for the remainder of Warren's men. Leena was surprised to see her this cozy with Edgar– or this naked.

Leena was also surprised to get a nasty little glare from her. Whatever Natalie's problem was, it could wait, and Leena chose to ignore it. Given Edgar's other stances, she was rather surprised to see him surrounded by nude women.

"Edgar," Leena called out.

"Yes, yes," Edgar grumbled. He took a sip from a cup of dizzy water, nodding as he did so. "You're looking for the lofu, Six, yes?"

"Yup," Leena said. "Trying to catch up with him before he hurts anybody else. You know the whole story, I guess?"

"Whose version?" Edgar asked as she stood. He was very well-dressed for being someone with naked women at his side. His robe had changed again since the last time Leena had seen him. It had more layers, which made him look bigger than he was, but whether this was intentional or not was hard to say.

"Version?" Lenth blurted out. "What do you mean, version?"

Edgar turned to the Natalie and the other woman lying around his pillow throne. "This might be boring for you ladies. Feel free to move into the next room." They stood. Natalie didn't bother to bring her covering with her, although the other didn't bother covering up very well, more interested in picking up her three flimsy, colourful books.

"I know the version that Mike would want known," Edgar said, taking his time, allowing his ladies to depart, "and it seems you support that position. Leena, your pet lofu here, his name is...?"

"Lenth. So you can quit calling me lofu. I've spent my life helping to make sure we all don't suffocate on our own breath. Others that you call lofu have been feeding you, keeping your water pure, and keeping the lights on."

Edgar raised an eyebrow and turned to Leena. "Your lofu has been sniffing?" He turned back to Lenth. "The things you speak of are gifts from Actual, brought to us all by Messenger. It is foolish to be ungrateful to Actual."

"Did Messenger say that?" Lenth asked with a furrowed brow. "Ugh. Not important right now. Do you know where Six is?"

Sipping once more from his dizzy water, Edgar paced in front of his pillow-throne slowly. "Hiding. He found Mike's welcome to be most unpleasant, holding him with his guards. It was only lucky that Six had weapons hidden on himself."

"Guards?" Leena spat. "There were no guards there! People were there to pick up food! No one tried to grab Six, they just couldn't get out of the way of him and his knives fast enough!"

"So you say," Edgar said, "and I'd expect nothing less from Mike's woman." Now Edgar was just being a jerk. Blame the dizzy water. Edgar was always saying how bad it was, but he was drinking it today. Great. The day a lofu showed up in a killing mood, and both Edgar and Mike had decided to be drunks. Between the dizzy-water and the women, Edgar's ideals didn't seem to apply to him, at least here in this den.

Lenth spoke up. "I was there. Six almost killed Leena, then ran off slashing through a crowd!"

"Mike's woman and a lofu!" Edgar chuckled. "Convincing indeed!"

"If the word of a 'lofu' isn't any good to you, then why are you defending one?" Lenth asked.

Leena huffed and stared. "He doesn't care about Six one bit, he just sees a chance to make Mike look like a bad guy. That won't work, Edgar. There were too many people there who saw everything. Too many hurt. Six needs to be taken care of, or thrown back down the elevator, at least!"

Edgar was silent, looking at his clasped hands.

"Edgar," Lenth said. "He's killed a lot of people for no good reason... in both the Citizenry and below. I'm not looking for revenge's sake. I just can't sit by and let it go on."

"No good reason?" Edgar asked. "It sounded like he had some very compelling reasons. Did you know a man in a black rubber suit made him work for his whole life, and the man in the rubber suit was controlled by your precious Providers?" *What the heck were these lofus doing down there?* Leena thought.

Lenth lowered his head. "True. Actually, I came from a very similar situation as Six. I bet he got shocked by his Rubberman more than once, when he didn't do what he was supposed to. And he told me that his Rub—" Lenth paused, lost in thought for a moment, then continued. "No. Even then. Then he went on killing Providers who had no connection to him."

Edgar peered at Lenth with quiet skepticism. "You do not hate that you were used by the Providers for their daily needs?"

"It's...difficult. I didn't take a lot of time to think about it before I met some. They're people. Most of them pretty nice. And don't forget, they're also making *your* daily needs. If they were using me, it was for your sake, too."

"Again with this blasphemy against Actual!" Edgar threw up his hands and faced the banners around him.

"Uh, Edgar," Leena spoke up, "you should worry less about where Lenth thinks food comes from, and more about where Six thinks it's going."

Edgar looked at Leena with a quizzical glare. "Explain."

Leena took a breath. Hopefully Edgar wasn't too drunk to listen to reason. "If Six feels like he's been used, and is out for blood, and he thinks like Lenth does—that Citizens are living off of his work...why do you think Six would stop at raging against Providers?"

Edgar grimaced. "He said Mike's men were—"

"You *talked* to him?" Lenth asked.

"Oh, lovely!" Leena said. "And how many of your own armed guards were standing around when this little chit-chat took place? Wanna know how many people were armed when Six cut into Mike's followers? Nobody but Six!"

"And why should I believe any of this?" Edgar bellowed.

Looking at the floor and shrugging, Lenth calmly replied, "—because every Citizen and Provider is a likely target to get stabbed to death next?"

"Yup," Leena said, nodding impishly at Lenth and Edgar, "that's a good motivator."

Edgar looked around as if spotting snippets of wisdom out of the air around him. He drank the last dribbles of his dizzy water and tossed the cup onto the pillow-throne.

"Edgar," Lenth implored, "I don't understand the conflict between you and Mike all that well, but this is more important than your...whatever it is."

Edgar stared at Lenth with one eye closed and pointed at him for a moment before letting his arm drop lazily back to his side. "Huh!" Edgar walked over his pillow-throne to get behind it and pulled out his spear, with its little decorative stained rag near the head. He beat the shaft of his spear against his chest twice to punctuate himself. His clothing had something hard under the top layer, and it made a dull clank noise when struck. "We sort this out now," Edgar said.

"What?" Lenth gripped his sword a little tighter, looking a little panicked, and readied to defend himself.

"Relax, lofu," Edgar said, walking past him. "I don't leave home without Gungnir."

"Who?"

Not bothering to break stride, Edgar raised his spear over his head. "Gungnir! I got the name from a book!"

Leena prodded Lenth to get moving, and found that one of the two guards following behind. "You and your book collection. Where did they come from?"

Edgar still didn't bother to turn back to face them as he answered, "They've been around for longer than anyone can say." He pointed his spear up to the top of the elevator shaft. "Likely from Actual originally. I'm not sure."

"Or Providers?" Lenth asked, catching up.

"Huh. I suppose that is possible, but it seems unlikely that a lofu could make such things."

Lenth sighed in resignation, then asked, "Aren't we going to go see Mike?"

"Yes. Yes," Edgar said, "but first we get Six. It just makes sense, no?"

"What?" Leena said. "You've been keeping him here?"

"Yes, I ran into him," Edgar said. "After some difficulty with introductions, he explained that he was attacked outside of the elevator, and had to fight his way out. He climbed the wall of the Refuge, trying to hide. So I helped him clean up, and he offered to help with the next meal. Very nice fellow, really."

Leena looked over to Lenth. He seemed to know Six somewhat. Lenth looked perplexed by what Edgar was saying, but kept his mouth shut.

"Oh," Edgar said as they came to a nook in the Refuge, where he expected to find Six. "Dead person."

Some guy was laying, face down in a pool of blood. Smears and hand-prints told a pretty obvious story of struggle.

There was no way out, other than how they had come in. Lenth and Edgar's guard both readied themselves for a fight, making weapons ready, looking around.

"Boys, relax," Leena said. "From the look of the blood, this happened a while ago. Edgar, who's this guy?"

Edgar knelt down by the body and pulled him over by his shoulder. The wound left the floor with a wet sound, and oozed out more blood. "Eh, I know him. Is a good guy. Is...name starts with a 'D', I think. Eh, Daryl? Doug? Something like Doug. Dave?"

"You don't even know?" Lenth asked, still facing away, scanning around for signs of Six.

"I'm going to go with 'Dave'," Edgar said.

A woman ran in from around the corner. "Robert!" she cried, running to the body's side, collapsing to embrace him.

"I was close," Edgar said, standing back up.

Lenth knelt by the woman and spoke softly. "Excuse me. I'm trying to find the person who did this. Do you know—?"

She turned her head to Lenth, bleary-eyed with shock. "The lofu?"

"Yes," Lenth sighed, "his name is Six—"

"I know. Damned lofus! We should kill them as soon as they pop up!"

"Six is not like most of us," Lenth said quietly. "Do you have any idea which way he went?"

She shook and settled in to cry under Robert's chin.

"He said before that he didn't want to come here," Edgar said quietly. Everyone moved away from the body and the grieving woman except for Lenth.

"Is there...can I do something for you?" he asked. She only replied with a brisk hand motion, shooing him away. Edgar pulled him away. "I'll have the guards deal with the body and all," Edgar said. "Six saw that the elevator shaft went further up and said that he was trying to go up more. I told him all about Actual, and he said he had a lot to think about."

"Then we have to get to the elevator!" Lenth exclaimed. "Actual is in danger!"

"Six can't use the elevator, stupid," Leena said.

"No, the great Actual is beyond harm," Edgar rumbled, "but just maybe Messenger is in danger, if you believe such a thing is possible. Certainly Mike is in danger."

"Oh, what the fuck do you care about Mike, Edgar?" Leena spat.

Edgar leaned his head to the side. "I do not hate Mike- I simply know I would be a better leader. Mike is popular because it was he who killed a horrible leader. If—"

"Is anyone else coming?" Lenth asked as he walked off briskly.

"Where are you going?" Leena asked.

"To the elevator, of course."

"No," Edgar said. "I'll go, and I'll send my guard to bring a few more guards to join me. You two go to Mike's."

Leena glared at Edgar for a moment. "You're right. Lenth, up we go again." Leena jogged out, and the stunned lofu caught up quickly.

"Leena, why is going the wrong way such a good idea?"

"Elevator doesn't come unless it's a regular time to drop off supplies or Messenger is called. The machine to call him is at Mike's."

"How would Six know that?"

"Ask the dead guy. Doug, David, err..."

"Robert."

"Right. Robert might have told Six anything."

Leena was happy to more or less ignore Lenth, even when he tripped on the ramp. Twice. When they made it to the den, they heard a voice coming loud and clear from the other room.

"—And we could have him there in ten minutes."

"It's Six. It has to be," Lenth whispered.

Leena nodded and they readied their weapons, creeping as quietly as possible towards the bedroom. As they came in, they saw that the weapons rack had been ransacked. Half of the weapons were dumped on the floor, and most of the rest were hanging haphazardly.

They tensed up as they heard a crash from the darkened little doorway in the corner, followed by two more crashes.

"Fuuuuuuck, fuck, fuck, fuck..." Leena whispered to herself.

The murderous lofu Six stepped out of the communication device room, with bloody hands and arms, and the sword that Edgar had given Mike. Speckles and gobs of blood reached all the way up to his face.

"What have you done, Six?" Lenth asked, weapons in hand.

Six smiled wide and tilted his head. "I just called for a ride, is all."

"That's all?" Leena growled, staring at Six with restrained rage. "Then what's the blood about? I've seen Mike use the machine a lot of times, and it never bled."

As if he hadn't expected anyone to notice the blood, he shrugged, holding the sword out to the side. "Oh. Oh yes, there were some problems," Six said, "A difference in opinion of what should be said to the machine. Did you know it doesn't talk back? At first, I thought they were shy, but I think the talking back part might be broken."

Leena brought her machete forward, holding it with both hands. She shifted her weight back and forth, looking for her chance to approach. It had been a while since she'd been in a real fight, but she felt no less capable today. Especially if Mike's safety was at issue.

"Huh, I guess I should have expected this," Six said.

"Is Mike in there?" Lenth asked.

Six glanced back behind him. "Yeah. Well, someone is. I never got his name."

"Is he dead?" Leena almost choked on the word 'dead', only truly considering the idea as it came out of her mouth. The blood seemed to bear an obvious answer, but foolish hope demanded that the question be asked.

Six smiled wide, looking around with mock incredulity. "What am I, a doctor? Do you want to rush in and see if you can help? Fine by me. I'll get out of your way, but you need to get out of my way first. A nice wide path."

Leena clenched her jaw. How many steps would it take in a frantic dash to get at him, and drive a blade into his gut?

Out of the corner of her eye, she saw Lenth looking around, apparently considering Six's offer. Maybe it was best- for now. She had to get to Mike, sooner than later. A fight with Six might not go as quickly or as smoothly as she wanted. It was tempting, though.

Six leaned his head towards the exit, raised his eyebrows, and asked, "Well?"

Leena yelled gutturally, and moved the machete to one hand, before moving back, out of the way. Lenth followed suit.

"Interesting company you're keeping, Lenth," Six said, dashing to the exit. Leena rushed into the communication room, and saw more than she'd feared.

Mike was spread out on his back, throat hacked open so deeply that bone was visible. His clothing, the walls, the floor, so bloodied. Bloody hand smears on the walls and floor told of a long struggle, but the damage to his neck- and the amount of blood- told of Six just playing after Mike had died.

Her machete dropped, and she looked at it, only now noting how much her hands were shaking. Her legs felt weak too, and she dropped to her knees.

Surrounded by the blood of her love, she felt tears coming. She felt the need to curl up in a ball and sob.

No. Not yet. She'd faced monsters before, she'd killed killers before. The mighty Sledge died, just as dead as anyone else. This putrid lofu scum would be no different.

Actually, never mind, it would be different. She'd killed Sledge quickly. Six wouldn't be so lucky. She curled up the pain into a tight little ball of rage, and screamed a warcry she hoped even Actual would hear.

Lenth came in. For all her 'summoned strength', she couldn't pull herself up to face him. She was still trembling.

"He's going to the elevator," Leena said in a squeak. "Go." She wanted to say 'go catch him, and hold him down for me to carve up.'

"Come with me," he said.

"No," she whispered. She'd come when she stopped shaking. A glance forward at Mike's brutalized body was making that difficult.

"I get it," Lenth said, "I do, but you can't stay here. At least come as far as another person. Don't be alone with this."

"With this? With Mike?" Leena finally turned away from Mike's body. As she turned, her knee came up from the blood, and she felt it trickle down her shin. She eyes widened as reality struck a little deeper into her mind. A desperate rasp, too rough to be a cry, came from her as Lenth helped her to her feet.

"We have to go," Lenth said. She accepted Lenth's hand up, but she still felt weak and heavy as she rose.

When they got out onto the ramp, Lenth hollered, "There he is!" Lenth pointed towards the bottom of the ramp.

Okay, okay, hard time. Push Mike's body out of your mind, focus on catching Six. Don't think about why. Just get him. Get him now, get it together, *go, go*! Leena gripped her machete, and bolted.

Focus.

Just the ramp, that's all that she had to worry about this second. Run, don't trip, don't think, run. She heard Lenth behind her trip and flounder. Sounded like a nasty fall. Push it out, he's fine. Run, run.

"Wait for me!" he called out momentarily.

"No!"

"We have to stick together!"

Too bad, Lenth. Running. Running. It didn't matter, as shortly after she got off the ramp, Lenth caught up. Her dashing had also caught up with *her*. Lenth didn't look tired, but she was feeling pretty wrung out already.

"Gonna...get...him..." she said between breaths.

"Don't get caught alone with him," Lenth said. She felt like giving him a speech about what she planned to do to Six, but she was too out of breath for idle banter. Focus on running.

Frig, Lenth was barely breaking a sweat, and she felt pretty spent. Were lofus all this fit? Six might be more of a threat than she was counting on. Well, of course he was, he overpowered Mi– *stop, don't think about it. Six probably ambushed him. There's no way Mike would just let… stop, don't think about it.*

Don't think about his head nearly hacked off. Don't think about the smears on the floor where Mike had been desperately grabbing for hope as he bled out, and Six repeatedly– *don't think, run. Run. Run. Damn it, run.*

Don't think about how she wasn't there to help when– *Stop this now*, and run, run.

128

Getting closer to the elevator shaft didn't show where the elevator itself, or Messenger were. Ahead, a couple of Edgar's guards jogged into view, also headed for the elevator's building. After a glance to Leena, Lenth easily broke out some extra speed, leaving her behind so he could go talk to the guards.

Everyone still running, Lenth talked to the guards. Lagging behind, pretty wiped out, Leena couldn't hear them well, but body language told her enough.

Lenth looked back to Leena, limping and holding her middle due to runner's cramp. He turned to the guard he'd been talking to. "Hey, I'm good to go ahead. Can one of you guys make sure Leena stays safe?"

The guard turned back without breaking stride. He tapped the other guard, and pointed back at Leena. "You, go look after her." The second guard nodded and started jogging back towards Leena.

Leena dropped her pace to a walk, and looked to Lenth with arms spread. "Seriously?"

Lenth just waved with a sheepishly apologetic smile. He turned, and started dashing towards the elevator. Lofu Lenth was fast, and still not showing signs of being tired. He'd been holding back for a while now to protect Leena.

"Condescending prick" she thought to herself, with only a bit of legitimate resentment.

The guard who came to 'keep an eye on her' stood nearby now, ready to run with her. Her side still burnt. She took a moment to catch her breath, and felt the need to justify her state. She pointed back up to the ramp.

"Ran... all the way... from up there..."

"What happened?" the guard asked.

Leena pointed again. "Other lofu... Six... and Mike... he... Mike..." Tears were pushing their way out, and her heavy breathing threatened to turn into sobbing.

No. No breaking down. Not yet. No time. Not yet, not yet. Gotta get him.

Leena stood, and forced her breathing to get in line. "Let's go."

The guard, who hadn't been running nearly as much, kept pace easily. Leena was still on the edge of exhaustion; but she pushed forward.

After shoving through some Citizens attracted by the fuss, she made it to the loading bay.

Lenth was here, Edgar was here, Six was here, holding a guard up as hostage with a knife to his throat. A few other guards were here as well. Everyone had obviously been arguing and yelling.

Leena scrambled in beside Lenth, glad to be able to stop and catch her breath. "Are we talking about killing Six?" Leena gasped. "I stake claim! He killed Mike! I have the right!"

"Which Citizen did he kill first?" Edgar asked. "It would be the right of—"

The elevator behind the closed door slammed down about a centimetre, the weight of it shaking the room. That answered where Messenger was.

"Lenth," came Messenger's voice finally, "who was the first person that Six killed?"

"Why are you asking him?" Six snarled. "It was my Rubberman! Manager, whatever. He killed my Brother by smashing the grating down on him, so I killed him *right back!*"

"Six, you told me that story," Lenth said, "but are you sure it wasn't an accident? My Brother died because of a mistake that maybe my Rubberman made, but I don't—"

"*What do you know?*" Six jostled his hostage in agitation, pressing the dull blade firmly on his neck. "Lenth, they turned you into one of them, a mindless Provider!"

"Augh, Six, you've gone way too far!" Lenth implored, "Even if your Rubberman meant to kill your Brother, that might explain your killing him, but what about the rest? What about attacking Diane? She did nothing to you! Or your other Brother, Eyes?"

Obviously, these two had some kind of history down below, which they dragged with them up into Citizenry. *Stupid lofus.*

The elevator groaned loudly, rising by the centimetre lost from the previous movement. Everyone in the loading bay shut up again, and Messenger spoke. "Lenth, Six. Give your weapons to a Citizen, and then all Citizens will leave the loading room."

"Then we can get on?" Six asked.

"Yes. Weapons and Citizens leave now."

Many Citizens were already obeying the voice of the Messenger. Among the handful who still lingered, Leena and Edgar stood at the forefront.

"What, you're just going to leave?" Leena said. "You can't just take off after all of that!"

"It's for the best," Edgar stepped up to say. "As long as Six never comes back here, it's good enough."

"The hell it is!" Leena wasn't about to let Messenger just make off with Mike's killer. She readied her machete and stepped forward, unconcerned about the hostage.

Before she got close to Six, he pushed his hostage away with a firm, flat-footed kick to the backside. The hostage went sprawling forward before scrambling off.

"I'm fine to settle this with you, little girl!" Six snarled.

"You worthless sack of blood," Leena snarled back, side-stepping to plan an attack. "You think you're the only killer in the room? Before Mike took over, do you have any idea how hard I had to fight? How many had to die before we got any peace from the savages?"

"I'll give you peace!" Six screamed. He charged at Leena.

She deftly sailed under Six's thrust, then sprung back up with her machete sliding up.

Six dodged by hopping back, but only well enough to avoid a fatal strike. A new streak of red now decorated Leena's blade.

With a throaty bellow, Edgar threw himself shoulder-first into Six. Six's hissing snarl ended with a pained grunt as they landed on the floor.

"Giant moron!" Six grunted. They struggled, Edgar's robe concealing most of their violence.

"Get off! I had him!" Leena yelled.

130

Just as Leena and Lenth were about to get into the fray, Edgar sat up, a fresh gash on one of his forearms. With one hand, he held Six down by his wrists.

Six still held his knife, wet with a streak of fresh blood. Six spat up at Edgar's face.

"You hold him still," Leena said, "and I'll gut him!"

"I want him alive," came Messenger's voice.

Edgar held his free hand out to Leena, signalling her to stop.

"Why?" Leena asked Edgar. "Why do we care what Messenger wants? This fucker slaughtered Mike, and I want the deserved justice!"

"Justice is for the one wronged first," Edgar said, "and you should care what Messenger wants. He is our link to Actual, and without him, we would quickly starve."

Yeah. She knew that. Being reprimanded like she was a child wasn't improving her mood any, but the reminder was valid. Leena reluctantly backed away and lowered her weapon. "Fine," she grumbled, "but I want a piece when others are done with him."

"I'm glad you see it that way, Citizens," Messenger said. "Now, as I said before, search Six and Lenth for weapons, remove them and yourselves, and we'll be going."

While Edgar roughly turned Six over, Lenth started handing over his arsenal to Leena.

"You're going?" Leena said, still regaining her composure. "I thought you were planning on staying. Isn't that why you came in the first place?"

Lenth made a tight-lipped face and looked away. "Well, not really. I came to explore. To find out what was up above where I was. Now I guess the only thing up is—"

"Actual!" Six scrambled away from Edgar, and got to his feet, up against the elevator door. "See, I knew you and I had the same ideas! Going up!" Six banged on the elevator door twice. He winced, and put his hand against his arm where Leena had managed to cut him. It was difficult to tell what was his his blood, and what was Mike's.

Edgar, bloodied from holding down Six, was backing away from him, holding two confiscated knives. "Messenger, you will have to communicate with a new leader now if Mike is dead."

"And the asshole wrecked the device after calling for you," Leena mumbled. "Can we get another?"

There was a moment of silence before Messenger's voice came from the door again. "It should be possible. It may take time. Next time I come, have the old one here so I can take it away first."

"Many thanks to you and Actual, Messenger." Edgar said with a bow as he reached the doorway. "Coming, Leena?"

"Edgar, Leena," Lenth said, "work together, all right? I don't see any reason for the ... uh...unfriendliness to continue."

Leena eyed Edgar. Yeah, of course he'd want to be leader now. No chance. She could almost see Edgar thinking the same thing about her, the way he looked her up and down with... not disgust, but not exactly respect either.

"Ehh, I guess he has experience," Leena said.

"And doubtless, Leena will retain Mike's followers," Edgar said. "An alliance of convenience would make some sense. We'll see."

"We'll see," Leena agreed. She forced a smirk at Lenth.

"I might see you all again," Lenth said. "I'm sorry about Mike."

"Yeah, he was my favourite of my eight men."

"Eight?" Lenth said.

Oh, it was too easy to tease him. She immediately felt like crap for saying that, though. Sure she had interest in other men, but Mike was more than just the favourite. She wasn't quite sure how to be without him. He had been a constant for so long. No tears, not yet. Not around the killer. Or Edgar, for that matter.

"Can we just get on with it?" Six wailed and winced in pain.

Lenth patted Leena on the shoulder. "Be safe."

She nodded. "You too. If you come back this way, I might have time and be in the mood to 'educate' you a little." She forced a smile, punctuated with a wink, then turned to exit with Edgar.

The door closed behind them, and she heard the little click of the lock. Edgar continued on to the Commons, but Leena stayed to hear the inner door open. The voice of Messenger talked with the two lofus. Some of it sounded friendly, some less so.

Lofus spoke to Messenger. Not through any massive closed door, not through some machine. Right now, they were face-to-face with the Messenger of Actual.

What does Edgar think of this? Will he call it blasphemy? Certainly Lenth had a lot of notions about things that conflicted with common knowledge, and Edgar most of all will be eager to dismiss it all as lufu-nonsense and heresy.

Leena also noticed that the lofus, at least Lenth, were physically much stronger and faster than her. And she herself was no slouch among Citizens.

It all made her question the name "lofu". Lesser others from under? If they're so lesser, why are they so strong, and permitted to talk so casually with Messenger?

Maybe some of the truths were wrong.

Did it matter? Mike was still dead, and whether lofus were garbage or not wouldn't change that. It was time to go home and cr... no, she couldn't go home. Oh damn, Mike's body was still there. And all that blood! That was the last place she wanted to go.

She heard the elevator come to life, groan, and hum away, fading towards the infallible, the Actual. Surely Messenger was not going to bring lofus before Actual.

Surely.

Wouldn't that have driven Warren crazy? For a fraction of a moment, Leena wished Warren could be alive just to see *lofus* surpass his grand plans.

In the middle of all her unimportant thoughts, the truth which she was desperately trying to avoid sat in her mind. Unmovable, eternal, colossal, the most horrid truth waited patiently at home to be addressed.

Back home, her beloved lay dead in a lake of his own blood.

Warren wasn't here, Edgar wasn't here. -it was as good a time as any to collapse. There in the hall, just outside the door to the loading bay, she felt tears drag her to the floor, slumping in the corner. If she wasn't strong, if she didn't stand up for the way Mike saw the Citizenry, that jerk Edgar would happily take over.

Edgar was no Warren – that might not be *so* horrible, but it felt wrong. She'd have to make a speech. She'd have to do the thing Mike would do.

Not yet. Right now, crumple. Cry. Wish she'd gutted Six. Crumple, cry, crumple.

She stared at a spot where the wall met the floor. An unimportant crease in the world to focus on. Time inched along, and that was fine. Right then, if all the time in the world slipped away, that would be okay. As long as it left her alone.

She heard her name. No, not worth responding to. If it wasn't miraculously Mike's voice, it didn't matter. Was he that important to her? She knew he was pretty important, but had no idea what losing him would feel like. And she left his body just... hacked open like that. He was dead.

For all the threat of Warren's rule, it was some crazy lofu that crawled up and got him. So senseless. If it had been Edgar or one of his followers that killed Mike, at least it would make a little sense. Still terrible, but it would make sense.

The voice that had called her name was talking. Had it been talking all this time? Who cares?

A person sat beside her. Whatever. Then an arm around her shoulders.

"Leena." It was Jen. Leena reluctantly ended her little trance to look over at Jen.

"Hi," Leena said flatly.

"It's true, then?" Jen asked.

134

Chapter Eleven

Stand

Leena burst out sobbing there in the loading bay, and leaned into Jen.

"No, no, no..." Tara, Jen's other half was here as well, and knelt down to grab Leena's hand.

"Bad lofu's gone," Leena mumbled between sobs. "Messenger came and took him and the good lofu away."

Tara and Jen didn't press her for more information, only sitting with her for a bit. After a while, Tara spoke up. "Let's get you home, okay?"

Jen shook her head immediately, apparently knowing why.

Leena looked up. There was a handful of other Citizens standing in the hall, looking at them.

"No," Leena said, asserting her voice to a mix of misery and feigned strength.

"Tara, she can stay with us," Jen said, "at least for a while."

"Thank you," Leena said dragging herself to her feet while staring down the Citizens ahead, "but I have something I need to do."

"Can we help?" Jen asked.

"Just stay nearby, okay?" Leena walked forward, and the Citizens parted before her. She walked out, seeing confused faces around her as she went. She stepped out into the open Commons and walked with a firm stride to the same platform at which Mike had announced Lenth and Six's bloody arrival.

She brought herself to the top of the platform and knelt as Citizens gathered in front of her, as well as others coming along, seeing that something was happening.

She stood slowly, fists held out at hip height, and screamed, "*CITIZENS!*"

The word came out with anger, and misery. She didn't stop her tears. The Citizens around her were silent. She could tell that some knew. Some seemed to be fighting tears as well. Jen, for one, didn't fight it.

Leena took a deep breath and screamed again, raw and ragged.

"*CITIZENS! Help me!*" She looked at them all.

Concerned murmurs came from many directions. Jen and Tara stepped towards her, but she held out a hand to stop their approach.

"*Citizens, Mike...*" she took a deep breath, "*has been killed. By the lofu we'd been looking for.*"

Gasps came from some of those who didn't know, or didn't believe the rumour. Some yells about lofus joined in the mix.

Leena held up her hands. "Now, now. He was a lofu, but a lofu helped catch him. Seems like lofus are a mixed bag. The point is, the threat is gone... but so is Mike."

A slurry of sympathy, anger and confused remarks flowed from the still-growing crowd.

Leena fought the image of Mike's body and gathered her strength, both mental and physical, and she screamed again- as forcefully as she could-

"*SO I NEED YOU TO HELP ME.*"

She looked across them all, trying to read their expressions as much as they were trying to read hers.

"Mike was *strong,*" she cried, spreading her arms, "and he knew I was strong. He knew *you* were strong. He *loved* you people for it. For all his asinine joking, he loved you. He knew we could be strong, that we could be good to each other. That we could look out for each other!"

Another wave of tears hit her, and Jen was soon at her side, grabbing a hand.

"So be *strong. Together!*" Leena yelled. "Keep up what he showed us we could do! If we let that strength die, then that part of Mike dies too. I need you to keep him alive for me! So *help me!* Help each other!"

From in the crowd, it was Cody who raised his fist. "*For Mike! Citizens Strong together!*"

"*Citizens strong!*" echoed a woman. "We survived Warren together, we're strong together!"

"*Citizens strong!*" Tara said gleefully, fist in the air.

"*Citizens strong!*" said another raised fist in the crowd.

"*Citizens strong!*" came four more.

"*Citizens strong!*" came a few dozen.

"*Citizens strong!*" came them all.

A chant grew. Leena clutched her chest, and raised a fist. "Thank you," she whispered.

A chant melted into cheers, while Jen came up to hug Leena, followed by Tara. Leena saw that Jen was crying, but forcing a smile. She got an arm free, meaning to wave Cody over, but the crowd seemed to see it as a call for everyone.

Soon, it was a scene she remembered seeing Mike in the middle of. Suddenly his memory assaulted her. He wasn't here. He was still on the floor back in the den, ripped apart.

She felt herself weaken, and having a hard time caring if she collapsed. She held onto Jen, and accepted help from Tara as well.

"Can we go?" she said, under the noise of the crowd, "I want to go. Can we just go?"

Sleep hadn't come easily, as supportive as Jen and Tara had tried to be. Leena decided she was awake, or at least, that she'd given up on sleep. Jen stayed by her side, while Tara and Cody went to tend to Mike.

The first time they came back, their faces were grim, and they spoke in muted tones.

"Well... we got started," Tara said, "and, well... I don't have to tell you it's bad. We want to... you know... be able to send him to Actual in a... respectful way."

Leena looked into her lap. *'Respectful'*. A nice way of saying that Mike was an unspeakable mess. "Guys," Leena said without making eye contact, "thank you. I know... I know it's not easy."

"We got a bit of help," Cody said, "but it didn't seem right to let in everyone who offered. Oh, we have someone cleaning up the broken communication device, too. Messenger wanted that, right?"

Leena nodded. "Anything going on over at Edgar's Refuge? I kinda feel like I should go talk to him."

"Why?" Jen scoffed. "If he hadn't been so chummy with that murderous lofu, then he probably —"

Leena waved her hand to stop Jen. "He couldn't have known what would happen. He's an idiot, but there wasn't any... I mean, he didn't mean for any of it to happen."

"I don't imagine he's grieving a ton, though." Cody said. "It's not up to you to go to him. If he had any sense of remorse, he'd be here to see if you're okay."

Leena smirked. "Maybe he's giving me space out of respect."

"I feel the need to go snoop," Cody murmured.

"Ditto. But we have work to do, still," Tara said.

Cody sighed. "To be blunt, Mike... Mike's not not going anywhere. Meanwhile, what are people saying over in the Refuge?"

Leena shook her head. "I don't like having to think like this. About this kind of thing. We're talking about me against Edgar to be the biggest leader in Citizenry, aren't we?"

"I'm not saying Edgar would lead in a terrible way, necessarily," Tara said, "but he's always been a bit... negative."

After a quick bite, Cody. Lara and Jen spoke together in hushed tones, facing away from Leena. Leena didn't feel the need to snoop about what they were saying. Knowing them, they were trying their best to be considerate of her feelings. As much as she hated people feeling the need to 'guard' her, she appreciated the notion enough to tolerate it right now.

One way or another, they decided that Jen would be 'just hanging around at home' while Lara and Cody headed back to the... the mess of Mike. The image of how he looked when she found him jumped back into her mind. It made her draw her knees in a little tighter, and tune the world out a little more. She tried desperately to think of nothing, but of course, this only allowed the worst thoughts to drag themselves across her mind all the more.

Of course, Jen hanging around at home was a transparent excuse to be on-hand for Leena, and they both knew it. Leena wanted to speak up. To thank her. But the urge to just stare into the wall was too strong.

At some point, Jen offered to get her something. Anything. Water? Food? Dizzy water?

Leena did her best to grunt 'no' in a polite and grateful way.

Jen knelt in front of her, and tried to get her attention.

"Leena."

It wasn't even a question, so Leena didn't feel the need to reply at all.

"Leena, hey, look at me."

That would mean raising one's head. Besides, she could already see Jen's lower half just fine. Mission accomplished, she looked at her. No, that wasn't good enough. Jen put her finger under Leena's chin, and gently lifted until they made eye contact.

Leena felt the burn in her eyes, and found herself blinking a lot to prevent tears from spilling out. Jen reacted to the painfully obvious misery, and lunged forward to hold Leena.

"I just don't know what to say," Jen said.

"My Mike is gone!" erupted from Leena with sudden sobbing.

She knew it wasn't going to stop any time soon, and there was no control. She hated the weak, mewling sounds that came from her. She hated being weak. She hated not being there to help Mike. How his killer had held her at knife-point. She hated how she let him walk by her just before she found Mike dead. She hated how she had her chance to gut him, and failed. She hated feeling like she was Jen's problem at this exact moment. She hated Six, but with Six gone, she turned anger's runoff onto herself.

And that horrible weak sound kept going. Her lungs hurt from it, but she couldn't stop it. It felt horrible, and necessary at the same time.

The next day, a Citizen came to Jen and Tara's place, looking for Leena. "That lofu is back. The one that's okay. And Messenger. They want the broken communication thing."

Leena looked over to the caved in metal box that had been delivered the night before. Mostly clean. "Yeah. I... I'll bring it to him," Leena said. Jen and Tara weren't here to object. They and Cody were making a big push to finish cleaning her and Mike's place ... well, just *her* place now.

138

She thanked the Citizen and sent him on his way before picking up the broken communication machine, and heading toward the Grand Elevator. It was too unwieldy to carry with one arm on her hip, especially with a broken edge or two. As she shifted it around, a few pieces clattered inside.

Could Messenger fix this? Maybe Actual? What else could they fix? Not people. They couldn't fix people, or they'd come back, right?

Would they?

Feeling foolish for thinking it, she imagined Actual above, fixing the broken people sent to him, then sending them to a new life. The seductive notion of Mike ending up somewhere alive took her rationale on a small vacation. What would he be doing now if he were up in Actual's world? Would he miss her?

Would Warren and Sledge be there?

No, idiocy. All of it. Would Actual fix Mike maybe, and not people like W... no.. idiocy. All of it. All of it.

She entered the building, and made it to the loading bay, locking the door to the rest of Citizenry behind her. The elevator door ahead seemed to watch her as she approached. And in effect, it was.

"I knew it. You're here," Leena called to the door. "You're back, aren't you? Lenth? You *are* in there, aren't you?"

"Leena!" It was Lenth's voice.

"Lenth, I brought the communication thing. It... it's been cleaned. You remember how it was. A couple of the tinier bits might be missing. Can you come out? I locked the other door. Messenger? I'm not armed or anything. I won't try to get on the elevator. Just let me see Lenth, please?"

She stood in silence for a moment, wondering if she'd been heard. Just as she took breath to repeat herself louder, the reply came from Messenger.

"Go stand on the other end of the hall."

She obeyed, dashing over to the door to Citizenry, and stood attentively. The elevator door clicked. It slid to the side, open enough for Lenth to get through.

Messenger was there. Never before seen so plainly by any Citizen, as far as Leena knew, and there he was. Lean, a touch older than Lenth or herself. His skin was rather dark, and with a reddish hint to it. His straight, black hair hung loosely around his face. Leena knew some people with dark complexions, but not quite this dark. It only stood to reason that Messenger would be unique.

Messenger. *This is the Messenger, servant of the Actual.* And here he was. Again, the contrast of Messenger traveling with a lofu struck her. Did all lofus get to see Messenger like it was a normal part of life? Impossible. Right?

Messenger spoke again with a deep tone that called for reverence.

"Stay on that end, Citizen. Lenth, proceed as you wish."

Lenth smiled a bit and jogged out towards Leena. Messenger collected the communicator which Leena had left by the Elevator door.

"You've been okay?" Lenth asked as he neared Leena, "with Edgar, and everything? I mean...there's peace at least?"

Leena nodded. "Yeah, yeah. He thinks he's the greatest and whatever, but I think I can keep him in check, at least. And you? And Six?"

"Six is caught. Haven't decided what to do with him yet."

What to do with him? Leena had an idea. "Bring him here and let me mash his head in!"

Lenth smiled and held her. A bit overly friendly, maybe, but she allowed it. "Oh, it's messy complicated," Lenth said, "and he's dying anyway, if that makes you feel better."

She backed away, and grimaced. "Not a lot better. What's killing him? Some kind of giant metre-long spike being slowly driven into his face?"

"Leena!" Lenth stifled a laugh.

"I'm not kidding! Much. What is it then?"

"To keep it simple, he's poisoned. The kind of thing they can't fix."

"Well, good," she said. "Will he suffer?"

"Actually, yeah, it sounds like it, quite a bit. I'm not sure what it'll end up like, but it could easily take weeks."

"Well, good. He deserves it," Leena said.

This sentiment made Lenth's expression sour a bit, but he didn't go so far as to refute it. "Overall...how are you doing?"

"It's...it's all right," Leena answered. "Six did a lot of damage. It didn't just affect me. Others lost people. I have to be strong for em all, y'know? He did a lot of damage."

Lenth held her again, and this time, she held him too. This lofu idiot was an okay sort of person.

"I have a stupid question, Leena. If you could change something about what Citizenry is like...well, what would you change?"

Leena looked over Lenth's shoulder to the open gap in the elevator door. "A lot, I guess. Nothing I can wrap up in a little package. I don't know. It just feels like things are wrong. Like they've always been wrong."

Lenth let go and gently backed away. "They are, and they have been, and not just in Citizenry."

"You're going?"

Lenth nodded. "I have a pile of junk to deliver, I guess."

Leena's face melted to a hollow, stunned look. "Deliver? You..."

Lenth glanced up.

"What are you now?" she asked in nearly a whisper. "Are you a..."

"No. I'm not sure what I am right now, or what I'll become."

What he'd become? She was hinting at Messenger, even if it felt ridiculous. What else was there? Lofu, Messenger, Actual. Something else? What else? Something beyond the knowledge of Citizens.

The notion of a wider world almost pushed her to ask about the dead. Even if Mike hadn't been sent up yet, it was only a matter of time.

Lenth broke the moment of silence. "Don't look at me like that."

Leena pointed a finger towards the elevator. "If you're going to be a...then one day you'll be..." Her now-timid finger pointed up.

He put his hands on Leena's shoulders. "When you put it like that...it's a little scary."

Then it was true. A lofu has a chance at becoming the Actual, assuming Lenth wasn't just talking nonsense- Where does Citizenry fit in with all of it?

140

Leena shook her head with slow, tiny flickers of disbelief."Don't forget all of us down here, okay? When you're everything."

"It's not going to happen for a long time. If it even ever does."

"Don't forget."

"Never."

"Leena, can I come over to your place?" Cody asked boldly. It had now been less than a week since Mike's death. While Cody was agreeable enough, she certainly wasn't ready to 'play' with anyone. Not for a long while yet.

"Cody, I... really? No. I'm grateful how you helped clean up my place and all, and you're a great guy and all, but I thought you would already realize-"

"What?" Cody backed away, hands open in front of him. "No, no, no! That's not what I meant. I want to..." Cody looked around to see if anyone was in earshot, then continued a little quieter than before. "I want to check out some of the construction in your place. To see if I missed something."

"Your new place not working out so well? Are you regretting giving me the one I'm in?"

"No, nothing like that. Heck, mine's bigger... but they *do* share similarities. I just wanted to see if you had some of the things I found in my place."

Soon they were at Leena's threshold, and Cody walked ahead briskly. He grabbed Sledge's sledgehammer, which was by the weapon rack in the bedroom.

"Woah, Cody, what's going on?"

"Eh, just needed something hard." He held the handle close to the head, and started tapping it on the wall, moving a few steps to the side, tapping, step, tap tap...

"Your swing sucks, Cody."

"I'm not trying to break a wall. Yet. I'm just looking for somewhere I might be able to."

"*Go break your own walls, then!*"

Satisfied he hadn't missed anything here, he planted the hammer's head on the floor, and leaned on the handle. "I did!"

"What?"

"Broke a wall. Well, not broke, but found a place I could pull open. I was looking for another thin wall here. But nope. Just my place has it, I guess."

"Ugh. Don't tell me you found a bag of crazy meds."

"Nope... well not yet." Cody smiled.

"What not yet, *what*?"

Cody smiled wider. "Come see."

The walk to Cody's was roughly as long as one could go across Citizenry without taking needless twists and turns. Down Leena's ramp, straight across the Commons, passing the Grand Elevator building, to Cody's ramp, and up.

The interior of Cody's den was longer inward than Leena's, in that there was no wall between the front room, and the room Leena used as a bedroom. The door at the end would be analogous to the room where the communication device had been kept. Where Mike...

Cody's den was considerably less tidy than Leena's. A pile of bedding could be seen in one corner, but everywhere else was bits of... things. Metal, mostly. Much of the metal was scrap from Warren's tower project. Boxes saved from food deliveries, neatly folded flat, sat in a pile by a suit of clothing that had been cut apart in very specific-looking pieces. None of it meant much to Leena, except that it was obviously Cody's doing, and seemingly meeting some specifications only he understood.

Cody walked behind a pile of standing corrugated metal sheets, which might have been intentionally set by Cody as a wall. He must have cleaned them. They looked much nicer than Warren's junk ever did.

Leena followed Cody, and saw the gap. His wall had a tunnel behind it. A slab of wall stood nearby. Not a wall piece that had been made of scrap... this was a section of *real* wall, thought generally immovable. The nearby 'tunnel entrance' told her that this was the kind of thing Cody had been looking for at her den.

"It's dark. Let your eyes adjust," Cody said as he slowly walked in.

"Looks like a great place for crap-sniffers to hang out," Leena said, "only smells like dust, though." As her eyes adjusted, she could see that the floor was fairly tidy, other than dust. The walls were typical, but untouched by daily damage of living, or art of the bored. Above, the ceiling had typical lights installed, but they were dark. Ahead ten or so metres, sat more scrap.

Cody's little wall of corrugated metal outside wasn't salvaged from the Commons- it was from this tunnel.

"Where does it go?" Leena asked.

"Won't know until I get there. It heads directly away from the middle of Citizenry, so I doubt it'll end up anywhere we know already."

"Lofus?"

"Lofus are down. We're facing sideways."

Leena smirked. "Okay, if not Lesser Others From Under, maybe Lesser Others From Sideways."

"Lofs? Heh. Why do others necessarily have to be lesser? Not that I expect to find anyone in here. Cut off from food and stuff."

Leena went over to the pile of blockage. "They might have their own source. For that matter, who knows? Messenger might also deliver somewhere else than just us. Hey, how long have you been working at this?"

Cody shrugged. "Only found it two days ago. And honestly, I kind of want to keep it a secret."

"Okay." Leena didn't need any explanation or reasoning. If she'd found something like this, she'd be inclined to keep it quiet too. "So, why tell me?"

"You're a good gal, and besides..." Cody went over to a chunk of blockage, and yanked on it. It was wedged between the ceiling and floor.

"So you trust me and my hulking muscles." She flexed for effect. While no weakling, her muscle tone was not extraordinary. "We should have brought the hammer," Leena said. She didn't actually want to be seen flouncing about with that thing, though.

Cody patted his arm. "I was thinking if we both rammed it with our shoulders at the same time..."

Leena nodded, and they took position about a metre away from each other and the target metal.

Cody bounced a couple of times to boost his morale. "Okay... and..!"

They both lunged sideways at the metal. A dull, resonant sound was their reward.

"Again!" They stepped back again, and lunged to a similar sound. This time with a tiny scrape sound.

"Progress! All right! Again!"

Leena tuned the other way, to abuse her other shoulder a bit. And they rammed, resulting in a slightly bigger scraping sound.

"Look!" Cody pointed up, and a noticeable scrape could be seen on the ceiling. "One more good one!" They lined up for another ram, but Leena stepped back a little further, and pulled Cody back, too. He nodded.

"Ohhhhh kay... one more.... and...." They impacted the metal sheet, and it toppled back onto other debris with a symphony of clangs and bangs. Leena began to chuckle in victory, but suddenly found it more pragmatic to jump back. She and Cody got out of the way as some smaller pieces came loose from behind the defeated wall, and toppled down to their feet.

Leena looked out towards the Commons. "Do you think anyone heard that?"

"No."

"No?"

"No. I managed more noise than that with some of the other pieces." Cody held up his right arm to show a long cut healing along his forearm. "And I think I might have given a shout or two when one of those other pieces cut me."

"Oh wow. That's a pretty long cut," Leena said. She'd seen deep cuts in a similar place result in death. "Did it bleed a ton?"

Cody shrugged. "On one end, a bit, yeah, but most of it isn't really much more than a scratch. Looks worse than it is, and it doesn't look all that bad. That's what I get for trying to move awkward chunks of metal all alone."

"Allllll awowwwwwwne!" Leena snickered. "Is that a hint that you'd like a hand moving some of this other crap out of the way?"

"Heh. I didn't mean it that way, but honestly, if you don't have anything else going on right now, I'd appreciate it."

The large piece they had to ram loose simply wouldn't fit through the opening into the main den. They wedged it sideways (and not *too* firmly) against the wall, out of the way. Most of the other bits were small enough to be easily carried by a single person, but at least Leena's assistance made things go faster.

Of note, they found some bright orange cones with an opening on the narrow end, and a squarish formation on the wide end, so they could stand about half a metre tall. They were fun to kick, fun to peek through or talk through. It made one's voice sound funny. Must have been some kind of toy.

It wasn't long before they spotted a wall behind the clutter. A few more pieces moved, and they saw that it was a door. With more pieces moved, they could get a proper look at it.

It was not so grand as the Grand Elevator's door, but it looked like similar metal. That is, it looked thick and shiny. About a metre and a half wide, white, with only the hint of hinges on one side, and a metal little panel securing it on the other side.

The panel had a handle on it, and a grouping of metal buttons with numbers on them.

"It's like they're daring me... offering me a game..." Cody said in a strange, hushed awe.

"They?"

"Whoever made this. If they didn't want people to get through, they wouldn't give us this little contraption to figure out." Cody stared at the panel, smiling. "Or for that matter, they could have just made it a wall or something. No, this is a challenge."

"Would 'they' be Actual?" Leena asked.

Cody smirked, and glanced upwards. "I suppose that's a reasonable possibility, hm? It would all beg the question *why*, though. But maybe that's part of the reward for getting through. Finding out why."

"What if you're just not supposed to get through? Maybe it's dangerous."

"So, what, you think I should leave it alone?"

"Ha! As if. As if I don't want to know– and as if you'd give up because *I* said so."

Cody smiled again. Smiled at Leena, and Leena felt it.

Her expression went blank. If Mike were still alive, he'd be okay with it if she jumped Cody right now. He would. They had an understanding. But dead? No, not now. Maybe never.

"What's wrong?" Cody asked, glancing at the door. "Are you that worried something bad's in there?"

"Well. Yes, there is a risk," Leena murmured, staring down, wringing her hands. "But it just seems like the kind of thing ya gotta push through. You know ..." she glanced into his eyes. "Eventually."

With a nod, maybe not of *full* understanding, Cody went over to the metal buttons, and pressed a few. Nothing seemed to happen. Not a light, not a sound. He looked up at the dark lights above. "The inside metal might be dark metal."

"Dark metal?"

"Yeah. Know the lights that light up the Commons, and our dens?" Cody pointed randomly at the ceiling, and out towards the Commons.

"Yeah, and sometimes they go out, and we ask Messenger for new parts."

"Yeah, well under what we usually see, there's tiny metal strings covered in rubber. They make the lights work."

"So, the light comes in through little rubber-metal strings?"

"No. That's what I thought the first time I opened one up," Cody said, eyes shining, eager to explain his process. "I tried to see the light in the strings, but it kind of bit me– but not really. Hard to explain. There's a different kind of light you can't see, riding the metal somehow, and when it gets to a bulb, the

144

bulb changes it! And if you touch the *metal-light*, it hurts! I'm not doing that again, so I only touch it through rubber, like they're in already."

"You bloody lost me, Cody. What's all this have to do with the door?"

"I think it needs metal-light. Those bulbs over there? They're from my den. They work in the ceiling out there, but not here. This area just needs metal-light. I'm not sure though. If I can open the thing on the door with the buttons, I might be able to get a better idea. In the mean time, I need to find a way to get metal-light to the dark metal here."

"I'm guessing you can't carry it in a cup," Leena said.

"No. In fact, for your safety, note that I've found that water and metal-light do *not* get along!... or do they? Oh, I have an idea. *Oh!* I have ideas!"

"Okay. They are?"

Cody looked around with quick little glances. "They are... I need to think about this for a bit. I need to... and... hmm...."

"Well, okay then, Cody. Maybe I should leave you at your new little hobby?"

"Ah. Yes, maybe. Okay. I can I think... maybe..."

"See ya, Cody."

"Hm? Yes, hm."

Leena started to leave, and found Cody was trailing right behind her but scarcely looking where he was going.

"I thought you were going to stay here and think," she said with chuckle.

"Yeah, I am. I mean, no, I want to see some stuff, to see what I can work with."

"You need stuff from the Commons?"

"I'm not sure. I think I need to invent a cup to put metal-light into."

"But you said—"

"Guaah," Cody shook his head. "Yeah, I knew what I said, but I'm talking about something to get the metal-light from one place to another. Not a cup. I'm pretty sure."

"You don't sound like you know what you're doing, Cody."

"I don't. Not all of it, not yet. That's why I'm thinking."

The two cleared the den and made it onto the ramp, when Leena spotted extra activity by the Grand Elevator building.

Edgar's robe made him stick out, leading a few guards, and a handful of other Refuge-dwellers. They were headed to the building, and one Citizen was coming out of it, carrying– a communication box! Messenger had just been here!

"Oh, no, no he doesn't!" Leena broke into a run, and when Cody figured out why, he picked up his pace to keep up. They got to the Citizen with the communication box moments after Edgar.

"Leena! You needn't have bothered yourself, I can handle it." Edgar took the box from the Citizen who had carried it. The Citizen didn't look sure about it, but didn't protest, either.

"Edgar, give that to me," Leena snapped. "It would have gone to Mike, but I claim it since he can't."

Edgar lowered his head, and said calmly, "It would not be well suited to being in your possession. You're alone."

Leena stood up stiff. She looked over her shoulder to Cody, back at Edgar, then again to Cody. "Cody, am I alone?"

With a mildly sheepish smile, Cody answered. "Nope, you're not alone."

Leena shifted her stance and put her hands on her hips before addressing Edgar. "Yeah, I don't feel overly alone. I think maybe Jen, Tara, and a few hundred others might feel I'm not alone."

"Very well," Edgar said, "you are not alone. But you are scattered. Unorganized. Undisciplined. If you were not any of these things, you or an associate would have been there, ready to receive the communication device. I and those loyal to me can more capably handle the responsibility."

Leena pointed at the Citizen that had carried the communication box. "What, this guy is your buddy?"

"I can't sit by the Elevator myself all the time, you realize-" Edgar said, "You could have as easily had someone there if you'd been organized enough, or even been there yourself. What is it you were doing that was more important than guiding the Citizens?"

Leena glanced up to Cody's den for a split second. No. Edgar doesn't need to know anything about that.

"I see," Edgar said dryly, looking at Leena and Cody. "That's unsurprising, I suppose. Mike would be *so* proud that you've moved on."

"Not that it's your business," Leena snarled. Let him think what he wants.

Edgar shook his head. "You demonstrate the sort of attitude that leads to people like Warren coming into control."

"What did you say?"

"Your body. You use it like a toy. That sort of thing makes others see it as a toy. A toy that can be taken."

Leena bared her teeth, and snarled, "What I do with my body is my business! And you talk pretty quick for someone who keeps two barely-dressed women with him when he's in his room!"

Edgar didn't have a retort at the ready for that, but didn't seem rattled. He just turned, communication box in-hand, and left through his little pack of followers, and the guards trailing him.

Resisting the urge to clobber Edgar (partly due to his nearby guards), Leena stomped off. Cody kept pace beside her.

Where to? Busy stomping. Aimed reflexively to home. Home, where Mike died. No. No, thank you. Not there.

Back to Cody's? That might be productive. Nope, too pissed off to be productive. Screw it, she'd go to Tara and Jen's.

Cody followed along with no particular invite, but welcome anyway.

"Should have taken it from him," Cody said, a handful of metres along the walk.

Leena shot Cody a cold, quick glance. "Yeah. Well, he had guards with him," she grumbled. She gave Cody another look– a bit softer, in case she was being too snippy with him.

"Would they have actually been a problem?"

Leena chuckled. "Thanks for the confidence, but I don't think I could have taken out Edgar, his guards, and any other refuge-dwellers who chose to get in on it."

146

"I would have helped," Cody said with a shrug, "but no. What I meant was, I think you could have made a point that it should be passed on to you. Mike... Mike was yours, not his, after all."

What a way to slap her mood into another mode; suddenly, unintentionally, but decisively, with a mention of her relationship with Mike. "Yeah... well... I don't think Mike's name holds a lot of weight with the Refuge-dwellers."

They walked a few more moments in silence, half-way to Tara and Jen's, when Cody quietly broke the silence. "Well, it should."

"Others appreciate him still. It's not like Citizens will forget him." Leena's words came without emotion. She needed to step back from that edge a little. "To be fair," she said, "Edgar was planning an attack on Warren for quite some time. Mike and I just got involved by accident, almost, and it gave Edgar a good opening."

"Maybe," Cody said, "but when it came to Warren and Sledge, who got the final blow?"

"Who's blowing who now?" Jen jumped into conversation as she joined the walk.

"Oh! Hi, Jen! We were just coming to your place," Cody answered.

"You're coming over for a blow?" Jen said. "You're going to be out of luck with Tara and me. We're not so much into what you have going on down there. Have you tried–" Jen stopped herself, and tried to not glance at Leena.

"Edgar took the newly-delivered communication box," Leena said.

"Edg... -what? Why? No, never mind. He feels he deserves it or something?"

"I guess," Leena said. "We talked less about his feelings on it, and more about how I'm not good enough for it, and don't organize people or something."

Jen's mouth scrunched up, and her eyes widened. "Did you try punching him?"

"Crossed my mind. He had guards and stuff, and *they* had spears and stuff."

"*Tara!*" Jen jogged ahead a few steps; they were basically there. "Tara, did you hear what that jar-sniffing sack of crap did now?"

Tara stepped out of their shack, with a wave for the trio who'd just arrived. "What, now they want to do the filling themselves?"

"Huh?" Leena said as they came to a stop before Tara. "Filling what?"

"You haven't gone to get water lately?" Tara asked. "Edgar has a couple guards standing around all four Commons taps."

While a few out of the way people had sources of water, like the ones in Mike and Cody's dens, most Citizens went to one of the equidistant faucets on the outer edge of Commons, usually to fill jars or bottles to take home to their shacks, or to wash up right there.

"He what...? Why?" Cody blurted.

"Guard said it's for Citizen safety!" Tara huffed.

"What kind of made-up crap is that? Was anyone ever in da..." Leena stopped herself. Yes. People have been in danger there. In Warren's days, women were wary to get water alone. But things had changed. Right? "I bet he plans to be handing out the food the next time we get a batch."

Everyone's thoughts immediately went to Warren's gatherings.

"What do you think he plans to do there?" Jen asked quietly, almost to herself.

"Nothing." Leena stood stiffly and looked towards the Grand Elevator. "we're going to be there first. When's the next shipment? Probably a week and a half?"

"We're going to be there?" Cody asked.

"Edgar's unimpressed with my organization skills? Let's be organized. Every second, we'll be there, ready to accept Messenger. Edgar has a person there? We can have two."

"With weapons?" Tara asked.

Leena looked to her hip and the knife that hung there. It was the one that had been a gift from Warren, given freely when he was happy on white powder. "Yes. But not in-hand. Ready, but not eager."

Chapter Twelve

Farewell

The loading bay room to the Grand Elevator was much as it ever was- perhaps the cleanest, least damaged room in all of Citizenry. As Cody and Tara walked towards the elevator door, the man sitting there stood, taking his spear in hand. Apparently he hadn't earned one of the guard outfits.

"Alright, we'll be here now," Cody said.

"Edgar wants *two* people here now?" the guard said. He didn't question that they were carrying a knife and sword instead of one of the spears that seemed to be common for Edgar's guard.

"This will be better," Tara said. "There's two guards at the water sources. One here seemed a bit off."

"Huh. Good point. I guess I'll head back to Refuge," the guard said, strolling to the entrance. Cody and Tara watched him go, and breathed a sigh of relief.

"Okay. How long until ole' Eddy barges along?" Cody leaned back against the Elevator's big door.

"Depends on if that guy just goes right home, or talks to Edgar first or something."

Only a small amount of time passed before a need for conversation arose between the two.

"So... Cody. You and Leena? Anything there?" Tara raised an eyebrow.

"Edgar assumes so, but no."

Tara was unmoved. "Why? Are you interested?"

Stifling a chuckle, Cody gave a short nod. "Sure. And before, something was maybe going to happen, but then Mike died..."

"You and Leena *and* Mike were...?"

Cody couldn't stifle this chuckle. "Hah, no, not my thing. But as cool as they were with playing with other people, right now, she... she's not in a playful mood."

Tara huffed in disappointment. "Maybe later."

"Maybe later, she might have ideas other than me," Cody said with a smirk and a nudge towards Tara.

"She likes girls too? Well, not me, I'm taken!"

"So you and Jen don't play with others, then," Cody observed.

"Nope. I'm too greedy, I want Jen all to myself. Jen feels similarly."

"Adorable," Cody said in earnest.

"Thank you, I know I am."

"You're the lippy one, aren't you?" Cody said with a smirk.

"Yup." Pleased with herself, Tara resumed quiet guard duty.

Not far off, Leena stood and watched the outside of the Grand Elevator building. Edgar's guard left, and he seemed all right with the situation. She silently congratulated Tara and Cody. She had wanted to go herself, but figured she was too recognizable.

Besides– organization. Delegating duties. She could do that. She *has* done that. Or was it just good friends stepping up at the right times?

With the area seeming clear of complications, she went into the Grand Elevator bay to see them.

"Hey guys. Things went well, it seems?"

Cody nodded. "Yup, didn't even have to fib. Let him assume Edgar sent us."

"Ha, who's organized now, huh?" Leena bobbed up a couple of times, grinning.

Tara smiled reservedly. "Hopefully, us."

"She's on it," Leena said, glancing to the entrance. "Have some faith in our girl." Leena had every faith in Jen's dedication, but now that it had come down to it, Leena wasn't overly confident in her ability for the task she'd been given– or the plausibility of it.

Leena, Tara, and Cody all sat, their backs against the Elevator's door, and held their breath. They didn't have to wait long.

The sounds of indignant footsteps came from the entrance, down the hall from the Commons.

Sure enough, Edgar appeared with three of his guards in tow. As soon as he entered the loading bay, he pointed at the trio forcefully, his robe's sleeve flopping angrily. "*Leena! I should have known!*"

"Known what, Edgar?" Leena replied cheerfully, "that if you wanted to control the water, I might want to make sure food was safe?"

"I'm not *controlling* the water! I'm keeping it safe!" Again with dramatic pointing, this time out towards the Commons.

"How kind. Not that it seemed all that necessary. Allow me to help out by keeping the Elevator safe. Not that it seems all that necessary."

Edgar stood and stared for a moment of silence before finally speaking again. "My people have this. You can go."

"No, I'm quite content here. You can put a person back here, that's fine. But my people are staying."

Edgar leaned his head to one side, and leaned on his spear- which had attained a few new little decorations since Leena had last seen it. "I don't think the three of you can adequately —"

"Leena, we're here." *Jen's* voice came from the hall behind Edgar.

Leena smiled meekly, and whispered to herself, "that's my girl."

"*My* girl," Tara whispered back with a wry smile. "Get your own."

Edgar turned to face Jen, as his guards shuffled out of the way. Behind Jen, a crowd of Citizens, many casually armed, clogged the hall. At least a dozen were visible before the corner of the hall obscured others.

"You brought him?" Leena called to Jen, her bemused smile gently fading.

"We did." Jen walked forward, giving Edgar no heed, stepping around him. Right after, it was Edgar who had to move, as the crowd was following up behind Jen, and they were less able to maneuver around Edgar — especially since they were carrying something.

"Mike." Edgar said grimly. The crowd were carrying a long bundle of re-purposed cloth, enough layers of dark blue so that no garish blood could be seen.

With all the dignity they had to give, and many a heavy heart, they brought Mike's wrapped body forward slowly amidst the group. They stopped before Leena, who, still seated, looked up at Mike with tears building.

Mike was set down with his head pointed towards Leena, who now would not look anyone in the eye. Tara took her hand, and gave it a small squeeze before standing to look at Edgar.

"Since you took the communication box, you'll have to call for Messenger to take Mike," Tara said calmly.

Edgar watched quietly for a moment as Citizens wandered past him to go sit near Mike. "You'll leave, after he's taken?" Edgar asked.

"Why?" Cody asked. "We have enough people to take care of the loading bay."

"And these were *fast* to gather," Jen added, implying there were even more people whose loyalty to Mike had transferred to Leena.

Edgar nodded with a patronizing little half-smile. "I have a call to make, then."

He turned to leave, and Leena broke her silence, "Say hi to our friend, if you talk to him. Or tell Messenger to say hi to him."

"That lofu?" Edgar sapped.

"That lofu is a good friend of the one closest to Actual," Leena said. "Maybe Lenth isn't so 'lesser' for a lofu, hm?"

"Don't push your blasphemy so far," Edgar grumbled as he finally left.

Once he and his people were clear, Leena let out a relieved sigh. "Thank you, everyone."

Jen sat on the other side of Leena, and took her other hand.

"I don't like that," Cody said, looking out the direction Edgar left. "That's going to be a problem." He caught Leena's eye. "Maybe I should just go keep busy. Keep my mind off of Edgar. Busy with a hobby. You know the one..."

Leena sighed again. "Some hobbies *are* important. Some hobbies might go smoother with some assistance."

Looking at Mike's wrapped body, at Leena, and her two close allies, Cody knew they couldn't... or perhaps just shouldn't be helping with that hobby at this moment. "Can you recommend anyone who might be suited to help, or should I just wait for you?" Cody asked.

Many supporters sat about the room, most of whom could probably be trusted to know about the tunnel in Cody's room. Probably. But even a well-meaning person might blabber too much.

"Did anyone here help restore Mike and mine's den?" Leena asked to all of the people in the room.

A few hands went up from familiar faces that Leena didn't know exceedingly well.

"Kim, Leon," Cody said, picking two, "either of you want to help me out again? Different kind of thing." He kept eye contact with Kim and Leon, hoping he was communicating the potential gravity of the task.

Leon stood, and nodded, stepping up towards Cody. After resting her hand for a moment on Mike's body and giving Leena a sad smile, Kim stood with Cody as well.

As the three left, Jen turned to Leena. "What was that all about?"

"Maybe nothing. Might end up important," Leena said. "I'll fill you in later." She gave Jen and Tara's hands an extra little squeeze. Tara and Jen glanced at each other. Between them, Leena kept her gaze fixated on Mike's body.

In the relative quiet that followed, occasional murmurs of conversation trickled through the other seated Citizens. Leena heard something about Edgar, in concerned tones, and bits about Mike in sad nostalgia. Leena knew Mike was well liked, but there was love in this room. She wondered what Mike would think. If he'd even take the idea seriously.

He would, certainly. Just as certainly, he'd make a joke about it.

Finally, the sound of the Grand Elevator drew near. No one stood, taking their cue from Leena.

The rumble and the shake seemed all that more pervasive in the relative quiet, as the Grand Elevator settled into place. When the sound ended, Leena spoke,

"Hello, Messenger."

She heard the sound of the little door he looked through. A moment or two of silence before he spoke. "Citizens. Please clear the loading bay."

Instead of obeying immediately, all eyes went to Leena.

"Go," she said to everyone with a nod and a minimal smile, letting Jen and Tara's hands go.

Tara looked a bit skeptical, but Leena only nodded at the concern.

Soon, every Citizen besides Leena had filed out, with Tara closing the door behind them.

It clicked. The lock was set remotely by Messenger.

"You're Leena, correct?" Messenger asked.

"Yes." She still sat, facing away from the Grand Elevator, towards Mike. "Is Lenth with you, Messenger?"

"No. Though I have news you will want. Six is dead."

Leena smiled grimly, and patted Mike's wrapped body. "Oh. Yeah, Lenth told me he was poisoned or something."

"As it turned out, he actually wasn't. In the end, it was Actual who ended his life."

"*Actual?!* How did that happen?"

Messenger was silent for a moment before replying. "Six's reasons were a little complicated. He was a victim before he was a killer. We tried to give him a chance at a life. It did not go well."

Leena stood and faced the little slot Messenger peeked through. He stepped back, which allowed Leena to see a bit more inside. The interior of the Grand Elevator was a large room, with rounded walls. She had seen Messenger himself before with his dark skin and yellow outfit– not all that different than the blue that every Citizen had.

At this moment, Leena came to appreciate that he might be just a person. Maybe not some inherently powerful being.

A strange mix of comfort and anger brewed inside her. "Do you understand? Does Actual understand? What goes on in Citizenry? What Warren was doing?"

Messenger walked out of view. "You live. You eat, you breathe, we make sure you can. Beyond that, it's never been a huge concern."

"*It's not great in here!*" Leena cried. "Even after Warren and his people are gone, there's... there's bad things coming together. I don't know how life is up there, or below with the lofus, but things aren't great here!"

Another moment of silence before Messenger spoke. "Did you know, Citizenry used to be the most fortunate of all? It was a rather glorious place. A privilege to live in. I have seen pictures. It was a long time ago. Actual says that the early Citizens eventually became restless, and things began to decline. He says that in contrast, lofus... well, we don't call them that. Providers, Subjects, Engineers... they've always had to work. For the most part, that has–"

"Wait, wait, so what Lenth said... was it true?" Leena asked, "Lofus keep Citizens fed?"

"And breathing, and in the light. Actual and I get them what they need to do it. But they don't need a great deal."

"*Why?*" Leena shouted. "Why would they do that? What do they care wh-... this is... We're all told Actual provides everything, and lofus..."

Messenger walked back into view. "Among all the people, some groups, such as the Citizens... over time invented ideas that made the world work for them. It is not helped by the fact that old rules stop truths from reaching everyone. There are reasons, for everyone's safety. You *can* know, however, that everyone contributes to our survival, and that it would all slowly break down if Actual did not do what he does for us."

"Truths..." Leena walked back slowly, stumbling to avoid Mike's body. It was so much to absorb. "Everyone contributes... everyone except..."

"Yes. Citizens. Most of you are descendants of the most fortunate from the time long ago. Wealth provided luxury, and so it was that you do not work. And the children, and childrens' children, and so forth... they became increasingly restless, and eventually... violent."

"So.. we used to be the lucky ones," Leena said softly, "and now..."

"Instead of keeping people out to protect Citizens, we are forced to keep you in. To protect everyone else."

Leena knelt beside Mike's body. "But we had hope! Mike was *so* not like Warren! He made people feel good about... helping each other! About looking out for each other!" She gazed at the body, as if hoping Mike would pop up and deliver a stirring argument in support of Citizenry.

"If he was as good as you say... he might have made a lasting difference if he'd lived longer," Messenger said in reverence.

Leena stood hastily, face quickly reddening. "*And he's gone now because of some crazy lofu YOU brought to us!*"

Messenger sighed deeply. "I know. I am truly sorry for your loss. Six was... unusual. I'd never seen the type. His violence affected many– many outside of Citizenry as well. The Provider levels and such are very safe in general, but one can not have guaranteed safety all the time when someone like Six can come into being."

Leena hadn't been listening too intently, pacing around, smearing the odd tear off her cheek. "So when you take Mike... he's not going to go live with Actual, is he? No one pops back to life, do they?"

"No. I'm afraid no–"

"*Then what the heck is the point of it? What happens? What really happens to the dead?*"

Head lowered, Messenger spoke from wisdoms taught, not experienced. "When the dead remain unattended, the decay can make the living very sick. We take care of them, and Mike does have a contribution to make for everyone yet. Something we will all do after we die."

"*What? What can he do now?*"

"Do you really want to know? I taught Lenth because he was arguably ready. He... was not overly glad to hear the truth. Because it involved his recently deceased Brother."

Leena's eyes darted between Mike and Messenger. "And Lenth. He eventually became all right with it? It's something horrible, isn't it? I mean, I have to find out eventually, it'll drive me nuts. But it's something horrible, isn't it?

Messenger's expression turned terse, and he stared at the floor. "Everything that dies... people, and wasted food products, old trees.. (we'll get to the idea of trees)... they all get put unto a place to become what we call 'compost'. It is eventually turned into a thick, lumpy, dark, powder that no longer looks anything like the things and people that decayed to create it."

Leena's eye were already wide with horror, but she remained quiet to hear the rest.

Messenger continued. "The compost is mixed with older compost and... dirt. From it, some people as far down as where Lenth grew up, help grow 'plants' of different kinds. Plants are alive, but they do not move, speak or think. They do not have blood, skin, muscles, bones, or bodies anything like ours, and come in many different shapes."

Leena reeled silently, imagining the unmoving living... things... growing covered in rotten bits of Mike. "They sound horrible!"

Messenger smiled sadly. "Actually, being in their presence can be very relaxing and peaceful. Some types are low and meek. Others grow tall, many times bigger that a person. You get to see how our departed loved ones help create the food we all need to live. Without moving, they absorb what they need from the dirt and compost, and slower than the eye can see, create our food's ingredients."

Was this what Lenth had been trying to tell her? She didn't listen. Why listen to a lofu? But now, in sickening detail, the great Messenger himself was laying it all out.

"It's... it's always been like this?" she asked.

"As long as anyone can remember."

"So... all my life..." Leena staggered back from Mike's body, pointing, and her voice raising in volume and pitch to near panic, "*the food discs I've been eating...!*"

"Take a deep breath, Leena. I know it's a shock, but it is the natural, peaceful end to our lives, making way and providing for new lives."

Leena couldn't take her eyes off Mike. Her hands clutched over her mouth, she trembled, breathing in fast little gasps.

"Close your eyes. Deep breath," Messenger tried to soothe.

Leena rushed to Mike's body, and collapsed by it, holding him, and sobbing. "No, no, no. Lenth tried to tell me! Say it's a lie, Messenger. My Mike can't... no...!"

"Mike is no longer there," Messenger said. "That is just his body. Your Mike has been gone since Six..."

"I can't just keep Mike?"

"I told you. You and many others would get terribly sick. And as he decays, you'll wish you last saw him more like this."

"Maybe you're lying!"

"Why would I lie about this?"

"I don't know! I don't know a lot of things!"

Messenger nodded. "True. But as of now, you know more than about half the people I tend to."

"Half?"

"Citizenry consists of almost four hundred people. Correction. After the purge of Warren's men, more like three hundred and a bit. The rest of the people outside Citizenry, number in the thousands."

Leena rose to be seated on her knees, a hand still resting on Mike's chest. "The lofus... they're not lesser than Citizens, are they? Not at all."

"I have to admit," Messenger said quietly, "aside from Six, and a friend of his, I've only known the *Citizenry* to give rise to killers."

"We're the lessers, aren't we?" Leena whispered. "Citizens, that is. Do others have a name for us? What do they call us?"

"Just *Citizens*; those that know you exist."

"Different truths for different groups..." Leena uttered in a near whisper.

Messenger looked the defeated Leena up and down. "Something like that."

Leena paused, still trying to absorb everything, still with her hand resting on Mike's chest. "Do people out there... who know about us... hate us?"

With a sigh, Messenger gave a slow nod. "A few. Some people have come to visit, and been hurt badly. And people know you don't make anything."

Staring at Mike Leena swallowed hard. "We're... we're violent and useless. Those who know we exist... think we're all violent and useless."

Messenger only replied with silence, giving Leena a moment to ponder.

"*I want to be useful,*" she finally squeaked out.

"If you have intentions like those you attributed to Mike, you might be the most useful right here." Messenger looked through the Grand Elevator's peek slot, out to the loading bay, to Leena, and beyond.

Being useful within the Citizenry would almost certainly mean standing up to, or even outright opposing Edgar. "I can't just freely repeat the truths you've told me," Leena said.

"No?"

"Some would be upset by the ideas. Some think the Actual is kind of everything. Warren was trying to get to Actual. Edgar here... still... he's making himself a big deal, and he's not kind to people who think differently. A little bit violent ...and worse than useless."

"Well then. You sound busy. Be safe, Leena."

"Is there anything you can do to help?"

"No. Not without violating many important rules." Messenger knocked on the Grand Elevator's door which separated them, for emphasis.

"How... how about Lenth?" Leena asked. "Can *he* help?"

Messenger was quiet for a moment. "He is bound now, much as I am."

"I see. So we useless, violent, lessers from upper... need to sort it out on our own."

Messenger gave a single solemn nod. "I'm sorry."

Leena turned her attention to Mike's body, merely sitting by his side with her hand on his chest. After a moment, she sighed heavily, and asked, "I guess it would be stupid to ask, and I'm pretty sure I know the answer... but this compost thing. He won't suffer, will he?"

"Correct," Messenger confirmed, "all of his suffering ended the moment he died."

Leena smirked a little at Mike. "*Taking the easy way, huh, lazy?*" she thought "*Well... goodbye. This is it. Guess you're not off to meet Actual or anything...*"

The realities of the compost and food system suddenly stuck her again, and she wondered how long until someone was eating a food disc that owed its existence to Mike's body. Her precious Mike, reduced to something so mundane, so forgettable as a bite to eat. The thought caved her chest in, and with a gasp, tears pushed their way out.

"*How am I supposed to deal with this all?*" she screamed abruptly.

"The way I did. The way Lenth did," Messenger said. "Time."

She leaned over to hold Mike closer, and cry. Being this close, she could smell the blood in his wrappings. The absolute, plain reality of his death pushed Leena slowly, forcibly, up onto her feet. "Okay. I'm... I'm going. I'll lock the bay door behind me so you can take him." She took a few paces to the door, leaving Mike behind, never to see or touch him again. She turned and pointed to Messenger. "You tell Actual! You Tell him how Mike was good, and he fought to stop the violence. He did a lot of good things. He meant a lot of things to a lot of people. He gave them hope. Because...

...because it's not great in here."

158

Chapter Thirteen

Empty Hand

From the Grand Elevator's loading bay, the hallways to the Commons were empty. She'd expected to see a few of Mike's people... arguably now her people, milling about. At least a couple to re-establish guard.

There was no one.

As she rounded the corner to see the Commons, she saw Edgar, and half a dozen of his men– all armed with spears, and their recently improved uniforms. They had metal shoulder pads, shin guards, a belt made of the same old blue material, and a loincloth-like adornment that served no purpose besides trying to look important. A random assortment of other Citizens lingered about, but which of them were loyal to whom was difficult to say.

"And why did that take so long?" Edgar demanded, clutching his spear.

Leena was feeling drained from her conversation with Messenger, and her final farewell to Mike. Shoulders low, in no mood to deal with Edgar's crap, she gave a deep sigh as she assembled an answer in her head.

"We talked about stuff. A lot of things I didn't know. Things *we* didn't know. And you wouldn't believe me anyway, so let's just... let's just be done with it."

"*Unacceptable!* What did you talk about?"

After another sigh, she replied. "We talked about Mike a lot. Messenger is kind of an understanding guy. We talked about where our dead end up, and how important it is."

"Important," Edgar said, nodding. "Actual needs their assistance when he brings them back- up above?"

Leena shook her head slowly, and listlessly. "Actual... isn't directly part of it. And... I don't think they go up. And definitely never come back to life."

Edgar's face distorted in disgust laced with horror. "Heresy! Blasphemy!" These were words it seemed that only Edgar had much understanding or appreciation of. "Tell me the truth about what you talked about with Messenger!"

"That's the truth. It gets more complicated, and deals with our food, and how it gets made. The whole thing is kinda... I'm still trying to accept it. I'm considering not eating for a while."

"You cannot spread such falsehoods among the Citizens!"

"I hadn't planned on telling you, cuz I knew it'd piss you off, but you kept nagging, and–"

"Guards! We're taking her to the Refuge!" The two innermost guards approached Leena with their spears at the ready.

"Seriously?" Leena mumbled.

"You will be taught the proper respect for the truths of Actual!"

Leena rolled her eyes and rambled, too fatigued to know when to keep her mouth shut, "Messenger said there were different truths, and a lot of them were made up. By us, by different kinds of Iofus, by –"

"*There is one truth! Straying from it is blasphemy!*" Edgar insisted.

With the guards prodding her to follow Edgar's indignant march, Leena followed along.

The surrounding Citizens looked on. Some looked curious. Some angry. Some concerned. Leena didn't manage to spot any familiar faces, though that didn't mean there weren't some in the group somewhere.

"*Those who don't recognize Actual's absolute might and benevolence,*" Edgar began yelling to everyone as he walked, "*those who destroy their minds with sniffing, or dizzy water, those who commit physical impurities casually with any body they can, those who oppose order- they need to be taught! To become in line with the whole! Only in this way can we keep ourselves worthy of Actual's gifts!*"

Edgar's rant become less focused and less loud, but he never truly stopped, rambling all the way to a small shack inside Refuge where Leena would be held. There was a panel of sheet metal that served as a door, but the only thing that would keep Leena from leaving were two guards– and relative proximity of others.

"Tomorrow, not long after Citizens wake, Leena will be made a public example of how disorder is dealt with!"

"What?" Leena yelled. "*What, are you going to beat me? Kill me?*"

Edgar said nothing else, and left Leena there in the 'closed' shack under guard standing outside.

After Edgar was gone, Leena decided to speak to the unseen guards. "Hey. So why you following this goon?"

The guards didn't reply, and other conversational attempts fared no better. She gave up for a little bit, and eventually, the door was unblocked so someone could hand her a cup with water, and four food discs.

"Hey guard, while I was talking to Messenger, he told me a bit about how our food is made. Quite a bit. Wanna hear?" Silence was the reply. "Nah... I didn't really wanna hear it either. It's not that pleasant. And if you knew, you might get tossed in here."

Leena let that sit out there for a little while with no reply. She paced her little enclosure for a bit, sipping her water, still not ready to face food discs again. She stopped, and turned to the blocked doorway again. "You guys... I guess *all* the guards... must miss Warren a lot. Missed your chance to be his guards? Get invited to his get-togethers?"

"Edgar is nothing like Warren!" one of the guards finally replied.

"Gettin' closer every day," Leena said grimly. "He's got his own stack, guards... gonna be doing bad things to me of some kind in a public gathering... tell me, does he still keep those two naked ladies by this fancy seat back there? What do *they* do for him? It's their idea though, right?"

The guards mumbled irritably between each other. A disagreement? Leena couldn't make it out. Wistfully, sarcastically, she wandered her little space, and called out, "*Down with Warren! All hail the new Warren!*"

"Be quiet in there!" one of the guards hollered in.

"Kay... quiet..." Leena said softly. "Bein' quiet." And for a while, she was, until she had a question. "I was just starting to wonder... remember the day almost everyone went hunting any of Warren's goons, and killing them? Bad scene. Shouldn't have gone down like that. Mike hated that it happened like that. He was eager to give out a lot of second chances. But what I wonder is.. that day... the guys that ended up being Edgar's guards... were they hunting Warren's men that day... or were they hiding from the hunt?"

This got under the skin of at least one of the guards. "Warren was despicable! The way he treated people was inexcusable!"

"*If that's not just talk, then act like it!*" Leena spat. "Don't stand there enforcing Warren-like things!"

"Keep your mouth shut! What do you know?" the guard barked.

"What do I know? What do *I* know? Do you even know who I am? That sounds like a big ego, but seriously, do you have any clue who set Warren up for his fall? Who took down his giant goon? You wanna stand with the guy who finally finished Warren? You can't! He's dead!" By this point, Leena was screaming furiously. "*Mike's dead, and Edgar loves it! Know who doesn't love it?*"

From outside, a little further off, a new voice was heard. "Us."

A clear voice, and confident. And... Jen?

"We'll be taking Leena now, thank you," Jen's voice called out.

More mumbling from the guards. Nervous mumbling, and then, "We're not afraid to use these spears!" the guard called out.

"We were." Who was that? Cody's friend? Leon? "We didn't come here to hurt anyone, so we left the blades at home. We just want Leena. Who, I'm pretty sure, doesn't particularly want to hurt you either."

Leena smiled. For one, Mike's influence seemed to have spread a little. And second, she was glad she hadn't bothered threatening the guards at any point, wrecking Leon's pretty speech.

"Oh, and just in case, we brought a bunch of us. We'd all like to go home," Jen said, "with Leena."

After some more grumbling, the 'door' was removed, and Leena could now see the sizable mob that had come to pick her up. Jen, Leon, and a few *dozen* other familiar and not-quite-as-familiar faces. Most of them erupted in cheers upon seeing her.

Leena walked briskly to Jen for a hug, and a few others joined in.

It was then that Edgar made himself heard. "*What's going on here! Why isn't she in the holding shack?*"

"Yeah, what *was* going on here?" Jen countered. Leena marvelled at how much Jen had come out of her shell in recent months, blossoming in a world without Dan, or Warren's goons and rules. "Why *was* Leena being held? What did she do to *you*?"

"*She's a heretic! Defying the will of Actual!*" Edgar ranted.

Leena stepped forward. "Who made you an expert? I recently had a nice long chat with the Messenger, and in it, I learned more than you ever thought you knew! I don't claim to know what Actual wants, but if he's anything like Messenger, he's probably not into publicly beating captives to make a point, or scaring people into obeying!"

Edgar was too busy ranting his own truths to hear much of what Leena was saying, but at least one person heard.

One of the guards looked at Leena, looked at Edgar, then tossed his spear on the floor in Edgar's direction before going over to stand with the mob. "Yeah. Your whole thing reeks a bit, Edgar. Smells a little too familiar."

"*Weak!*" Edgar wailed. "*Your weakness and lack of faith in Actual will undo you all!*"

As the mob began filtering out with Leena, she called back to Edgar, "Our weakness just took a prisoner and one of your guards using words, reason, and not a drop of blood. Don't be a Warren, and you won't have to worry about 'weak' people causing you troubles."

As the mob moved through Citizenry, Leena noticed they were taking a very inefficient path. Instead of going through clearer areas, Jen directed them through thicker concentrations of shacks and minor structures.

Jen got close to Leena and spoke quietly, while looking around constantly. "Okay. Here's Cody's plan. I'm going back to your old place with most of these people. Meeting up with Tara and some others. We're going to build. Your ramp is getting a makeover. You're going with Leon, and try to go unnoticed up Cody's ramp, and meet with him and that Kim girl. He's been busy. There's a shack ahead on the right. See it? As we all pass by, you and Leon get in, and stay hidden until the group is long gone. If we're lucky, any of Edgar's buddies will assume you came with us all."

"Whoa, what's this all going to –"

"No time, here's the shack, talk to Cody."

As they passed the shack in question, Leon gently pulled her aside. The shack had a little bit of a turn just inside the door which made a spot where Leon and Leena could wait and not be seen by anyone unless they came directly inside.

The group's tone changed. Most of them knew a step had been taken. Many were talking more, but in lower tones. A quiet wave of restrained enthusiasm.

This was the first time Leena got a good look at Leon, and he was certainly close enough now. In this odd little nook, she got a *very* good look.

"Leon. So, how long have you known Cody?"

Leon smirked, and gave a little shrug. "Forever-ish. He's my *maybebrother*."

Leena nodded. Between forceful fathers and difficulties in keeping a family together at all during Warren's rule, and that of his predecessor, *maybebrothers* and *maybesisters* were common enough. They were treated and loved as siblings no matter what.

"I can see it," Leena said. "Your faces have a lot of similarities. Around the eyes.. chin... I'd judge it a bit more than maybe." Indeed, the longer she looked at him, Leon looked like a slightly younger, lankier version of Cody.

Waiting for the group to pass, Leon told Leena, "You know... I probably shouldn't say this... but he... he kinda likes you."

Leena blushed with a smile she couldn't entirely hold back. "Yeah. Yeah, I guess I knew that. I think he's pretty neat, too. Not horrible to look at, smart, kind..."

Leon raised his eyebrows, and looked around. "Aha! So... are you two going to be... a thing?"

Leena swallowed, and any mirth drained from her face. "Maybe. But not soon. I... if Mike were still alive, it would already have been a thing, I think. But right now. I... I'm not ready. I think I'd like it to be a thing. Eventually."

"I guess he *is* smart," Leon said.

"Eh?"

"Oh... he said pretty much the same thing. I was trying to encourage him to talk to you about it, and he told me to shut my face, because it was a bad time for you."

Leena smirked again. "Well... goes to prove the smart and kind thing again. If you find yourself telling him things that you *'probably shouldn't be saying'*, tell him thank you."

Leon snorted. "Is this how it's going to be until you two become a thing? Sending goofy little passive messages through me?"

"I'll try to spare you."

"Good. If it becomes a habit, I'll just close you both in a shack together to shut you up until I'm an uncle."

Leena rolled her eyes with a small, bemused smile. She was pretty sure children were not in her future, but it was an amusing notion.

The sounds of the mob had vanished for a good while, and they decided to step out and start towards Cody's ramp. Before they did so, Leon gave Leena a headscarf, made of course from the inescapable blue cloth.

"We can make you less noticeable. Tie your hair up in it- we can try to hide it all."

"Won't a big blue head-thing look suspicious as well?"

"Yeah, it's a gamble, but at least from a distance it'll probably be more of *'oh, look at that lady with the blue thing'* as opposed to *'Oh, there's Leena, that lady everyone knows and Edgar hates.'*"

"Blue-head-lady it is, then."

With no small effort, they managed to get the bulk of Leena's black hair, which was partly wavy, and partly more curly, into the cloth. The majority of the resulting blue lump of cloth hung off of the back of her head.

"How's it look?"

"Like we shouldn't dawdle to Cody's."

Much of the walk *to* the ramp was shielded by scatterings of shacks and other scrap, but once they got on the ramp itself, they felt that much more exposed.

"Stop looking over your shoulder," Leena said. "it makes you look suspicious, and this blue thing on my head is doing that enough as it is."

Leon grunted. "Yeah... it's not like I can get a good look at every spot someone might be looking up at us. Still... I'm not used to this sneaky stuff. Onward, mysterious blue-head-thing lady."

Once they were up the ramp, they stepped into Cody's den. It was filled with even more scrap than before. Leon had to take a moment to navigate through the dense rubble to get to the back half. Sheets of metal, sheets of... it looked a lot like the walls of the Citizenry, the ones that had been in their places forever.

Leena had never seen this material as anything but part of immovable walls, and the one in the back of Cody's den that was loose. She doubted that anyone she knew had seen it loose before, either. It was a little unnerving to be able to grab a big chunk and flip it over more easily than scrap metal. One side of the panels had little pieces that probably were made to connect to surfaces.

Her mind went to the Grand Elevator loading bay. The walls there– she now understood that they were made of these panels, and figured that if a person were to somehow rip them loose, the back sides would look like the back side of the panel in her hand.

"Cody's been calling them Actual-metal," Leon said, "like... placed by the Actual when Citizenry was made, or whatever."

Leena smirked, "Edgar would like that idea. Or hate it. Especially if it's not sitting on the wall, and being handled like this."

"Hey Leena!" Kim's voice. Coming from... somewhere.

"Hey Kimmie," Leon called back, "open up!"

"Yeah, uh, hang on a second."

Scuffling and moving of unseen objects could be heard nearby. Leon faced a nondescript wall. Leena was sure this was where Cody had brought her through before, but it looked like a very solid wall now. And then, not so solid. The section jiggled loose, and Leon helped push it in, as Kim pulled from inside.

Kim and Leon shared a little hug and a peck, before Leon turned to Leena. "Okay, give Kim the blue-head thing. Me and her are going to your old den."

"Oh, I get it..." Leena said, "to anyone who'd been watching, a guy and some lady with a blue thing covering her hair came up, spent a minute inside, then left. Will this work? I mean, Edgar himself used someone who looked like me to sneak me around once."

"Yeah, but we're not sneaking you, we're sneaking blue-thing lady. Whatever. Should all be different enough to trick anyone watching if they're not watching *too* close. We're basically in the clear now," Leon said. "If someone stops blue-headed-thing lady now, or sees her up close, *poof* it was Kim all along! They ask about Leena? We have no idea where she is, didn't you hear? A big group took her from Edgar's refuge to Mike's old place."

Leena blushed a little. "And I... simply vanish. To where, though?"

Leon pointed his thumb deeper into the passage. "Go ask the man with the plan. New-blue-lady and I gotta go. You're going to have to push the wall chunk into place. I can't pull it all the way closed from the outside. See there at the bottom? That'll kinda click into place, and poof, it's a wall until you dislodge that bit from the inside." Leon and Kim began dragging the panel shut, and Leena started pushing from inside.

"Thanks guys," Leena said. With three people pushing, the panel closed fairly quickly. Sure enough, with the last little nudge, the bits at the bottom of the panel fell about half a centimetre into the floor, solidifying its position.

Leena headed in deeper, again seeing the dead lights overhead, but a tiny bit of light came from ahead; enough to get by. The big, thick door sat ahead, but somehow, Cody had managed to open it. The little section with buttons hung defeated from its usual spot on the door, held up by a few of those rubber strings with metal in them that could carry that *metal-light* that Cody had talked about. A few of the rubber strings dangled to the floor, then in the door, and further down a hallway.

Leena followed the strings a short distance, until the hallway branched into two. Two of the strings went one way, the other two went the other way. A glow of light came from either direction.

"Hey Cody! Can you hear me? Left or right here?"

Cody's voice came from the left. "Leena! You're here, you made it! Hold on, I'll be right there!" Soon, Cody came around a corner. He wore some strange things on top of his usual clothes.

Around his waist clung a belt, dark brown in colour, and heavy looking. It rattled a bit when he moved, due to several random-looking things attached loosely to it. As he approached, he took off two bulky chunks of clothing. Gloves, easily twice as big as anything Leena had seen in any armour collection. They had very specific sections of greys and black, and after Cody got them off, he folded them together and hung them from a section on the belt.

"Well! Somebody found some toys!" Leena chuckled.

Cody chuckled in kind, grinning mischievously. "Yup!" He hopped a little, and jostled the belt with his hands. A hammer, a couple kinds of gripping tools, a roll of grey tape, a roll of the rubber string with metal in it, and things

Leena had only seen *after* they'd been mangled into small daggers. "Opening that big door would have been a lot easier if I had some of this stuff."

Leena looked at the floor, and gestured to the rubber strings. "Didn't find a cup to carry metal-light?"

"I think I found better, for what I'm doing with it." Cody jiggled the roll of rubber-insulated wire on his tool-belt. "I've managed to get metal-light out of the door, and with this stuff, I can send as much as I want where I want it. I'm guessing if I did find some kind of *metal-light-cup*, I'd have to worry about how much was in it. The door seems to have an endless supply if I use the strings. I could also probably run rubber-metal strings from lights in the front den now that I have all this, but then the secret door wouldn't look so secret."

Leena peered at the roll of rubber-metal string on Cody's belt. "Hey, it's got words on the sides."

"Care to try to read it? I never got too hard into reading," Cody said.

Leena knelt down to see it closer. "Well, there's a pile of words, but three are a lot bigger than the rest... first is long... I, N, S, U... oh screw this one. Next word's about as long, but the last is short. W, I, R, E."

"Weeree?" Cody guessed.

"Why-ree?" Leena attempted. "No wait, I betcha this is one of those *E*s than hang out at the end and don't do anything."

"Whyr?"

"Whyr? Sure, *whyr* not?" Leena said with a sheepish smile.

"That's bad."

"But *whyr*, Cody? *Whyr* is it so bad?"

"You're obviously in need of sleep. You've had a stressful day, you're going strange."

"Yeah, whatever. So, do I get the tour?"

Cody looked both directions. "Okay, boring side first." He led to the left, and after passing through a doorway only slightly smaller than the other, (which looked like it didn't need a ton of convincing to open) they were in a fairly large space, roughly the size of Cody's front den. Overhead, a few wires ran into the lights, so that they could serve their purpose.

Re-purposed food boxes served as metre-high dividers, and from a standing position, it was pretty easy to tell what the sections were for.

One was home to a supply of food, jars of water (presumably not dizzy water) and a little pile of assorted weapons. A couple daggers, three swords of varying quality, and a spear. There was enough space for a semi-sorted pile of smaller metal scraps and clothing pieces.

Three sections had heaps of cloth for use as bedding, pretty common, but the last four had a chunk of solid furniture. They weren't sofas like she had in her home den. They were about the length and width of a sofa, but a little taller than the middle parts of the sofa. The ends and sides had no backing or special edge.

On each one were unusual pieces of cloth. One of them showed that the cloths were a bit bigger than the top padded section of the furniture, as if made specifically for this purpose. Each bedding piece of furniture had two different pieces of cloth. A thinner white one, and a thicker dark grey one with a lighter trim on one of the narrower edges.

Each of the pieces of furniture also had a white soft piece about twice as big as a head.

Cody jumped onto one of the pieces of furniture, quickly pulled the two cloth pieces over himself, and dropped his head onto the soft white thing. He then faked a few snores. "Seriously? These are just too good." He pointed at the cardboard separators. "I want to replace those with taller metal or something, like small shack walls. Give people a little privacy, y'know?"

"Damn, Cody, you've been busy!"

"This? I got Leon and Kim and a couple others to do a lot of this. I've been busy on the *other* end." He hopped up, and led down the right hallway branch.

Following along, it wasn't long before another turn aimed them further away from the Commons. The walls here were different. Not the usual smooth white, but a rough grey pocked with imperfections that were so regular, it had to have been intentional. Further were bulkier, red metal beams that framed the hall, still being mostly embedded in the grey.

Cody tapped the grey wall as he walked. "Yeah, this seems to be behind anywhere that the 'Actual-metal'– I'm reconsidering that term, by the way– is mounted. But this grey wall is hard! I can see how the Actual-metal gets mounted on it, but it would take a tool that... Well... I don't think a sledgehammer would cut it."

"Made by Actual, then?" Leena smirked.

"Sure, why not? -But not by any Citizen, that's for sure. This is... we're dealing with stuff not specifically meant for us to mess with, put here long enough ago that none of us even know any stories about it."

"Messenger told me a story..." Leena mused, "that Citizenry used to be a lot different. When it was first made."

Cody stopped, and looked at Leena. "Was... was Messenger there when it was all made? Is he that old? Makes sense. He *is* Messenger. He'd be as constant as Actual, I guess."

Leena frowned. "I'm not sure. He said he saw a picture of it. Maybe he wasn't there. He was telling me so much, a lot was kind of a blur... there's still a lot of things he didn't clarify."

"Did he clarify this?" Cody pointed ahead. The grey hall split into three directions. The left one continued on for quite a distance, had a rail-guarded staircase going down, and a metal door across from it. Ahead had several metal doors before stopping at a ladder that went both up and down, and right went a fairly short distance towards the Commons, ending at a big metal door much like the first one that Cody had to overcome.

"Cuz if Messenger gave you a map to *this* place, I'd appreciate a peek."

By the time Kim and Leon made it back to the other ramp, which had become simply known as "*Leena's stack*", several Citizens, including Jen and Tara, had already disassembled their own shacks to bring the material to become part of the new stack.

Edgar had already claimed a great deal of the available metal to be had for his stack, the Refuge, but Mike and Leena's den had the advantage of having the ramp. As long as the bottom area around the ramp was secure, the entirety of the ramp was pretty much secure. This meant a lot of floorspace to be had without building a perimeter around it... the downside being that doing anything on the ramp itself meant dealing with the slope.

Tara had watched most of the movement of the group going to Edgar's, and returning. From where she could see on the ramp, the concealment of Leena's path went just as planned. Not many in the group had known the whole plan. Cody and Jen had expressed concerns that someone in the group might be keen to tell Edgar all of it. Just maybe.

For the benefit of any such person who might benefit from closure to the ruse, Tara went down to greet Leon and Kim as they arrived.

"Hey guys," she said to them, "did you find Cody?"

"Naw," Leon replied, "he must be scrounging old sniffer dens for metal or stuff, probably."

Tara then 'noticed' Kim's headwear. "Kim... what's... going on with your hair?"

Leaning her head, Kim fiddled with the edge of it. "Not workin' for ya?"

"Hate to say I told you so," Leon said.

"Aw crap." Kim raised her voice and looked around at anyone nearby. "Hey, anyone! How does this thing look?"

No one gave a particularly good response, and one woman said "Mehhhhhhh..."

"Aw crap, okay, you all win." Kim yanked the cloth off of her hair, and toyed with it in her hands. "I'll keep trying headband stuff. I'm so bored of just tying it back at different heights and stuff."

Performance complete, and the blue-hair-thing now retired, Tara moved on to actual business. "So, Kim, Leon, you were going to bring your shack over here and make it a part of things?"

"Yeah," Leon replied. "You and Jen gonna help us haul it over?"

"Jen's pretty busy up top, but I'm with ya. I figured out a thing I can do with cloth to drag metal better, it'll be easy. Well... easier."

There were nearly seventy people now living around the base of Mike's ramp/*Leena's stack* and a third of them had been there since shortly after Warren died. People coming to Leena's now generally felt uncomfortable with Edgar, his rants, and his guards.

Yet the notion that Leena's stack might eventually need guards too, had crossed the minds of many. They had the weapons for it. Not a matching set of spears, but a mix of weapon types were available. Between Mike's original collection and the odd weapon donated by joining Citizens, they were not particularly short on things to poke people with.

Not many people were keen on copying Edgar's attempts at a uniform, but the notion of some kind of armour was accepted as more practical. Some people had begun trying to make some, either alone, or in small groups. Shoulder pads with light metal, or a couple layers of cloth (with maybe a piece of cardboard inside) to cover the torso were being made with increasing quality as experience grew.

Of course, the metal ones seemed more logical than a padded front, but metal supply (and cutting) were big issues. Most metal armour was made from pieces that happened to be about the right size– which also made them pretty useless for something like a chunk of wall.

Tara had taken up the hobby of sorting materials into small piles of likely uses. Spear heads, swords, armour pieces, walls and barricades... scrap unused cloth also got sorted by size, but not purpose. A hairband needed a pretty standard size, but for making armour pieces, it was a little more varied. Potential bandages, unfortunately, might need almost any size. Enough of an unknown that it wasn't worth dwelling over.

The new medical bag that Messenger had brought was in their possession, along with its bandages and pain-killers. That jar of white powder was still missing. Maybe it had been consumed by an opportunistic member of Warren's stack, or some lucky crap-sniffer.

It was just as well that they didn't have all the other things that were in the old bag- Everyone had *some* idea of how to use a bandage at least. Mysterious little bitter things to eat, and liquids liable to make you throw up violently, on the other hand, were not in great demand.

When Leon, Kim, and Tara got back with the metal, they immediately started rebuilding the shack as part of the outer wall. Others were expected to bring more metal suited for wall sections soon, which would allow the wall to be complete – even if not as tall as Edgar's, or reinforced yet. It seemed smaller until you count the ramp area, and the upper rooms. It made it pretty difficult to compare.

Once Leon and Kim's shack had been dealt with, Tara went up to go talk to Jen. Jen was sitting on the sofa, which had been moved to where Jen could sit and watch the top of Cody's ramp, and not be seen from Edgar's Refuge. In her lap lay bits of metal that she had been folding, using cloth and bits of cardboard to guard her hands, into various useful small things. Things like spear heads, blades, and armour pieces for limbs.

"Hey there," Tara said, wrapping an arm around Jen from behind. "Anything going on over there?"

Jen reached back to wrap her arms around Tara's head, and steal a kiss. "Naw. Cody and Leena haven't peeked out, and no one else has gone over since blue-head-lady and Leon visited."

"Blue-head-lady is no more, by the way. We made a show of it," Tara said.

"Yes, I heard parts of it. Do Kim and Leon have any info about how Cody's stuff is doing?"

"Sounds like Cody just keeps finding new things. Things he's fascinated with, but didn't make any great impression with Kim. Leon just got in, traded Leena for Kim, and got out. No lingering."

Jen grabbed Tara's arm which was across her front to the shoulders, and gave a squeeze. "Ooh, do you think Cody and Leena are getting a lot of *work* done right now?" Jen purred with an exaggerated seductive tone. "Working up a sweat, tiring themselves out?"

"Doubtful," Tara cooed, "but we're going to have to work on sleeping arrangements around here."

"Yeah. Well. I still want news from over there," Jen sighed.

"We agreed. Edgar will be watching too close for a while. No casual running back and forth for a now. We build, and we wait."

Chapter Fourteen

Full Hand

Deeper in Cody's den, down the stairs, and through some more halls, many rooms were discovered. Few had much in them. Many were only a few metres in size, a few were several times bigger, and had machines in them that Cody took mental note of for picking at later.

The darkness was a continuing issue. They had found a thing that had a small light on one end, but the bulk of the device looked rotten, and was inoperable. Cody had picked it open, and found little cylinders that looked the most rotten. "Metal-light cup. Betcha anything. Got too old? Can metal go bad like that? Or was it the metal-light?"

Barring any miraculous hand-held light that ran on metal-light cups, they were forced to bring along an awkward unused ceiling light, and run a 'whyre' all the way back to the furthest source of metal-light. Thankfully, in one of the rooms, they found a much bigger roll of wire, tall as one's knee, and held together by wood (a material they'd only really known from furniture in Leena's den, and still didn't know the name for), not thin metal. The wire itself was a good deal thicker.

They finally came to a door of sorts. It was at least four metres wide. Instead of a solid door, it was a rigid wire mesh with supports of metal running about diagonally. The handle to the door was at the bottom.

The mesh allowed Leena and Cody to look through. The other side couldn't be called a room, as it had no floor. Only darkness presented itself from below.

The ceiling was about a metre higher than the ceiling they were under now, and on it, some bulky machine clung. It had a few prominent round parts, and from these round parts, wires almost as thick as one's wrist dangled down into the darkness. The wires also fed into the far wall, by the ceiling, and rested on another barely-visible round part before they were swallowed by the wall.

"What is it?" Leena asked.

Cody bit his lip. "I... I have a thought, but..." Cody tried to lift the handle at the base of the door. It refused to budge.

"*What?* Were you planning on jumping down?"

"Just testing," Cody said, then pointing to a little panel on the wall, with a single button on it. "I think *that* might have something to do with opening this up."

"Is this... is this a Grand Elevator?" Leena balked at the thought, "I mean, no, I saw through the slot of the Grand Elevator. This one's not nearly as big."

"Lesser Elevator, then," Cody said, self-satisfied. "Get it? It's less big, and also it only goes down from here, so it goes to the... oh crap... *oh crap, this might go to lofus!*"

Leena drifted over to the button, and rested her hand on it lightly.

"*What?* Are you insane?" Cody yelped.

"Lofus... after my talk with Messenger..." Leena began, "they don't sound so '*lesser*'. A lot of the things we think Actual does for us... I think lofus do the actual work for a lot of it. Making our food... and... taking our dead, at least. Probably more, if that weirdo Lenth had any clue what he was talking about."

"*A lofu killed Mike!*" Cody gasped.

"I... I know. But *that* lofu, Six, killed a bunch of lofus, too. They hunted him for it. Warren wasn't so nice to lofus the few times one came up. It... maybe some of them can help."

As Cody winced, Leena pressed the bulky button firmly, and... nothing. Cody sighed in relief.

Leena pressed the button a few more times, to no result. "Broken?"

Cody tapped the lighting fixture they'd been carrying around. "Betcha it needs metal-light."

"Can you?" Leena asked meekly.

Cody stood especially upright. "I... possibly. But really... should it be done? *Lofus*, Leena!"

Looking down the elevator shaft, Leena sighed. "Messenger said... *they* all work. They all do things to keep everyone... even us... alive. What do *we* do? What do you think they think of us? Six was apparently a really uncommon thing to happen. Us? We kill all the time. We do horrible things." she whispered.

"That was Warren's people!" Cody reminded her.

"Yeah. But I've killed too. Lots of good Citizens killed the day everyone hunted down Warren's people. Citizens are... we're killers. We're ... bad people."

Cody stammered and fumbled for justifications. "But you killed who, Sledge? He totally deserved–"

"Yep. But *they* don't know all that stuff. They know Citizens kill. And we don't work for food and things." Leena sighed, "If they fear us... hate us..."

"*Then why go right TO them?!*"

Tara and Kim were on semi-official guard duty. They sat on either side of the opening to the completed wall to 'Leena's stack'. No uniforms, no standing at attention- just sitting on small piles of cloth, and keeping an eye out. The casual approach was very intentional, as to not appear over-zealous... but there was a schedule. Guards were now an established thing.

It was these casual guards that first saw a quartet of Edgar's guards coming through the Commons. At a volume that the approaching Edgar guards wouldn't be able to hear, Tara called back into the stack, "Got four Eddies coming to visit. Be ready, be calm."

Tara stood when the approaching guards were undeniable. Her lengthy sword, ripped from the best scrap, hung from her hip. She leaned against the edge of the gate, and gave a signal for Kim to stay seated for now. She could hear more than a few allies finding positions behind her- out of direct view. Ready. Calm.

The Edgar guards seemed intent on just walking right in, but Tara made a single step of getting in the way. "Okay, fellas. No Eddies wandering 'round in here with weapons. I hope you understand."

"Is this Leena's stack, then?" the front 'Eddie' asked.

"Yes, it's her home, but we hold this place for Mike. For those Mike would want to keep safe," Tara said.

"Edgar made a stack, and called it a refuge," Jen said, coming forward from inside. "but I'm still not sure what it was a refuge *from*. Warren was gone, and Mike never made a threat of himself... leaves me wondering what Edgar felt he needed to hide from. Or maybe be just wanted a stack like Warren had."

The guard didn't have a response to that, so Jen continued. "Then suddenly, after Warren, a new stack pops up, with a loud-mouthed leader who thinks he knows what's right for everyone, sets up very Warren-feeling guards, decides on a public beating... other people saw a new Warren, and wanted a place of their own to be safe from new-Warren."

The Eddies looked uncomfortable, but the front one spoke up. "We're here to talk with Leena."

"She's not here," Leon said, making himself known from around a corner.

"You said this was her home," the lead Eddie said.

"Yes, it is," Leon said, faking indignation and confusion, "but she's not *in* it right *now*. Are *you* home right now? No. People *go* places, go for *walks*, go get things, *strrrretch* their legs. From time to time."

"We can pass on a message," Tara said.

"Edgar wants to talk to her," the lead Eddie said.

"Then he should have come himself!" Leon said sardonically, "Of course Leena isn't here, which would have made it a waste, but he didn't know that. But of course, I hear he's very busy being good and noble and surrounded by naked women and sipping the dizzy water that he thinks is so bad. Sounds like a good way to pass the time. Frankly, no wonder he sent you boys instead of leaving all that."

Jen took a hard stance in the middle of the gate, hand on the hilt of her sword. Kim stood, bringing a spear upright which had been casually hidden under cloth on the floor. Several people milled about behind Jen, including Leon. They all looked ready. And calm.

"Are we done, here?" Jen asked.

The Eddies looked about, realizing how outmatched they were as more of Leena's people seeped out of nooks and crannies, many casually holding a weapon of some type, or wearing it on their hip.

"I... I guess we are," the lead Eddie said with a nod. "Let Leena know, Edgar wants to talk." The Eddies turned, and headed back they way they came. The further they got, the more that Leena's people returned to what they were doing before.

"Whee, we win," Tara said flatly to Jen, who still stood in the middle of the gate.

"Doesn't feel like a win," Jen said. "we're now official. We showed some strength. Edgar's probably not going to be too keen on it."

"This gate needs a door," Kim said.

Jen nodded. "A strong one."

A few hours passed, and no further visits came from Edgar's Refuge. Some scrap was re-purposed with the aims of a door for the gate, but it became clear that more large metal would soon be needed.

"I wonder if Cody has any we could use?" Jen mused.

"I guarantee it," Leon said "It's just laying around his den, last I saw. Might have more from the back, too."

"Sounds like a perfect excuse to go for a visit," Jen said.

Jan had kind of fallen into the position of leader of Leena's stack, at least with Leena absent, and Tara convinced her to stay behind.

"Take Leon with you," Jen suggested. "I think I kind of like Kim at the front gate. I'll ask someone else to partner with her while you're gone."

And so Tara and Leon took a leisurely stroll over to Cody's ramp, poking random bits of scrap on the way; partly to actually be looking for stuff to claim later, partly to be *seen* doing so. To not look overly intent on getting to Cody's. In case it mattered.

When they finally got up the ramp and into Cody's den, the mess of material lay before them, much as before. "Yeah, some of this metal, we can take for sure," Tara said.

"Yeah, what about the Actual-metal chunks?" Leon said, nudging a sheet of comparatively pristine wall, taken from further in.

Tara sneered at it. "Do we want to be dragging that right across Citizenry? If someone recognizes it for what it is..."

"True. Suspicious enough we're hauling out a fresh little supply of normal metal," Leon bemoaned. "In fact, the Actual-metal should probably be stored further in, in case Eddies sniff around here too hard. Speaking of which..."

Leon went over to the sealed wall piece that led deeper inside, and knocked fairly hard.

"How far in do you think they might be? Will they hear?"

Leon shrugged. "Hope so. We made pretty darn sure it won't open from this side." He gave a couple more hard bangs, and while they waited, they picked out which metal sheets they wanted to take back later.

"Can we just dump these off the ramp instead of dragging them all the way down?" Leon whined.

"Oh crap, can you imagine the noise?" Tara chortled.

"Ah, maybe we don't want *everyone* in Citizenry watching us."

"Maybe not, huh."

With all the jostling of metal, Leon and Tara managed to miss the sound of the sealed wall opening.

"Tryin' to sleep in here! You wanna sniff your crap jars in peace, go somewhere else, ya crap-sniffin' crap... sniffers." Leena teased.

"Leena! How's being nowhere treatin' ya?" Tara said as she and Leon got themselves inside. "For that matter, how's being nowhere with *Cody* been?" Tara leered.

"Ohh, I have so much to tell you." Leena said with a bit of wonderment in her voice.

"Whoah, crap, I was kidding!" Tara said. "Kind of. Really?"

"No, no, no," Leena said waving her hand dismissively. "I mean something we found here, and what Messenger told me before he took Mike."

Cody caught up, and they went to the resting room to talk. Leena was eager to share the information with people she could trust to not beat her for heresy.

She did her best to communicate her understanding of the compost and food system, with strange living things that didn't move, and about how lofus helped these living things make food.

About how many, *many* more lofus there were than Citizens. How they all worked at things to help everyone. About what Citizenry used to be, and what many lofus thought of Citizens now.

Stunned, and struggling to absorb the amount of information that flew in the face of such long-running assumptions, Tara only came out with "...but Actual..."

"Actual," Leena nodded. "He's important, but he only keeps the lofus organized. Gets them things they need. I don't know what... I mean, if lofus make food, what else do they make? What *can't* they make?"

"Actual-metal?" Leon suggested.

"That's a guess I made too," Cody said, wandering in from the hall, "Could be all metal, really. Maybe the metal-light. It all brings up a lot of questions."

"Which brings me to the other big thing," Leena said, almost in a whisper. "Something we found *here*."

Cody frowned, and gave a heavy sigh.

"Meds? Weapons?" Tara asked.

Leena raised her eyebrows and smiled slightly. "An elevator."

"Like... like to go to Actual?" Leon stammered, "After all that effort Warren went to–"

"*Nope!*" Cody boomed, "this one only goes *down!* Assuming I can fix it."

"*What? Well, what good is that, then?*" Leon squeaked.

"Messenger pretty much told me that even though he'd like to, he can't help us," Leena said, "because of his rules."

"And you think Iofus *will* help?" Tara asked, shaking her head slowly.

"They *have* been helping us," Leena said, "all our lives. Our food, and who knows what else. Even if *some* of them hate us, I... I gotta hope some of them can make that extra step, if I find a Iofu anything like Lenth."

"And if you find one like Six?" Leon asked.

"Messenger tells me that people like him are so rare, that it was the first like him he'd seen."

"Okay..." Tara pondered. "Say you get down there, and meet the friendliest, most helpful Iofu ever. What kind of help do you want from them?"

"Well, I'm not about to ask them to kill all the Eddies," Leena answered. "That would just push the negative ideas they have of us. Maybe they can put people somewhere else... maybe use this Actual-metal to turn Citizenry into two totally separate sections. I don't know. If they're so great, they might have ideas."

Cody frowned in thought. "So stupid it's smart. I mean, if there's so many of them, maybe they... I don't know."

Leena smiled cautiously. "So... think it's a good idea now? How long until you can fix the elevator, y'think?"

Cody sighed in frustration, and shook his head.

"That bad?" Leena responded.

"Worse than that." Cody shook his head again. "It was easy. I did it when you had your nap."

"*What? Really?*"

"I popped that button cover, wired it up, the button lit up, and the bulky thing on the ceiling holding the cables made a short noise. A growl-noise, but not particularly a broken noise."

"*Cody! You're amazing!*"

"*Don't get too excited*, it's not like I tested it. Even if it works, it probably makes noise all the way down, and I didn't feel like attracting Iofus!"

"Can... can I try right now?"

Tara yelped, "You're crazy!"

"At least bring a weapon," Leon said, "and you shouldn't go alone."

"No, no weapons, I don't go down looking like I wanna kill people."

"But at lea–"

A pounding came from the sealed wall. Cody sprang to it first, followed closely by Leena.

"Who is it?" Cody demanded.

"*It's Jen! Let me in, Leena's stack's been attacked!*"

They scurried to open the wall and bring Jen in, careful that some Eddie wasn't following or watching.

"What? I haven't even seen it yet, and it's been attacked?" Leena agonized.

"*Four of ours dead, two of theirs, and they took Kim!*" Jen cried, latching onto Tara for support.

"*What?*" Leon wailed, "Where...? Are they taking her to Edgar's Refuge?"

"*Worse.*"

Leena re-opened the wall, and patted the knife on her hip. "*Now* I need a weapon."

The four marched to the spot where Warren had put on so many of his dreaded gatherings. Sure enough, a crowd was forming, feeling almost like the warm-up for a riot than anything. The pole for guests of honour now held Kim.

Nearby, Edgar stood with his beloved decorated spear.

"If any care for this woman," he said, swinging the dull shaft of his spear hard into Kim's abdomen, "they'll go get the heretic Leena!" Kim doubled over as much as she could, and gave a defeated groan.

When Leena arrived, she called out to Edgar, "Hey, Warren!"

"Leena!" Edgar bellowed, "Such disrespect! Are you prepared to accept the punishment as a heretic, or must I punish *this* heretic all the harder?" He gave Kim another strike to the midsection, and she responded with a shrieking sob.

Leon cried out to his love. If Kim responded, it was amidst unintelligible heaves of pained weeping.

"Holding a friend and beating her isn't a great way to win my acceptance!" Leena yelled. "If you beat *her*, what for me? Or any other Citizen not loyal to your Refuge? What other Warren-like thing do you have planned? Do you have your own Sledge now, or do you plan to do it yourself!?"

"Do not compare me to that monster!" Edgar bellowed. "He thought he was an Actual! What higher crime can be done?"

"What about assuming you know what Actual wants, and trying to force it on everyone?"

"*Denying my authority is denying Actual!*" Edgar ranted.

"I disagree!" Leena scoffed. "Why don't we have a nice calm talk about what Messenger told me! Better yet, how about I tell everyone right here where our dead go, and who really makes our food?"

"Lies and heresy! You can't be reasoned with! Guards! Take her!" To punctuate his order, he drove the tip of his spear into Kim.

With her final mewling cry, chaos erupted.

Leena turned and ran, making sure Cody, Tara, Jen and Leon were with her. Leon was in shock, and needed to be yanked by the arm hard to get him moving. Even still, his unblinking eyes seemed to look nowhere as tears pushed forward.

"Tara!" Leena yelled as they ran, "I'm going for the elevator. We need help bad now." she gasped for air, trying to yell and run at the same time. "You

177

stay here, help people, survive, hide, pretend to change sides, whatever, just stay alive. Remember what I told you about what Messenger told me! Be careful with it!"

Tara nodded, and winked, stopping as Leena headed for Cody's ramp. Tara turned to the approaching guards, and waved her arms. "That bitch is crazy! Help me!"

Despite looking perfectly fine, she got at least one of the guards to stop, at least for the moment. Jen stopped when Tara did, unsure of what was going on in all the yelling. She was confused but a bit relieved when the remaining guards soon passed her and Tara by in favour of chasing Leena.

Possessed by rage, Leon tackled the nearest guard, not even thinking to draw his blade first. His target guard went down, not expecting the attack. Leon landed several vicious blows, but he didn't anticipate the next guard- or his spear.

It drove through Leon's ribs deeply. Collapsing onto the first guard, the spear wrenched out of the hands of the second guard. A wet, desperate scream came from Leon as blood surged into his lung.

Tara looked to the ramp. Leena and Cody had a strong lead. "Jen, we can't do anything here now! We need to run and hide!"

"Wh... where?"

"Run first."

Chapter Fifteen

Run

The wall was still open; closing it while it was empty would have meant a huge ordeal to re-open it. Leena and Cody got in, and pushed it into place, with a locking click.

The voices of the guards quickly followed, as the front den was searched.

"We have a little time," Cody said. "Let's grab some food supplies before we try it."

"Cody... he... Kim... and four were killed earlier?"

Cody sighed, and bit his lip. "And... and my maybe-brother."

"Leon? I didn't see that... oh, Cody... I'm... *I should have just surrendered!*"

Cody shook his head as tears came to him, and he grabbed Leena tight. "No... no... pretty good chance it wouldn't have made a big difference in the long term."

A strike was heard at the sealed wall. And another.

"I knew that wall looked too clean and perfect," Cody said with a sniff. "We need to hustle."

They dashed to the living space, gathered a couple sizable bundles of food, and a jar of water each. As they passed the intersection, it sounded like the guards had given up on the wall, at least for now.

"Maybe you shouldn't come with me," Leena said. "Here, maybe you can get people in here to safety. Maybe you can do some good things."

Cody shook his head, putting his tool-belt on. "They're never going to leave my den alone now. Besides, if the elevator messes up, you need me."

"Yeah," Leena bit her lip and sighed. "I might need you."

With the exact activities of the guards outside unknown, they made haste to the elevator. The button glowed on its little panel, and the panel hung loosely with a couple of wires hooked up to something inside to provide power. Cody held up the little panel to steady it, and turned the button to Leena. "Your idea, you get to press it."

The first press of the button seemed to do nothing.

"Harder," Cody said. Leena added her other hand to Cody's to brace the panel. She pressed harder, sinking it further against the panel. The cluster of machinery began its loud grumble, turning its wheels, and pulling the big cables attached.

"That's... good?" Leena said with an innocent smirk.

"Yeah. I... let's assume so. It didn't fall apart, and it's still going. Noisy though." Cody glanced down the hall towards his den.

"Think the guards can hear it?"

"Hard to say," Cody said. "It's far enough away, even if the sound gets that far, it might not even sound like it's coming from our little sealing wall. And if it does, we'll just have to hope the wall stands up to them."

Leena looked to the direction the guards would come from. "The elevator's loud enough, I don't know if I'd hear guards over there even if they were battering it."

Cody leaned on the grating door, and did his best to peek down. "Should have been watching all along. Do you see anything moving?"

Looking down, Leena squinted hoping to see their ride. "The big wires kind of wiggle. A little. Other than that..."

They waited, and Cody broke the silence, such as it was with the motor running. "I hope Jen and Tara and... I hope people are okay."

Leena reached out to hold Cody's forearm. Of course, she knew Leon was on his mind, but it was hard not to worry about the survivors. Even if one was caught, and told Edgar how to get into the wall... they don't actually *have* any methods that work from the outside.

"Why do good people keep dying?" Cody whispered to himself.

Leena sighed. "Because... because I don't think it's the lofus that are lesser."

Cody's expression soured. "That hopeless? We're just all garbage?"

"We have a lot of garbage living in the same place," Leena said, "It... it gets the rest of us dirty. Cody... have you killed?"

Cody shook his head.

"Well, good. My nice, clean Cody."

"And you? Sledge, I knew that one."

"Just him," Leena said, "but I've been close to killing others. That Six lofu... and I got sucked into that hunt for Warren's men... even if it was sort of a necessary thing. Even if Mike hated it. And before that? I've badly injured a few. People who needed it. So... sometimes I feel pretty *lesser.*"

"Maybe it's not *what* you do, but *why*, that makes someone lesser. You're... so strong," Cody said, looking into her eyes, "it's really amazing how _"

180

"Lights!" Leena blurted.

"Huh?" Cody looked down the elevator shaft. Dim and distant still, one steady light glowed, and a dimmer one blinked. Together, they lit up a section of the elevator shaft they were at... and they were indeed getting closer.

"Well, that kind of implies that it's working," Leena chirped.

"At least it's working at dragging up a couple of lights," Cody quipped.

"No, no... look closer... you can see a solid shape under the lights."

Cody grasped the grating and pressed close to attempt a better look. Leena put her hand over Cody's.

"Thank you. For helping me with this crazy plan."

Without daring eye contact, Cody smiled a tiny bit. "It's... some of it's a kind of crazy that I'm getting used to."

Still with her hand on Cody's, they watched the lights get closer, and waited. Leena sighed, and said the inevitable. "I'm... sorry about Leon. He was a pretty good guy."

Still with his eyes down the shaft, Cody grimaced, and nodded. As it got closer and closer, they could make out more of the shape. The bottom was solid, but the sides appeared to be made of grating. The top was just beams of metal for attaching the big wires to.

"Fingers off the grate. In fact, let's step back a bit," Cody suggested.

The elevator rose to their level, its metal grating creating a dizzying effect to watch as it passed behind the nearly identical metal grating door. It came to a sudden stop at the top with a resounding clang. The light that had been blinking stopped.

"Well, less noisy than the Grand Elevator," Cody commented.

"One day," Leena said flatly, "this elevator will grow up to be a big elevator like its momma, and it'll have its own little Messenger, and bring little food discs to feed to little Citizens, and–"

"I didn't realize you'd been sipping dizzy water, Leena."

"Meh. Okay. Well... open up..." Leena reached down to the handle of the door and pulled up. It was stiff going, so Cody helped by carefully pulling up on the grating, then grabbing the bottom edge. The door lifted the grating side of the elevator also, and they receded most of the way into a ceiling slot that couldn't be seen before.

"After you...!" Cody held up the bottom of the grates, but found they had no will to fall on their own, so he released his needlessly chivalrous grip. The other three walls were also metal grating reinforced with metal beams, and the floor was an odd, solid metal with a systematic pattern of uniformly-sized and shaped bumps. Overhead, the metal beams didn't close off the top, but only served to attach to the big wires, and mount the two lights.

Another small panel awaited on one side, with two buttons very much like the one that called the elevator. One up, one down.

"Here goes..." Leena pressed the down button, and braced for a jolt... but nothing happened.

"Maybe if we hold it down," Cody suggested, giving it a try, and holding the button down. Nothing. "I hope I don't have to run a wire to this. That would be difficult to get- then again, if these lights have metal-light, I assume, I can probably just–"

The grates rattled and whined as Leena pulled the door and the front side of the elevator down.

"Oh, oh, duh," Cody said, hopping over to get a good look at where the handle settled in. "Oh, see, right there, they work together, I see, clever, cute and simple."

Leena leaned against the side opposite of the buttons. "Who you callin' *simple*? Okay, give it a go!"

"Fingers out of grating? Okay!"

Cody slammed the button, and the machine above awoke once more, and the secondary light began its blinking again. The elevator gave a jostle that neither of them could anticipate. Leena fell back a few inches onto the side, and Cody tumbled forward. The disorientation of the world sinking beneath them made it tricky at first to get their bearings.

As Cody rose to his knees, Leena went to him, and got down on her knees to match. "Might be safer to be closer to the ground if it shakes us again," Leena said.

"Probably won't," Cody replied. "We didn't hear it doing any random rattling noises on the way up... just when it stopped. All the same... everything feels kinda..."

"Yeah. Knees it is. Or..." Leena slid sideways to have a seat, legs off to the side. Cody shrugged, and did the same.

"So. I guess we have a while," Cody said. "What do you think's going on out..." Cody looked up. While not fast, they'd already traveled a distance that made the top feel pretty far away. "... Going on *up* there?"

Leena grimaced a little, shook her head and shrugged. It's wasn't as if they'd be getting new info for quite a while. "Is this a horrible mistake? Should we have just stayed behind?"

Cody sighed, and patted Leena's ankle. "Either way, things are getting ugly up there. This plan... might flop. Might not help, might get us killed nice and quick. But maybe we can do a lot more good like this than up there in a knife fight."

Leena bit her lip. "That's what's going to end up happening, isn't it? It's going to end up as some huge fight right across Citizenry."

"Maybe. How many are with Edgar, and how many with us? I never got a good count. And there's all the people who hadn't chosen a side yet. If this gets big, they're going feel a lot more like picking a side as things get worse."

"It's all too... how did it get like this?" Leena asked herself, "What happens if when we eventually get back, and our friends are... and the only people left are Edgar and his guards?"

"Then we turn right around and leave."

"*And go where?*" Leena cried.

"We should keep that in mind when we get down there. Maybe there's a place for us if things go badly up in Citizenry."

"Optimist."

"I'm not the fool who wanted to go ask Iofus for help," Cody chuckled.

"No." Leena forced a smile and looked into Cody's eyes. "You're just the idiot that went along with the fool that wanted to go ask Iofus for help."

"I guess I am."

They were quiet for a bit, and the hum of the machine, now quite a bit farther, was nearly soothing.

"I should have counted how long it took to get up," Cody mumbled softly to himself.

"Maybe," Leena responded just as softly.

Cody sighed, and looked at the floor. "Sometime..." he paused to swallow hard, "sometime, are we going to be... an 'us'?"

Leena gave a small chuckle. "Seems like, eventually. It's the popular opinion. I think we have to. I'd hate to disappoint."

Starting to blush, Cody mumbled a bit. "Oh darn, fated to be romantically involved with a beautiful, amazing..."

Leena clumsily interrupted. "I'd say I don't want to rush, but it's been no rush at all, has it?"

"Still a lot of fresh wounds," Cody said. "Mike... now Leon..."

"Eventually, these wounds are going to be excuses, given enough time," Leena said, "Especially Mike. If he isn't already." She smiled slightly, looking into nowhere.

Cody sighed, and dared a peek at Leena's eyes. Just a peek. "Can I ask a... an awkward question?

"More awkward that this?" Leena said with a smirk.

"Very."

"Well darn, Cody, do it."

Cody's breathing deepened from nerves, and he forced out the question he feared. "...do you... do you still love Mike?"

Leena sighed with a grimace. "Well. Yeah, of course. That never meant I can't love others. He and I were always clear on that."

Cody knew that much, but everything had changed. "Can I compete? Am I stuck in second place? I mean..."

"Feeling nervous?" Leena smiled with understanding. "I'll be honest. If he were still alive, and even if I ended up loving you more, he'd probably still be my main guy. Loyalty and all."

"Not a great situation for me, there..."

"Me either," Leena said with a nod. "I'd feel guilty. I think I'm going to end up feeling that no matter what."

"So, our *unavoidable* 'us'... we're doomed to suffer?"

Leena smiled, holding back a small laugh. "No way is totally painless. That's life. And we can't ever build on wishing for a perfect situation, or a perfect past, okay? Neither of us can fix it. We just... we just move forward."

"Just move forward," Cody said with a smirk and a small head shake. "Oh yeah, how's that done?"

Leena moved forward and pressed her body against Cody's. She put her hands around his waist, and pulled him in firmly. "A little like that, maybe." She looked into his eyes, and they shared a long gaze.

Cody took a moment to catch his breath, having it knocked out of him in surprise. "Oh, is it my turn now?"

Leena bit her lip, and squirmed a little against Cody. "I think so."

Cody leaned in, and kissed the side of Leena's neck, making her gasp lightly.

"Oh... oh no, I think we just became a thing," Leena whispered.

"Terrible!" Cody said, leading kisses to her cheek, but pausing there, not yet heading for her lips.

"I'm skipping my turn. I think you've got a good idea going," Leena whispered.

Cody ran a hand up Leena's body, cupping a breast briefly through her clothes before going further up, stoking along the unkissed side of her neck as his lips reached hers.

"Ohh," Leena gasped softly between delicate kisses, lips scarcely doing more than grazing, "yeah, I think there's definitely a thing here now."

The elevator jolted to a stop, and through the door-grate, and secondary grate for the bottom floor, they could see into a small room with a door about the same size at the elevator's door.

Leena gave Cody a squeeze, which he returned. "Feel guilty yet?" he gently joked.

"Only because that happened when there's so much awful stuff is going on," Leena said, "and Leon."

Cody gave a small nod. "The elevator gave us time. And now—"

"And now we move forward!" Leena got into position to heave up the elevator door and the grate of the bottom floor. "Welcome to lofu-territory."

"Smaller than I expected," Cody said, surveying the little room.

"Dork" Leena went the whole three metres to the room's other door, and like the elevator, it had a handle at the bottom to lift. Except it wouldn't. Cody helped. It didn't open, but a sound caught Cody's ear.

He went over to one part of the bottom edge, and felt the door in that spot. Three screw heads stuck out, and Cody merrily pulled a matching screwdriver out of his tool-belt. "Good thing I brought it, or I'd have to take the elevator back up to get it."

The screw was really tight, but after a couple of attempts and some creative positioning for leverage by Cody, it started to move. It was rough going, then a bit easier, then *too* easy to turn. "It's not coming out right now. The other end is spinning too, so the little bits aren't... okay... This might take a while." Cody switched to pliers, pulling the screw towards himself, About five millimetres of the screw's shaft had been showing for some time now. He turned the screw with the pliers, keeping tension towards himself so the other end wouldn't be able to turn.

Finally, Cody, the pliers, and the screw went tumbling suddenly backwards, and there was a little '*plink-ink-ink*' of a small bit of metal hitting the floor on the other side.

"Okayyyy, that was one of three!"

"What a pain!" Leena said "I saw how you did it. Take a break, I'll work on number two." She reached for the required screwdriver from Cody's belt, and couldn't resist turning the motion into a little bit of an embrace. "Nope, behave, focus," she said softly to herself.

Taking a cue from the contorted position that Cody had gotten into before for leverage, Leena took a similar approach, eager to get some progress before Cody felt the need to take over. When he tried, he was shooed away. Soon she was at the stage to need the pliers. This part was notably harder, but she managed it, falling backwards into a waiting Cody.

He took his pliers back to put in his belt, but he found himself doing it slowly. Having his tools back would mean getting back to work for screw three, which was less attractive than the pile he was currently in with Leena.

"This is kind of difficult," he said with a playful smile. He gave one of her curves a restrained squeeze, and went over to the third screw.

After initial loosening, there was a much bigger 'clonk' in the door. "I think we broke it."

Lifting the handle to the door now got them about a centimetre of opening. Below the screw, they could now see some kind of metal hook lazily latched into a hole in the floor. On the floor just beyond, they could see the two metal nuts they had already overcome. Letting the door down a little gave the metal hook a little more freedom, and a screwdriver pushed the hook the side so it wouldn't hook into the hole as they pushed up again. The door moved up much more freely, and opened with little effort.

Beyond, a wide hall much like the Grand Elevator's loading bay stretched before them. A few small doors and an elevator-sized door dotted the hall before it branched off into two directions.

It was well lit, and so clean. The walls bore no crude paintings, no damage. The floor, no stains of blood or anything.

"So. This is what *lesser* looks like..." Leena said.

Cody picked up the two bolts off of the floor, and reached up to the mostly-open door, and started repairing their dis-assembly.

"Why?" Leena asked.

"Might be smart to leave it looking like it hasn't been messed with. I'm only going to tighten them as hard as my fingers can."

Leena ducked under and reached to close the elevator door.

"No," Cody said, "Leave it open. If it works like it does upstairs... if Edgar gets into my den, the elevator won't work for him unless this door is closed, I'm pretty sure."

"Then we were very lucky that it was closed down here when we wanted it to come to us," Leena said.

"Yeah, no kidding."

The two of them left the little elevator room, and closed the room's door. From this side, the metal hook that locked it could be moved with another little handle. It didn't feel as tight, since the screws were not in tight either, but they closed the latch anyway.

"Okay, boss. What now?"

"We find someone," Leena said, "and hope they don't feel like killing us."

"What do you think? Go in a random door, or wander the halls?"

"I don't know..." Leena pondered, looking around. "The hall is a little creepy. Let's try a door. One of the smaller ones."

The nearest door was unlike anything they'd encountered before. It was plenty big enough for a really tall person to walk through, and wide enough two people might be able to stand side by side in it. A little label at eye-height read "*B1 STORAGE 08: LIGHTS, CABLING*". The handle was a hip-height bar of metal, which swiveled up when she yanked on it. The door swung much like the big doors in Cody's den, but much lighter.

They cautiously entered. It was a big room, twice as high as the hallway, and filled with shelves that stood in rows. A ladder with wheels sat between a couple of rows, reaching upper shelves. They shelves themselves were about half filled with cardboard boxes much like the ones that their food came in, but in different sizes. Some were much smaller, some wider, some thinner...

Cody went up to one that was open, and peeked inside. About a dozen carefully packed light rods– the glass ones that went into the light things that were in the ceiling. He darted over to one with a bit of thick wire sticking out. Peeking in the little hole the wire was sticking out of, it was apparent the box housed a whole roll of the stuff. Both boxes had many, many, identical but sealed boxes. Further boxes of different types made Cody's eyes widen with curiosity.

"Oh... oh, I could play in here."

"We're not here to play," Leena said playfully. "Or loot. But wow."

"Right, right. Looking for lofus."

"Yup. But maybe we shouldn't call them that, especially to their faces."

They went back into the hall, and went into a big door that had to be opened by a handle at the bottom. They found a broad selection of wall pieces. Actual-metal, metal grating much like the elevator had, thin sheet metal, bulkier types, a material they couldn't even guess at, with paper stuck on one side.

"Hey, let's build a stack right here. I... if we had even a bit of this in Citizenry..." Cody said wistfully.

"We could make so many things," Leena said, gazing at the heaps of raw, perfect materials, "My ramp that looks like crap? I think I see the stuff it's *supposed* to have on it. Frig, do you think the lofus built this place themselves? Like, the hallways and the elevators... and everything?"

"I..." Cody's eyes betrayed the pace his mind was racing. "Not with just this stuff, but we've seen so few of these rooms... and the tools they'd need to get it all to fit together so... *oh fuck! The tools!* They must have such wild tools, just to attach the–"

Leena laughed. "Oh boy, you need to calm down. If we ask nicely, maybe they'll upgrade your belt."

Giddy almost to the point of bouncing, Cody's mind explored ideas and things that might be possible using abilities and materials that made halls and rooms such as these.

Feeling the need to yank Cody's chain a little, and decidedly charmed by his glee, she slid up very close, and whispered, "I wonder what I'd look like wearing your tool-belt and nothing else?"

Cody blinked, and looked Leena up and down. "Wha... don't do that to me. I... my brain. Wait, we're a *thing* now! That's a very possible thing that could happen!"

Leena giggled softly. Seeing Cody this excited was getting her a tiny bit excited. The temptation to exacerbate the excitement was pretty strong. She grabbed Cody by the belt and pulled him close. She rested her lips on the side of his neck, and whispered. "I was joking, but I've had worse ideas, the more I think about it. But not now."

"Now, looking for lofus." Cody said with resolve that didn't reflect the position of his hand on Leena.

"Nyaaaha. Yes, lofus." Leena composed herself and led out the door. Cody followed, adjusting his tool-belt as Leena shut the door. When it was closed, she stood and noticed Cody staring down the hall.

A woman, thirty or so metres away, wearing an outfit much like their own, but yellow instead of blue. Like Messenger's. The woman stood there and stared.

"Uh... hello?" Leena called out.

The woman wrung her hands and shifted her weight. "Are you two lost? Where are you supposed to be?"

"Kind of lost, I guess. We're looking for," Leena stammered, trying to avoid the word *lofu*, "looking for the group of people who make the food, and ... and do the other things. And... well, we're from Citizenry, if you've heard of it..."

The woman's stance changed immediately. She was prepared to fend off an attack, or run, or... or something! "I think you mean Providers. I– I'm one, you've come to the right place... what... what do you want?"

"Providers? You... you're called *Providers*?" She'd heard the term before, but now it all clicked. A wave of humility and gratitude swept over Leena for a brief moment, before feeling herself to be so much lesser in comparison. "th– thank you... but I'm looking for help."

"What kind of help?"

"It's Citizenry. Good people... could be..." She thought of Jen and Tara, hopefully well hidden right now. Her voice cracked as she fought crying. "People could be dying right now, and I can't stop it from happening. Please..."

The Provider staggered, unsure of what to do. She leaned towards one of the branching hallways, and called out, "Roland! *Roland!* Come here, quick!"

"Roland?" Cody said, "Who..."

Soon enough a male Provider, also in yellow showed up. He saw Leena and Cody, and gawked for a second. "Woah. Hi?" He turned to the woman Provider and asked, "what's this? Subjects? They look kinda –"

"Citizens," she replied. "They say they're from Citizenry, and are here looking for help."

"Wh... we should tell Gabe or someone!" he said.

The woman nodded. "Yes, I'll go get a hold of Gabe or someone, you stay here and watch them."

"Me?"

"You're a guy. If they start a fight, you can fight better if they get angry or something," she said as she ran off.

"That's... sexist?" Roland said, "and... there's two of them?" He turned to Leena and Cody. "So... you're... Citizens. How, uh... how's that workin' out for you?"

"Badly," Cody said, putting an arm around Leena. "That's why we're here."

"Ah," Roland said, quite happy to keep his distance. "Ya hear things about Citizenry."

"We were working to make it better," Leena said. "Stopped a lot of bad stuff... but new bad stuff started anyway."

"So... you're like... *good* Citizens," Roland said.

"That's not so rare. You don't have to say it like that," Leena said. "For a long time, the bad ones were so many, the good ones mostly had to hide. Then a good one helped get rid the worst... Warren and his men... but then that good one was killed. By one of *your* people."

Roland inhaled audibly, and stepped back. "You're talking about Six."

"Yes. Six. You knew him?"

Roland cocked his head. "Knew *of* him. You bet. While he was loose around here, he was a terror. No one really felt safe."

"Then imagine living with a couple hundred like him, and they controlled who got food." Not that Leena felt it was quite accurate to equate Six with Edgar or Warren's crew, but at the moment, it was splitting hairs.

Soon, a group of Providers showed up. Five of them, and four carried spears of a sort. Even Providers had need of guards, apparently. These spears were very different. They didn't look sharp, but they had a few other things attached; some kind of wire, and a round canister of sorts.

Cody put it together, and almost smiled. "Metal-light cups," he whispered. He put out his hands. as if to stop them, and said, "We're not here to hurt anyone. Just please don't bite us with the metal-light."

The one with no spear stepped forward a little. "Bite you with... is that some kind of Citizen-speak? Whatever. I– I'm Gabe. I help run things a bit around here. And you are?"

"Cody."

"Leena. Lenth and Messenger know me," Leena said nervously. "They'll tell you we're not violent."

"Leena? As in *Leena*-Leena?" Gabe smiled. "Well, Lenth's talked about you. Well, assuming you *are* her."

"I assume I am!"

"Well, Lenth and Messenger can't be reached all that fast. I'll certainly try," Gabe said, "but for now, for everyone's safety, will you agree to come to a room to stay while I wait for either of them to come?"

"Like... closed in a room like prisoners?" Cody asked.

"Well... yes, it'll be locked. It's got a bed and chairs, and I'll get you some food and water. We'll make you comfortable. If we're lucky, one of them will get back to us quickly."

Chapter Sixteen

Some Truths

The Providers asked Cody to give up his tool-belt, which he was not keen to do, until Leena pointed out that most of the stuff hanging off of it could be used as a weapon. He still wasn't *keen* about it, but reluctantly allowed it, as if he had a say in the matter. They also had to give up the water they had brought, but the food rations were permitted.

The room they were brought to (a trip which involved a short trip on a *whole other type of elevator- [!] which was even smaller but much nicer inside,*) was simple. Clean and tidy like all of the lofu places had been so far. The room had a bed, much like the ones Cody found in the back areas of his den, and a couple of chairs, which had to be explained to them. Why sit on those rigid things when you could sit on the padded, blanketed *bed*?

A box with a little supply of food discs was provided, and shiny, metal containers that had water– once one knew how to open the things.

Also prominent was a large panel of black glass on one wall. They could see their reflections in it, which was a pretty new experience. If they weren't so worried about friends above, they might have played with the reflections more.

Leena grabbed a food disc out of the box, so as to not deplete the little supply she carried on her hip, and sat on the edge of the bed. "So, feel like a *lesser one from upper* yet?"

With a huff, Cody sat next to Leena, and flopped back. "Already I've seen so much that begs me to learn more about it. Materials alone... you just *know* there's so much we *don't* know."

Leena held up her food disc, now with a small bite out of it. It would seem that lofu... er... Providers, ate the same thing as they sent to Citizenry. They obviously knew how they were made, and ate them anyway.

"I still can't believe it's dead people," Leena said, her thoughts finding a way to her mouth.

The door opened, and Gabe came in with one guard. "It's not that simple-it's not like it's just people, and it's not like they haven't decomposed, been processed as c – "

"As compost, and then fed to giant living things that can't move that make the stuff that goes into these," Leena completed in her own words. "Okay, but what's going on right now? I need to find a way to help Citizenry."

"*Leena!*" She knew *that* voice. Lenth came in, wearing Provider yellow. "You seem to know the facts, but until you see a tree... 'giant living thing' up close, you can't really *get it.*"

"Lenth, good to see you," Leena said, giving him a friendly hug. "Do they have you dealing with trees? Feeding them the..." It had been a good while since she'd seen him, and he seemed a bit more confident. Maybe it was just that he was in an area more familiar to him than Citizenry.

"No, I don't feed the trees. I... well, I'm learning to feed the lights."

"Metal-light." Cody smirked. "Getting the light to go through the wires and *do* things."

Lenth turned his attention to Cody. "Metal-light? Do you mean electricity?"

Thinking back to the words they'd only half-read on his first roll of wire, things suddenly clicked. "... yes! I think so! Elec..."

"-Tricity. Yup. Oh, and you are?" Lenth asked.

"Cody. I'm..."

"Ah, one of Leena's many men," Lenth said.

Cody was taken aback a little, and Leena chuckled. "Oh, *Lenth*, I have to be honest, I gave you the impression I 'kept' a bunch of men just to see your reaction. I've only ever kept at the *most*... like three at the one time."

"Oh, well, that's *much* more reasonable than... what had you said? Eight?"

"Whatever. Hey, you find yourself a lady, Mister-Innocent?"

"Yeah, actually. Her name's Karen. She's smart, kind–"

"Tsk," Leena joked, "couldn't save yourself for me, huh? What's this Karen got that *I* don't?"

"A full bodysuit made of rubber, and the abilities to mildly electrocute people, or render them unconscious by gassing them."

Leena blinked. "Oy, fuckin' lofus..." she whispered to herself.

"*Anyway!*" Gabe clasped his hands. "There's a problem in Citizenry bad enough that you found a way here which, by the way, I'm very curious if we can expect more Citizens pouring out of..."

"We sealed a wall behind us," Cody said, "and if they get through that, they still have to deal with the elevator, which, we left the gate open, whiiich, we hope makes it unusable from the topside. I guess they could climb down the wires... but it's a long way for climbing!"

190

"Show me. We can walk and talk about Citizenry's problem," Gabe said, opening the door. He, Lenth, and the guard came along as Leena and Cody led them back to where Gabe found them.

"Let me guess," Lenth said as they got underway, "Edgar?"

Leena huffed. "Edgar. He... pretty much wants to control whatever he can, and calls people he doesn't like 'heretic' and a bunch of other words that only really seem to matter to him. He took me as a prisoner, and was going to publicly beat me or something until friends came and got me out *peacefully*, I'm proud to say. But then he took another friend, tied her up and demanded to see me. Before I know it, Kim's tied to the pole, getting my beating, Edgar kills her, and everything went crazy. Last I saw Citizenry, Edgar's guards were chasing down people, Leon got killed, and it was... it was chaos.

"I had to escape to get here, and now I have no idea what else happened, or who's still even alive, and I'm so worried for Jen and Tara, since they were apparently making a stack in my name, which I never even got to see, and... and..."

"Woah, Leena, slow down, take a breath." Lenth said. Leena found Cody's arm around her, and she only then realized that somewhere in her spiel, she'd begun crying.

"He's hunting my friends in the name of his precious Actual," Leena squeaked out.

"Actual?" Gabe said, "Why Actual? Did Actual send some kind of message for all of this?"

"I don't think so," Leena said. "I had a long conversation with Messenger at the Grand Elevator not long ago, and he was on my side in all this... but said he couldn't help because of rules."

They'd reached the door to the elevator that Leena and Cody had taken, and Gabe opened it up. The elevator was still there, open and empty.

"Phew. When was the last time *this* sucker was used?" Gabe pondered.

"An hour ago or so, by us," Cody replied.

"Yes, yes, but before that. You're lucky it worked at all, or didn't drop you half-way through. I'll have some people check it over, and set some kind of barrier to keep unwanted visitors away."

"But how would we get b– oh..." Cody mumbled.

"Grand Elevator," Lenth said. "You know, being allowed on it is kind of a big deal. It's parked not so far away. It's how I got here, and Messenger took me. So... maybe we should go talk to him."

Gabe looked at Lenth, and back to the elevator Leena and Cody had used. "You've got *that* situation then, Lenth? I should stay here and deal with this elevator."

"Sounds good. I'll catch you later, Gabe."

"Don't be a stranger, Mister-Engineer," Gabe answered. Lenth smiled and nodded, but with a hint of sadness.

As Cody, Lenth and Leena walked, Leena asked, "Stranger? Engineer?"

Lenth shrugged. "I mentioned my duties these days were about electricity? That's the Engineers. They have a separate section you can only get to by the Grand Elevator, kind of like you can only get to Citizenry by Grand Elevator. I... rarely get to socialize up here."

"Rules."

"Yeah."

"They can be bent," Leena said. "You're here right now, and *I* certainly didn't use the Grand Elevator to get here."

Lenth nodded. "A fellow named Contact is in charge of the Provider levels, and we haven't involved him at all yet, unless Gabe has reported the situation. If we were sticking hard to rules, we'd be involving him a lot more, but I'd rather not. Bendy rules! Whee!"

"Why don't you want to involve Contact?"

"He's... he does a job that's needed, but the way he thinks about Actual always was a bit unsettling. Like he's some huge unknowable force from above."

"Woah. Sounds a bit like he might get along with Edgar," Leena said. "Contact doesn't yell and call people 'heretic' that he thinks don't respect Actual enough? Kill them?"

Lenth took a deep breath. "No, no he does not. In fact, because I've talked to Actual, Contact kind of treats me as if I was something extra special. Which is *also* kind of creepy."

"You talked to... I knew that. Yeah," Leena said as they entered the Grand Elevator loading bay. "So who... what is Actual, anyway?"

"A nice old man who lives on the top floor, and gets us things we can't make ourselves. Light bulbs, computer stuff. Mostly complicated things. The occasional chunk of machinery..."

Cody was grinning. "I think I want to get to *know* Actual."

Lenth gave a laugh. "Oh, Contact would give you *such* a speech for that attitude."

"And Edgar might stab him," Leena added, sucking the levity out of Lenth. Lenth knocked on the door to the Grand Elevator. The little peeking hatch opened, and Messenger's eyes looked out at them.

"Lenth, you brought a couple... Leena? Leena? What are you doing here?" The peeking hatch closed, and a little metal click sounded off before Lenth, (and from the inside, Messenger,) started to slide the massive door open. Leena noticed how here, he didn't need the opposite door of the loading bay locked to do this. Messenger did not see Iofus as a threat. Citizenry. *That* was the threat.

"Leena, what are you doing here, and... how?" Messenger asked.

Seeing the Grand Elevator open so wide like this was unsettling and somehow amazing. This big, round white room, which had provided for everyone she'd ever known for her entire life was now presented as plainly as if it were pretending to be just any other room... and failed to be as mundane. The man inside, Messenger, felt like its core. As if they were nearly one.

They stepped inside, and closed the massive door behind them.

"Hey Messy," Lenth said, "things have gotten really bad in Citizenry."

"Alright, stop right there," Messenger interrupted. "Firstly, I still haven't heard how our lovely Leena got here. Second, I have no ability to go in and crush her enemies and see them driven before her, and third, for crying out loud, don't call me 'Messy', especially in front of others."

Leena put it together. Messenger... Messy..."M.. messy?" she thought out loud, trying not to smile.

192

Messenger sighed, and pointed at Leena with an open hand. "See? This is why. Citizenry is lost to me now, I'm sure. Any sense of gravitas is destroyed."

"No one's expecting you to lead an army of Providers into Citizenry," Lenth said.

"We're not?" Leena said, "I mean, I'm not sure what I expected, but brute force maybe with those...uh... 'electricity' spears?"

"We have *four* of those 'spears'," Messenger said, "and Citizenry has unfortunately been a home to conflict and violence for generations. I can't throw Providers into it when they could get killed, and still not solve anything. And no one's answered how Citizens are leaking into Provider levels!"

"Gabe's sealing it up right now," Lenth said. "Leena and Cody here found a freight elevator that's been neglected for quite a while, and took a ride."

"*This* is the freight elevator!" Messenger exclaimed, reaching out to the Grand space around him.

"The one I found was a lot smaller," Cody said, "and bare metalley-er– and rectangular."

Messenger pinched the bridge of his nose and sighed, muttering, "oh, *those* things."

"Maybe we need to go talk to..." Lenth smiled sheepishly and looked up.

"Really?" Messenger's stance relaxed, almost in defeat. "You know, he's old. One day, not so far away, I'll have to take his job. Then you'll be coming to *me* with this crap." He pointed with his open palm again at Leena, then Cody. "Citizens... seeing Actual. Really?"

"I remember you once took a Subject to see him," Lenth said.

"That was different. And for that matter, a Citizen is a much higher threat than the average Subject, Six not withstanding."

Leena was unsure what a Subject was. Lenth had said that he worked below Providers, so maybe it was another group like Engineers. Not a threat, but separate. Likely something to do with rules of some kind.

Lenth threw an arm around Leena. "She's no threat to Actual. And her friend... I... I don't know this guy."

Leena moved out from under Lenth's arm, and threw her arm around Cody. "This is Cody," she smiled. "He's mine." Cody smiled sheepishly.

"He's certainly no Six," Messenger muttered. He went over to a panel on the inside of the Grand Elevator, and opened it up. The parts were a little different than the one Leena knew, but it was obviously a communication device. Messenger held down the speak button on the microphone piece.

"Hello Actual? Are you there? It's me." Messenger put on a set of headphones to listen for replies. After a bit, he spoke again. "Messenger to Actual? Hello?" A short moment later, Messenger's expression and stance relaxed a little, and he spoke to the Actual.

"Yes. Well, remember the issue in Citizenry I told you about?... yes. It has apparently gotten much worse. Maybe. It's hard to tell, but two Citizens found their way into Provider levels to seek help. No, not him, thank goodness. I'm guessing he's at the middle of the problems."

There was a longer pause as Messenger listened, then replied, "Yes, that's essentially what I told them. Oh. Really? Well, I certainly hadn't thought of that. It's not exactly... Yes. I... I guess we'll see. Right. Then we'll be en route presently."

Messenger put away the communication device, and turned to other nearby controls.

The Grand Elevator shuddered to life. This was something Leena had heard many times from the outside, usually from the other end of the loading bay, and through an extra door.

Being in the middle of it was something entirely different. If the other elevator moving was a rattling shock, this was a shift in perceivable reality.

"Going up," Messenger said.

It felt like a very, very long time going up. Leena wondered if it might be good to stop at Citizenry, or if Messenger would just kick her out and forget the whole thing.

She didn't even dare ask when they were passing it, but the urge to run in and check on friends was painfully strong.

But no, they'd certainly been going up longer already than the other elevator had spent taking them down. Sure enough, they soon reached the top.

"Actual level," Messenger stated.

Cody raised an eyebrow. "Part of me wishes I could rub this in Warren's face."

"He should have just asked nicely," Leena said.

"He did, if I recall. Asking nicely would not have done it, Citizens," Messenger commented. "There is need. I'd say it was just your story, but Edgar regularly talks to... *at* me through the communication device, and–"

"What?" Leena knew Edgar had the new communication box in Citizenry, but it sounded like he was using it for unintended purposes. "What does he call you about?"

"Nonsense- going on praising me, and especially Actual. He pledges all kinds of promises if I continue delivering food, like I've been already doing since I became Messenger. He speaks of unfit Citizens that don't believe everything he says about Actual, whether it's true or not, and says they'll learn or be punished. Things like that. It lends extra gravity to your claims. I just recently picked up a few bodies. Some were his own people, some his 'hated enemies'."

Leena gasped. "*When? Who were they?*"

"Just before I went to get Lenth to bring to you. He didn't give me their names. Three women, two men."

Leon, Kim, Jen, and Tara all came to mind immediately. "Messenger, did one kind of look like Cody, and another with–"

"Honestly, I didn't get a good look." Messenger interrupted, "and they... many were not in great shape."

"Do you mean... the faces..." Cody asked meekly.

Messenger looked down grimly. "I don't think there were mutilated on purpose, if that's what you mean," he said, "but two had... notable injuries on the face, and there was blood on almost all of them. There looked to be no effort put into cleaning them or such."

Leena screamed and punched the wall. "*If he still thinks they're going to meet almighty Actual, you'd think he'd at least wipe their faces first!*" She turned to Messenger. "*Why allow these lies to go on?! You could have told us any time that we don't get revived or anything!*"

Messenger sighed. "It was decided long before my time that the notion gave your people peace with death. It... is not a unanimously popular opinion."

Leena composed herself with a deep breath or two, and muttered, "Well– rest assured that I'll try to spread the truth when I get the chance."

Lenth spoke up. "May I suggest you see the trees first? Get a feel for them, and *then* you tell people... start with the trees. How they silently help us, but need our help too."

"You've thought about this, Lenth," Messenger said. "You want to make it part of the lessons?"

Lenth nodded in response. "Yes. But I don't want to put too much on my *students* minds all at once. Introducing them to their Manager has been big enough on its own so far."

"Are we going *in*, or are we just on the top floor to chat in the Elevator?" Leena asked, "I don't mean to be snippy, but–"

"Of course. Time is a factor." Messenger began heaving open the door, and Lenth joined in.

The loading bay was similar to the one going into Citizenry, and Provider levels, but this one was the most pristine of them all. Messenger opened the opposite door, and they moved into a space that was strangely smooth. The walls stood as smooth and glossy as glass, a gleaming white. They curved a little, widest at shoulder height by a dozen or so centimetres more than at the floor, then tapering back in to meet the ceiling.

At the ceiling's edge ran a stripe a few centimetres thick– and such a light, almost clear blue. It almost looked like if Leena could reach and touch it, it would be liquid. The ceiling itself had nonsensical white metal shapes mounted on it, which were positioned to block the lights behind them– but the light flooded the room anyway. Even the floor was unusual, like one large dark glass sheet with tiny bits of shiny metal in it.

It was beyond Leena's imagining. She figured it would be just a similar place as the Provider levels.

Cody was smiling wide again. "Somehow... someone... used something... to *build* this!"

"Let's not keep Actual waiting," Messenger said as he led the group down one of the few passages from this space. They took a hallway that, -much to Cody's disappointment- looked a lot more like a Provider area.

They went down a fairly ordinary-looking hall, with fairly ordinary-looking doors, which had little labels and sometimes simple pictures to describe what was on the other side. One little sign had the simplified appearance of a person. The next door's sign showed a similar person, but with a triangle from the hip to the feet instead of legs.

They got more confusing from there. One with a picture of some kind of chair... maybe... one with a stick with– hair at the bottom next to a... thing.

195

They were getting sillier. The doors soon went back to plain words, most of which didn't mean much to Leena.

They stopped at one such door near the end of the hall, so presumably the words on its sign were important.

"Adm–" Cody started to sound out slowly, only for Lenth to complete it for him.

"Administration. Means *boss*, kind of."

Messenger opened the door to a wide room with a few tables- with some strange machines on them- a few chairs, a very wide sofa... and an old man in Provider yellow. For all his grandeur, he looked quite normal.

"Messenger, Lenth," Actual greeted them. "Oh, Lenth, things go well at the Reactor?"

"Always learning, Actual. My lessons for my old unit go well too, though I'm taking it very slowly still, like we agreed."

"And now you break more rules," Actual laughed, gesturing to Leena and Cody. "I've never actually seen a Citizen. I don't think one has been up here in... oh, a long time."

"We're real," Leena said, hit with a sense of worthlessness. "If you don't know us, that might explain why things have been the way they've been. For a long time."

"Citizen..." Messenger used his sternest, most proper voice, "Are you implying that all the killing could have been stopped by Actual? Or myself? That we let it happen because of sheer... disdain? Neglect?"

Eyes still lowered, Leena held her arms in, seeming smaller somehow. "I... I'm just trying to understand. I thought we had the violence under control, but it just keeps rising up. I'm guilty too, but I still don't understand. So many worship you- and do awful things saying it's for you, or you'd want it."

Actual went over to the nearest chair and sat, chin in hand. "There's no group of people I can risk to go in and solve your problems. And as you said, I suppose problems would simply rise up again."

"So you're not going to help us?" Cody said.

"I didn't say that, no..." Actual sighed with furrowed brows. "If you returned to Citizenry, would your lives be in danger?"

Leena raised her eyebrows and nodded. "*I'm* especially at risk, probably. He hates me a bit. The group that Edgar leads sees my friends as enemies, because Edgar's version of *you* says they should be."

Actual breathed in sharply. "I could kill them all," he said plainly. "Maybe you could sneak your friends out, and I could cut off the air. Citizenry is quite big, it would take a while, but eventually, they wouldn't be able to breathe, and then they'd die. Or maybe we could poison the food, and warn your friends. How does that sound? Would that fix everything?"

Leena staggered back, horrified. The great and mighty Actual would do such a thing? "*Are we so disposable?*"

"Hm?"

"*I know we're worthless,*" Leena said, nearly screaming. "*I know we don't do anything useful, but can you just throw us away?*"

Actual frowned, and sat upright as much as his old bones allowed. "Not even if it were just this *Edgar's* people?"

"They're people! We're all people! When my friends rescued me from Edgar's guards once, they basically did it with only talk, and one of the guards joined us. His people aren't just violent garbage. If one can be convinced... I mean, he's a person! A person I don't even know if he's alive right now!"

Actual kept his eyes on Leena, but leaned towards Messenger and said to him calmly, "You know, for a savage, she seems rather thoughtful. Not *quite* the violent beast the rumours say about Citizens."

"You're... teasing me?" Leena said meekly.

"No, young lady. Testing you. Fine, fine, you've won me over. But the fact remains that unless you can safely talk all your enemies onto your side, I don't see a way to intervene. I do see a few options for you."

"What kind of options?" Cody asked, assuming he was also eligible for the offer.

"One is work. The Providers could find you a role in the Units, I'm sure. I have a feeling Lenth would want to make your unit one of his special projects."

"What does all *that* mean?" Leena cried.

Lenth cleared his throat. "You'd be confined to a living area like I once was, and given some kind of job. A duty to do something to help. And Actual is right; I'd want to take your Unit on as a project, to educate you on some of the knowledge I never had as a Unit Subject."

"But we'd be trapped..." Cody commented.

Lenth nodded. "A few rooms, reasonably comfortable, but yes. It wouldn't include running around Provider areas. At least not for a good while."

"Trapped, but useful." Leena wasn't overly keen on the idea. Being useful was intriguing, but on such strict terms...?

"If possible," Lenth continued, "I think you might be well served as a gardener of some kind, taking care of those plants that make our food."

That sounded uncomfortably like it would involve the dead. "What's the other option?"

Actual turned in his chair, facing to the left, staring off to something not in the room. "The choice we gave Six."

"*Death?*" Leena yelped. *"I can get that in the Citizenry!"*

Actual smiled sadly. "No, his death was only necessary because he was too afraid of the path, and lashed out. I had to kill him to save... " Actual gestured to Messenger and Lenth.

"We offered Lenth the same thing, but he decided to stay," Messenger said. "Something we couldn't allow Six to do."

"No one's actually saying what this option is!" Cody said. "Stay? Go? Where?"

Lenth, Messenger, and Actual traded glances.

"What time is it?" Lenth asked. "Where's the Enemy?"

Actual tapped a part of the boxy machine on the nearest table. The biggest part, with a black glass section, sprang to life with an array of words and imagery painted in light that made no sense at all to Leena.

"Still early enough, if you don't dawdle too much," Actual said. "You wouldn't even need suits, for a short look."

"You won't be coming, Actual?" Messenger asked.

"I'll leave it to you boys. I'm feeling pretty stiff today."

Messenger nodded, his face telling of a deep concern for Actual. "Okay people, let's go."

Chapter Seventeen

The Big Truth

Not far from the room with the glass-like walls, Messenger and Lenth led Leena and Cody into some kind of storage room. It was filled with miscellaneous supplies– from stacks of new folded clothes, to cups, to wall pieces, and items Leena had never seen before.

Messenger opened another wide door that opened with a handle at the bottom, only to reveal a smaller space before a near-identical door. He bent to unlock it, then lifted this last wide door from the bottom edge, only by a dozen centimetres or so. He was holding his other hand out to keep everyone away from the opening, then knelt down to peek under.

"Yeah, it's fine. The Enemy is far enough. It will be a while before it arrives."

"Wh... what enemy?" Cody asked quietly, lest this enemy hear him, and rushed over to attack. Any enemy that made Messenger nervous was worth taking very seriously.

Messenger got a solid grip on the bottom edge of the door. "Maybe the Enemy is easier to explain after you see the Battleground." Messenger heaved up the door, and it rumbled up out of the way, into the doorway's top edge.

With a waft of warm, strange-smelling air, the room beyond spread before them. It had no walls, it had no ceiling. Colours blended in unimagined ways above, darkness giving way to blues, then to golden yellow as they flowed from the brightest edge in the distance. Beneath them a dry, cracked, light-brown, dirty floor spread as far as they could see. A length of metal grating stood not too far away, but no other structure was to be seen.

"Battleground?" Leena asked as she stepped forward to grab a bit of the crusty floor, which came apart in her hands, falling into dust. "Who fought here?"

"There were once a great, great many more people than there are now. They were divided into groups, and they had weapons that did this," Messenger said, pointing to the expanse all around them.

To Leena, 'weapon' meant a blade. "What do you mean? What did this? What... what exactly did it do?"

"The people then fought using fire; great heat and force-" Lenth explained, "and they had machines that could instantly make a fire that would kill millions of people."

"Millions? How many is that?"

Messenger did a little rough math. "Picture everyone you've ever seen in Citizenry as a group. Now make a hundred of that group... what, before Warren and his people were killed off, that was like ... four hundred? I forget, let's round up to five hundred. Nice workable number. Now imagine double that. That's a thousand. Now get *that* crowd in your head. Now make a thousand groups of a thousand people each. That would be one million. A good-sized settlement called a city might have five million or so. And they could destroy it all in an instant."

Messenger picked up a clump of dirt, held it up. "A... a city. Five million people..." He struck the clump with his other hand in a way that sent crumbling dust out to the vastness of the ruined world. "And then this. There were many cities. One guess is that there were eight or nine thousand million people... nine 'billion', before the big battle. Before the war."

"Ridiculous!" Cody stammered. Even trying to imagine such a number was impossible... being able to easily kill them all was too terrible to try imagining.

"Then explain a place like this. Our ancestors lived here. And explain the Enemy." Messenger pointed to the lightest part of the sky. Indeed, a colossal light loomed far away, pushing out the brightest hues. "That energy is from the Enemy. To just *look* at it directly when it is any closer causes pain. The power it displays, even at a great distance, it must be much like the weapons that were used."

Certainly, as mesmerizing at the light was, Leena noticed her eyes ached if she looked too long. She looked back inside. "And... we're all hiding from it! Our ancestors lost, and survived!"

Cody looked back inside also, then back again to the vast empty. Certainly, this emptiness wasn't here before the war. Obviously, it used to be all hallways and rooms like the Provider areas, with an occasional larger space like Citizenry... obviously even the ceilings had been destroyed to such an extent that the nearest ceiling was too high up to see. "Such... such destruction. I... some time... I want to build."

Leena scoffed a little. "I don't think happy building time is what Actual had in mind. I think he means that we could just... go."

"Out here?" Cody yelped. "Into this, with the Enemy running around?"

"It doesn't run, it flies." Lenth corrected.

"Oh, that's *so* much better! Some bright burning enemy swooping down at us sounds like a great time!"

"It doesn't come down, it attacks from up high," Messenger said. "High, like up *there* high." He pointed in a direction they hadn't paid much attention to, and in a flash, Cody turned to face some terrible unknown.

Distant, and blending into the sky, was a round white-ish shape, like a circle with a slim portion sliced neatly off. Even at a great distance, it was obviously badly damaged.

"A dead enemy?" Leena guessed.

"Maybe," Lenth said. "I often think it was a weapon of our ancestors, which has been destroyed by the Enemy. When the Enemy is farther, and it's darker here, this one here is easier to see, so it has at least a little power left... but sometimes, even in the dark, it isn't around at all. Or is a different shape. At first, I thought it was trying to repair itself, but a soon as it's a full but scarred circle, it shows decay only a few days later. Decay, or a loss of power. I think the little lights have something to do with it. They show themselves as it gets darker. Tiny lights just as high, and so, so many."

"What idiocy," Cody said softly. "Who would make weapons like that..."

"We have one," Lenth said. "We keep it sealed tight. It makes all of our electricity. Otherwise, we'd be in the dark, our air wouldn't move, water wouldn't move, elevators wouldn't move..."

"And our ancestors didn't use it to fight?" Leena asked.

"I suppose they chose peace." Messenger replied.

"And that's working out for all of us," Leena sneered.

"We lived. So what are your thoughts right now?" Lenth asked. "Work in a Unit and learn what I can teach, or go out into this place?"

"*This place?!*" Leena yelped, "with the Enemy 'attacking from a distance', this other thing, tiny lights that show up in the dark, and is there even a food supply? This is insane!"

"There are ways to avoid the Enemy's power," Messenger said. "We'd give you a supply of food and water to take with you, and we have these full-body rubber suits that can withstand the radiation of the Enemy when you can't find a hiding place."

"Full body r... Lenth... like your girlfriend?"

"Very similar," Lenth answered, "although the kind she uses isn't made for radi–"

"Lenth, Lenth, Lenthie, Lenthilolo..! I want to talk about your girlfriend's weird abilities..."

"I'm sure it breaks a lot of rules, Actual," Leena said with the humility of need, "and it might forever change things. But things right now..."

Actual held a fist tightly in his other hand, and sighed. "Yes. This would be... a change. And I appreciate that your plan risks so few people... but what a risk!"

"So, we can do it?"

"I don't know if you've considered what a lasting change this could be."

"I have," Leena said gently but firmly, "and I hope it *is* a lasting change. I see the dangerous repetition. It has to be broken up somehow."

Actual looked to Lenth and Messenger for opinions. Messenger shrugged with a smirk. "I'm willing to play my part."

"Same here," Lenth agreed.

Actual chuckled. "Ohhh my... what will you tell Contact about this?"

"If we feel the need to ever tell him, we can honestly say it was the will of the Actual," Lenth said with a smile.

"Oh, he'd eat that up," Messenger said.

"Is this a *yes*?" Leena chirped.

Actual nodded. "Just don't make me look like too much of a fool."

When Cody was finally given official permission, his project was already half done, thanks in no small part to getting his beloved tool-belt back. "Messy, I just need one of those cans. Then this part is done. I have no idea how to do the other part. Well, I have an idea, I just don't have the stuff."

"Don't call me Messy," Messenger said grimly, "but I'm pretty sure I know all the parts you need. Lenth, this thing he's building is going to be in your care. Is it all making sense?"

"As long as the filter is good, it's all looking simple enough."

"That thing is really, really creepy," Leena said.

Lenth chuckled. "Try growing up with one living in your ceiling."

Chapter Eighteen

The Big Lie

The familiar rattle and boom of the Grand Elevator echoed once again in the loading bay of the Citizenry. The guards there, Edgar's guards, stood to accept orders from the Messenger, spears in hand.

In his best officiating, authoritative, booming voice, Messenger spoke. "Tell the Citizens. I will be bringing Actual to speak to them. Tell them to gather in a place not far from the Grand Elevator, but out in the open of the Commons."

The guards took a moment to absorb what they'd just heard. "I'll tell Edgar, you tell... uh... everyone!" They scampered off, only to halt, hearing the Grand Elevator open freely behind them.

In front was Messenger, in his usual yellow clothing. Even those who had not seem him directly through the peeking slot knew of his stern expression, dark reddish skin, and yellow clothing. Much farther back stood Leena and Cody.

In between... something dark, alien, and almost menacing. Almost all black, with unstoppable-looking boots, gloves to match, hands clasped in front of himself. All of it under an all-encompassing cowl, with presumably a human face in behind. Maybe?

The outer eyes were round, four centimetres wide with thin silver trim and a thicker black edge, but a vast darkness in the middle. No mouth, no nose, but a round metal grate the size of one of its eyes.

One of the guards gawked a little longer than the other, but they were both soon back on mission, running off to tell of his coming. "Actual, Actual!" The one not running to Edgar yelled as he ran, "The Actual is here! Messenger, too! Everyone! Come!"

Messenger led the procession, and as Citizens came to look, Messenger held out his hands to keep them at bay. Not that many looked eager to go touch the Rubberman-suited figure that followed.

Once about twenty metres from the Grand Elevator building, Messenger stopped, and held out his hand to a nearby guard. Confused for a moment, the guard guessed correctly and handed Messenger his spear.

Messenger used the spear to sweep a circle, about four metres in radius around Actual. He pressed hard enough to leave a faint scratch in the floor. Following Leena and Cody's lead, everyone stayed out of the circle, leaving just Messenger and Actual within it.

Across the circle, behind a few other people, Leena spotted Jen and Tara. Jen had a cut above her eye, with some swelling around it. But she was alive. They were both alive.

Messenger held the upper part of the spear's shaft, steadied the other end on the floor, and used his foot to bend it in half, leaving the thing broken on the floor. The guard looked quite stunned, even offended maybe, but did not otherwise react.

Actual raised a hand. He moved it and the direction of his stare slightly as if he were calling out to everyone. Messenger nodded as if he heard. "Actual wishes to see the one you call Edgar."

The crowd murmured, and one asked loudly, "What, can't he talk?"

Messenger turned to the Citizen with an incredulous expression. "Citizen, why would you expect to be capable of hearing the voice of the Actual? This is part of the purpose of my being. I convey his messages."

This was heard by the approaching Edgar, for whom the crowd parted. He stopped just inside the circle.

"You are the Edgar?" Messenger said, after a slight head tilt by Actual.

"And you're Actual?" Edgar said brusquely.

Actual bowed his head. After a moment of silence, Edgar began to speak, but Messenger forcefully held his hand out to silence him. Messenger was busy 'listening' to Actual. Messenger soon spoke for him. "You praise me, you claim to know my wishes and my will, yet you cannot recognize me. Your devotion is admirable, but what you do with it is shameful and tragic. These are troubling paradoxes, don't you think?"

"I know what the Citizens need!" Edgar hollered.

Actual stood more upright, and Messenger spoke. "They need to be degraded? To be hunted? To be killed?"

"*If need be! If they do not praise you honestly!*" Edgar was growing red in the face, rattling his spear as he spoke.

Actual raised his hands, and brought down fists by his sides. And Messenger spoke with force. "*I crave no such praise! I seek no such deaths!*

Citizenry was on the path of true peace until you defiled my name with YOUR wishes!"

Edgar's face was awash with anger and fear, and anger won. *"We'll see if you're just some infidel!"*

Edgar's spear came down from a high swing, aimed at Actual's head.

Actual caught the shaft in his hand.

And Edgar screamed.

Edgar's grip tightened on his spear as his face contorted, and Actual took a step forward as Edgar's knees buckled. Sobbing, trying to plead for mercy, and unable to release his own spear, he felt the power of Actual.

Actual released the spear, tossing it aside. Edgar was now able to let go, but he was a quivering, sobbing mess.

Messenger stepped forward, raising one hand open above his head as if about to hurl some invisible sphere. "Is it to be death, Actual?"

The Citizens gasped at Messenger's raised, open hand. What deathly power would flow from it to end the great and mighty Edgar?

Actual shook his head slowly.

Messenger looked at Actual, as if listening for a moment. "Yes, Actual." Messenger turned to Edgar. "Edgar, you've been granted mercy, which you so seldom granted to others. Be grateful for his kindness. Do you accept that this is The Actual?"

Edgar, still on his knees, still a trembling wreck, and trying not to sob outright, nodded. "It... is clear, Actual."

Actual then shifted his stance toward the crowd.

"Then hear my words," Messenger relayed, "and find no need to imagine them. My first rule is to not kill. Those who *do* are to be brought before Messenger at the Grand Elevator, who will represent my will. Similarly, purposeful harm and degradation is not to occur. I had hoped these ideals had been taken to heart after you removed the one you called Warren."

Actual turned to Leena and Cody, and Messenger spoke. "When these two were brought to me, I told them of what must be done in Citizenry. Citizens have always been afforded luxury, and to not work. This has led to a lack of direction, and to boredom... far too often this has led to cruel acts. It is my hope that contributing back to the realms that have helped feed you... will give you greater purpose."

Actual looked across the Citizens for a moment before Messenger uttered his words. "Remember three things; kind, wise, and strong. Let kindness guide you first, to consider your fellow Citizens and act in their benefit, as they act in yours. You have seen what cruelty does. It brings no benefit. No power that is worth having. With the power of cruelty, you will be hated, and your days will become joyless.

"Wisdom, to act with reason and fairness. Wisdom is the servant of kindness, and grows from it.

"Strength, last. Not to benefit yourself, but to be strong enough to help others. Strength to uphold kindness. Strength is also to be the servant of kindness. Strength used *against* kindness leads to ruin."

Actual forcefully held up a hand with one finger held high.

"Kind." Messenger decreed.

Actual held up a second finger, his hand raised not as high.

"Wise."

Actual relaxed his arm, his hand to his side, as if an afterthought, and a third finger was held out.

"Strong," Messenger said with firm, measured calm. "Fare well."

As Messenger stopped speaking, Actual raised both hands, and from his sleeves gushed a nearly invisible vapour. Discreetly, Messenger, Leena, and Cody held their breath until most of the surrounding Citizens had melted into peaceful slumber, copying the gentle decent of the other Citizens. As the vapour spread, Citizens farther from Actual felt sleep seduce them.

From under his coat, Actual produced three compact masks for the other three to wear over their noses and mouths.

Cody gasped for air the loudest. "Think we got 'em all? Looks like a huge group to me!"

"We'll have to be quick- and careful," Messenger said. "It would be ideal if we found them all. Let's get moving."

Chapter Nineteen

The Awakening

Edgar awoke, groggy but fine, in a heap of Citizens. An empty circle sat in the middle where the great Actual had been.

As others woke, Cody and Leena 'woke' from pretend sleep. Many mumbled as they woke, some wondering if it had been a dream.

Leena held up her hand, holding up another finger for each of the three words she spoke. "Kind. Wise. Strong." She heard someone respond with an exact repetition. "Kind. Wise. Strong."

Edgar sat up, but held his head low. Nearby, one of his own guards repeated the words. Edgar looked around himself. "My spear…! Where…"

"Mine also!" said a nearby guard. Other had similar realizations.

"My knife!"

"My sword!"

"My spear!"

Leena smiled, and gave a joyous laugh. "Spears aren't needed to be kind!"

Edgar was among the first to his feet. His hand still ached from where Actual's power had come through his spear. "Miracle," he mumbled, awed but troubled. "Miracles all… miracle I was spared."

"He forgave," Leena said. "He knows about Kim, and probably all the rest. He forgave. He was kind first."

Edgar's breathing was heavy, and he stared at the floor. "Actual forgave. I'm certain some others will not."

"Well," Leena started, "the rest of us aren't allowed to kill or torture you, so I guess we'll have to *try* to forgive." The words nearly choked her as she spoke, but she wouldn't see a repeat of the hunt for Warren's men.

Next, to find more of her friends and see if they were okay. Forgiveness might become far more difficult if they weren't okay.

"You know, I still wasn't sure about me being your voice until we were doing it," Messenger said to the rubber-clad man in the Grand elevator with him, "but I think it really added to your mystique!"

With the Rubberman mask held under his arm, Lenth chuckled. "I sure can't compete with *your* voice. And you did awesome all around!"

"I'm calling the *actual* Actual," Messenger said, "and reporting success."

"Let's hope it sticks. Speaking of sticks, did we ever decide what to do with all these spears and junk?" - Junk which they were up to their ankles in.

Messenger smiled, and shook his head. "I'm sure we can find a way to recycle them somehow. What's going to be trickier is deciding on consistent rules for when they inevitably come to me to decide how to handle problems like murders. I expect they'll come to me for lesser things as well."

"So, you're going to be much more... involved with them, I suppose," Lenth said.

"Oh, don't make me regret this," Messenger chuckled. "This Messenger job just got more complicated than I agreed to initially. I blame you. And your buddy-girl Leena. Nice work catching Edgar's spear with your hand, by the way. Much more dramatic than just *touching him* with that hand."

As Lenth took his gloves off, the wire in the one glove's palm yanked loose from a '*metal-light can*' in his coat, and the other glove yanked loose a control for the sleepy gas. All the powers of his love, Karen– sort of, which gave Leena the idea. "I'm just glad it didn't shock *me* instead!" Lenth laughed, "Heck, for a second, I thought it was going to *kill* Edgar."

"It would have been essentially all right if that were the case," Messenger said, "but yes, if we wanted to teach '*kind*'..." He smirked, and looked at Lenth. "Leena and Cody didn't seem any more interested in exploring the top outside than you were."

"Well, of course not. Up there is amazing, but their loved ones are here, and they're needed."

Messenger gave a single nod, and looked upwards.

Chapter Twenty

Purpose

In the coming days, fresh metal sheets were dropped off at the Citizenry by Messenger. Immediately, Leena and Cody led other Citizens in building a box out of them at the spot where 'Actual' had spoken. A box with no lid, ten metres long and wide, and five metres tall.

When completed, with top edges having been beaten into a bit of a lip to make them safer, a ladder was secured to the outside. Leena reported completion to Messenger with the communication box, which Edgar no longer kept for himself.

Soon, carts filled with rich, black soil were delivered. Leena knew it was the product of compost. Aside from dead people, it was made from every bit of wasted food and excrement, but it was now something very different than what Leena imagined.

Sticking her hand in it was... pleasant. Its scent could even be called pleasant as well. The legacy of those lost. Citizens began to fill the new big metal box with soil.

Edgar arrived. Worried whispers preceded him. A knife was in his hand. Leena knew there was a chance that a few blades would be missed in their hurry to get them all before people were due to wake, but of *all people* to find one now...

Edgar stood where he had people watching him, not far from the new garden box. He raised his knife high in the air.

"Actual has left me this," he called out, "and I understand. He forgives me, but I see in the faces of so many... that I am not forgiven."

He looked over to the fresh soil. "I know my place. I will find my repentance where I am destined."

Leena stepped forward, hands dirty from the soil. She looked at Edgar with stoic eyes. "Edgar, what's going on here?"

"Leena. I leave you the communication box, and my den, if you'd have it. Your clever man can have my books." He turned to address everyone nearby.

"Let it be known, I was not murdered. No sin need be confessed to Messenger." He stared at his knife, held in both hands in front of him. "You may mourn or rejoice in my passing. I must accept either."

With that, he thrust the knife into his neck using both hands. A yell became a gurgle. He collapsed almost immediately, and his blood spread quickly. His pain wracked his body, and he curled up abruptly on the floor, spreading a smear of blood in the process before he stopped moving at last.

The few dozen Citizens nearby responded with shock, but no cheers, nor cries of anguish. It was merely done.

Leena stepped forward, and knelt, putting a hand on his shoulder, draped in his cloak of importance.

"Call Messenger," Leena said to the nearest Citizen. "Tell him about this. Tell him I... I'll have his body ready in an hour or so." She stood to address the nearest few Citizens. "I need some cloth to bundle him in. And his knife. It's going too." She raised her voice so any nearby could hear.

"If anyone else finds a weapon that Actual missed, don't try to guess why! He came to speak to us, and told us not to guess his will! If you've any sense, you'll give it to Messenger, or turn it into a gardening tool or something! Finding a blade is not a sign to kill yourself, or anyone else! Have some sanity!"

"Maybe in *his* case," a nearby Citizen started to say.

Leena interrupted him.

"He's still bleeding. Go get some extra cloth."

She looked down at Edgar's body, his face frozen in pain and shock. She took a moment to close his eyes. "You belligerent thing," she said softly, almost affectionately. "Found a way to be pompous to the end. I guess you didn't want to be just a gardener."

***

More soil arrived, and Edgar was taken. Messenger commented that Edgar could be safely buried at the bottom of the garden box, and it would be a natural way to compost, but Leena chose not to do that.

After more and more soil, the box was full, the garden was ready, and seeds were provided. The seeds were soon arranged in carefully laid-out sections for the short-root crops. This left one space for the only crop that needed the depth which they had built the box for.

Messenger had said that he'd soon be altering the lights directly above the garden to give the plants the kind of light they'd need, whatever that meant. He reminded her about the delicate ways to water, and the time-consuming and careful pollination that the Citizens would have to do for some of the plants.

In time, almost all of the crops needed to create food discs would grow here. Not in enough quantities to account for all of the Citizenry's needs... not yet. Not with just one garden box.

The next day, a Citizen came running to Leena from the Grand Elevator building. "Leena! Leena! The Messenger calls for you!"

She stood from the soil, finding that her spare time somehow led to sitting in the garden, waiting for green to appear. It was still too soon. "All right. I know what this is. Let others come too. Make sure Cody's told."

Between the time that the Citizen had left the loading bay and the time anyone had returned to it, Messenger had unloaded the cargo. He returned to the Elevator, where he still maintained his distance from Citizenry, as per the old custom.

When Leena arrived in the loading bay, followed by many, she stopped a metre away from the little delivery. The miracle bestowed upon them. She got on her knees in front of it, almost as if she were addressing a child. Several of the nearest Citizens followed suit, transfixed on this object.

"It... it's alive," Leena said, a question as much as a statement.

"It is a tree," Messenger's voice replied. "Young ones are called saplings. This kind live at least four years. When it reaches maturity, this kind of tree, a papaya tree, will be much larger than a person, and provide things called papayas until it grows too old. They will be its gifts to the Citizens in gratitude for raising it. Its 'offspring' will be able to do the same in the future."

"If it's alive, does it have a name?" Leena asked.

"I told you, it is a papaya tree."

"And I am a person, but I have my *own* name."

"It does not talk," Messenger said. "It does not *need* a name, but if you choose to name it, that breaks no rules. People have been known to talk to plants. Some people think it even helps them."

Cody stepped up from behind a few other Citizens. "I think we should name it Mike."

Leena turned to Cody with tears forming in her eyes. She nodded as other Citizens softly voiced approval.

Leena took the cloth containing the sapling's roots and some soil in her hands and stood. "Thank you, Messenger."

"Mind your garden well, Citizens."

Carrying the sapling, Leena led a flurry of Citizens trying to get a good look.

"When I was way with Actual and Messenger, I was told that we shouldn't touch the green bits on top too much," Leena warned, "and even then, very, very gently."

She slowed her stride when children came to see, and had to repeat the rule about touching the leaves. The children were very fond of introducing themselves to 'Mike'. It made Leena smile, but also made it hard not to cry.

When she reached the garden box, climbing the ladder was tricky with the sapling in one arm. While Citizens offered a hand to help up, none seemed to think it proper to ask Leena if they could carry the sapling.

Holding the sapling so close, the leaves caressed her face as she ascended.

Rows for the other crops, all facing the centre where a hole had been dug, seemed to call the sapling to its new home.

She gently removed the cloth of the bundle, and some of the soil fell loose into the hole. Cloth tossed aside, she lowered the sapling into the hole, and patted soil left around the edges over the sapling's base.

Cody's arm draped around Leena's shoulders, and with his other hand, he passed her a cup of water. Inexperienced but instructed, she dribbled water around the trunk and the area the hole had taken up. She stood and turned to see Citizens standing behind her. As many as could fit on the garden box behind her.

They cheered, and Leena laughed, wiping her eyes. "Okay, okay, too many people are walking on the other crops," she said. A stream of sheepishly apologetic people headed back down the ladder.

Leena turned to embrace Cody. "I think I'd better hang out around here for a while. Make sure the curious don't accidentally do harm."

"I think I'll stay with you."

"That... that sounds pretty good."

And the Citizenry found purpose.

And for now, the Citizenry found peace.

The Rubberman Series began with:

RUBBERMAN'S CAGE

Lenth grew up in a lie.
Apparently there's more than five people in the world.

Four Brothers live their lives in an enclosed habitat, as directed by the silent Rubberman above them. When they disobey, they get shocked. This is normal. It always has been.
When a Brother dies, they learn of death. When he is replaced by someone new, they learn they are replaceable.

When the ceiling above the ceiling cracks open, Lenth plans a journey beyond the known universe:

A third floor. Up.

Also check out the Lifehack series:

Starting with *Lifehack*, continuing in *Watching Yute*, and concluding in *Echoes of Erebus*. Love, loss, nanotech-driven evils, and a madman who refuses to accept death as the end.

LIFEHACK

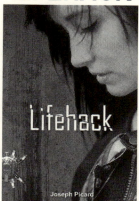

Regan has her ups and downs.
- Dumping her girlfriend: Down.
- Moving in with her loving brother: Up.
- Waking up to a plague of undead: REALLY down.

After the undead began roaming the neighborhood, Regan lost track of her brother. She's spent the last two years searching for him. In the meantime, she's fallen in love, only to be told, "Sorry, I'm straight. And you're a lunatic." There's a psycho out there somewhere who caused the outbreak, using nanotechnology just for the fun of it, and Regan intends to hunt him down.
Oh, and the crush she still has on the straight gal? Dangerously distracting, especially when there's a zombie around every corner.

WATCHING YUTE

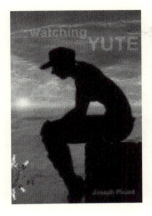

Change. Loss. Consequence.

An ideal post opened up for Lieutenant Cassidy Stanton when she wanted a fresh start. She expected a measure of peace, guarding a historic temple in the middle of the desert.
She didn't expect to find a new girlfriend; maybe even a soul mate.

She didn't expect to be in the crossfire of a terrorist, a cowardly scientist, and a fleet of microscopic invaders.

She didn't expect to lose.

ECHOES OF EREBUS

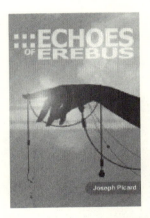

Sarah's got daddy issues. He lives in her head, built her out of fish, and killed millions of people.
But he's really sorry.
Honest.

A father that lives in your head wouldn't be so bad if he wasn't the killer of millions. At least it's comforting to know that he didn't murder the fishes used to create your body.
Or the seagull.

Sarah hides her illegal nanite origins in an effort to build an ordinary life, but the legacy of Dad's horrors makes it difficult. Especially when new but familiar zombie-like abominations begin to appear in the city.

Find Joseph Picard's books at ozero.ca, Amazon.com, and Audible.com

About The Author

B.C. Lower mainlander since 1992, Joseph has always tinkered with art, music, and writing.

He chose to focus primarily on writing in the early 2000s, and his short stories have since evolved into character-driven novels of science-fiction and broader speculative fiction.

In 2001, he found out that cars are harder than mountain bikes, and has been a paraplegic ever since.

Miraculously, this has not altered his career arc as a quarterback, basketball star, pole-dancer, or kung-fu movie stunt double.

Thankfully he has that whole 'life-long-nerd' thing to fall back on.

With a daughter, Caitlin, born in 2007, and a son, Lachlan, in 2011, free time has become a very valuable asset, and most of it gets poured into writing.

Find Joseph Picard's books at ozero.ca, Amazon.com, and Audible.com

Please Email much-appreciated feedback to Joseph: joe@ozero.ca
or even be as wonderful as to post a short review online!

Facebook: www.facebook.com/ozerobook

Made in the USA
Columbia, SC
09 March 2018